THE LAST DAYS
VOLUME 1

Gathering Storm

Books by Kenneth Tarr

The Last Days Series
Gathering Storm
Pioneer One
Promised Land
End of the World

Other Books
The Hive: Amerika, Best of All Possible Worlds

Middle Grade
Birdlegs

THE LAST DAYS
VOLUME 1

Gathering Storm

Kenneth R. Tarr

This is a work of fiction, and the views expressed herein are the sole responsibility of the author. Likewise, certain characters, places, and incidents are the product of the author's imagination, and any resemblance to actual persons, living or dead, or actual events or locales, is entirely coincidental.

Gathering Storm (Last Days Series #1)

Published by Truebekon Books

ISBN: 978-1493683710

Printed in the United States of America
Year of first printing: 2013

To my wife, Kathy, and my daughter Rachel, without whose continual support and inspiration this novel would not have been written.

Chapter 1

The lemonade vibrated in the glass sitting on the arm of the chair. Steven stared at it a few seconds without understanding the cause of the unusual movement. It reminded him of the pools of water which trembled just before the great tyrannosaurus appeared in the movie Jurassic Park. The picture frames began to rattle violently on the walls. He looked around the room trying to figure out what was happening. Then he realized it was nothing more than a small earthquake, similar to the one he had felt in California while visiting his sister and her husband the summer before. Still Steven was surprised. He had lived in Provo all his life and couldn't remember experiencing a single earthquake. His three children, who had been playing Parcheesi on the kitchen table, rushed into the living room, eyes wide with excitement. First Andrew, then William and Jennifer.

"Dad, did you feel that?" Andrew said with a mixture of fear and enthusiasm.

William rolled his clear blue eyes and smacked his lips at the obvious naivety of his eight-year-old brother. "Of course he felt it, stupid, what do you think?" At twelve years old, William loved to set his younger brother and sister straight. He was into disaster movies and was constantly trying to convince his father to let him see them on television and at the local movie theater.

William pushed past Andrew and came to his father's chair. "Hey, Dad, do you think there's going to be a bigger one in a little while?" he said hopefully.

"I don't know. I suppose we might get some aftershocks. William, please don't call your brother stupid."

William ignored his father's reprimand. "Gosh. I hope so. Some huge ones! Magnitude 8.5. That would be cool."

"Cool? I'm not sure that floods, fires, destruction, and death are all that cool." Steven looked at ten-year-old Jennifer, who was standing ten feet away, holding one hand over her mouth. "Don't worry, Jen, it'll be okay. There's no danger."

"Do you think Mom felt that earthquake?" she asked.

"Clear down in Arizona? I don't think so."

A wave of bitterness came over Steven. His ex-wife, Selena, had abandoned the family two years ago to join a polygamous cult in Arizona, and she had not bothered contacting them since. He had often cursed the fact that he had consented to go with Selena to a series of lessons given by the polygamous "prophet" Colton Aldridge on Monday nights in Springville. He had not agreed with many of the things he had heard and had tried to discuss them with Selena, but she had refused to accept his objections. He'd learned later that she had secretly attended other meetings sponsored by the same group during the day. Obviously, Aldridge had seduced her with promises of a new life of spiritual ecstasy.

The reason she had given him for leaving was that she was unhappy living an unfulfilling, humdrum life with a man who did not care about spiritual things. She told him she wanted to obey God in every way and that included living the celestial law of plural marriage.

Since Selena's departure, Steven had blamed himself many times for the disruption of his family and the loss of his wife. And yet after all that time, he still could not stop thinking about her, especially at night. He couldn't understand why she had stopped loving him, and the pain was so great that he had become sullen and depressed. It had taken six months for him to get past his own pain enough to see the sadness and disillusionment in the eyes of his children, and now it was only because of them that he struggled to keep things going.

There was a loud rap at the door and Steven dragged his weary body out of the chair and went to see who it was. Opening the door, he saw a tall, skinny woman in her mid-fifties. She had her gray hair in a bun and wore thick glasses that made her eyes resemble those of a giant fish.

"Good afternoon," she said. "Is this the residence of Brother Steven Christopher?"

"Yes."

"Are you Steven Christopher?"

Who else would I be if this is the residence of Steven Christopher? he thought. "Yes, yes," he said, his voice betraying a touch of impatience. He tried hard to control himself, knowing his irritation was mostly due to his fatigue and his sad memories of Selena.

"I'm Sister Florence Goodrich. The bishop of this ward, Ronald Justesen, sent me to welcome you. I visit all the new people. Did you feel that earthquake? Were you frightened? Please don't be afraid. Earthquakes never cause much damage in Utah. Oh, maybe you already know that. You just moved in, didn't you? You look awfully tired. I help maintain the ward list. I know our membership better than the bishopric. Why don't we sit down and talk?" Before Steven could invite her in, she walked past him into the living room. She continued to whip out short, staccato sentences as she headed for the couch. "I get the entire history. Family members. Ages. Talents. Likes and dislikes. Problems. You know, all the general stuff to help the bishop. Without me I don't know how the ward could function."

Never before had Steven seen anyone talk so fast and say so much without even taking a breath. "Please sit down, Sister Goodrich. How can I help you?"

"First of all, welcome to the Grandview Second Ward."

"Thank you very much. I really appreciate that." He felt he was now under complete control.

The three Christopher children sat on the floor in a circle around their visitor, clearly fascinated by her appearance and personality.

"When did you move in, Brother Christopher?" she asked.

"We started two days ago, on Monday, and we're almost done."

"Where did you move from?"

"Harbor Park. On the west side of Provo."

"Oh yes. That's a nice subdivision. Didn't you like it there?"

"The house was too small. Only two bedrooms and one bathroom and I've got three children. Now each child has his or her own bedroom. Besides, I got a great deal on this house and it's close to my parents and my brother John and his family. The kids can walk a few blocks and see their grandparents and their cousins whenever they want."

Sister Goodrich smiled sweetly at the three children. "My yes. That's very important, isn't it, my little darlings?"

Once again William rolled his eyes in disgust and Andrew and Jennifer looked at each other in disbelief. Florence didn't seem to notice and barreled ahead without missing a beat. "How fortunate for you, Brother Christopher, that you didn't have to travel very far. All you had to do was pop your belongings into a truck, drive a mile, and then zip up the hill. I'm glad the weather has been so nice. It can get very smucky sometimes in May in Utah County. I remember once back around the turn of the millennium that we had a blizzard on this same date, May 15. You couldn't see five feet in front of you. That's when my brother, Richard, and his wife, Emily—bless her dear heart—and their six children came to stay with us for a week. Heavens! Was that a living nightmare. But my husband and I—his name is Brigham—love them all so much. You'll meet Brigham at church on Sunday, I'm sure."

Steven heard the word smucky and little else. He had always been amazed at the ability of women to invent expressive new words. The only other thing he noticed was that Florence had the unique ability to think by association and thus get lost regularly in her own chatter.

"You had some questions to ask me?" Steven said. The children had moved closer and closer and were almost touching Florence's feet.

"Oh, yes. Um, let's see. How many people do you have in your family?"

"There are four of us. Me and three kids."

Florence hesitated noticeably. "Uh-huh. Only four of you? You don't have a wife?"

"No, I've been divorced about a year. There are only the four of us."

"But your children. The poor angels with no mother to take care of them."

Steven could see that she was itching to ask about the divorce but didn't dare. He smiled in spite of himself. Fortunately, he had instructed the children to say nothing to strangers about the problems between him and Selena.

"What's the next question, Sister Goodrich?" Steven said with growing impatience.

"Oh, yes. What are your children's names and ages?"

"Well, the boy on your left is William. He's twelve years old. The one on your right is Andrew. He's eight. He was baptized two months ago. And my daughter, Jennifer, is ten."

Florence muttered as she wrote, "Jennifer. Ten . . ." She looked up at Jennifer and exclaimed, "My, she's a raven-haired beauty, isn't she? Such dark eyes, oval face, and olive skin. I'll bet she favors her mother."

Steven suspected that Florence was fishing for information about his ex-wife. "Yes, she looks very much like her mother." In fact the resemblance was so striking that when Steven looked at his daughter, he was often reminded of Selena, and it was a continuous source of disquiet in his heart. He noticed that Florence had no special praise for his sons and he glanced at them to see how they were taking all the flattery heaped on Jennifer. Thankfully, he saw no obvious signs of irritation.

"You know," Florence continued, "we have another Christopher family in our ward—John and Tania Christopher. They're only about thirty and already have five delightful children. I bet they'll have ten or eleven little spirits by the time they're forty. Do you know them?"

"Yes, John's my younger brother."

"Oh, that's right, of course. You did say that one of the reasons you moved here was to be closer to your brother. How wonderful. They are *such* a nice family." Her voice was coated with honey. "And Tania is *such* a lovely lady and *such* a good wife for John. It must be hard on you not to have—"

She stopped abruptly and changed the subject. "Well . . . now at least, we have a new bachelor in the ward. One so young and good looking. Tall, dark, and handsome, as they say. I'm sure the unmarried females in our ward will want to know you're available." She winked at him and chuckled knowingly.

Steven felt anger and bitterness sweep over him and he struggled to control himself. "Available? I'm not sure I'm ready for that."

"Of *course* you are. Remember what the scriptures say about it not being good for a man to be alone."

"Dad doesn't want another woman," Jennifer said firmly. "And he's not alone. He has us."

Florence's mouth gaped in surprise, and Steven, seeing how rattled she was, decided to change the subject. "What's the next question, Sister Goodrich?"

Florence consulted her list. "Let's, uh, see now . . . What kind of work do you do, Brother Christopher? I ask this because the ward likes to know what talents its members have."

Steven wondered what Bishop Justesen would think of all these questions. "I'm a freelance translator."

"How exciting!" she cried. "What's a freelance translator? What do you translate?" She snickered at her own wit.

Steven didn't get the joke, but he was determined to get it over with. "I translate Japanese and French documents into English. Sometimes I interpret."

"Oh. See how talented you are. And French. It's such a beautiful, romantic language. Our single sisters will love to hear that, I'm sure. I took two years of French a long time ago but I don't remember a thing. Our teacher simply couldn't—"

"Do you have any more questions, Mrs. Goodrich?"

"My yes, lots of them." She looked at her list. "Where do you work?"

"I'm a freelance translator, which means I work at home by myself. I use a computer."

"How nice for you, Brother Christopher. I'll bet you make lots of money with all that freelance talent. That must be why you're able to afford this beautiful new home on Grandview Hill. My husband and I live in a tiny little house down the street, but we're truly grateful to the Lord for what he has given us."

"I'm sure you are," Steven said. "Well, it's getting late and I know you have other things to do."

"But I still have several questions to ask."

The front door burst open and John Christopher stormed into the living room. He was obviously excited. "Did you feel the earthquake, Steve? The news report said it was 3.5 on the Richter Scale. It was probably just a fore-shock and there'll be a bigger one soon. I'm sure of it." John finally noticed Florence. "Oh, hello, Sister Goodrich. I didn't see you sitting there." She gave him a cold nod, but John ignored her and said to Steven, "Like I've told you a million times, the end is near. There's crazy weather all over the earth and it's going to get worse—much worse. And there are hundreds of other signs."

Florence jumped to her feet. "I've got to go now, Brother Christopher. It's been so nice of you to give me a moment of your time. Besides, I'm sure you want to talk to your brother."

She hurried to the door as if someone had just announced that there was an outbreak of Ebola Fever in the room. Steven figured she had already heard John's doomsday ideas before and was doing her best to escape, completely forgetting the rest of her questions. When Florence shut the door, Steven felt grateful John had showed up when he did.

"Looks like you scared her half to death," Steven said, grinning. "Why did she leave so fast?"

"She's like most Mormons when it comes to the signs of the times. They simply don't want to think about it. All I do is to warn them that the Second Coming is really close and they run like scared rabbits."

"Maybe it's the way you talk to them. You tend to state your ideas in an absolute manner and you're always harping on the same subject. Perhaps you should be a little more subtle."

John's face turned red with indignation. "I simply tell the truth, but they don't want to hear it."

Steven decided to change the subject. He loved his brother and didn't want to make him angry. "Okay, John, but you said something about an earthquake, 8.5 or something?"

"It was 3.5 not 8.5. If it had been 8.5 there would be devastation every-where. For Pete's sake, didn't you feel it?"

"Yeah, the house shook a little. It wasn't serious."

"But don't you see? That's a foreshock. There might be a big one any minute now. I'm thinking we should pack up our families and get out of this area. That's why I got the rest of the day off from work. If it's a major one, it might destroy Deer Creek Dam or Jordanelle Dam in the canyon and flood all of Utah Valley within no time. Thousands of people could drown."

Steven glanced at his children and saw the frightened look in their eyes. "Calm down, John. There's not much chance of us getting an earthquake that's big enough or close enough to make those dams fail. It's a far-fetched idea. You're getting excited over nothing."

"That's what everybody says. Look, Steve, all I can do is warn you. Now it's up to you. The lives of your children are in your hands. I've got to go now because there isn't much time. I'm loading my family into the car and heading for high ground in case of a flood." John rushed for the door but stopped abruptly and returned to the living room. "Oh, yeah, I forgot. The news report also said that a series of huge tsunamis are hitting the west coast. They're over sixty feet high and people are drowning all over the place. Don't you ever listen to the news? Like I said, the end isn't far away."

Suddenly Steven felt sick to his stomach. "I wonder if Christine and Chad are in danger." Christine was their 29-year-old sister who lived in Pasadena, California with her husband, Chad Renwick, and their three children.

"I called them a while ago and they're fine," John replied. "They live too far from the ocean to be in trouble. See you later, Steve." Without waiting for an answer, John hurried out the door and drove away at a high speed.

Steven sat down and took a deep breath. He was happy to hear his sister's family was all right, but he always felt exhausted after hearing John go on about the signs of the times and the Second Coming of Christ.

"What did Uncle John mean when he said our lives are in your hands?" William asked.

"Don't worry about it. You know Uncle John. He loves to scare people. That's why everybody accuses him of being Chicken Little, always proclaiming the world is coming to an end. John says he does it on purpose because it's human nature for people to do nothing about such things unless they're scared to death. But sometimes I think that's how he gets his kicks. I never take him seriously and you shouldn't either."

"What's all that stuff about people drowning on the West Coast?" Jennifer asked. "And what are tsunamis?"

Steven tried to remember an article he had read on tsunamis in the *National Geographic*. "Um, let's see . . . They're giant sea waves caused by earthquakes under the ocean. They can cause serious damage but only along the coast, and we're hundreds of miles from the ocean. John said they were over sixty feet high, but he always exaggerates everything. Probably, a lot of surfers are riding on top of those waves."

Andrew was shocked. "You mean there are guys dumb enough to go surfing on top of monster, killer waves?"

Steven laughed at Andrew's description. "Yes, you'll always find crazies willing to risk their lives for a thrill."

"But, Dad," William said, "are we going to have a giant earthquake here like Uncle John said?"

"No, we are not. John doesn't know what he's talking about."

At that moment the pictures on the walls began to vibrate again. The children yelped and ran to their father. The shaking lasted fifteen seconds.

"Was that the big one, Dad?" Jennifer said nervously when the movement stopped.

"No, it was only a little aftershock. That suggests the worst one was the first quake."

"They were both pretty scary," Andrew said. "I hope we never get another one."

"I doubt we'll feel any others," Steven said. "And if we do, they probably won't be any worse than those we had today."

The children seemed relieved and satisfied when they saw their father's nonchalant attitude. The family continued putting things away the rest of the afternoon. Since their mother's desertion, the children had become closer to their father and seemed to enjoy helping him do things. Adversity had tightened the bonds of their love.

That evening Jennifer and Andrew prepared supper as a special treat, while Steven checked on them regularly to make sure they didn't burn the house down. When Andrew proudly brought each plate to the table around seven o'clock, William groaned and Steven stared in amusement. First, Andrew presented a huge bowl of spaghetti which resembled white glue, with specks of burned hamburger sprinkled on top and red sauce that lay in pools around the edge. Next came a casserole made of potatoes, cheese, several kinds of legumes, and more of the burned hamburger. Finally, he brought a tray covered with olives, pickles, carrot sticks, celery, fish sticks, and candy bars. Jennifer completed the menu by placing four bottles of root beer on the table.

"I bought the soda pop from the money I earned myself," she said happily.

"Gosh!" Steven exclaimed. "What a feast." He threw William one of his strongest I-dare-you-to-say-something-smart looks, and William's mouth snapped shut. But that didn't prevent the boy from frowning and holding his stomach.

Steven ate slowly and carefully, determined to praise every part of the meal. He was amazed to see Andrew and Jennifer gorge themselves as if they were eating the finest delicacies at a world-class Parisian restaurant. William excused himself early and headed for the living room.

"That was delicious," Steven said when he had finished. "Thank you very much, kids."

Andrew beamed. "You're welcome, Dad. Would you like us to fix supper tomorrow night too?"

"Oh, no. I think I can handle it. After tonight I think you two need a rest. We'll save your talents for a special occasion. Let's go watch TV, if there's anything good on."

Steven plopped into his favorite armchair in the living room, while the children jumped onto the couch. He touched a button on the console built into the arm of the chair, and half of the south wall lit up. The giant television was only four inches deep and was completely recessed into the wall. When a popular sitcom comedian, who was famous for telling dirty jokes, appeared on the screen, Steven changed the channel immediately. The children complained loudly as they always did whenever he switched channels. The family used to enjoy several good programs on television, but the programming had degenerated rapidly in recent years. Complete nudity, both male and female, was now legal for viewing, and Steven never allowed the children to watch TV without supervision.

Nudity was not the only thing currently promoted by many television stations and by dozens of "progressive" organizations. They also supported legalized abortion, infanticide under certain circumstances, immorality, euthanasia, and homosexuality. In reality, Steven believed the entire value system presented by television programs, advertisers, and politicians had become corrupt, godless, and self-seeking, and the only way he could protect his children from tainted values was to carefully monitor what they watched. Unfortunately, that eliminated nearly everything except news reports and programs on KBYU and KUED.

After bouncing from channel to channel all evening, Steven tucked his children into bed at ten o'clock, reminding them that they had to return to school the next day. Then he sat down to watch the evening news on Channel Two.

"Our top story tonight," the anchorman said, "concerns the giant tsunamis rolling onto the coast of California. We have reports coming in which describe waves higher than sixty feet striking the entire coast line. Our Los Angeles correspondent, Vern Reynolds, reports."

The scene changed to show a small man bundled against the weather. He was standing on a hill overlooking a black and forbidding ocean about a mile away. Around him there was a chaotic spectacle of people running in all directions, screaming and crying. "Here at Huntington Beach we have just been hit . . . gigantic tidal wave, estimated to be over seventy feet tall. The authorities warned the people in the coastal region twelve hours before the first tidal wave hit, and people have been evacuating the coast ever since . . . three this morning.

"Unfortunately, they couldn't take . . . beach properties with them. We ourselves are in danger and will move to safety within the next few minutes. There are reports that some of the waves have flooded vast . . . miles inland. The authorities estimate that there have been about six thousand casualties so far and three hundred thousand people left homeless. Most of the casualties resulted . . . fact that many people refused to heed the warnings and others purposely came . . . to see the excitement. This is—"

Again Steven saw the face of the anchorman in the studio. "It seems our transmission from Huntington Beach has been interrupted. Vern Reynolds used the term tidal wave but these waves have nothing to do with the tides. Their real name is tsunamis, which in Japanese means harbor waves. Usually they are caused by massive earthquakes or vast landslides under the sea. These mighty movements of the earth push a series of waves outward in all directions like a pebble does when it's dropped into a pond. They travel up to six hundred miles per hour depending on how deep the water is. While they are at sea, they are only one to three feet high and are hardly noticeable. In fact, tsunamis can pass under a boat without the passengers even realizing they are there. But when they roll up to a coast, they often rise upwards to incredible heights and cause great damage like these tsunamis are now doing along the Pacific coast."

The newscaster paused as someone handed him a piece of paper. He examined it quickly and said, "I just received another report that tsunamis are also devastating Hawaii and the east coast of Japan, but we have no particulars at this time. KSL will keep you informed about these deadly tsunamis as we receive additional information. Back to you, Marsha."

Steven was surprised to see that John had not exaggerated the situation on the Pacific coast.

"Thanks for that report, Tom. Now we turn to more pleasant things. Our Middle East correspondent, Claudia Akim, reports that Israel and two Arab nations, Jordan and Syria, will soon cooperate in a project to desalinate water from the Dead Sea to provide fresh water for new farms in many desert locations. This shows that the peace accord signed by Israel and its Arab neighbors sixteen months ago is still bearing fruits. Many leaders in the Middle East credit this accord to US president James Miller. His efforts are described by many commentators as a masterpiece in diplomacy."

"That's right, Marsha," the male anchor said. "England's prime minister, Arnold Bradbury, is quoted as saying that President Miller and Henry White, our ambassador to Israel, accomplished a miracle in bringing the peace talks to fruition, and that their efforts may well lead to a new age in Arab-Israeli cooperation and understanding."

Steven felt sleepy and he shook his head to stay awake, wanting to hear the rest of the news. Since his stomach was still upset from supper, he slipped a couple of Tums into his mouth.

"Now in national news," Marsha said, "the National Association for the Advancement of Colored People, or NAACP, reports that blacks have made great strides in recent years. The percentage of blacks now employed exceeds that of whites and they earn as much as whites in most professions. Other reports indicate that job and educational opportunities for minority groups in this country are becoming plentiful."

"Yes, Marsha," Tom said. "Some experts feel that there is also a general growth of tolerance in this country in the last decade."

Steven turned off the television. *I believe in tolerance*, he thought, *tolerance for other races and religions, but the trouble with the world today is that it's so tolerant toward evil that it often ends up promoting it. Oh well, I'm too tired to think about it now.* Steven checked on his children and then went to bed. As he lay on his back in the dark, he thought about John's dire predictions. John always went too far. For him the end of the world was always right around the corner. People had better get ready now, both physically and spiritually. If they don't, they'll perish in the plagues and devastations of the last days or burn with the wicked at Christ's Second Coming.

Yet nobody seemed to take John or his predictions seriously. Actually, none of the people Steven knew, including members of the Church, ever talked about the end of the world. Or if they did, it was as if it were an event that would take place some day in the remote future. Nothing to worry about for a few decades or a hundred years. Even though John got a lot of flak for being a fanatical alarmist and fearmonger, and people ridiculed him behind his back, Steven figured that in a way he deserved what he got. It was obvious that the world in general was pretty wicked, but there was a lot of good too. Steven could easily point out many acts of kindness and love every day. No, it would be a long time before the world became ripe in iniquity as the scriptures foretold.

Feeling a pleasant numbness overcome him, he lost track of his thoughts. Soon his mind created a vivid image of his ex-wife Selena. He saw her dark beauty and her deep brown eyes, and his heart raced and burned at the same time. With all his might he yearned to hold her and it was with great agony that he realized he would never hold her again. In spite of himself, he still thought of her as his wife. He saw this image and had these same feelings several nights a week, and each time he had to struggle to get rid of them. The only way he could go to sleep was to force himself to think of something pleasant such as the family vacation he was planning for this summer.

As he imagined himself camping near the river in Provo Canyon with his children and enjoying the peaceful, majestic scenery, he drifted into sleep. Then in his dream he glanced up and saw something strange—something horrifying. It was an enormous wall of water moving downstream toward him, pulverizing everything in its path. He awoke with a start and sat up in bed bathed in sweat. He wiped the perspiration from his face and condemned John for making wild predictions and bringing more turmoil into his life. He was especially angry with himself for allowing his brother's silly ideas to upset him.

Chapter 2

"But, Dad, why do we have to go to school?" William moaned. "We haven't gone for three days, so why can't we stay home the rest of the week?"

"Yeah," Andrew said. "We're still not done moving. What about all those boxes sitting in Uncle John's pickup in our driveway?"

Jennifer agreed with her brothers for the first time in weeks. "I think it's dumb to go back to school in the middle of the week. It's much smarter to have a few days to prepare and start on Monday."

Steven laughed at their arguments and he continued to drive toward Westridge Elementary. "In the first place, you played more than you helped me move. If it hadn't been for John and the elders from Harbor Park, I would have been forced to hire some help. In the second place, it doesn't matter which day you enter school. Conclusion—you're going to school today."

From that moment on, the children sulked until Steven dropped Jennifer and Andrew off at Westridge Elementary and William at Dixon Middle School. Fortunately, Steven finished the trip rapidly because the children were attending the same schools as before, and he knew the way. The only trouble he had was finding out where William was supposed to catch his bus from their new home.

As soon as he returned home, Steven unloaded John's pickup and drove the empty truck to his brother's house a short distance away. He was surprised to see that John and his family had not yet left for high ground. After giving Tania the keys to the truck, he walked home and spent the remainder of the morning organizing his office in the basement. In the afternoon he forced himself to boot up his computer and download a French document that a Provo cosmetics company wanted him to translate into

English. He could do it much faster now that he had a super computer and a sophisticated new program which instantly gave a rough translation of the text. Instead of going through the laborious task of typing every word, he could scan the French text, wait a few seconds for the rough translation to appear, and then concentrate on expressing the exact meaning and feeling of the original into English.

Steven was proud of his skill in translating and knew it was unusual for a translator to be proficient in two foreign languages. After studying French and Japanese for many years at BYU and Yale, he had spent a total of five years in France and Japan. He had passed the American Translator Association exams in both languages at BYU without any trouble, but it had taken him another eight years to build up his reputation. At this point he was widely known internationally as an expert translator, and he often did work for US Government agencies.

Sometimes he got a break from translation when he was asked to interpret for visitors from France or Japan, who desired to tour Utah companies or travel to sites of special interest. The extra stipend he received for this work gave a boost to the family budget.

By the time school was out at three o'clock it had begun to rain—a steady, moderate shower that seemed to refresh the world. The children arrived home within a half hour and Steven fed them ham sandwiches and milk. After the snack he piled them into his blue Chevrolet and took William to karate, Jennifer to dance, and Andrew to Grandma's house, which was only a quarter mile away on Grandview Hill.

He was dragging by the time he got back. He wondered how it was that a 36-year-old man could be so exhausted all the time. *It must be all this hauling I do*, he thought. *But that's my life—the family chauffeur.* He felt ashamed that he had never appreciated the fact that Selena had relieved him of most of that burden when she had lived with them.

Steven worked as fast as he could because he had to pick up the kids around five. One more hour before the next interruption. At the end of the hour, he quickly searched the French dictionary on his computer for the English equivalent of the French expression "SIDA."

"Let's see," he said out loud. "It's . . . oh yes . . . 'AIDS.'"

He typed that abbreviation in and got up immediately to leave. It was still raining and he felt nervous as he unplugged the electric cable which charged the car's batteries. He thought, *I hate to plug and unplug this thing in the rain. What if I get electrocuted? Maybe I should get an old gasoline-powered buggy like John's. All he has to do is jump in and turn the key.*

Steven continued complaining to himself as he whipped out of the driveway. *Maybe I should get married again. Then I wouldn't have to waste so much time running all over town. Yikes! What am I saying? Even this is better than marriage. I'll never make that mistake again, no matter what anyone says.*

He picked up the children at their different locations and headed for home. As he entered his driveway, he noticed John's green truck parked in front of the house. John was nowhere in sight. Steven led the children into the house, wondering what John was up to now.

"Where on earth have you been?" John shouted as they entered the kitchen door.

"Picking up the kids."

"So you don't know," John said. "Don't you ever watch TV? I told you it would happen. I knew it. I drove right over after work to tell you the news."

Steven grabbed him by the shoulders. "Calm down. Just tell us what happened."

"It hit Tokyo at four o'clock this afternoon. They've been dreading it since 1923."

"What hit Tokyo?" William asked.

"An earthquake, magnitude 8.4, right in the heart of the city."

Steven felt sick. "You're kidding, right?"

"Kidding? No, I'm not kidding. There's devastation everywhere. Hundreds of thousands of people dead. They don't know the exact number. The city was leveled. Even their new, reinforced skyscrapers. I told you the great devastations of the last days were beginning, but you wouldn't believe me."

Steven sank to the couch. The children were frightened by his bloodless face and piled onto the couch next to him. No one understood better than Steven what this meant. "Sit down, John," he said weakly. "Tell me what you know."

"I'm afraid I don't know much . . . At 8:02 a.m. Japanese time—that's 4:02 p.m. our time—an earthquake measuring 8.4 on the Richter scale hit Tokyo. It's epicenter was right under the city. It hit at the worst possible time, during the morning rush hour. The quake lasted about sixty seconds and there have been several strong aftershocks. There are fires everywhere in the city."

Steven was dazed and couldn't say a word. For decades the experts had declared that another quake would strike Tokyo someday. It was a question of *when* not *if*. Some scientists believed that the cycle was about once every seventy years, meaning it was long overdue from their point of view.

"Dad, are you okay?" Jennifer said with a worried frown, her voice trembling.

"Yeah, I'm fine." Her words had brought Steven back to reality. "Let's turn on the TV and see if we can find any reports." He touched the switch and everyone watched while the television came alive.

". . . not all in yet," the newscaster said, "but it is estimated that there have been at least a half million casualties in Tokyo alone. And the totals are mounting every minute. Most of the casualties have resulted from collapsed buildings, falling glass, and from the fire that is raging in the city. The fires are especially bad because of the high winds in the area. All essential services in the city have been disrupted, including gas, water, power, and sewer lines. Since there is no water, and most of the firefighting equipment has been destroyed, the authorities have no means of fighting the fires. There are hundreds of water storage tanks on the outskirts west of the city but the trucks bringing it in cannot penetrate very far into the city because virtually every street is blocked by tangled masses of debris . . . I repeat again, a massive earthquake has struck Tokyo at 8:02 a.m. today, Tokyo time. We will bring you a complete report on the regular Channel Four six o'clock news."

Steven flipped to several other channels and received three more reports giving essentially the same information. He turned the TV off and looked at his children.

"Could that happen to us, Dad?" Jennifer said.

"I don't think so, sweetheart."

"Sure it could, Jen," John said. "We live in an earthquake zone and there hasn't been a big quake in Utah for centuries. Some geologists believe that when there's a lack of quakes, the pressure builds up and you get a really big one sooner or later."

William's eyes were alive with excitement. "Gee whiz, I hope so. I've heard that during a big quake the earth can open up wide and swallow you up." He seemed delighted to see Jennifer and Andrew cringe.

Steven scowled at his older son. "No, the earth doesn't open up. You've been watching too many movies. As for you, John, were you asleep yesterday? We had two small quakes, remember? Doesn't that count for releasing pressure?

"Not necessarily. They were probably too small to do any good. It's possible they were only foreshocks. It happens all the time, and then—wham! The big one."

"Look. I'm no seismologist, but even I know Utah gets hundreds of quakes over a period of a few years. They usually measure from about 1.5 to 5.5 at the most, and people don't even feel the majority of them."

John said, "Steve, you're not listening to me. It's getting worse. We're close to the end of the world and it's prophesied that the Lord will speak to this wicked and unbelieving world with the voice of lightning and thunder and earthquakes."

"Okay, that's enough," Steven said. "We've been through this many times. You're scaring the kids." He decided to encourage John to go home. "By the way, what happened yesterday? I thought you were going to take your family to high ground in case the dams break in Provo Canyon."

John gave him a sheepish grin. "Hah! That was a dumb idea. Tania reminded me that we're already on high ground here on Grandview Hill."

Steven had been so upset by John the day before that he hadn't even remembered they lived on a hill. "Yes, of course. Trust a woman to set us straight. But still, are you completely prepared for the big quake you think is coming?"

"You know we're ready. But I can take a hint. You're trying to get rid of me." John headed for the door.

Steven followed him and said, "I'm sorry, but I've got so much to do." As he waved good-bye, he noticed it was still raining. The rain no longer seem refreshing, but rather ominous.

After supper the children went into the boys' bedroom to play video games, and Steven turned on the television again to check for further reports on Tokyo. Every station was covering the disaster, and he stopped at Channel Five to hear their report.

"The fire is still ravaging the city," the anchorwoman said. "Yesterday a cyclone drove west across Sagami Bay and caused violent winds and torrential rains in Tokyo. Although the cyclone moved on to the Sea of Japan during the night, there are still winds estimated at fifty miles per hour over Tokyo, which are fanning the flames and driving them throughout the city."

"That's right, Marsha," the anchorman said. "Some witnesses say the fires have overtaken several pockets of thousands of people taking refuge in supposedly safe places, but the fire is burning up the oxygen in the air and is suffocating people en masse. It's especially tragic when we realize that Japanese authorities are helpless to do anything. Believe me when I say this is one of the worst disasters of all time."

Steven was sick at heart. This catastrophe reminded him of the great 1923 Tokyo earthquake which had taken one hundred and fifty thousand lives and destroyed 2.5 billion dollars in property. But this time it was much worse because greater Tokyo had a population of sixteen million and was much more developed. Even the super skyscrapers, which were designed to be earthquake proof, had collapsed like so many dominos. The soft fill materials in east Tokyo made the devastation even worse in that part of the city. His cell phone rang and Steven turned down the television so he could answer.

"Hello, Steve."

"Julie!" Steven was pleased to hear the voice of his younger sister who lived in Manti with her husband, Mike Godet, and their four children. Julie, who was thirty-four, was the second oldest child in the Christopher family after Steven. He had always been close to her.

"You've heard the news?" Julie asked.

"About Tokyo? Yes, I'm watching the reports now."

"Oh, Steve, it's so awful. Those poor people. Are you okay? I know how much you love the Japanese people."

"It's hard to take," Steven said with tears in his eyes. "At least none of my Japanese friends live right in the city. I'm trying to get up the courage to check on them."

"I'm sure they're fine. Please don't be upset." Julie hesitated. "Why did this have to happen to so many innocent people?"

"I don't know. I really don't know."

"Mike and I were concerned about you, and I decided to call."

"I'm all right. Thanks for your concern. You don't need to worry."

"But I *do* worry," she said. "Well, I'll let you go. I'm going to call Mom and Dad, and the other members of the family."

"No need to call John. He's already been here with the news and a reminder that this is one of the great judgments of God."

"That figures. It's just like John to scare people with more doom and gloom. Good-bye, Steve. I'll call again in a few days."

"Thanks, Julie. See you later."

Steven walked over to his chair and turned off the television. He couldn't bear to watch the scenes of destruction anymore. He had always wondered why it was that people seemed so fascinated with the morbid and violent. As he sat in the chair, he tried to imagine what might result from the Tokyo earthquake. He had read a book and several magazine articles during his studies at BYU which predicted that if a major quake struck Tokyo, it would cause untold damage and loss of life and would paralyze the economies of almost every nation in the world. To rebuild Tokyo, which would cost trillions of dollars, Japanese institutions would have to sell their overseas investments, especially several trillion dollars in US government bonds. This would result in a worldwide panic to get rid of T-bonds. It would be especially bad now because the dollar was weak against the yen. US interest rates would rise and the stock market plummet, followed by all other world markets. Steven hoped these dire predictions were exaggerated, but they made him feel uneasy nevertheless.

He tried to contact six Japanese friends on his cell but he couldn't get a connection. He went downstairs to his office and sent them e-mail messages, hoping to get responses soon. At nine o'clock he went into the boys' room to check on his children and found the boys still playing video games and Jennifer doing her math homework.

"Okay, kids, it's reading time."

After the children begged to continue what they were doing for a few more minutes and he refused, they jumped onto William's bed next to their father. Steven was pleased to see that despite their protests they always loved having him read to them. From a table near the bed he grabbed his copy of *Les Misérables* by Victor Hugo and began to read. He would have preferred to read it to them in the original language, but somehow he never seemed to have time to teach them enough French. The story was exciting and full of action, and the children asked him question after question. Jennifer and Andrew expressed great sorrow for the trials and pains of the hero, Jean Valjean. At ten o'clock their eyelids began to droop, so he put the book away and tucked them into bed. It always seemed strange to Steven that this was the time he felt the most guilty—guilty for not wanting to pray with them and for the other mistakes he made as a father. Guilty also that he had not been a good husband.

In his own bed Steven listened to the rain on the roof, feeling unbearably lonely. It was coming down harder now. In a way, he almost wished John was right, and that the time had finally come for something new and unusual to happen, even if it resulted in great changes and perilous events. It was so tiring to do the same thing every day and to bear the entire burden of the family. On the other hand, he doubted that he was ready to face the challenges or worthy to endure the trials. Hoping to fall asleep quickly, he avoided thinking about Selena and the Tokyo disaster and focused instead on the comforting sound of the rain hitting the roof.

During the next two days, Steven was happy to receive e-mail messages from all his Japanese friends indicating they were all right. He finished his translation for the Provo cosmetics company and received a long Japanese document from a new client. This client urgently requested that he translate it immediately and forward it to a major investment broker. Before Steven began the translation, he perused the document and saw it dealt with the potential economic repercussions of the Tokyo earthquake. The economist who wrote the report concluded that many Japanese investors expected the disaster to have extremely negative effects on world markets. Steven finished his translation at 5:00 p.m. on Saturday and immediately sent it to the broker in an e-mail attachment. The rain continued without ceasing. Steven was surprised and irritated. He couldn't remember a time when it had rained this steadily in Provo for more than an hour or two.

His irritation vanished when he heard a soft movement behind him. "Dad, I was wondering if you could do me a favor?" Jennifer said in her sweetest voice. She wrapped her slender arms around his neck.

Steven knew Jennifer was an expert at manipulating him, but he still found it hard to resist her. Even the boys sometimes sent Jennifer to talk to him in order to get what they wanted. "Yes, sweetheart, I'll do anything you want. Well, almost anything."

"Are you done with your work for a while?" she said in the same voice.

"Yes, thank heavens. What do you need?"

"I was kind of wondering if you'd like to take the family to the movies tonight since you're not busy. It would be like a family outing."

Steven was anxious to please her because she was usually helpful and considerate. "All right. I'll get the newspaper so we can pick a movie."

"We've already picked one."

"Okay. Which film is it?" Steven became suspicious when he spotted the boys peeking through the door of his study.

"It's an old thriller movie called Titanic." Then she added quickly, "It's supposed to be one of the best movies ever made. They're showing a rerun at the Pleasant Grove theater."

"Titanic! That's a pretty frightening movie, and I understand there are some bad scenes in it."

"I know," Jennifer said, "but the newspaper said the movie theater edited out all the bad parts."

Steven laughed. "If they edited the movie, you can be sure Paramount Studios will begin foaming at the mouth and mobilize their army of high-paid lawyers to defend their rights. They've done it in the past."

Jennifer didn't seem to understand what her father was talking about. "So can we go?"

"The film still has some disturbing scenes. Do you think you kids can handle it?" Steven wanted to protect his children, but he didn't want to overdo it. Jennifer nodded her head vigorously. "Okay, are you ready now?" Before he got the words out, the children screamed their delight, pounced on him, and pulled him up the stairs.

Steven had seen the movie and had been horrified at the sight of hundreds of helpless people running desperately in all directions, crying and shrieking as they faced certain death. And later in the water, their screams gradually turned into anguished moans and finally—silence. These movie scenes reminded him of the scriptural prophecies about the last days when the spectacles of bloodshed, suffering, and devastation would be far greater than anything that had occurred before in the history of mankind.

After the movie the children wanted to stay up and watch a late-night TV film, but Steven insisted they go to bed to be bright and fresh for church the next day. They wailed almost as much as the people on the Titanic but went to bed anyhow.

Chapter 3

Sunday morning Steven and the children were nervous when they arrived at the Grandview Second Ward because this was their first Sunday at the new ward. Since it was still raining, they hurried from their Chevrolet to the protection of the building. After walking through the doors, they saw a tall gray-haired man in his fifties heading their way. "Good morning," he said with a warm smile. "I'm Bishop Justesen. Welcome to our ward."

"Thank you. I'm Steven Christopher and these are my children, William, Jennifer, and Andrew."

"Oh yes. We've been expecting you. You're John Christopher's brother. John's a good man and we enjoy having him and his family in our ward. Since he's a supervisor in the Provo City maintenance department, he gives us some great advice on how to get along with the city."

Steven wondered if the bishop was really as pleased to have John in the ward as he said. "Yes, John's very talented and also quite a character." Immediately Steven felt guilty for those words. He knew he was a little ashamed of John and often tried to distance himself from his brother and to show everyone that he—unlike John—was normal.

The bishop didn't seem to notice that Steven had said anything out of line. "I knew you moved into your new house the first part of the week because we got a special report from Sister Goodrich. It was everything I could do to stop her from singing your praises. She's a wonderful woman and a great help to the ward. But if you don't watch out, she'll try to marry you off to one of our single women." The bishop chuckled.

Steven laughed and Jennifer glared. "It won't be an easy thing to do," Steven said. "Bishop, can you tell me your meeting schedule?"

"Yes. We have sacrament meeting at nine. Then Sunday school and priesthood, in that order. Priesthood is held in the chapel. Let's see. You're an elder so then you'll meet in room six today because the elders and high priests are having a combined meeting. Your oldest boy will meet with the deacons in room four and your other two children will go upstairs to primary. For Sunday school class go to room ten."

"Thank you. I think we can find our way. Is that right, kids?" The children nodded.

"All right, but if you have problems ask any member for help. Once again, welcome to our ward. I'll ask my secretary to give you a call in a day or two to arrange a meeting." He waved as he hurried into the chapel.

At 11:00 a.m. Steven took Andrew and Jennifer upstairs to primary and set out for priesthood meeting with William. As they descended the stairs, Steven caught sight of Florence Goodrich in the foyer below, or rather she caught sight of him. The instant she saw him, she stopped talking to a pretty young blonde of about thirty, smiled broadly, and dragged the blonde toward him.

"How delightful to see you at church this morning, Brother Steven Christopher," she said in a loud voice. "This is Sister Mary Fleming. Like you, she is not currently attached to anyone. Her husband ran off last year with some little redhead, and now she's sharing a house with Sister Andrea Warren, who—in spite of all my efforts—is getting to be an old maid. You'll have to meet Andrea. She's such a card. Well, now. I've got to hurry off to Relief Society—I'm giving the lesson—so I'll leave you two alone to get acquainted." She sped down the hall looking quite pleased with herself.

Steven's face was hot with embarrassment. Obviously Sister Goodrich wasn't wasting any time in trying to get him hooked up with one of the "available" females. "It's, uh, nice to meet you, Sister Fleming," he stammered.

"I'm glad to meet you also, Steven," she said. "Sister Goodrich has told me a lot about you and your family. I'm sorry she's so blunt. That's just the way she is."

"Oh, no problem. Uh . . . yes. I guess I'd better get going or I'll be late for my meeting," he said lamely. "See you later." As he turned to go, he caught a glimpse of her shapely figure.

The pretty, green-eyed blonde was clearly disappointed. "Oh. Yes. We can talk again sometime."

Steven flew into the chapel like a condemned man trying to escape the guillotine. He and William quickly spotted John near the front and joined him. Steven was relieved to see that this ward appeared to be like every other ward he had attended. During the short meeting Steven tried to pay attention to the announcements but was unable to stop thinking about Mary Fleming. When the opening session was over, several men came up to Steven and William and welcomed them to the ward. Soon William left for his quorum meeting with one of the men, who was the deacon's advisor, and Steven and John hurried down the hall to find the adult priesthood class.

When they reached their destination, Steven was surprised at the size of the room, which was easily large enough for the forty men in attendance. As John led him to the back of the room, he said, "Let's sit off to the side back here so we can talk without being overheard." Steven didn't argue because he was feeling somewhat uncomfortable. He noticed that the ages of the men ranged from about twenty to eighty-five years.

After the prayer, Homer Billings, the high priest group leader, stood up, welcomed the members, and turned to Steven, saying, "Today we have a new member with us. The bishop welcomed you in the other meeting, but I didn't catch your name. Would you like to tell us a little about yourself?"

This was the part Steven hated the most, and he wanted to be done with it as soon as possible. "Yes. My name is Steven Christopher. I'm an elder. I have three children. We just moved from Harbor Park. I'm a freelance translator in French and Japanese. I'm the brother of John here. I'm happy to be in this ward because it seems very friendly. And that's about it." He dropped to his chair immediately. Although Steven had been a member of the Church all his life, he had never felt completely at ease introducing himself in priesthood meeting or Sunday school class.

"We want to welcome you again, Brother Christopher," the group leader said. "We can always use another good man. What did you say your wife's name was?"

Steven's face turned a bright red because he always felt embarrassed when asked that question. "At the present time, I'm not married."

Some of the brethren looked surprised, but the aging leader went on as if he hadn't heard a word. "That's wonderful, Brother Christopher. Thank you." He gazed at the floor with a blank look and his counselor whispered something in his ear. "Oh, uh, yes. Today's lesson will be given by Brother Russell Mikkelson. He'll announce the subject."

Steven had developed the habit of observing human behavior and the ways people express themselves, and he was always fascinated by what he learned. He believed this habit helped him create more sensitive and accurate translations. He watched as Mikkelson, a balding man of forty, nervously shuffled his notes.

"To start with, brethren, I want to warn you that I was too busy to prepare this here lesson until late last night. Since I didn't have no time to make up a proper lesson, I thought we could talk about current events, so to speak. I did the best I could to jot down some notes, but I was hoping mostly to get you brethren started and let you run with it. I hope you will all join in." Steven liked the man immediately. Even though Russell wasn't educated, he seemed to be humble and honest. "I was especially thinking about the terrible earthquake that happened three days ago in Tokyo. Who would like to say something about that?" Several hands went up and Russell nodded to one of the men.

In a low voice John said to Steven. "This is Michael Stark. He drives trucks for LaCrosse Enterprises here in Provo. Excellent man. Well informed about everything."

Michael said, "Brethren, I believe the destruction of Tokyo will precipitate an economic collapse in the United States and most European nations within the next few months. This collapse may bring about the destruction of the US government. As you all know, the fall of the government has been prophesied." Michael was a short, chubby man with a full head of blond hair. He wore a string tie and cowboy pants and boots.

"Where do you get that from the scriptures, Brother Stark?" another man said.

"That's Floyd Madsen," John whispered. "The poor sap thinks he knows everything about religion because he's a history professor at BYU. He's your typical liberal who pooh-poohs everything."

Steven frowned. He looked around and was relieved that no one seemed to be able to hear John. He did not appreciate John whispering to him and describing the men who were talking. He listened more intently, wondering whether or not this group could discuss a controversial issue without becoming upset with one another. In the past he had seen many doctrinal discussions degenerate into arguments because the men couldn't disagree without becoming angry. He also noticed the worried look on the group leader's face.

Michael picked up his triple combination and flipped pages until he came to his reference. "Turn to Revelation, chapter 13." He waited a few seconds. "Note that the introduction to chapter 13 in the official LDS scriptures says that the beasts represent degenerate earthly kingdoms. Next, turn to Revelation 19:20." He stopped until they found the reference. "Here you see that the beast and the false prophet are cast into hell, or in other words, they are destroyed. Now when you look at the scandals, bribery, corruption, and abuse of power which are rampant in this country, you'll all have to admit that the American government has become a degenerate kingdom and is ripe for destruction. I believe this government must fall first before the unholy New World Order can gain total power in the earth."

"Like I've been saying all along," John muttered.

Steven examined the faces of those present and saw disbelief or shock on most of them. The poor group leader looked as though he was about to have a stroke.

Floyd said, "I understand what you're saying, Brother Stark, but I'm not sure we should make definite predictions on the basis of the Book of Revelation. It is full of imagery and symbols and probably no one fully understands their meaning. Besides, didn't Joseph Smith say we shouldn't concern ourselves with interpreting the meaning of the beasts? No, I think there are millions of good people in America at this point in time and it will be a long while before this country will be obliterated, if ever."

Michael Stark shook his head and said, "I didn't say America would be obliterated. I said the US government would be destroyed."

At that moment a young man with black hair and a short beard raised his hand and was recognize by the teacher.

"Byron Mills," John mumbled from the corner of his mouth. "He's a building contractor who sees himself as the ward scriptorian. Good man but a bit pompous."

After pausing a few seconds, Byron turned and looked at Michael. "The trouble is, Brother Stark, you're not looking at the entire text of Revelation. If you read carefully from chapter 12 through chapter 19, you'll see that Babylon the great Harlot, which represents all false philosophy and religion, is destroyed before the beast. In chapter 17, verse 16 we read that it is the beast or the degenerate governments which eat and burn the great Harlot. Then in chapter 19 we see a description of the great war of Armageddon, after which the beast is cast into the lake of fire and brimstone. I conclude, therefore, that what you said about the fall of America is not possible yet. Firstly, because all worldly religion and philosophy, in other words Babylon, has not been annihilated at this time, and secondly because Armageddon hasn't taken place yet."

Steven was intrigued by the imperious manner with which Byron punctuated his words. He noted that Byron had completely ignored Michael's explanation that it was the government which would fall, not the entire nation. He searched Michael's face and waited for the fireworks. He almost hoped that Michael would have a good answer because he had always had a soft spot for the underdog, except in the case of John.

"Don't you have something to say, John?" Steven whispered.

"Don't worry. Michael can handle these guys any day."

Stark said, "Byron, it's possible you may be right about the meaning of the Book of Revelation, but as Floyd said, it's difficult to understand what it means in detail. However, there are many predictions from latter-day prophets, including Brigham Young and Wilford Woodruff, which state that the US government will fall before the building of the New Jerusalem, Armageddon, and the Second Coming."

"You know," another man said, "I don't think it matters who is right."

"Lyman Jones," John murmured. "He figures he knows all the answers."

Lyman was a sixty-year-old man with a bald head and a paunch. "Now listen to what I'm going to say, brethren. I'm not going to repeat it. As you all know by now, I'm the best darn cop in Provo and you'd better not mess with me." Everyone laughed. "Especially since I'm only five years from retirement." The laughter grew louder. "All this stuff about the horrible events of the last days really isn't important. People get too caught up with doom and gloom, storing food and guns, moving into the mountains for protection, and building underground bunkers and nonsense like that. But the truth is, all we have to do is go to church, say our prayers, pay our tithing, do our home teaching, and be an all-round nice person. And that's it in a nutshell."

Steven was amused because he had heard that definition of righteousness many times before. He knew that obeying the fundamentals was essential but there was more to it than that. One of the scriptures he could remember from his missionary days was the *Joseph Smith Translation* of Hebrews 6:1, which says, "Therefore not leaving the principles of the doctrine of Christ, let us go on unto perfection . . ."

Apparently John could bear it no longer and raised his hand. "I appreciate all the opinions which have been expressed here this morning, but I should remind this group of the words of Brigham Young who said that a man's opinion isn't worth a straw. I guess he meant that what really counts is the revealed word of God." Steven noticed that John had adopted the diplomatic tone of Floyd Madsen and was obviously trying to discredit the opinions of Lyman Jones. "And the scriptures clearly state that the true saints of God will know the signs of the times and the *season* of the Second Coming. They will look forward to that coming with happiness and joy. In other words, it's very important for us to recognize the signs of the times."

"Where do you find all that in the scriptures?" Floyd said.

Steven was delighted. All this reminded him of his mission. In those days when anyone said, "Chapter and verse," it was the same as a challenge.

John thumbed through his quadruple combination, marked neatly with all the colors of the rainbow. "Okay, look in Doctrine and Covenants 45:39." John waited until they all seemed to have it. "Note that the Lord says he who fears him shall look for the great day of the Lord—that's the Second Coming—and for the signs of that day." None of the brethren said a word. "In Doctrine and Covenants 35:15 it adds the idea that it is the poor and meek who will look forth for the time of Christ's coming."

"Now as to the time of Christ's coming, Paul the Apostle tells us that the faithful saints will know the general period of time. Turn to I Thessalonians 5:1-6." Again John paused to give them time to find the reference. "In verse 1, Paul says he doesn't have to write to the Thessalonians about the times and seasons of Christ's coming because they already know about that. In verse 2 he says the Thessalonians know perfectly well that the day of the Lord will come as a thief in the night, which means the Second Coming will surprise the wicked, not the righteous. We can see that idea more clearly if we refer to Doctrine and Covenants 106:5-6. In verse 5 Christ says his coming will overtake the *world* as a thief in the night, and in verse 6 he admonishes the saints to be righteous so his great day will *not* overtake them as a thief."

John paused and looked around the room. "Are you all following me?" A few of the brethren nodded and others were busy flipping the pages of their scriptures. "Okay, let's go back to I Thessalonians, chapter 5. In verse 4 Paul also cautions the saints to not let the Lord's coming catch them by surprise. But why? Because if they are caught unawares, it's a sign they are wicked. And in verse 6 he declares that the saints should watch for the Second Coming."

"Wait now," Lyman said. "You may be right that people should study the signs of the times and look forward to the Second Coming, but I don't agree with you that the saints or anyone else can know the time of his coming. We've all heard of the scripture which teaches that no man knows the day or the hour, but you seem to be saying the opposite."

"Not at all," John said. "No man knows the day or the hour, but the righteous will know the *season,* or the general time period, because they are studying the signs. So Christ's coming will not surprise them. But just because we know the season, it doesn't give us the right to make specific predictions. We shouldn't tell people that Christ will come four years from now during the summer."

Since no one said a word, John continued. "A little while ago I mentioned what our attitude should be toward Christ's coming. It's not enough for us to look forward to that day. If you read the book of Isaiah, you'll see that great prophet taught over and over that the righteous should *anticipate* the Second Coming with hope and joy. If we are prepared, that is, if we are righteous and fill our lamps with the oil of the Holy Spirit, then the idea of Christ's Coming will fill us with joy. It's only when we do these things—seek righteousness, learn the signs, and joyfully look for Christ's coming—that we will be truly inspired to repent and make our lives holy." John sat down next to Steven.

Steven had never seen John so precise and calm. Reluctantly, he admired his brother at that moment. He almost snickered when he saw Byron Mills frantically searching through the Topical Guide in his Bible.

"Hah! I've been in the Church for sixty-five years now," one of the high priests blurted out without being recognized by the teacher, "and I've never heard of those scriptures, so maybe John could give them to me again after class."

"That's Buford Hanes. He owns a small restaurant down on State Street," John whispered as he smiled at Hanes.

Floyd, however, didn't seem quite so satisfied. "Well, John, that was very *enlightening*. But I don't think God wants us to spend half our life studying the signs of the times and analyzing every unusual event. We need to spend that time doing good to our neighbors and magnifying our callings. And what does Paul mean by times and seasons? If the term one day sometimes means a thousand years in the scriptures, what on earth is a season? It might mean the same as epoch or age. And to say we should look forward to the Second Coming with hope and joy is, in my opinion, not being completely realistic. When this world approaches the end there are going to be millions—perhaps billions—of people destroyed, and some of them will be righteous. It's only natural for good, faithful people, like those in this room, to be nervous and scared. I think it's dangerous to take scriptures out of context and draw hard and fast conclusions. To understand the whole story, we have to look at all the scriptures and also the words of our leaders."

Russell Mikkelson, the teacher, looked at Steven and said, "What do *you* think, Steven? You haven't said a word."

All eyes turned upon Steven. He had been enjoying this discussion immensely, but now he felt as though every man in the room was waiting to see what he was made of. Was he crazy like his brother or a normal, rational person like Floyd?

Steven said, "Well, I don't know for sure. I haven't given it much thought. The only thing is, I don't think John ever suggested we become fanatical about the signs of the times or the Second Coming. And I can't recall him saying we should spend half our life worrying about it or neglecting our church duties. As for Brother Madsen's analysis of the expression 'season,' I'm not sure it's especially accurate. And one thing I know for sure, John never quotes scriptures out of context or ignores the guidance of church leaders. That's all I have to say."

Steven felt like an ignorant dope, but at least he hadn't abandoned his brother. John leaned over and thanked him for his support.

A man with a round, swollen face, and a stomach that flopped over his belt, raised his hand and waved it vigorously. "I'd like to say something,"

"Nolan Carson," John whispered. "A prospective high priest and a postal supervisor. Gets most of his info from TV."

"I've only become active in the last six months and I don't know if what John here says is right or not. I'll have to study it out for myself when I get time. But one thing I can say for sure is we're definitely living in the last days. There's sin everywhere you look. I watch TV a lot and I see some programs that embarrass even me, and believe you me, I'm no puritan. And that's not all. There's tons of crime and pregnant teenagers. Even the public schools ain't safe no more because doped-up crazies are getting guns and shooting little kids. And that's not all. The weather seems to be getting worse every day. There's more storms, quakes, tornadoes, and volcano eruptions than ever before. So I'd say Christ will probably come within the next five or ten years. And take my word for it, that scares me half to death because I know I ain't ready. I ain't got one drop of that precious oil John talked about."

"I agree with Nolan," Michael Stark said. "The Second Coming isn't far away. The reason I say this is because there's a deep-seated, pervasive moral degeneracy in our society. I'll give you one example from a hundred I could mention. The lottery, which is no more than a form of gambling, has become one of the main sources of income for all the states in the union, including Utah. And the excuse for accepting this corruption is that lottery money helps support the schools and provides so many other great benefits to millions of Americans. Without that money those benefits wouldn't exist."

"Wait a minute now," a young elder said at the front of the room. He got up and walked to the blackboard as if he wanted to write something on it.

John whispered, "Gregory Millman, Elders Quorum president, nice guy but usually sticks to all the politically correct ideas."

Gregory faced the class and said, "The world has always been corrupt. I'm not so sure it's worse now than before. Look at the decadence of the Romans and the Greeks. The violence of the Assyrians and Huns. And as for natural disasters, the earth has always suffered them. I don't see them getting worse now than they were hundreds of years ago."

Steven was intrigued to see that the brethren were now making comments without waiting for the teacher to recognize them. Although he had seen a few sparks in their eyes, so far they had done well to control their tempers.

Byron Mills jumped in. "At this point in time I believe the world is pretty wicked but it isn't nearly wicked enough to be destroyed by the Lord. I go along with Floyd when he says there are millions upon millions of good people in the world. That's why the Church is still sending out a hundred thousand missionaries every year."

A handsome young man sitting on Steven's left laughed. "Yes, but the number of attacks against our missionaries has greatly increased in recent years. Don't forget the six missionaries who were shot down in cold blood last month in New Zealand. The police said it happened because they were Mormons. And the Church has pulled out missionaries from five countries already. Because of that—and for other reasons—I think the world is becoming a much more dangerous place, especially for Latter-day Saints."

"That was Quentin Price. He's a doctor in Provo who moved into the ward three months ago," John said. "I'm not sure about him yet."

"In some ways that might be true, I suppose," Floyd said, "but when you look at the big picture, you have to admit there is more peace now than at any time in history. It seems the nations of the world have finally realized the futility of war. As a history professor I have ample opportunity to study these things."

Steven thought about television. The cartoons were so violent that he would not permit his children to see them, and the soap operas and sitcoms portrayed all forms of immorality and violence, including grotesque murder. The most shocking part was that the television writers seemed to delight in scenes where acts of simulated brutality were inflicted upon helpless nude women. He wanted to raise his hand and correct Floyd, but he didn't do it, figuring someone else would make the point.

"I agree," Lyman said. "As a cop I see a lot of bad, but I also see many acts of kindness. And even if there is a lot of evil, it doesn't mean the end is near. Remember that the Lord promised Abraham to spare Sodom and Gomorrah if he could find as few as ten righteous people in those cities."

Michael began to search through his scriptures again. "Hold it. I'm trying to find a passage." He searched frantically but without success. "I can't find it now, but it indicates that even though the wicked will be burned by fire at the Second Coming, those who are living a terrestrial or a celestial law will be spared. Isn't that right?" Several men indicated their agreement. "Well then, that means there will probably be millions of good people who will survive the burning. So not every person on earth has to be wicked before Christ comes. That means the Sodom and Gomorrah comparison is not valid."

Lyman frowned and mumbled something under his breath.

"Oh, I think this old world is pretty far gone," Buford Hanes said. "It's getting so you take your life into your hands if you walk down the street at night, especially in large cities like Provo and Orem. I think the Second Coming is real close. Probably within ten to fifteen years."

"Personally, I think we still have a *long* way to go before that happens," Floyd insisted. "The Lord won't come until men are ripe in iniquity as the scriptures say. Think of all the advances in science and technology, all the efforts by government everywhere to make our lives safer and happier."

"But think of all the illegal drugs everywhere, the prostitution, the disgusting programs on TV, the greed and dishonesty in business, the corruption in high places, the lack of moral values among the people, and the growing crime and divorce rates." It was John, countering Floyd's speech. Steven saw that everyone was surprised, but still he detected no open anger.

Floyd continued as if John had said nothing. "And we have to remember that bad weather and natural disasters have always been with us. What is happening now, even in Tokyo, is not unusual. In fact, if you look at things from an historical point of view, everything is perfectly normal."

At that moment the entire building began to shake violently. The men grabbed on to anything they could find for support, their faces stiff with shock and fear. Their chairs rocked back and forth. Most of the Bibles and lesson manuals fell to the ground. With a loud grinding sound, two of the walls split open. The big blackboard hurtled from the wall onto the floor. The men looked helplessly at one another and around the room, not knowing what to do. A shower of plaster dropped from the ceiling, and a plate-size chunk struck Floyd on the head. The vigorous shaking continued for forty long seconds. Then it ended as suddenly as it had begun.

After a long moment John said quietly, "I think you're right, Floyd. Everything *is* perfectly normal."

The brethren were scared to death, but they still burst out laughing. When the laughter had subsided, Homer said, "That's the third quake we've had in five days." He looked at several men in the front row. "Will you brethren go and check on the women and children to make sure they're okay?" After the men rushed out the door, he turned to the teacher. "You might want to finish things up now, Russell."

Russell looked at an elderly high priest sitting nearby. "I wanted to ask Brother Clark what he thought about our subject for today."

Heber Clark paused and looked at the floor as if he were trying to remember what he wanted to say. Then he looked up and said, "I'll make it short because I know you all want to check on your families. I believe the world is ripe in iniquity and the great events we see today, including the disasters, are proof that the Second Coming is very close. The greatest proof, however, is found in the wars of ideology which rage all around us every day. Today more than ever before, Satan is continuing the War in Heaven, except now he uses false philosophies, false religions, and evil governments to win the souls of men. This is the most important sign of the times. I believe the judgments of God will start with his own people because they need to be chastened. And when it happens, some saints will betray their religion, but hopefully the majority will repent and complete the great work the Lord has given them."

"Thank you, Brother Clark," Russell said. "I guess that's it for today."

As Russell sat down, the high priest group leader, Homer Billings, stood and, with a sly grin on his face, turned to Floyd, who was still brushing the plaster out of his hair. "We need to say a closing prayer now and, Floyd, I think you should offer the prayer for us."

"I think you may be right," Floyd said.

Chapter 4

After the closing prayer, the elders and high priests left immediately to check on their families. No one was seriously injured, but Bishop Justesen announced that the remaining meetings would be canceled. He didn't know how much structural damage the building had suffered and wanted to have it checked by professionals. Steven and John went out the rear door with their families and waded through the flooded parking lot to their vehicles, which were parked close together. Steven saw that the rain had turned into a drizzle, but the wind was blowing hard. As John struggled to open the door of his black SUV, Steven called out to him. "John, why don't you and Tania bring your family to our house instead of going home? We'll whip up something to eat, play some games, and talk about things."

John seemed pleased. After consulting with his family, he shouted, "Okay, they'd like to come. See you in about ten minutes. I want to check on the house first. Oh, by the way, thanks for the support in there."

Steven returned a wave, and William and Andrew hooted with delight. Though the streets were partially flooded and crowded with members anxious to get home, it took only four minutes to cover the distance. They hurried into the house, removed their coats, and sat down to catch their breath. A few minutes later John's family arrived. Their five children piled onto the second couch next to their mother, Tania. Steven and John checked the house for earthquake damage and found a few problems, but nothing they couldn't fix. Steven had purposely waited for John to arrive because his brother was an expert at anything having to do with building and repairs.

"Whew!" Tania said. "Won't this rain ever stop? It's been coming down steadily since last Wednesday. That's unusual for Utah County, isn't it?" Tania came from Cedar City.

"It sure is," John said. "It's raining everywhere, from Ogden to Saint George. But we have to expect crazy weather these days."

"At least the rain feels warm today," Tania said. "Before it was so cold."

John said, "What did you guys think about that quake? I'd say it was about VI or VII on the intensity scale. On the way to your house we heard a report on the radio which said the quake had a magnitude of 5.0 and did minor damage throughout the city. The epicenter was right under Orem."

"I was scared to death," Tania said. "I'm still trembling. I thought the end of the world really had come."

"Yeah, man, it was shake, rattle, and roll!" William hollered with delight.

Patrick—John and Tania's ten-year-old—agreed. "Boy! That was the coolest thing I have *ever* been in."

Jennifer scowled while Andrew and John's other four children remained silent, looking around furtively as though they expected another quake to come at any minute.

John laughed. "Tania, you should have seen what happened to smarty pants Floyd Madsen."

"Tania gave her husband an icy look. "You shouldn't use disparaging terms to describe your fellow man, especially in front of the children." She waited but when John said nothing, she demanded, "Well, what happened to him?"

"He was busy spouting off some false doctrines when the quake hit and a big slab of plaster clobbered him right on the head. He sure looked silly." Even Tania couldn't resist laughing with the others at the idea of Floyd covered with plaster. John turned to Steven. "That sure shut him up, didn't it?"

"He was certainly embarrassed."

"So what did you think of priesthood meeting in this ward?"

"It's been quite a while since I've enjoyed a priesthood meeting that much. You have a lot of men with strong opinions and they aren't afraid to express them. I was surprised when no one lost his temper. I was even more surprised that someone didn't take it upon himself to chastise the others for arguing. That usually happens when Mormons discuss a difficult issue, even when they do it in a pleasant way."

"Yeah, they're a good group," John said. "Even though most of them don't know much."

Steven frowned at his brother. "One thing though. I wish you wouldn't give me your opinions on the character of each of the brethren. You should let me decide that for myself."

"I'm sorry. I thought I was helping."

Tania shot John an angry look. "What was the lesson about?"

Steven replied, "The last days and the signs of the times."

"Oh no. That subject always seems to get people worked up. We had an interesting lesson in Relief Society too."

"Why don't you tell us about it?" Steven suggested.

"Sister Goodrich, the teacher, asked the class what they would do if they knew the Savior was waiting outside to interview each of them. At that the sisters became silent and thoughtful. Before long most of them said they'd be excited and happy. But some looked as if they were waiting in line for the gas chamber at a Nazi death camp. They said they'd be scared to death to face Jesus. Sister Goodrich made the point that we wouldn't feel such fear if we were truly prepared and worthy to meet the Savior."

"Then the earthquake hit. All of us jumped from our seats as if the end of the world had come. A few sisters tore out of the room frantically to check on their kids. Poor Sister Goodrich had to spend the rest of the period calming us down by reading scriptures on peace and serenity."

"Hey. That sounds almost as interesting as our meeting," John said.

Steven got up and found his cell phone. "I'm calling Mom and Dad to see if they're okay."

"Good idea," John said.

Steven punched in the numbers and after several rings he heard his mother's voice. "Hi, Mom, are you guys okay?"

"Yes. It was pretty scary but we're fine. We didn't go to church this morning because we weren't feeling well. The earthquake broke some utensils and a couple of picture frames, but that's about all."

"I was worried about you. I'm glad everything is all right. John and his family are here. I was going to invite you and Dad to join us, but maybe you don't feel up to it."

"No, I don't think we should come. We've got the flu or something. But how do you like your new ward?" Before he could answer, she added, "Say. Maybe you can find a good wife there."

Steven ignored her comment. "Look, Mom, I'd better let you go. Take care of yourselves, okay?"

"We will, dear. Don't worry about us. Good-bye."

The screen went dark and Steven returned to his guests. They spent the rest of the day eating good food and enjoying games with the children. The earthquake and the rain were soon forgotten. After his brother and sister-in-law left in the evening, Steven put his children to bed and began to read the newspaper reports on the Tokyo earthquake. But he couldn't bear the gruesome descriptions of death and destruction and quickly put the paper aside. He thought about the meeting he had attended that morning and was surprised to find himself wishing the other meetings had not been canceled.

He was especially impressed by the powerful testimony of Heber Clark and by his belief that the most characteristic sign of the times was the intensification of ideological wars. He also wondered why Heber had said the judgments of God would begin at his own house when it seemed clear to him that most of the saints were obedient. At least in comparison to him.

"It's about time something exciting happened around here," Andrea Warren said. "Life can sure be boring sometimes."

Mary Fleming leaned back on her couch and said, "Yes, but I'm glad it was only a small earthquake. I'd rather not have the problems people are having in other places."

"Good point. Michael Stark told me the death toll in Tokyo is nearly six hundred thousand people, and that hundreds of other people were killed in several quakes in California."

"Well, while you were taking your nap this afternoon, I heard a special news report which said serious crime was up fifteen percent from last year and a lot of militia groups are defying the federal government."

"Militia groups? I didn't know there were more than a few of them around."

"The report said there may be as many as several hundred thousand dissidents in this country getting ready to wage war against the government. There are even several large groups in the wilderness of southern Utah and northern Arizona."

Andrea yawned and blinked her eyes, obviously getting tired. "Oh, they're too far away to bother us, and anyway I doubt they could ever do much against the government. It would be like a fly trying to kill an elephant."

The conversation lagged for a while, and then Andrea said, "By the way, Florence Goodrich told me there's a new bachelor in the ward."

"Oh?"

"Yes, a good-looking guy, to use Florence's words, named Steven Christopher. It seems he's John Christopher's brother."

"Oh, yes. I think I met him in the foyer today at church. I guess we have three or four bachelors in the ward now."

"The trouble is, this bachelor has three young children. That alone would scare away most single women."

"That's true," Mary said. "It would take a very special kind of woman to take on that responsibility. I don't see myself as special, of course, but I'm sure I could be a mother to a man's children if I loved him and trusted him and he—"

"Right! A very special kind of woman." Andrea gave a little smirk. "But I guess he might be worth it . . . Anyhow, Florence said she introduced you to Steven."

"Yes, she did."

"Why didn't you tell me?"

"Why should I? It really wasn't that important."

Andrea studied Mary's face a moment and said, "What's he like?"

"Nice."

"That's it?"

"No, uh, he's about six one or six two, has dark brown hair and blue eyes, and he looks very fit."

"According to Florence he's thirty-six years old, is a freelance translator, and he's been divorced for about a year. It seems his ex-wife abandoned their family two years ago and joined some polygamous cult in Arizona."

Mary's eyes opened wide with surprise. "Where did Florence learn all that?"

"Oh, you know Florence. She has her sources," Andrea said, laughing. "What Steven's wife did isn't all that unusual. I've heard three or four stories where married LDS women ran away to join polygamous groups . . . What's the matter with them? Are they crazy?"

"I don't understand why they do it. All I know is *I* wouldn't do it."

"Do you like this new guy?"

"Certainly. I like everyone."

Andrea rolled her eyes. "You know what I mean," she said, frowning.

"I just met him!"

"I only ask you that question to see if I would like him, because we seem to have the same taste in men. If he's as fantastic as Florence says, maybe I should go for him myself. All those kids make it harder, but I'm sure I could adapt and become a good mother for them."

"Andrea, you make me laugh. It's hilarious to hear you talk like that now when you've always said you don't *need* or particularly *want* a man. But let a new bachelor come into the ward and whammo you talk about being the mother of his children. The fact is, you're thirty-one years old and you still give every man you meet a hard time."

"That's because every available man I meet is either sick, stupid, wants a second mother, has no job, or can't control his hormones."

"Come now. You're exaggerating."

"Listen, I'm not about to hurry and marry some slob simply because of the belief that I need a husband to get to the celestial kingdom."

"Yes, that would be foolish, but if you're waiting for the perfect man, you'll never get married."

Andrea glared at her roommate impatiently. "Enough of that! Are you interested in this guy or not?"

"Let's say I wouldn't mind going out with him if he asked. The problem is, after the betrayal of his ex I wonder if he would allow himself to get involved in another relationship."

"He will. Men have short memories and strong hormones. If a great looking woman like you shows she's interested, he'll come around sooner or later. He'd be crazy not to. You're young, beautiful, intelligent, blonde, and you've got a killer body."

Mary laughed but quickly became serious. "There's something you're not considering. Maybe *I* don't want another man. Remember, my ex betrayed me too, and it will be hard for me to trust again."

"I thought you had gotten over that. Your ex-husband was a creep from the word go. He didn't even want to have children. Most men aren't like that. Look at Steven Christopher. According to Florence, he's a hard worker and a responsible father. I'm sure he'd make a wonderful husband and you'd make a fantastic wife and mother."

"You are too much to believe. Talk about inconsistent. A minute ago you said that every available man you meet is a slob and now you say most of them are noble souls. And you talk about Steven as if you've known him for years when you haven't even met him."

"Okay, okay, but you get my point. All I'm saying is you should be cautious but give Steven or some other guy a chance." Andrea yawned again.

"You look tired. Why don't you go to bed? It's getting late."

"Maybe you're right. I'm so tired I can't keep my eyes open. We'll have to discuss all this another time." Andrea dragged herself out of her chair and headed for the bathroom.

As her friend disappeared from view, Mary called after her, "And why don't you take your *own* advice?"

Gilbert Hoffman forced himself out of bed at one thirty in the morning on Monday, after only three hours sleep. He staggered into the kitchen and prepared some quick-brew coffee. After gulping two cups, he wobbled back into the bedroom.

His wife Edith rolled over in their bed and looked at him through bleary eyes. "You've got to go again? You checked it three times yesterday."

Gilbert started to dress. "I know, but it's been raining nonstop and I don't want to take any chances."

"My gosh, you're such a fanatic. Dear Lord, tell me why I had to marry a dam tender. Gilbert, the stupid dam is okay. Come back to bed."

"No," he said shortly. "The lives of thousands of people are in my hands. I'm going."

Gilbert finished dressing and hurried out the door. He swore when he saw the rain coming down in torrents. He went back in and grabbed his umbrella and raincoat. Usually the drive from his house in Provo to Deer Creek Dam took about a half hour, and he felt an urgent need to hurry. He tried to calm himself as he climbed into his car. *What's the use of getting all shook up?* he thought. *I've been checking the dam several times a day since Wednesday and everything is under control. Saturday night I opened both spillway gates about ten percent to handle the increased volume in the reservoir. It's idiotic to fret like this when nothing is wrong. Maybe Edith's right—I'm nothing but a fanatic.* And yet he couldn't shake the nagging feeling that something wasn't quite right.

Gilbert looked down at his speedometer as he headed north on University Avenue. He was going sixty miles an hour in this weather. He had already run three red lights and now he was exceeding the speed limit. He slowed to forty and told himself over and over to take it easy. Like most people, Gilbert talked to himself out loud when no one else was around, and when he was nervous or worried he chattered incessantly. After entering the canyon, he was forced to slow to thirty-five.

"Blast this road! Mud everywhere. Hard to see in the dark with all this rain. At least the wipers are working . . . Holy cow, I'm starting to slide. No, it's okay. Only a few miles to go." He slowed to twenty-five as the road became worse. The trip seemed to take forever. "A lot of good it did to widen this road and build tunnels and everything." He swore again and slowed to fifteen miles an hour. "Finally! The campground . . . and there's the power plant." He checked his watch. "It took me forty minutes to get here." He drove down the small road to the power plant at the foot of the dam, got out of his car, and walked over to the Provo River. The water volume looked normal, so he hurried back to his car. He drove up the hill to the dam and parked his car in the small parking lot at the top of the dam near the spillways. Grabbing his umbrella and his powerful flashlight, he walked across the two-lane highway to the first spillway.

"It sure is dark tonight. Hard to see a lousy thing, even with *this* flashlight." He leaned over the rail and pointed the bright beam of light at the huge gate at the top of the first spillway. He directed the light down the spillway. "Good. No obstructions." He proceeded to the second spillway. "Looks like you're okay too." He walked to the upstream side of the dam to check the water level. "A little more than three feet below the top of the dam. In an hour or two I'll radio in. They'll probably want me to open the gates a lot more." He went back to the road, which crossed over the dam, and began to walk the 1,304 foot length of the dam, checking the downstream side for damage or leaks. In spite of the raincoat and the umbrella, he was soaked by the time he reached the end. As he walked back he checked the upstream side for anything unusual. *Great!* he thought when he reached his car. *Everything appears to be normal. I guess I was worried for nothing.*

But Gilbert was a very careful man. He decided to wait in his car instead of returning to Provo. He turned on the car's motor and heater and lay down on the seat. He was wet and uncomfortable, but he fell asleep almost immediately. A half hour later he awoke and checked the reservoir's water level again. There was not much difference, so he returned to his car and tried to doze off. This time he couldn't fall asleep in spite of the fact that he was exhausted, and he debated as to whether or not he should drive back to Provo. He was positive the dam was all right but that nagging feeling wouldn't go away. Finally, he decided to play it safe. He would drive east to Heber for coffee and a bite to eat and be back to check the dam within fifty minutes.

Gilbert felt better to be on the road. It was three forty and sunrise was only about an hour and a half away. There were a few small landslides partly covering the right side of the winding road and an occasional vehicle coming from the opposite direction, but he was able to continue at a good pace. When he reached Heber he pulled into the Tri-Mart convenience store, which was open all night.

The clerk seemed happy to see him and smiled broadly. "Hello, Gilbert. It's good to see you," she said. "What are you doing here at this hour?"

"Hi, Mavis. Just keeping an eye on the dam."

"Do you think there's any danger?"

"No, but it's been raining steady for over four days and I'm not taking any chances, especially since the rain is so warm."

"Yeah, that warm rain sure melts the snow pack fast," Mavis said. "I'm glad you're so conscientious. I wish you were up there watching our monster."

"Jordanelle?"

She shuddered. "Yes! It towers over us like some huge beast ready to belch forth billions of gallons of water and drown us all. I feel it there day and night, watching us and waiting for the right moment."

Gilbert knew Jordanelle was only six miles away and made many people in Heber nervous. "Don't worry so much," he said. "It's perfectly safe." He remembered all the controversy surrounding the safety of the dam when it was built and wondered if it really was safe.

"That's what all you government employees say. Look, let's not talk about it anymore. It really depresses me. What would you like?"

Gilbert paused a second. "I think I'll have a cup of coffee, a ham sandwich, and two packs of those small chocolate-covered donuts."

"Let me get those things for you, Gilbert. You look awfully tired."

"Why thanks, Mavis, that's sure nice of you."

Gilbert talked to Mavis while he ate his food. Then he ordered a second cup of coffee, reluctant to go out again in the downpour. After his second cup, he said good-bye, opened the umbrella, and ran for his car. He thought about Jordanelle Dam as he made his way out of town. *A hundred and four billion gallons of water when the reservoir is full. Think what it would do to this valley if it failed. And it would finish Deer Creek in minutes!*

The idea made him shiver. Feeling an urgent need to get back to his dam, he stepped on the gas in spite of the weather and nearly skidded off the road several times. He reached the small parking lot on the far side of the dam at four thirty. Immediately he grabbed the flashlight and jumped out of his car, forgetting his umbrella. "Wow! The water's two feet below the crest of the dam. That's going up fast." He returned to his car and radioed to base. "Falcon to base. Over." He repeated the message three times.

Seconds later the radio crackled. "This is base. Go ahead, Falcon."

"Our little doe is slightly over maximum fill. Shall I drop her a bit?"

Gilbert waited impatiently, knowing the base operator was getting the go-ahead from the powers that be. "Poor dumb lackey can't make the obvious decision himself. We wouldn't want to usurp the big guy's authority."

Three minutes later the base operator came back on. "Falcon, this is base. Over."

"Go ahead, base."

"You are authorized to open the gates sixty percent. The boss says to watch the water level and advise in one hour, or sooner if the water continues to rise. Over."

"Message received. Release at sixty percent and advise on water level changes. Over."

"Ten-four, Falcon. Base over and out."

Gilbert was impressed because that was releasing a lot of water. The report from satellite imaging had shown an unusual accumulation of moisture in these mountains, and with the warm rain the snow pack must be melting fast. He felt a wave of relief as he climbed out of his car and headed for the small blockhouses which enclosed the mechanisms to raise the gates. Fortunately, the torrent had turned into a steady drizzle. He unlocked the door to the first blockhouse, switched on the light and set the control to sixty percent. After pausing a moment, he made up his mind. "I'm opening this baby up eighty percent, no matter what. It might get a few feet wet but I'll sure feel a lot better." He reset the control and flipped the master switch to energize the huge electric motor which raised the gate by means of two flat cables. As the gate raised, the roar of the water rushing down the spillway beneath the blockhouse steadily increased.

Gilbert hurried to the next blockhouse, set the control to eighty percent, and energized the second motor. As before, the water rumbled louder and louder and the entire blockhouse vibrated. He left the blockhouse and looked over the rail. What an awesome sight to see the immense power of that stream of water plunging to the Provo River below! After watching for a while, he looked up and saw at the first lights blinking on in the town of Heber six miles away.

In the sleepy town of Heber, Billy Ashworth dragged her head from beneath a pillow, blinked a few times, and gazed wearily at her husband. "What time is it, Charles?"

"It's about five." He had just thrown cold water on his face and was wiping it with a towel.

"Why are you up at this hour?"

"I have to go in early today." The boss wants to complete that big house on the east side this week."

"Oh no! You poor man. But it's still raining. I can hear it on the roof."

"It's all inside work now. The rain won't slow us down. At least not much."

"Do you mind if I go back to sleep?"

Charles laughed. "Not at all. You had a tough day with the kids yesterday."

Suddenly there was a deafening roar like a train approaching and the house began to shake violently. The windows shattered and objects throughout the room crashed to the floor. The floor rose and fell like a series of ocean waves. The ceiling sagged and threw plaster everywhere. In spite of the rumbling,

Billy could hear her children screaming. She tried to stand but was thrown to the ground. Charles went to help her but was smashed to the floor on the other side of the room and was powerless to move. It seemed as though the earthquake would never end, but in reality it lasted less than a minute.

"That was a big one!" Charles said as he got up to help his wife.

"The children!" she screamed.

Before they could rush from the bedroom, all three of their young children ran into the room and threw themselves on their parents, sobbing with fear.

"It's okay, guys," Charles said. "Take it easy. It's over."

Billy was calmer now that she saw her children safe. "Oh, Charles! The house!"

"Yeah, there's a lot of damage. But it would be laid out flat if I hadn't built it myself."

"Charles, the dam!" she cried.

Panic struck at Charles's heart. Struggling to control himself, he said, "It's probably okay. They would have sounded the alarm. We've got a good system here." Charles didn't bother to turn on the radio or the TV. He knew the media would never get the message to them in time if the dam failed.

"But what if the alarm was destroyed by the earthquake?" Billy said frantically.

Charles hadn't thought of that. He saw the terror in his wife's eyes and made an instant decision. "Let's go—*right now*! Are the packs and blankets still in the car?"

"Yes. Everything is ready."

Charles and Billy grabbed their children and carried them outside to the car. They didn't bother to dress. Billy was wearing a nightgown, and the children were dressed in pajamas. Charles wore nothing but shoes, garments, and work pants. They didn't stop to pick up possessions. They could always come back if nothing happened to the dam, but a few minutes wasted now could mean their lives. Outside they saw half-dressed neighbors rushing frantically in all directions. Many of them were piling into their cars and driving away at top speed, some heading east and others going west. Still others were running for safety with small children in their arms.

Charles drove east on 200 South, dodging people fleeing in the street and ignoring the desperate requests of some for a ride. He realized that if he stopped to help anyone, he might be sacrificing the lives of his family. He felt guilty but knew all those frantic people had been warned, as he had, to prepare an escape plan in case of emergency. Charles went faster as he exited the town, knowing the road would end before the foothills. When they reached the end of the road, they dragged their children and the supplies out of the car. Billy picked up the two younger children and Charles carried the seventy-two hour kits and the blankets. The oldest child, who was eight, carried his own pack. They began the long ascent up the mountain slope. Charles heard other people on all sides of them frantically climbing upward as fast as possible. Years ago Billy and Charles had decided they would climb at least three hundred and thirty feet to a small cave that would give them shelter.

They had almost reached the cave when they heard the terrifying roar of billions of gallons of water crashing toward Heber City. From their vantage point high above the valley, they looked below, straining to see what was happening, but they could only see fleeting reflections of light on the surface of a black ocean of water surging across the valley floor. It was as though they were watching the sea at night from a low-flying airplane. With horror Charles thought of all the helpless people being swept away to their deaths far below by one of the most awesome forces of nature.

"I hope everybody got out in time!" Billy shouted above the roar of the water.

"I'm sure most of them did if they made an escape plan like the city advised."

"I . . . I'm cooold," the smallest child said, shivering. Billy wrapped her children in blankets.

"What about the people in Provo, Dad?" the eight-year-old boy said in a loud voice.

"They'll be okay. The authorities have plenty of time to warn them." Charles knew many people would die that morning, but he didn't want to upset his son.

"How much time *do* they have, Charles?" Billy asked.

"About forty-five minutes, I think."

Gilbert Hoffman glanced one last time at the water flowing down the Deer Creek spillway and turned toward his car. *I'll wait around a couple of hours to watch the water level. Home base will be glad to get reports and I'll be happier too.* He climbed into his car, turned on the motor and waited for the car to warm up.

At 5:02 a.m. the earthquake struck. Gilbert's car rocked violently and was hurled against the concrete wall enclosing the parking lot. The windshield crystallized but did not fall in. For a moment he feared the car would be flipped over the wall and down onto the spillway below. He hung on and waited it out. When the quake ended, he leaped from his car and ran onto the crest of the dam. He saw that the old concrete wall on the north side had been torn to pieces but he didn't detect a breach in the dam itself. He ran down the road, frantically checking the downstream side of the dam for leaks. The sky was becoming gray and he could barely see the slope of the dam. "Nothing. My baby's holding fine."

He ran back to his car and radioed to base. He tried for two minutes without success. As he sat there wondering what was going on, the radio came alive abruptly with static and catches of words. "This is . . . in Falcon. Jorda— . . . under water . . ."

Gilbert shouted, "Base, this is Falcon. I'm not getting your message. Come back, please."

"Falcon . . . dam failure . . ." Then the radio went dead.

Understanding hit Gilbert like a sledge hammer. He jumped out of his car and ran as fast as his chubby legs could go to the mountain at the west end of the dam. He scrambled up the rain-soaked slope, slipping and sliding and falling face first again and again. Covered with mud and blood, he struggled up the embankment, feeling a frantic desire to escape death. When he had gone high enough, he turned and sat in a puddle of muddy water. His heart was beating wildly and his lungs burned. It was then that he felt a pang of guilt for not using that three-hundred-dollar Exercycle like he should have. He looked down at the dim form of his beloved dam.

"Nothing yet. You're sitting there pretty as you please. Maybe you'll hold that water after all." He knew that what he was saying was impossible. When the hundred billion gallons of water from Jordanelle hit his dam, it would go right over the top and take the dam with it. The water of both reservoirs combined would make over a hundred and fifty billion gallons of water rushing down Provo Canyon toward the cities below at forty to fifty miles per hour. In the canyon the wall of water would reach a height of eighty to a hundred and twenty feet, depending on obstacles and the width of the canyon.

Transfixed, Gilbert stared at the dam and the water directly in front of it. He thought about his poor wife and daughter in Provo. They lived in a low-lying area which would be flooded for sure. He tried to contact them on his cell phone, but as usual he couldn't get a connection this far up in the canyon. With relief he remembered that the water control officials in Provo would probably know about the disaster and would sound the alarm. In the year 2000 the leaders of Utah County cities finally stopped making excuses and installed a state-of-the-art disaster warning system. He and Edith and Carmen, their fourteen-year-old daughter, had talked about the possibility of dam failure and flooding many times, and they knew what to do. As soon as the warning sounded, Edith and Carmen were to jump into their old Dodge Aries, which was kept full of gas and loaded with all types of emergency supplies, and drive about a mile to I-15 and head south as fast as they could go. In fifteen minutes they should be completely beyond the range of any flood waters.

He gazed at the dam so long and with such intensity that his eyes began to burn. He blinked them rapidly to relieve the burning and when he looked again, the water came. An immense swell filled the space below as if nothing had been there before, and a great wave suddenly rose high above the crest of the dam and thundered downward two hundred and fifty feet to the river. Within seconds everything beneath the dam disappeared. Gilbert strained to see the dam itself and soon realized that it was no longer there. The mass of water flowed past like some gigantic black leviathan slithering toward its prey. The roar was deafening. Gilbert wasn't a religious man, but for the first time in his life he prayed fervently for the people of Utah County. The people who lived peacefully and happily in the valley below.

Chapter 5

Steven awoke to a violent shaking. For a few quick seconds he thought it was Elder James, his missionary companion in France, who loved to wake him up by seizing him and, laughing boisterously, bouncing him up and down until his body completely left the bed. But then Steven remembered it was years later and he was at home. The entire house was rocking back and forth as if some powerful giant were trying to shake it to pieces in his anger. The dresser and a chair were knocked over. The pictures crashed from the walls. The walls and ceiling cracked in a dozen places. The entire room was a vibrating chaos. He lay there holding on to the sides of the bed to avoid being thrown to the floor until the earthquake finally spent its energy.

When it was over Steven dashed into the children's bedroom. Though there were four bedrooms in the house, all the children preferred to sleep in the same room. He was amazed to find Andrew and Jennifer still sleeping soundly in a room that was a complete shambles. William was lying on his back staring at the ceiling.

"Are you okay?" Steven said, taking his son's hand.

"Yeah, but I think that was the big one."

"I believe you're right."

"Dad, do you think the world's coming to an end like John says?"

"No, that won't happen for a long time." Steven sat on the bed next to his son and continued to hold his hand. Jennifer and Andrew remained asleep. "Try to go back to sleep, William. We'll clean up the mess later, okay?"

Steven heard a sudden piercing sound which hurt his ears. After a few seconds he realized it was part of the city's system of sirens which emitted a continuous blast.

William cried out, "What's that noise?"

"Warning sirens." Steven's other children awoke and sat up in bed, frightened and trembling.

"William, take care of Jennifer and Andrew. I'll be right back!" He hurried into the living room and switched on the lights and the television. The face of Mike Headrick appeared on the screen on channel 5 news.

"This is Mike Headrick with breaking news. Due to the earthquake we reported a few minutes ago, there has been a complete failure of both Jordanelle and Deer Creek Dams. A disaster alarm is now sounding in most cities of Utah County. It is estimated that a wall of water fifty feet high will reach the mouth of Provo Canyon in about twenty minutes, after which it will spread out and reach Utah Lake within thirty minutes. All residents living in low-lying areas of Provo and Orem are advised to evacuate their homes immediately and move quickly to higher ground. We advise you to take no possessions with you except blankets and survival gear."

"The flood will destroy every structure and object in its path. You will find safe places on the BYU upper campus, Grandview Hill, and the hills east of Provo, Springville, and Mapleton. In the north you will find high ground in the Highland and Alpine areas. Once again, this flood presents the gravest danger to your lives and you must leave for higher ground as soon as possible. Other areas, including Lehi, parts of American Fork, and all communities close to the Jordan River will be flooded within one to two hours, depending on their distance from Utah Lake."

Abruptly the lights and television went off. Steven figured that the earthquake or the flood had disrupted power transmission in the city. He was relieved that none of his family lived close to any of the flood zones. William ran into the room and flew into his father's arms. Jennifer and Andrew were not far behind.

"What's happening, Dad?" William cried.

Steven put his arms around all three of them. "The dams in the canyon have collapsed and a flood of water is headed for Provo."

"We'd better get dressed," William said as he whirled to go to his bedroom. "We've got to get out of here."

"Hold it," Steven said. "We're not in any danger up here on this hill. In fact the news report said this was one of the safe places in Provo." Steven picked up his phone to check on his family and found the device did not work. He turned to William and said, "I want you to take care of Andrew and Jennifer. I'm going to make sure Grandma and Grandpa are okay."

"When are you coming back?"

"In a few minutes. Watch the kids and don't worry . . . Above all, don't any of you leave the house. Do you think you can handle that?" The children nodded bravely. Steven left the house, climbed into his white Chevrolet, and drove to his parents' house. He found Sarah and Robert frightened and nervous but safe. They were busy cleaning up the mess caused by the quake. Steven was surprised and relieved to see that their house was not seriously damaged. His parents had heard the news reports of the approaching flood and asked Steven question after question that he couldn't answer. He finally told them he had to leave because the children were alone.

Before heading home, he drove south toward the edge of Grandview Hill. At regular intervals the sirens continued to sound for three minutes. There were people everywhere, hurrying in all directions. Some of the homes in the neighborhood were completely demolished and many others showed signs of serious structural damage. Most of them were dark, but a few were lighted by small home generators which rumbled nearby. From time to time Steven saw groups of men fighting small fires. When he reached the edge of the hill, he stopped his car and looked out over the southern portion of Provo City.

Sunrise had not yet come, but the entire area was bright with the light of fires burning everywhere and the headlights of hundreds of cars. It was frightening to see the cars caught in traffic jams on every street when death was approaching relentlessly from the north. He could see the silhouettes of crowds trying to escape on foot, and some of them were fighting their way up the hill toward him, carrying weeping children in their arms. Sick to his stomach, he turned away, feeling weak and powerless to help. As he returned to his house, he saw his children with their faces pushed against the big front window. When they spotted him, they clapped their hands with delight.

As soon as he entered the house, Andrew said, "Dad, are we going to get drowned?"

"No. We're safe here."

"Is there anything we can do to help the other people?" William asked.

Steven looked at him with frustration. "I don't know, son. I really don't know."

"I know what we can do," Jennifer said. "We can pray for them."

Steven was ashamed that he had not thought about prayer. "Yes, that's one thing we can do." They knelt and Steven asked God to protect the people of Utah County from the flood bearing down upon them.

Fred Wilson and his young family were in their old Chevy Suburban. They had survived the earthquake without serious injury and had heard the news report warning the citizens of the impending flood. Immediately they had left their home—located a mile south of the entrance to Provo Canyon—and were now proceeding south at an agonizingly slow pace in bumper to bumper traffic on University Avenue. Fred and his wife Rachel couldn't decide whether to continue south to Springville or turn off to the east and seek refuge on the BYU upper campus or the east bench. Fred kept looking at his watch. The newscaster had said the flood might reach northern Provo as soon as twenty minutes from the time of the warning, and already fifteen minutes had passed.

As the traffic continued to move at a maddening pace, the panic Fred felt became unbearable. He realized that in the last three minutes they had advanced no more than three hundred yards and things weren't going to get better. He checked his watch again and saw that twenty-four minutes had elapsed since the warning. He debated whether or not they should abandon the car and make a run for it. It wouldn't be easy with two small children to carry. He glanced through the rearview mirror constantly, afraid of what he might see at any moment. A minute later he saw it, the most frightening sight he had ever witnessed—a mountain of water rushing toward them like a giant tidal wave, engulfing and sweeping away everything in its path.

Frantically, Fred sought a way out of the traffic, but there was no escape. His family saw his sudden desperation and turned in their seats to look northward. What they saw made Rachel cry and the two children scream. Fred laid on the horn and rammed his vehicle into the one in front of him. The cars behind him did the same and the Suburban was rocked violently. People began to exit their cars and fight their way on foot through the wrecked vehicles in a mad attempt to save their lives. Fred tried to open his door but a van had slammed against the side of his car and he could only push the door open a few inches. At that moment he knew there was no hope of escape. He turned in his seat and, seizing both of his children, dragged them into the front seat next to him. He held them in his arms and waited.

The wave struck with indescribable force, swallowing every object in sight. Buried in a watery tomb, Fred felt the Suburban sweep upward violently, roll over and over, and slam at last into some massive barrier. Death came quickly to him and his family as the car was crushed against a concrete barrier. Then the wave continued its work of destruction, devouring the lives of thousands of victims still trapped on the impassable roads.

Later a Channel Four newscast, which announced the disaster to the nation, reported that in the early hours of Monday, May 20 an earthquake measuring

7.0 on the Richter scale had caused the failure of Jordanelle and Deer Creek Dams and within twenty-five minutes a flood of one hundred and fifty billion gallons of water had burst from the mouth of Provo Canyon and headed directly for the cities of Orem and Provo. As the water swept through the cities the height of the wave varied from ten to thirty-five feet depending on the obstacles it met. It followed the old stream bed of the Provo River between University Avenue and Freedom Boulevard but spread out gradually as it moved south.

The flood had destroyed every object in its path no matter how large, including houses, cars, buses, trucks, trees, buildings, bridges, the I-15 freeway, and thousands of people. Nothing could withstand its mighty power. It demolished all lifelines, including telephone, power, sewer, gas, and water systems, and it deposited soil and debris everywhere in vast bars twenty to thirty feet thick. By full daylight the entire flood zone was a scene of unbelievable devastation. After this general report, the TV newscast focused on several stories of individual tragedy.

What the news reports neglected to say was that there were many heroes who jeopardized their lives to save others in trouble, and there were some cowards, who turned their backs on drowning people to avoid risking their own lives.

Steven forced himself to prepare breakfast for the children. He wanted to charge out of the house and do anything he could to save others, but he was afraid to leave the children alone. He had heard that looters and marauders profited from such disasters to steal property and attack people while the police and other officials were busy rescuing victims and providing basic necessities. No, his children were his primary responsibility and he would stay home to protect them. To keep his mind off the disaster, he made a careful examination of the house to ascertain whether or not it had sustained serious structural damage. Reassured that the house needed immediate repairs in only four rooms, he stepped onto the front porch and saw people everywhere, shivering under blankets in small groups. Some families had no blankets and wore nothing but nightclothes. They were trying to keep warm by cuddling together. Steven's heart went out to them and he was about to invite as many as possible into his home when he caught sight of a man rushing toward him.

"Brother Christopher, Brother Christopher!" the man called.

Steven waited until he drew near and said, "Yes, can I help you?"

"I'm Greg Millman, the Elders Quorum president."

Steven remembered him now from the meeting the day before. "Oh yes! Come in, Greg. Please call me Steve."

"Thank you."

They sat on one of the couches and Steven said, "How can I help you?"

"In the last hour the stake presidency has contacted every ward in the stake and asked all church members to welcome into their homes the survivors who lost their homes in the flood. I understand this request comes originally from the prophet himself. All the stakes in Utah County will participate, and I'd like to know if you can help in this way."

"Absolutely."

"Super! How many families can you handle?"

"Let's see. I have four bedrooms. My children can move into my bedroom with me. I suppose we can take in at least three families."

"President Howard suggested that each member family try to accept two families if possible," Gregory said.

"All right," Steven said. "We'll take in two or three, whatever you think."

"I appreciate that. Do you have any supplies on hand?"

"We have several closets full of bedding and clothes and at least a six-month supply of food and other things."

"Great! Do you have any drinking water? As you may know, the water supply lines in Provo have been destroyed."

"I think we have about a hundred gallons, thanks to my mother."

Gregory looked pleased. "That's marvelous. Your water should last several days if you ration it carefully, and your other supplies may last as long as a month, depending on how you use them. Most of our members have next to nothing, and I have no idea how we're going to get supplies to everyone in need. We may have to house these families two to three weeks, possibly longer."

Steven was shocked that all his storage might last no longer than a few weeks. "I'm willing to share with those in need. I certainly don't take the credit for the supplies we have. My mother is always loading us up with supplies and every vitamin and herb known to mankind. She pays for it herself and makes my poor old dad haul it in."

Gregory laughed. "You're a lucky man, Steve. Listen, I'll get back to you in about an hour. I should have your assigned families with me by that time. Oh, by the way, the schools have asked that we not send our children to school until they notify us."

"All right. I planned to keep them home anyway."

"What about your work?"

"That's no problem. I work at home as a translator. I just use my computer."

"But there's no power. It might take weeks to get it back. Maybe longer."

Steven shrugged. "I have a small solar backup system. It'll power my computer and a few appliances. Communications are down so I can't use the internet. But I can still do word processing."

"That won't present you with problems?"

"Not as long as it doesn't last too long."

Gregory left. Steven sat there worried and somewhat troubled, not believing what he had committed himself to. *Oh, well,* he thought, *I wanted to help. I just figured that helping might be more exciting than this.* He heard a knock at the door.

It was Gregory once more. "Sorry to bother you again. I forgot to tell you one thing. I suggest you start on the outhouse right away. It's still cloudy and windy but the rain has let up, so you'll be able to work on it today." And he was off again without further explanation.

Steven stood there staring after him, not knowing what to say. He vaguely remembered what an outhouse was, and the memory was a disgusting one. He had seen a picture of one in some encyclopedia, but he had the distinct impression that outhouses were relics of the nineteenth century, and the idea of him building one himself was unbelievable. He had never built anything or repaired anything in his life, and screwing in light bulbs was the utter limit of his mechanical ability.

He decided he'd have to get John's help, or maybe one of the men coming to stay with him would know what to do. Hopefully. By twelve o'clock Gregory Millman had not yet returned with the homeless people. Steven fed his children some cold canned stew, milk, and bread. While they ate, he explained that soon they would have some strangers living with them. Maybe for several weeks. The children were very excited, especially at the prospect of sleeping in their father's room.

After lunch Steven sat down on his favorite chair in the front room, and while he was busy worrying about the outhouse problem, the front door popped open and a young man stuck his head into the room.

"Does everyone have his clothes on in here? Can I come in?" It was Steven's 22-year-old and not-yet-married brother, Paul, who prided himself on being the joker of the family, and who was a student in business at Snow College in Ephraim. Since spring semester had ended on April 30, Paul now lived with his parents and worked in their herb shop on State Street in Orem. He'd made the trip to Steven's home on his small motorcycle.

"Cute, Paul," Steven said. "Where were you early this morning when I checked on Mom and Dad?"

"I stayed the night with a friend."

"Are Mom and Dad still okay?"

"Positively. They have me to watch after them," Paul quipped. "Since John built their house like a fortress, it suffered very little damage."

"How are they taking the disaster?"

"Very well, especially Mom. I think they live for disaster. Right now their house is crammed with people, and Mom is shoving so many herbs down their throats they're starting to turn green."

"That figures."

"Mom told me to come here to check on you guys."

"You wouldn't know how to build an outhouse, would you?"

"An outhouse? What's that?"

Steven smirked at his brother as if it was incredible that anyone might not know what an outhouse was. "Man! Where have you been all your life? It's a small, freestanding structure that people use to take care of their natural needs."

"Oh! You mean a poop shack."

Steven quickly looked to see if his children were within hearing distance. He was relieved when he didn't see them. He couldn't believe how crude Paul could get sometimes. At the same time, he also knew Paul had a hidden side which was profoundly spiritual. Apparently the children had heard Paul's voice because they popped into the room all at once and swarmed over him. They had a special affection for Paul because he was funny and played games with them.

"Hi, Uncle Paul," they yelled in unison. "Can you stay with us for a few days?"

"Sure, if it's okay with your dad. That'll give me a chance to see whether or not he's doing a good job of being your father." The children laughed merrily and Paul gave each of them a big hug.

Steven was dismayed that Paul could tell jokes and his children could display such delight when thousands of people were dead or dying in the city around them. He noticed a big book in Paul's hand. "What's that?"

"As you can see, it's a book."

"I know it's a book!" Steven said impatiently. "But why do you have it?"

Paul handed the book to Steven. "Mom told me it would help you out. Look on page 60."

Steven read the title: *Back To Basics* by Reader's Digest. He turned to page

60 and saw in full color the plans for building an outhouse. Steven couldn't help but grin at his brother. "Mom thinks of everything, doesn't she? This is great. You can build it for me."

"I don't think so, big brother. I'll help but I won't do it for you. Mom's orders."

The front door banged open and John rushed into the room. "I told you, Steve, the end is near. This disaster proves me right. The Lord said his judgments would start in his own house . . . Oh, hi, Paul."

"Howdy, John. Looks like you were right after all. I'll bet the end comes this afternoon or tomorrow at the latest. It's probably too late for me to prepare."

"Always the joker, aren't you? This is not a laughing matter. The reports I'm getting on my CB say authorities estimate that fifteen thousand people were drowned in the flood, and about two hundred thousand are homeless. Property damage may be in excess of ten billion dollars."

Hearing John's review, Paul became serious. "I'm sorry, John. You're right. This is no laughing matter."

Steven took John by the shoulders. "I know this is no consolation, but the casualties are far less than expected. I heard one expert say several years ago that if the dams in the canyon collapsed, twenty-five to thirty thousand people might perish in this area."

"I know," John said. "For that we can be grateful. The casualties were lower because the authorities set up a great warning system, gave everybody good instructions on what to do, and warned them early. Fortunately, most people followed the instructions."

"Have you heard reports about what happened up there in the mountains?" Steven asked.

"Yes. There was a 7.0 earthquake on the Cottonwood Fault, which either runs directly under Jordanelle Dam or is a short distance from it, depending on who you prefer to believe. In the long run, it didn't seem to make any difference. The quake cracked the dam's foundation and it was completely breached within five minutes. The water flooded most of Heber Valley and reached Deer Creek Dam in about thirteen minutes. That dam failed immediately and the total volume of both reservoirs, which were filled to capacity because of the rains, swept down Provo Canyon. About one hundred and fifty billion gallons of water. You know the result."

After they discussed the flood for a while, John said, "I have to go. We're starting to search for the dead. Tomorrow we'll probably be asking for volunteers to help." He got up to leave.

"By the way," Steven said, "do you know how to build an outhouse?"

"I sure do, but you're on your own this time. There's wood and supplies in my backyard, and you're welcome to use anything you want."

"But what are you going to do about toilet facilities?" Steven said.

"I installed a bypass septic tank and water cistern two years ago. Don't you remember? You teased me about it for a week." He smirked a little and waved good-bye.

Now Steven knew he had been wrong to tease John. "Oh yeah, I forgot," he said as he watched John head toward his pickup.

John's report on the disaster left a profound impression on everyone in the room. Jennifer and Andrew had tears in their eyes, and William struggled to hold back his. Steven was so distracted that he looked up Gregory Millman's phone number and tried to use his landline phone for the second time, not remembering the facilities were out until he found the line dead. As he comforted his children, he heard a knock at the door.

It was Gregory. "Sorry for the delay. We've been running into all kinds of problems." Behind him was a crowd of people, carrying packs and blankets. "May we come in, Steve?"

"Oh yes! Please do."

Gregory seemed embarrassed. "You said you'd accept three families so I invited that many."

"The stake president changed the policy?"

"No, but some people refuse to welcome the flood victims, so we're asking those who are willing to take in more people. Is that a problem?"

"Nope. None whatsoever. They're completely welcome."

"Let me introduce you to the parents," Gregory said. You can get to know the children later. This is Douglas and Elizabeth Cartwright. They're investigating the Church. They have five children. This is Ron and Janet Loomis, who have five children. And this is the Simpson family." Steven wondered why Gregory had introduced the Simpson family differently, waving his hand in their direction as though trying to make them magically disappear. The Simpsons had two boys, one who was about fifteen and the other who appeared to be nineteen. Both of them sprawled out on one of the couches as if they owned the place.

"I want to welcome all of you to our home." Steven introduced himself, his children, and Paul.

"How many bedrooms do you have, Mr. Christopher?" Sybil Simpson said, wiping her eyes with a handkerchief. She reminded Steven of Olive Oyl in the old Popeye cartoons.

"Uh, we have four bedrooms."

"That's not very many," Sybil sniffed. "What are we supposed to do, jam an entire family into one bedroom?"

Gregory was obviously embarrassed. "We should remember, Mrs. Simpson, that this is an emergency. Everyone will have to make sacrifices."

"But I'm not well," Sybil complained. "I have a bad heart and a weak back." She put her hand to her chest and breathed heavily as if she were about to have a heart attack. "Mr. Christopher, would you please assign us a bedroom that is quiet and has a big bed?"

For a moment Steven was speechless. He looked at Mr. Simpson and saw him glaring at his wife. Then he found his tongue. "We'll try to make you as comfortable as possible, Mrs. Simpson."

"How many bathrooms do you have?"

"Two."

Sybil sighed. "I certainly hope that's enough." She looked around frowning and shook her head sadly. "How do you intend to keep this house warm, Mr. Christopher? It's still cold at night because of the bad weather and the gas lines were destroyed in the flood. I have terrible arthritis and I cannot bear to be cold. In fact, it's hurting me right now! Oh, dear Lord, why did this have to happen to me? I had such a big beautiful house, and now I have nothing. I might as well be dead!"

Steven glanced at Gregory's unhappy face and asked himself if he had made a mistake. But when he looked at the small children huddled at the back of the room, he knew he had not been wrong. "We have a nice fireplace and lots of wood, so I think you'll be warm, Mrs. Simpson. Also, I have access to all kinds of herbs and I may be able to find some remedies for your health problems."

"Absolutely not." Sybil cried, her face screwed up in horror. "I'd have to talk to my doctor first because I've heard some herbs are very dangerous. Why I wouldn't even take a vitamin without my doctor's permission."

Now there's a woman who thinks for herself, Steven thought. He remembered what his mother had said many times about doctors and herbs. She complained bitterly because the drug companies and the medical authorities were constantly trying to get the government to regulate the sales of vitamins and herbs by making it illegal to obtain them without a doctor's prescription. Sarah mocked the idea of giving doctors and pharmacists complete control over natural products when they knew absolutely nothing about them.

"Your doctor's office was in Provo?" Steven asked.

"Yes, I go to my doctor every two or three months," Sybil said. "He's such a wonderful man."

"You may not be able to see him for a while, especially if his office was destroyed by the flood," Steven said slyly.

"Not see him? But what about my prescriptions? Without my Prozac I'd die!"

Steven felt like hooting but forced his face to remain blank. Mr. Simpson looked as though he was ready to go out and sleep in the street, but the Simpson boys didn't seem to care what their mother did. Gregory simply stood there as if someone had told him to shut up. Out of the corner of his eye, Steven saw Paul at the back of the room pretending to weep and complain as he mimicked Sybil Simpson.

At last Mr. Simpson spoke up. "Sybil, we must be grateful to Mr. Christopher for his kindness and hospitality." Mr. Simpson was a short, bald man who was built like a wrestler.

Elizabeth Cartwright stepped directly in front of Sybil and said, "Yes, Mr. Christopher, we are so grateful to you for your kindness. We know it can't be easy for you to have so many people invade your home." Several others also stated their appreciation, but Sybil smacked her lips in disgust and held her tongue.

It took one hour for Steven to assign bedrooms and to help get his guests settled. Since there were only four Simpsons, he gave them the smallest bedroom at the back of the house—in spite of Sybil's angry looks. While Paul made a warm fire in the fireplace, Steven put several large buckets in the bathrooms as emergency toilets and asked his guests to use them instead of the regular toilets. Then he and Paul left to retrieve tools and materials from John's backyard so they could build the outhouse. They borrowed John's pickup to haul the lumber. When they returned, there were two other women standing in his front room—Mary Fleming and Andrea Warren.

"Brother Christopher," Mary said, "do you remember me?"

"Yes, Sister Goodrich introduced us yesterday at church." Steven wanted to add that she was one of the single females in the ward but didn't dare.

Mary flipped her long blonde hair away from her face and looked Steven directly in the eye. "This is my roommate Andrea Warren. We dropped by to see if we could help you in some way. We heard you were kind enough to invite a large number of homeless people into your home and we wanted to know if we could help. You know, fix meals, clean house, whatever you want. We don't have a lot of time because I'm a nurse and have to care for disaster victims, and Andrea has to watch over the family staying with us. However, we'd be happy to spend as much time as necessary helping you."

Steven was struck by how incredibly beautiful she was, especially her big olive-green eyes. And Andrea, who had blue eyes and short black hair, was pretty inviting herself. He wanted to say "yes" to her offer but couldn't think of a plausible excuse for accepting it. "That's very kind of you, Mary," Steven said, "but now I have three women in the house who can help me. Still, I appreciate your offer."

Mary smiled when she heard him use her first name, and she handed him a slip of paper. "If you ever need help, send your oldest son to this address, and Andrea and I will come as soon as we can."

"Thank you so much." Steven let them out. He was delighted that two attractive women were so willing to be of service to him. He checked his watch and saw that it was two o'clock. Not much time. He had to complete the outhouse before dark because it was one job that could not wait. Already his guests had filled two of the five temporary toilet buckets and had used six rolls of toilet paper. He grabbed *Back To Basics* from the bookcase, worked his way through the crowded front room, and joined Paul in the backyard. He was surprised and pleased to find four men waiting for him, Paul and the three fathers who were staying with him.

"Okay, Steve, what do we do?" Paul asked.

"Do any of our guests know how to build an outhouse?" Steven asked. They shook their heads, and Steven suspected they didn't even know what an outhouse was. His stomach tightened into a knot as he flipped to page 60 in the book. He had never done anything like this before and now they were all depending on him. He quickly read the first part of the instructions. "It seems we start by digging a deep hole in the yard as far away from the house as we can."

Paul laughed and said slyly, "Shall we alert the local building inspector so we can get a building permit?"

"That'll be the day," Steven growled.

They agreed to divide up into three teams. Douglas Cartwright and Ronald Loomis dug the hole, while Paul and Clinton Simpson built the outhouse framework. Steven had the job of guiding them with the book and building the base for the toilet seat. He removed one of the seat tops from a toilet in the house. As the work progressed, Paul went to John's house several times for additional materials and tools. From time to time the women brought them food and stopped to admire the work. After four hours of hard work they had finished their assignments.

Steven examined his finished seat with pride. "What do you think, gentlemen?"

"It's a beautiful thing to behold," Clinton said. "The base looks very solid and the seat is smooth and round."

"Yeah, I wouldn't mind sitting on that baby all day," Paul joked.

They all laughed and got to work putting it all together. An hour later they stood back and admired their handiwork. Then Paul ran into the house and excitedly asked the women to come and see their masterpiece. The women rushed out the door followed by a herd of children.

"That's simply wonderful!" Janet Loomis said.

"I'm proud of you all," Elizabeth Cartwright added.

Sybil Simpson frowned. "Do you mean we have to use *that* disgusting contraption if we need to, uh, take care of certain natural requirements?"

"Yep." Paul said. "If you've got to go, this is the place to show. We even installed a little window near the top so you can gaze at the stars while you're doing your duty at night. The window also helps to air the sweet little thing out because, as you can imagine, outhouses can get pretty fragrant." Steven flinched but couldn't resist grinning. He saw that everybody else was grinning too.

Sybil looked as though she was having one of her notorious heart attacks. "But what if it's really late at night and—"

"That's why we'll keep a flashlight in the kitchen," Steven said. "We installed a latch and a lock on the inside so you'd be as safe in this little domicile as in a pew at church. There's even a small cabinet at the side with ten rolls of toilet paper." Steven bit his lip. Paul's irony was starting to affect him.

"Yeah," Paul said. "The flashlight also helps to scare away the skunks and raccoons that lurk around here at night."

Seeing the shock on Sybil's face, Steven glared at his brother and said, "That's enough, Paul. We don't want to frighten our guests. There are no such animals on Grandview Hill."

One of Mrs. Cartwright's children pulled at her dress. She leaned over and the child whispered something in her ear. "Mr. Christopher," she said, "is it okay if the children use the toilet?"

"No problem," Steven replied. Instantly every child in the yard lined up in front of the outhouse.

"Whew! I'm glad we finished when we did," Douglas said.

"Yeah," Steven said. "I wonder when the kids will be finished."

Chapter 6

The following morning John arrived early and asked the men to help shovel debris and search for bodies. All the adult males and the two Simpson boys volunteered to help. When they reached their work site at the bottom of Grandview Hill, John asked them to work together as a team. He gave them shovels, gloves, protective masks, and some body bags. Hundreds of other workers were doing the same type of work. It was a terrible task because there were huge deposits of mud and debris everywhere, and the constant threat of disease from toxic waste and rotting bodies made them extremely cautious. Everyone was excited and grateful when the workers uncovered people who were still alive. Immediately they gave them first aid and tried to make them as comfortable as possible.

Steven's crew could only work around the periphery of the flood because a great deal of water was still flowing toward Utah Lake and it was deep in spots. It was disheartening and gruesome for them when they discovered the dead body of a victim, especially when it was a child. They worked like automatons, their clothes saturated with mud, stopping only when John arrived on occasion to check on them and to give them food and water. When they came home at five o'clock, exhausted and heavy with gloom, Elizabeth and Janet did their best to cheer them up, but the women were struggling with their own disillusionment and the difficulty of handling so many children jammed together.

Steven shuffled into the kitchen to find something to eat and was cornered by Sybil. "Mr. Christopher, we're trying to fix supper but there is no gas. Yesterday we ate from our seventy-two hour kits, but tonight we would like a decent meal. What are you going to do about it?"

Steven wanted to smack her in the mouth to shut her up. It was everything he could do to control himself. It wasn't only what Sybil said but how she said it that was maddening.

At last he said, "I have a Coleman stove in the basement. I'll get it for you."

"I certainly hope it has more than one burner," Sybil snapped.

Steven brought up a large Coleman stove with four burners and a gallon of fuel. He took the stove to the back porch, lit the burners carefully, and headed for the bathroom to clean up.

As he went through the kitchen Elizabeth caught his attention. "Mr. Christopher, I hate to bother you but I was wondering if there was any way we could wash our clothes. The clothes we have on are utterly filthy."

"I'm sorry, but we don't have enough water to wash clothes. As you know, we have less than a hundred gallons of drinking water and I've asked everyone to limit their consumption to a half gallon per day. Three of the closets contain emergency clothes and you're welcome to use any that fit."

"That's wonderful," she said. "I'm sorry we're such a burden."

"Please don't say that. You're not a burden at all."

Since both bathrooms were occupied by people trying to clean up, Steven had to wait a half hour before he could give himself a sponge bath. It was not an easy task because all he had was a wash cloth and a small amount of bottled water. As soon as he finished, he sat down on the front room floor and, surrounded by children, tried to forget the five lifeless bodies they had uncovered that day. Elizabeth Cartwright brought him a meal of beans and fish sticks.

Around nine thirty that evening, after putting the smaller children to bed, everyone gathered in the living room. There were twenty people, and most had to sit on the floor. Steven built a fire in the fireplace to give them warmth and light. He invited all of them to introduce and tell a little about themselves.

After the introductions they discussed the recent catastrophe. Many wondered why such terrible things had happened to this primarily LDS community. Others wondered what the future held in store for them, and how they could rebuild their lives. No one had perfect answers.

After the discussion, the guests retired for the night. Steven and Paul went into Steven's bedroom and found the children asleep. William and Jennifer were rolled up in blankets on the floor, and Andrew was lying on Steven's bed. Paul crawled into a sleeping bag not far from Steven's bed.

Steven was beginning to doze when he heard Paul rolling around in his bag. "Can't you sleep?" Steven asked.

"No. I can't get it out of my mind."

"What?"

"All those dead bodies. All those lives destroyed in a few minutes. I don't understand why it happened."

Steven tried to console him. "Bad things happen. Even to good people. I really don't know why either, but you're forgetting the people we rescued. Ten of them. If it hadn't been for us, they might have died too. Concentrate on that."

"Yeah. You're right. We did make a difference."

When another ten minutes had passed, Paul said sleepily, "Hey, man, I hope you know I love you. You've always treated me like a brother should. I don't know what it is, but you're a very special person."

Steven was touched by Paul's sudden tenderness and emotion. "I love you too. Now go to sleep. We've got a lot of work to do tomorrow. If John doesn't come for volunteers, we'll have to make some emergency repairs on this house."

Because of Paul's words, Steven was no longer sleepy. He wiped the tears from his eyes as quietly as possible and struggled with his feelings. He didn't believe he was a special person. In fact, he had no idea who or what he was. Except for his children, he saw no purpose in his life.

When he figured everyone was asleep, he lit the oil lamp that was near his bed and opened the scriptures he had brought with him into the bedroom. He started reading the Doctrine and Covenants from the beginning, marking all references to the conditions of the world before the Second Coming. By the time he reached section 7, he was tired enough to fall asleep.

Two hours later Andrew woke him up and asked to be taken to the outhouse. The night before, this had occurred several times. First, it had been Andrew, then Jennifer, and then Andrew again. William had insisted on going by himself. All night long Steven had heard a continuous parade of people moving from the house to the outhouse and back again as one parent after another led a child to the smelly sanctuary. He had heard it when he was awake and had sensed it when he was asleep.

Tonight the same routine repeated itself, until by morning he knew he had hardly slept at all. As he lay in bed, trying to wake up, he thought that if one flood could disrupt the lives of thousands of people so drastically, what would life be like when the disasters prophesied for the last days began in earnest and filled the whole earth?

John Christopher arrived at seven o'clock the next morning. Steven gazed at him through sore red eyes. "What are you doing here in my bedroom at this ridiculous hour?"

"Hey, calm down. The sun's been up at least an hour and a half," John replied.

"What sun?" Steven rolled over and looked at the soft rays coming through the window blinds. "Oh, yeah, *that* sun. So it finally decided to show its face for the first time in a week."

He climbed out of bed and slowly got dressed, trying hard not to wake the others. Then while Steven cleaned up in the bathroom, John waited for him in the kitchen. When Steven entered the kitchen, John said, "I'm sorry, Steve, but I wanted to give you some news before I leave for work. I've got a lot of emergencies to handle today. I'm still on the city payroll you know."

"You and your news. Don't you ever sleep? Oh, that's right. You can sleep. You've got all the comforts of home and nobody to bug you."

"Hah! What gave you that impression? We've got two homeless families staying with us."

Steven felt a twinge of guilt. "I didn't know that . . . I'm sorry, John. I didn't get much sleep last night. How many people do you have in your house?"

John did some mental counting. "There's my family and seven refugees. That makes fourteen people!"

Steven chuckled. "Only fourteen? I've got twenty-two people in here, and our food supplies are really taking a hit." He lowered his voice almost to a whisper. "And some of them aren't all that fun to be around."

"But you're the kind of person who can put up with all this. You've always had a lot more patience than me."

"I don't feel all that patient right now. Listen, do you want a crew today? If so, I'll ask for volunteers, but it'll take us an hour to get ready."

"No, that's one of the reasons I came a tad early," John said. "The National Guard moved in this morning and there are FEMA jackets everywhere. Last night the president declared this county a national disaster area. We'll still need volunteers, but not as desperately as before. Why don't you stay home today? I'm sure you've got a lot of problems to solve."

"Thanks, John. We do have repairs to make. I don't want any ceilings falling in on people. Also, it's only been two days and we're running out of supplies already. I never dreamed kids could use toilet paper so fast. I'm sure we had a hundred rolls on Sunday and now we're down to half a dozen."

"Speaking of supplies, they're flying in food, water, and medicine this morning by helicopter. As for toilet paper, I doubt they consider it an essential. It might come with the convoy of trucks arriving tomorrow afternoon, which is hauling in clothes and other provisions."

"Hah. They don't think toilet paper is essential because they don't have a house full of kids to take care of. We're going to have to do something about the toilet paper problem this morning, or else. Yuck. I can't bear to think of what will happen when it runs out."

"Yeah, things will get pretty ugly. At least we won't have to worry about paying for supplies because the Church is apparently footing most of the bill. The rest of the money is coming from the government and charitable contributions."

Steven felt a pang of irritation and jealousy. "Where on earth do you get all this information? In this house without electric power we seem to be as separated from the rest of the world as if we lived on Mars."

"Well, duh. Don't you hear that pleasant purr coming from down the street?"

"What purr?" Steven said, puzzled.

"That gentle rumble of generators. On this street alone there are three or four of them going."

"Oh. You have a generator?"

"Naturally. I believe in being prepared for all contingencies. I told you this before but you never listen to me when it has to do with nitty-gritty things. I have a big generator which supplies most of the electricity we need. As for the news I share with you, I get some information from county emergency management but the rest comes from TV and radio broadcasts. By the way, don't you have a small backup solar system for your computer?"

"Yes, course."

"Well, why don't you just power a radio with that?"

"I can do that?"

"Definitely. You do have a radio, don't you?"

"I think so. Somewhere around here. I'll have to look for it."

"Okay. Find it, plug it in, and voilà—news reports."

"You know, I really don't give you enough credit. Is that all the news?"

"No, I also have something very bad to report. I was saving it for last."

"Great. What is it?"

"The Tokyo quake is beginning to cause financial repercussions already."

"Repercussions?"

"Yes. There's serious concern that banks everywhere in the world will be forced to close, and the panic is causing a radical drop in the value of stocks on most markets, especially here in the states. Believe me, this is going to get a lot nastier than not having enough toilet paper. And the endless, government-created recession in this country and in Europe doesn't help things. The only thing propping up trade now is the Chinese market. But even that has been wildly volatile in the last few years."

Steven grimaced. "Can't our government just bail everybody out like it usually does by printing more money?"

"That's one of the major causes of instability. Printing more and more money just raises our deficit and causes inflation."

"I know. You're right, of course. To keep their jobs, government leaders tell the people they won't raise their taxes. They don't have to. They sneakily raise taxes by printing money and creating inflation. When people go to the store and find that everything costs twice as much, they're paying higher taxes that way." Steven shook his head in disgust. "Well anyhow, thanks, John. Is there anything else?"

"No, but I'll keep you posted. I've got to head out now."

Steven went back to his bedroom. After waking Paul and the kids, he went onto the back porch to light the Coleman stove so the women could prepare breakfast. By this time, a long line had formed in front of the outhouse, and Janet Loomis was hurrying across the lawn toward him with a worried look in her eyes.

"Mr. Christopher, I hate to bother you, but did you know that we have only two rolls of toilet paper left?"

"Yes, I'm afraid they are the last we have. My brother and I are going to see if we can find some this morning, and I understand there's a convoy of trucks coming tomorrow afternoon which might be carrying toilet paper."

"Umm, that means we might not get any for a long time. I really hope you're successful today. Shall I send Ron with you?"

"No, that won't be necessary. We'll try to do our best, Sister Loomis." Steven went into the kitchen and was met by Sybil Simpson.

"Mr. Christopher, do you have a portable toilet or some contraption we could use in our room so we won't have to use that abominable outhouse?"

Steven wanted to grab her scrawny neck and squeeze it until she turned purple. He had felt the same urge several times already but had managed to suppress it so far. Sure the outhouse smelled horrible and was inconvenient, but it was the only toilet they had. Besides, it was the only thing he'd ever helped to build and he was proud of it. Steven bit his lip and hemmed and hawed for a while until he knew his temper was under control.

Then he said, "I'm sorry, Mrs. Simpson. I don't have anything like that. Maybe your husband could make something." Steven was tempted to say she could always take care of her natural needs in some bushes at the back of the yard, but he didn't dare.

"Let this be a lesson to you, Mr. Christopher. A person should always be prepared for emergencies." She turned without another word and stomped out of the house, apparently heading for the "abominable" outhouse.

After breakfast, Steven and Paul set out to find some toilet paper or a substitute. As they drove down the first street, Steven checked the meter which indicated the charge of his batteries, and was relieved to see there was enough power to allow them to visit the Dumpsters of several supermarkets in Orem. However, after driving around for a half hour, they didn't find a scrap of paper in any of them.

"It looks as though everybody in Utah County had the same idea," Paul said with frustration.

"Yeah, but I'm going to try one more store about a mile from home."

A few minutes later, they drove behind a huge supermarket and jumped out of the Chevrolet near several giant Dumpsters. Paul heaved himself over the edge of one of them. At first he saw nothing but cardboard boxes, but after moving a few boxes out of the way, he said, "Is newspaper okay?"

"I don't know. I've never tried it. Why don't you test it out on yourself right now?" Both of them laughed at that thought. "Go ahead and grab it," Steven said. "It's better than nothing."

"Hey, there's two huge cartons of facial tissue down here. Looks like it was run over with a bulldozer," Paul cried.

"By all means get it."

They pulled the newspaper and tissue paper out of the Dumpster and stacked it in one big pile. After extracting a large roll of string from another receptacle, they straightened the rumpled sheets and folded them to the right dimension in order to tie them into bundles. As they worked, they laughed and joked at the idea of how their guests would feel, especially Sybil, when they tried to use the newspaper.

A half hour later they were almost finished when they heard the earsplitting screech of tires. Shocked, they looked up and saw a black car full of dark figures. Six toughs leaped from the vehicle and surrounded them, bristling with clubs and knives. One of them brandished a pistol in one hand and a knife in the other.

The guy with the pistol stepped forward and shoved his weapon into Steven's ribs. "Make one move, buddy, and you're a dead man." His huge earrings reflected sunlight as they bounced in time to the movements of his head. He wore dark Levis and a black leather jacket, and he constantly flipped his long brown hair out of his eyes. Steven figured he was their leader. "Give me your keys and your wallet." Steven and Paul emptied their pockets and the thugs swept up their valuables.

"You establishment types better get used to following orders," the hoodlum said. "Guys like us are taking over this country." He tried to pistol-whip Steven, but Steven ducked and the blow grazed the side of his head. Grabbing his attacker with his left hand, Steven slugged him in the mouth with his right. The thug retaliated by slashing his left arm with the knife. As Steven clutched his arm to stem the flow of blood, two other thugs slugged him with clubs on the back and the upper legs. Falling to his knees and fighting to remain conscious, he heard the sickening whack of blows not far away and the groans of his brother. He struggled to get up, but suddenly his head exploded with pain. His face thudded against the blacktop and everything went black.

Steven opened his eyes and saw a golden cloud floating high above in a dazzling blue sky. After gazing at the cloud for a while, he remembered where he was and what had happened. He sensed that his attackers had left. He moved slightly and a terrible pain shot through his neck and head. He struggled to get up but was so weak that he dropped back onto the blacktop. He thought of his brother and, in spite of the agonizing pain, rolled over and looked around. Paul was there ten feet away, lying on his back, but Steven couldn't tell how badly he was hurt. He thought he saw a pool of blood surrounding his brother's head. He felt his arm and was happy to discover that the bleeding had stopped. He lay there for another fifteen minutes, hoping to regain some strength. Finally he crawled to Paul and felt for a pulse in his neck. Paul was breathing roughly but didn't open his eyes.

"Thank God! You're alive." Steven shook him gently and patted his cheek. There was a bloody gash on his head, but it had stopped bleeding. He checked Paul's body for bleeding and found nothing more except a few cuts and scrapes. Steven was too weak to do anything else but wait. He tore a piece from his shirt and made a bandage for his wounded left arm. After what seemed forever, he heard Paul stir.

"Did we win the fight?" Paul muttered feebly.

Steven was overwhelmed with gratitude, for if Paul's wit had returned, he must be all right. He looked around and saw that his car was gone. The two brothers lay on the ground for a half hour until they recovered enough strength to get to their feet and begin the long walk home.

"Wait a minute," Steven said. He went back to the pile of newspapers and hefted a bundle. The effort left him breathless and wincing from pain. "Nobody's going to stop me from getting what I came for, at least not entirely."

"You're nuts, brother," Paul said as he picked up a small bundle. "We'll be lucky to make it home without carrying anything."

They had stumbled along for a block, every step sending jolts of pain through their bodies, when another car screeched to a halt not far away. Fearing a repeat of what had already happened, Steven looked up and saw a gray-haired couple staring at them.

"Can we help you boys?" the old woman said, kindness shining in her eyes.

"Yes, please," Steven murmured.

The brothers were a sorry sight. Their faces were covered with sweat and grime and their clothes were torn and stained with coagulated blood, but the elderly couple didn't hesitate to hop from their car as fast as their bodies would permit and rush to their aid. They helped the young men into the car and put the newspapers into the trunk.

"You boys look like you fell off Mount Timpanogos," the old man said. "May I ask what happened?" Steven related the story as quickly as possible. The old man offered to take them to Orem Community Hospital but Steven declined. He figured the hospital, if it hadn't been destroyed in the flood, would be swamped with patients.

"You were after newspapers, huh?" the woman said. "Harry, it's only a block away and it's so important. If they don't get that paper they'll have to use grass or leaves or anything they can find."

"No problem." The little old man took off like a race car driver. Steven held on for dear life as his chauffeur tore into the service area behind the market and jolted to a stop. "Now you boys stay right here. We'll get the paper," he said.

Within five minutes they whipped out of the service area, the car loaded with bundles of newspaper. As Steven gave directions to his home, the old man barreled down one street after another. Steven thought for sure the car would tip over as they rounded each corner, and was relieved when they arrived in front of his house.

"Here you are, boys," the old man said. "Did the trip scare you a bit?"

Since Paul seemed unable to say a word, Steven answered, "It certainly kept me awake."

"You didn't feel your pain quite so much either, did you?" the grandfather said with a cackle.

"No, come to think of it, I didn't feel much of anything," Steven said sincerely.

"Father, stop making jokes," the old lady said. "These boys are really hurting. They may even have concussions." She looked at the brothers sadly and said, "Are you sure we can't drive you to the hospital?"

They refused politely and, after thanking their benefactors, got out of the car painfully. Since they had been gone so long, most of Steven's guests spilled from the house to check on them. Paul asked the men to remove the bundles of paper from the trunk of the car. When the work was done, the elderly couple waved good-bye and sped away in their big Ford. The men carried the bundles while Steven and Paul limped into the house. They immediately stretched out on the couches. Janet Loomis brought them pillows, and everyone gathered around. Steven's children looked frightened as they examined their father.

"What happened?" Claude asked. Steven told the story again.

"What a terrible thing for them to do!" Janet Loomis said tearfully.

"Are you going to be okay?" Elizabeth Cartwright's eyes were full of concern.

"I'll think we'll survive," Steven said. "All we need is some rest and a few bandages."Douglas Cartwright sighed. "Some of the neighbors say there are bands of hoodlums roving all over the county, looting homes and robbing people."

"This kind of thing often happens in a community when the police are occupied with a disaster," Ron Loomis added. "In these days mob violence sometimes causes as much damage as the catastrophe."

At that moment, Steven caught sight of Mary Fleming standing behind the others. He was surprised to see her because he knew she had been busy caring for disaster victims.

After staring at Steven for a minute, she hurried forward and stood close to his couch. "We can talk about these things later, but first these men need attention. Steven, I think we should take you and Paul to the hospital right now to get X-rays and be examined by a doctor." Mary began to mumble in a low voice as if she were talking to herself. "Let's see, they may be able to see them immediately at Orem Community Hospital or American Fork Hospital. Especially if I go with them. On the other hand, those facilities may be swamped with injured people or even be demolished by the flood. We may have to drive all the way to Salt Lake."

"What about Utah Valley Hospital?" Sybil Simpson said.

"That hospital was almost completely destroyed in the flood," Mary replied.

Steven turned painfully and looked at his brother. "Paul, do you have any broken bones?"

"I don't think so. Just forty bruises, thirty cuts, and a huge gash on my head. Oh, and a bit of a headache. Nothing that twenty painkillers wouldn't take care of."

"Are you bleeding internally?"

"Well, I do feel something spurting around inside somewhere. No, actually my innards feel pretty solid."

"That's how I feel too," Steven said. "I'm sure that if we were bleeding internally, we'd have lost consciousness a long time ago. Okay, I gave us our X-rays and our physical examination. I'm sure the medical facilities are taxed to the utmost with real emergencies right now. They don't need to bother with us. Besides, there's no sense wasting good money on medical bills. What we need now is a bed."

Mary looked as if someone had committed the most appalling blasphemy and she was anxious to call the guilty to repentance. But when the initial shock had passed, she set her jaw, raised her head, and said, "Brother Christopher! Do you have a first aid kit? If you don't, I can go home and get mine."

"There's a good kit in that closet over there," Steven said, amused at her indignation.

Mary went to the closet and pulled the kit off the shelf. "I guess this will have to do," she sighed. "Now we need to find a private place so I can doctor you properly. You'll need to take off those bloody shirts."

In Steven's bedroom, Mary doctored the brothers with concern and tenderness, in spite of their heretical attitude. She worked on Paul first, and when she had finished, he fell asleep. Next she started on Steven and while she cared for him, he discovered he couldn't take his eyes from her face. Before long she noticed him staring and broke into a smile. "What?"

"You sure are beautiful."

Both of them blushed with embarrassment. Steven couldn't believe he had said that. He glanced at Paul, who still seemed to be asleep, and back at Mary.

"I've never had a patient talk like that before," Mary said with a smile, her face now crimson.

Steven felt a wild, overpowering urge to say something crazy when the bedroom door banged open and Sybil strode into the room.

"Mr. Christopher, I'm sorry you and your brother were attacked by those thugs, but I was wondering about the toilet paper. We used the last roll twenty minutes ago."

"That's why we brought home the newspaper, Mrs. Simpson," Steven said, sighing deeply. "It'll have to do for a few days until they bring us some real toilet paper." He purposely didn't mention the smashed boxes of facial tissue.

Sybil rolled her eyes and looked into heaven. "Dear Lord, please take me from this earth right now." At that she spun around and rushed from the room.

"Poor woman!" Mary said. "Some people can't cope with trials."

"Yeah. She's poor all right."

Steven fell asleep within ten minutes after Mary left, and he didn't awaken until nine o'clock the next morning. When he opened his eyes he was looking into those of John.

"I visited you last night around eight o'clock and they told me what happened. I went at once to Mom's house and she and Dad came with a load of herbs and doctored you. Mary Fleming was here all night watching over you and helping Mom. I think that young woman has a thing for you. You'd better not let her escape."

"Thanks for the advice," Steven said sarcastically. He sat up and stretched his arms. "Ooh! It still hurts, but I do feel much better. I was so tired and weak that I must have been asleep when they worked on me, though now that you mention it, I seem to recall something. Thought it was a dream. What did Mom do exactly?"

"Let's see. She changed Mary's dressings, covered the wounds with comfrey salve, and bandaged you up again. On your bruises she rubbed arnica salve, and I believe she got some goldenseal and arnica down your throat. Looks like the treatment worked. Is there anything I can get you now?"

Steven got up and started to dress. "No, I'm fine. Are we going to remove debris today?"

"What? You'd better stay in bed a few days until you recover. Mary said you might have a concussion."

"No. I'll be fine. All I have is some cuts and bruises, and a lump on my head. Doing some work will help me get strong faster, and I don't feel like working on the house without Paul's help. Don't worry. I promise to take it slow and easy."

"Okay," John said. "I know better than to argue with you. What about Paul?"

"Let him sleep. I think he was hurt worse than me."

After John left, Elizabeth fixed Steven some breakfast. As Steven watched her work, he enjoyed once more the warm feeling of having a woman around doing things for him, even if she was another man's wife. He noticed some of five-gallon bottles of water sitting against one wall of the kitchen. "I see they brought us water."

"Oh yes. Some elders from your church came in a huge truck and gave all kinds of supplies to everyone. I've been amazed at how much you people help each other, and others too."

"Thank you. I believe most Mormons are capable of great sacrifices if the situation requires it. Did they bring toilet paper too?"

"I'm afraid not. We're using the newspaper and the tissue paper," she said with a wry smile. "Frankly, I'm grateful we have it. If it weren't for that, what else would we use? Grass? Leaves? Towels? If we used towels or wash cloths, we'd have no way of washing them because we have no power or wash water. Yes, I'm very grateful for the paper."

"What about Sybil?"

Elizabeth grinned. "She uses it too, especially the tissue. What other choice does she have?"

Before Steven left at ten o'clock, he checked on Paul and found him still sleeping. He kissed his children good-bye and told them to obey Elizabeth and Janet and to expect him to return in four or five hours. Using his remaining means of transportation, a small motorcycle, Steven drove to the site where John usually worked. John, Claude Reynolds, Douglas Cartwright, Ron Loomis, and Clinton Simpson were already there. They were surprised to see him and tried to persuade him to return home, but he refused. Steven felt stiff and sore but had no severe pain. He was startled to see armed troops everywhere directing the work of restoration.

He had worked only an hour when he found her body under a collapsed wall. He dropped to his knees abruptly, unable to believe his eyes. It was the lifeless body of Florence Goodrich, the ward welcome lady. Gregory Millman had told him that some of the ward members were missing but since he knew very few of them, he hadn't given it much thought. But this was someone he had known, if only briefly.

Stunned, he held her in his arms and slowly cleaned the mud from her mouth and nostrils. He blamed himself for the way he had treated her, and he was ashamed that he had considered himself unfortunate because of the beating he had received. The other men gathered around him and, after gazing at the tragic scene for a few minutes, finally convinced him to lay Florence's body down and return home.

Chapter 7

During the following week the waters continued to recede and the labor of restoration went on. There were thirty thousand workers striving many long hours to find people trapped by the flood and to clean up the damaged cities. Most of the workers were volunteers who had escaped the deluge or who had rushed in to help from other parts of Utah and nearby states. At first they found an occasional survivor, buried in the debris but still alive, but as time passed they found nothing but bodies. As more and more corpses were discovered and carried away in trucks, a great fear fell upon the hearts of the people—the dread of disease and plague.

On Sunday the churches of Utah County that were still standing held brief meetings to pray to God to bless them with his mercy and power. The great question on the minds of the people of all denominations was why God had allowed such a disaster to happen. Some said it was beyond the understanding of man. Others said it was a lesson from God to teach men the fragility of life and the futility of placing one's heart on material possessions. Still others said it was God's judgment poured out upon men because so many had turned away from the Lord and placed their hearts on the pleasures and securities of Babylon. While many repented and offered their hearts to God, others denied him, declaring that a just and kind God would never permit the slaughter of so many innocent people.

Steven went out every day with Paul and his guests to do flood relief. The work was hard on the brothers but it also helped them recover more rapidly from their mugging. In the evening the men returned home exhausted and fell into bed without eating supper. The women had to wake them up later in the evening to give them the nourishment they needed.

In Hampshire County in the south of England, Gerald Galloway strolled across one of the fields of his estate with two of his grandchildren, Callie and Marcel. In order to enjoy the beautiful spring day, he was taking them for a short walk. Gerald was a fifty-year-old English billionaire of medium height with flowing white hair. He looked at his grandchildren tenderly and spoke to them softly, and their laughter echoed through the nearby hills. They left the field and walked along a trail bordered by tall hedges toward the veranda of Gerald's mansion.

"Hello there," Mrs. Galloway called from the porch when she saw them approaching.

"Hello, Grandma," the children called in one voice.

After they climbed the veranda steps, Elenore Galloway said, "Did you enjoy your walk with Grandpa?"

"Very much," Marcel answered. "Grandpa knows lots of funny stories."

Nine-year-old Callie clapped her hands with delight. "Yes! And he taught us a lovely French song. Shall I sing it to you, Grandma?"

"Oh, please do! I'd love to hear it."

In a small, sweet voice Callie sang,

"Dites-moi pourquoi la vie est belle.
Dites-moi pourquoi la vie est gaie.
Dites-moi pourquoi, chère Mademoiselle,
Est-ce que parce que vous m'aimez?"

Elenore hugged her granddaughter. "That was beautiful. You have such a pretty voice and your French is improving so much. I bet Marcel could sing it too."

"Of course I could," Marcel said. "But I leave that singing stuff to girls."

"That's probably very wise," Elenore said with a wink. "And Grandfather, isn't he clever to teach it to you?" The children agreed. "Well, I have to write a letter to your mum. Would you like me to send Madelaine out with a treat for you all?"

"Oh, yes, please," the children chimed.

As Elenore headed for the house, Gerald and the children sat around a small glass table sheltered by an umbrella from the bright rays of the sun.

"There now." Gerald said. "You two must tell your grandfather how you're doing in that big Parisian school."

The children were quiet for a moment and then Callie said, "It's okay, I guess, but the kids are pretty mean. Just because we don't speak French as well as they do." She began to pout.

Gerald took her hand to comfort her. "Mean! What do they do?"

Quickly Marcel said, "They poke you, call you names, and steal your stuff when the teacher isn't looking."

"Do you tell the teachers what they do?"

Callie's eyes grew wide with fear. "Oh, no. If we did, the nasty boys would do it even more."

"Yeah. Besides, the teachers don't believe you," Marcel added. "They tell us to go away and try to get along."

Gerald was angry. "Don't you worry. I shall write a letter to some friends in Paris and they will take care of the problem. Is there anything else that bothers you?"

"I wish we could live in the country with you, Grandpa," Marcel said. "The city really scares me."

"Scares you? But Paris has always been safe. When I go there I see policemen at every corner. I thought the only dangerous things in Paris were the crazy drivers and the sidewalks covered with dog droppings."

"That was a long time ago," Marcel said. "Now there are gangs everywhere. I've seen them attack old people and little kids. They run in packs in broad daylight, shooting guns and stealing everything they can get their hands on. The police used to walk around alone but now they travel in groups. But even the coppers can't be trusted. One day I was walking past this alley and I saw three of them beating some bloke in a bright red shirt. Boy, did I get out of there!"

Gerald was shocked. "Does this happen all the time?"

"Nearly every day in Paris, no matter where you go," Marcel said. "It wasn't that bad last year, but now it's getting worse and worse."

"I don't know why you're surprised, Grandpa," Callie said. "We see it in London too on the way to visit you."

"London too!" Stunned, Gerald gazed at the peaceful tree-covered hills surrounding his mansion. "I knew there was a great deal of violence in some cities, but I'm amazed to see it happen in Paris and London. Those cities have always been fairly safe. I guess I've stayed too close to home during the last few months writing my memoirs."

"Which home, Grandpa?" Callie teased. "You have forty or fifty mansions all over the world, don't you?"

"Don't exaggerate, little monkey. I only have six estates and a few other holdings." Callie's teasing made Gerald feel somewhat better. "Now I'm very worried about you two, and my other grandchildren as well. What I'd like to know is what you do when you see all the violence. Why have *you* not been put upon?"

"Callie and I know how to handle ourselves," Marcel said proudly. "We know when to run and where to hide."

Gerald was shocked. "I promise you I'll check this out," he said angrily. "I'll probably assign your dad to one of my other companies in a different city. Maybe it won't be too far from here and you can visit me more often."

"Oh, when? Tell us when!" Callie said, clapping her hands again.

"I'll get things moving today. I can't allow you to live in danger one more day. You'll be safe while you're here visiting me, and when you return to your parents, it might not be in Paris."

The children laughed with delight. Then, after they had hugged and kissed their grandfather, Marcel got a serious look on his face and said, "Grandpa, why are people so mean? Why is there so much violence?"

Gerald's face became hard. "I've told you before, Marcel. Many times. Have you forgotten already?" There was anger in his eyes.

Marcel looked puzzled for a moment, but soon his face brightened. "Oh, yes! It's because of the Jews."

"That's right. The Jews seek to rule the world and they are everywhere, infiltrating businesses, governments, and educational institutions. They are polluting the earth with their ideas and their religion and building their power in every nation on earth."

"Why are the Jews so bad?" Callie said, her voice trembling.

"They are bad because of their basic evil nature," Gerald snapped. "They are an inferior race. And that's not all! Do you remember the wicked thing they did about two thousand years ago?"

"No," Callie said, "what did they do?"

Marcel raised his hand straight into the air as if he were in his Paris classroom. "I know! They murdered the Son of God."

"Whose name was?"

"Jesus Christ, the Savior of the world," Marcel shouted.

"Yes, the Jews crucified their own Messiah and our God, Jesus Christ. And what must we do about it?"

"We have to stop them in any way we can," Marcel repeated from memory.

Gerald slammed his fist against the table top and bloodied his knuckles. "Yes, and I promise you I'll do it. The Jews will destroy the world if I don't stop them."

"Grandpa, you're scaring me," Callie said.

Gerald fought to control his anger. "Don't worry, little monkey, I won't let the Jews hurt you. Believe me, I'm the richest man in the world, and I've got the money and the power and the connections to punish them for what they are and what they're doing. I've been preparing for this all my life."

Callie looked up at her grandfather with tears in her eyes. "But won't the Jews be good if we love them like Jesus said?"

"No, little one," Gerald said, more calm now. "You can't love a Jew. If you try, he'll simply use it against you."

Madeleine brought three huge tumblers full of ice cream and root beer. The children squealed with pleasure and began sucking on the straws. Gerald looked at them tenderly and thought how happy they would be in the beautiful new world he would create for them.

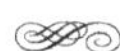

Two weeks later John arrived at Steven's house around noon in his green pickup and unloaded a heavy piece of equipment. Steven saw him from the front window and hurried out to the sidewalk.

"What do you have there, John?"

"It's an old generator I fixed up for you. It's got four 120-volt outlets and one 240-volt outlet. Sure works good after I got through with it."

"That's great, because my small solar system doesn't give us nearly enough power. But how do I use it?"

"How do you think? You know, for an intellectual type you can sure be dense sometimes. It's to give you power for your important needs, like the TV and the lights."

"Will it make my computer work, if my solar system fails?"

"Definitely."

"Terrific. Can you show me how to use it?"

"No problem," John said. "Also, I drove up north to get you some gas for the generator. There's twenty-five gallons in these containers." John pointed to five gas cans in the back of his pickup. "We can get more later if you need it." They unloaded the gas, some lumber, four long extension cords, and then rolled the heavy generator to the back of the house. John spied a place twenty feet from the house. "This will make a great spot for us to build a small shelter to house the generator. We can store the gas in the garage when we're done." John looked around, surprised. "How come it's so quiet around here? It's usually a madhouse."

"Because most of our guests have been able to make other arrangements during the last few days. The only ones still here are Doug and Liz Cartwright and their kids."

"Super. Now life will be easier for you."

"True, but I'll miss them too. Most of them, that is."

"Is Paul still staying with you?"

"Yes, but today he's in Orem helping Mom and Dad with the herb shop, and I expect him back at about six. My kids went along to help clean up."

They began to build the structure for the generator, and Steven was amazed at how fast it went up because of John's skill. They finished most of the work in an hour and sat on the grass to rest and eat sandwiches.

After eating, Steven lay on his back and stretched his legs. "How's the work going in the city?"

John shook his head in disgust. "It's a slow, miserable task. They say it'll take years to completely clean up the mess and rebuild the city. The mayor of Provo estimates that twenty thousand county people have already gone elsewhere to start over."

"That's terrible."

"Yeah. The federal government is installing dozens of trailer parks up on the east bench for some of the homeless families. The problem is, they'll probably become permanent homes for a lot of those people."

"I can't believe how blessed my family is for moving to Grandview Hill," Steven said. "And to think I was considering buying a house on 900 East."

"Man, it's a good thing you didn't," John said. "I hate to think of what might have happened. That area is still completely under water."

A half hour later they finished the shelter and John showed Steven how to start the generator. Next they plugged the extension cords into the generator and brought them to convenient places in the house. "Now you can use the TV and see what's going on in the world," John said, "and I suggest you do."

Steven studied John's face. "What do you mean?"

"There have been floods and tornadoes all over the United States east of here."

"There have always been floods and tornadoes," Steven replied, feeling the blood drain from his face.

"Yes, dear brother, but now they're a lot worse and they're hitting smack dab in the center of towns and cities. Two dozen communities have been hit in the last thirty days, and the death toll is in the tens of thousands. I told you we were getting close to the end and you wouldn't believe me."

"Do you think it's caused by global warming?"

"That's a large part of it. Because of global warming, there is violent, erratic weather all over the planet. The warming is caused mostly by manmade pollution. In some regions there's unusual drought. In other regions there's a great increase in rainstorms, winds, and flooding. Hurricanes and tornadoes are more frequent and more violent. Nowadays the weather regularly causes flooding on the East Coast and the Gulf Coast. The ice sheets at the North Pole, in Greenland, and in Antarctica are melting rapidly. In the near future the coastal regions in every country on earth will be under water."

"You don't think world governments can reverse the trends?"

"There have been some efforts in that direction, but it's not nearly enough. People are too hooked on their cars and conveniences. Industry always claims it needs fossil fuels to produce its products. Governments have to maintain current energy sources and are responsible to meet future needs. If they don't, the leaders lose their jobs."

"What about nuclear energy?"

John scowled. "That's the most dangerous source of energy there is. Think of Chernobyl in 1986. Think of Fukushima in 2011. At Fukushima one tsunami destroyed the nuclear plant with deadly results which will impact the population for decades. Think of what would happen in this country if we built more and more nuclear plants. With the increase in earthquakes and destructive storms, there's an increased chance of those plants being destroyed. And what's the final result? Armageddon."

"I guess I was trying to help a bit by installing a small solar system."

"And you did help. The problem is, the solar panels and solar equipment have to be manufactured, and manufacturing creates more pollution. Still, it's a step in the right direction. As soon as things return to normal, I'm going to install a wind turbine and a large solar system. I'm also looking into the possibility of other sources of alternative energy."

"Well, thanks, John. You've given me a lot to think about . . . I promise to watch the news tonight."

"You do that. Look, I've got to go now." John started to leave and stopped, "Oh, I almost forgot. Have you seen Mary Fleming lately?"

Steven knew what was coming and he guessed that his mother, who was always encouraging him to remarry, was behind John's inquiry. "Yes. She comes here nearly every day to check on us. It'll please you to know that I asked her to study the scriptures with me this Sunday night."

John shot him a glad smile. "Okay then! I suppose I'd better be running along."

After saying good-bye to his brother, Steven went into the house and continued cleaning up the mess from the large number of guests. At three o'clock a woman appeared at the door.

"Hello, I'm from Westridge Elementary. I'm here to tell you we are starting classes again on June 17. That's this Monday. Your daughter Jennifer and your son Andrew are on track at this time and we would love to have them come. School will only last three hours until the facilities become fully functional."

Steven was perplexed. "But I thought you needed water and power and rest room facilities to hold any classes at all."

The woman looked at him with indulgence. "Now, now, Mr. Christopher, don't you worry. We know things haven't completely returned to normal, but we want the children in school regardless. Believe me, we know what we're doing. We have two big new generators and we've made reasonable arrangements for the other necessities. Please be sure the children arrive on time at nine o'clock Monday morning. Oh, by the way, when you bring the children to school, please check first at the school office. There has been so much disruption, with the earthquake and the flood and all. So many new students and teachers! To make a long story short, we are still making last minute arrangements on room scheduling and other details." Without waiting for a reply, she turned abruptly and started down the steps.

"Yeah, sure," Steven said. As the woman reached the bottom of the porch he shut the door hard enough to let her know he didn't like her attitude. *You'd think the school district had more authority over Andrew and Jennifer than I do!*

That night they watched several television news programs, and Steven realized that John was not exaggerating. They saw reports on one disaster after another until Steven could take it no more. The children, however, were delighted that they finally had power for watching TV and playing video games. Jennifer and Andrew screwed up their faces when they heard they had to go to school on Monday. Things almost seemed back to normal except for the outhouse.

After church on Sunday, Steven spent most of the day reading a study on the Book of Revelation by an LDS scholar. He got nervous every time he thought about his study "date" that evening with Mary Fleming. At eight o'clock she arrived, but the children, seeing their father alone with a woman, were so inquisitive that Mary and Steven decided to take a long walk around the neighborhood.

He related to her the story of his life, and when he had finished she also told him her story. Steven found her easy to be with and was surprised that he wasn't embarrassed when both of them related the emotional account of the betrayal of their ex-spouses. She didn't seem embarrassed either. As he walked her home near ten, he took her hand, and she did not pull away. Then on her front porch he embraced her and kissed her on the cheek, in spite of the fact that he had sworn to himself during the day that he would never do such a stupid thing.

On Monday Steven woke Jennifer and Andrew and helped them get ready for school. He decided not to disturb William, who was sleeping soundly. It was a long walk to Westridge Elementary but they made it by nine o'clock. After checking on the new room schedules at the school office and taking the children to their classes, Steven returned home and continued work on a translation. In the meantime, Paul finished repairing a damaged wall in one of the bedrooms. At eleven thirty Steven and Paul left together to pick up the children from school. They waited at the front entrance for a while, and soon Andrew came running toward them.

"Where's Jennifer?" Steven said.

"I don't know," Andrew replied. "I haven't seen her."

After waiting until most of the children had filed out of the school, Steven was struck with sudden panic. He ran to the school office to check on Jennifer. "Do you know where my daughter is?" he said frantically.

"What's her name?" the secretary said with irritating calm.

Steven shouted, "I gave you her name three hours ago!"

"I'm sorry, but there are so many children," she said, shaken by his anger.

"Jennifer Christopher! She's ten years old!"

"Jennifer Christopher. I don't know . . ." She turned to another secretary. "Margo, do you know anything about a Jennifer Christopher?"

The second employee, a woman who was tall and skinny, approached smiling. "Oh, yes! Her mother came to pick her up a little early. I told her the child was in classroom sixteen."

Steven stared at her, unable to believe what she had said. He grabbed the counter to control his shaking and he couldn't say a word. Paul and Andrew had followed Steven into the office, and now Paul put his arm around his brother's waist to support him. "What did the woman look like?" Paul asked.

The scrawny secretary's mouth tightened. "She . . . she was a blonde of average height. She was wearing Levis and a blue blouse. She wore sunglasses and was carrying a large brown handbag."

"Jennifer's mother has *black* hair," Paul said.

The two secretaries looked as though they had just learned that the world was coming to an end.

"What's the matter with you people?" Steven shouted. "What do you do—release a child to anyone who comes popping in here? Don't stand there with your mouths open. Call the police!"

As the first secretary picked up a radio handset, the thin secretary said, "But the child seemed happy to see her. She was holding on to the woman's arm."

That shocked Steven and he didn't know what to think. Paul led him and Andrew into the hall to wait for the police. Andrew looked frightened and Steven took him into his arms.

With tears in his eyes the boy said, "What's the matter, Dad? Where's Jennifer?"

"We don't know, son, but I promise we'll find her soon." Steven hesitated to tell him that Jennifer had been kidnapped, but Andrew seemed to understand what had happened and began to cry. Steven snuggled him close.

"It's a good thing they have a radio here," Paul said. "Still, with the disaster to handle, the police may never get here anyhow. But wait." Paul rushed into the office and talked for several minutes to the secretary named Margo. When he returned he had a smile on his face. "I'm sure it was your ex who took Jennifer."

"Selena?"

"Yes."

"What makes you think that?" Steven said.

"Everything the skinny secretary told me convinces me it was her. She described a woman who was about the same height and weight as Selena. She said the woman had blonde hair and wore dark glasses. Since Selena used to visit Westridge to attend activities and special programs, I believe she was afraid one of kids' old teachers might spot her, so she went into the school office wearing a blonde wig and dark glasses to find out which room Jennifer was in. I'll bet she also wore the disguise so you wouldn't know she was the one who had Jennifer. She knew you'd come after her. Then just before she reached the classroom, she stuffed the glasses and the wig into the handbag so when she reached the classroom, Jennifer would recognize her and be willing to go with her."

"But Jennifer's teacher might have recognized her and not let Jennifer go."

"Well, maybe she hoped that Jennifer would have a new teacher. And even if she did recognize her, do all the teachers know that you and Selena got a divorce, and that you have custody?"

"No. I doubt that any of them know."

Paul said, "At any rate, Selena did the best she could to hide her identity. Now we need to talk to the teacher to get a description of the woman who came for Jennifer."

They rushed to room sixteen and found the teacher putting up student drawings on a display board. Steven related the entire story quickly. The teacher admitted that a pretty brunette with olive-colored skin had come to get Jennifer early. She confessed she did not know Jennifer's mother, but saw no problem since the child said the woman was her mother and went with her willingly. Steven sighed with relief. He had been so frantic that he was unable to think clearly. Thank God for Paul. He knew that if it was Selena who had taken Jennifer, at least his daughter would be safe.

Back in the foyer, Steven said, "I think you're right, Paul. I'm sure it was Selena." At that instant he was struck by the terrible thought that he might never see Jennifer again. "We've got to find them," he said anxiously. "Selena has no right whatsoever, after abandoning the children for two years . . . What I can't figure out is why she didn't try to steal Andrew too."

"Who knows? Maybe she didn't have time."

"Where do you think they are?" Steven said.

After considering the question for a moment, Paul said, "She may have returned to the polygamist colony in northern Arizona. On the other hand, she may have decided to relocate in an effort to throw you off the track."

They continued to discuss the possibilities until three policemen appeared and began to question them and the secretaries. One of the officers took notes on the circumstances, Jennifer's description, and that of the kidnapper. Paul told them they suspected the kidnapper was the noncustodial parent.

Finally, one of the officers said to Steven, "We'll send out an AMBER Alert as soon as possible. Now we need to question everyone we can at Westridge and in the neighborhood. It would be very helpful to have a description of the vehicle used by the kidnapper—or kidnappers. Is there any other information you can give us?"

Steven told him that he thought his ex-wife may have taken Jennifer to a polygamist colony in northern Arizona. The policeman noted that and told Steven the authorities would contact him as soon as they had any solid information as to Jennifer's whereabouts.

After the police left, Steven said, "Let's get the family together." They need to know what's going on. Maybe they can help us decide what to do."

Once the initial emotion was over, Steven felt confident and capable of making intelligent plans for the recovery of his daughter. They hurried home and explained to William and the Cartwrights what had happened and their plan to get their family together at John's house. It was the first time in a long time that Steven had seen William cry.

"I'd like to get in on this too," Douglas said. "It's the least I can do after what you've done for my family."

"Thanks," Steven said. "We'll need all the help we can get."

"I'm not staying here alone," Elizabeth said. "Let's go."

Steven's heart was moved with gratitude and he hugged both Douglas and Elizabeth. They all set out on foot for John's house. As soon as they arrived, Steven used John's radio to contact John, who was at work, and the other family members who had radios. Since Robert and Sarah Christopher had no radio, Paul took one of John's cars and drove to the herb shop in Orem to inform their parents. Within forty-five minutes the Cartwrights and all of the family members who lived in the area gathered in John's living room. After analyzing the kidnapping at length, they agreed it was Selena who had taken Jennifer, and they discussed where Selena and Jennifer might be.

"I believe Selena made arrangements to take Jennifer some place we're not acquainted with," Steven's father said. "She understands you could find her easily if she went back to that colony in northern Arizona."

"I disagree," John said. "I feel she'll return to the colony. If I know anything about polygamous men, they believe they are patriarchs who are building their personal kingdom when they have several wives and as many children as possible. Selena's husband would claim Jennifer as his child because she's the daughter of his wife, even though he has no legal right."

"I agree with John," Sarah said, "and I think we should go down there as a group and swarm all over them to get Jennifer back. Let's go! I'm ready right now." The others concurred with John and Sarah and began to make plans for the trip to Arizona.

Steven stopped them. "No, we can't all go. I appreciate your support, but a large group might alert them, and they'd hide Jennifer so well I might never find her. I believe they're at the colony also, but Paul and I will go alone. We'll contact you if we need anything."

Reluctantly the others accepted Steven's decision. Robert suggested they kneel in prayer to ask for God's help. As Robert offered the prayer, a warmth filled Steven's chest and he knew without doubt that they had made the right decision.

"What are you going to do when you get there?" John asked.

"I don't know," Steven said.

"You'll need a map, some money, and photos of Selena and Jennifer," John said.

"I picked them up before I left home." Although he had divorced Selena, Steven had never been able to throw her photographs away.

"Look, son," Robert said, "you don't even have a car. I want you to take mine."

John shook his head. "No, Dad, your car is electric and they might have trouble finding charging stations. I want him to take my power buggy. It's a souped up Mercury and it's got two oversized gas tanks. Steve should be able to get there and back without even stopping for fuel." John went to a drawer, unlocked it, took out a revolver, and held it out to Steven. "Take this with you. The world is getting dangerous, and I'd feel better if you had some protection."

Steven shook his head. "That won't be necessary. I don't want to resort to violence."

John put the revolver back into the drawer and locked it. "All right, but be very careful. You never know what you're up against out there."

"Thanks, John." Steven felt that his brother was being melodramatic again, but he didn't want to hurt his feelings. "We'd better go now. There may be a chance we can overtake Selena before she gets to the colony."

"Drive fast then," John said. "That car can take it."

"Believe me, I will!" Paul said.

As his brothers headed for the door, John called after them, "By the way, they expect to reroute telephone service from Orem into this area in a day or two, so if you need to contact us, try the phone first. Or try your cell."

"I'll do that, thanks," said Steven.

The family rushed out to the car and put some emergency provisions into the back. William and Andrew begged to join their father in the heroic task of recovering their sister, but Steven refused. He hated to leave his sons, but when Elizabeth assured him that she and Douglas would watch over the boys as if they were their own, he felt much better. After hugging his sons and telling them to obey Elizabeth, he promised that the next time they saw him, he would have Jennifer with him. At last he and Paul jumped into the blue Mercury, waved good-bye, and drove away immediately. They left an hour and a half after they had learned that Jennifer had been kidnapped.

Chapter 8

Steven and Paul were excited to feel the power and performance of John's Mercury as Paul drove north toward Orem. "If we ever have to make a run for it," Paul said, "this car will do just fine."

"No kidding," Steven agreed. "How are we going to get around the flood zone?"

"Let's drive to 1300 South in Orem and go west to I-15. I've heard they've repaired the freeway enough to let traffic through." Paul broke speed limits as he made his way north. "Do you really think we have a chance of overtaking them?"

"I doubt it. Not only does Selena have a good head start, but she may have taken an alternate route after she left this area."

It took them forty-five minutes to get past the Orem and Provo areas, and Steven was nearly frantic. But finally, near Spanish Fork, they were able to speed up. They were shocked to see large numbers of military vehicles and personnel at regular intervals as they sped south. From time to time they observed squadrons of black military helicopters flying north and south. As they approached Santaquin, they saw a contingent of soldiers blocking the exits.

"Look at those uniforms," Paul said. "What army do they belong to?"

Steven saw that the soldiers were wearing green uniforms with light blue hats. "They look like UN troops. I'm surprised to see them here. I thought they went to regions where different nations or ethnic groups were in conflict."

"It's probably because the United States, like a lot of countries, has been complying with international laws established by the United Nations. Some of those laws permit UN troops to enter a sovereign nation in special circumstances of internal conflict."

"That's unbelievable!"

They looked west toward Santaquin and saw a huge fire burning in the center of town.

"Check that out!" Paul cried. "I wonder if that fire has anything to do with the troops blocking the exit."

"I don't know."

After they had sat in silence a few minutes, Paul asked, "How do we get to Colorado City?"

Steven looked at the road map. "Let's see. We continue south on I-15, get off at highway 17, and go through La Verkin and Hurricane. From there we drive about twenty miles southeast to Colorado City."

"Did you ever go to Colorado City after Selena left to join the colony?"

"No, but I studied the map and other things I got from the library."

There was a short break in the discussion and then Paul spoke up. "What are we going to do when we find Jennifer?"

"I don't know yet. We'll figure that out when the time comes."

Paul continued in the right lane, driving a bit over seventy-five miles an hour. There was very little traffic on the highway. They had just gone by the Nephi exits when three powerful cars roared up to them. One of the cars moved up behind, another pulled in front, and the third came along their left side. It happened so fast that Paul was stunned and couldn't maneuver the Mercury out of their way. Within seconds a man in the backseat of the car next to them thrust a pistol out the window and fired several rounds at them. The brothers dropped low in their seats as glass showered them. A bullet grazed Paul's left shoulder but he hung onto the steering wheel with all his might and, unable to see clearly ahead, struggled to hold it steady.

The firing stopped abruptly as the thug fumbled with his pistol, apparently trying to insert another clip. Suddenly Paul saw a shoulder ahead which appeared wider than usual. It continued for about a hundred yards. Just as he reached it, he swerved the Mercury to the right and hit the accelerator. Partly on the road and partly on the shoulder, the Mercury swept past the car in front. When he had passed them, Paul moved the car back onto the highway and gunned it, quickly pulling away from their pursuers. Steven turned to see their enemies falling behind for a while and then beginning to overtake them again.

"Paul! Can't you go faster?" Steven yelled. "They're catching us."

"No problem. I'm toying with them."

"What? Toying with them? No, don't toy. This isn't the time to toy."

Instead of answering, Paul pushed his foot to the floorboard and John's "buggy" jerked ahead with a roar, rapidly leaving their attackers behind, almost as if they weren't even moving. As the cars became dots behind them, the brothers let out a yell of victory and relief.

"Thank God for John's fanaticism!" Steven called.

"Wow, this baby can *go*," Paul shouted.

Steven saw blood soaking Paul's shirt at his left shoulder. "You're wounded. Let me see." He reached around Paul and tore his shirt open wider. He examined the wound and saw it wasn't serious. "Just a flesh wound."

Steven removed a first aid kit from the glove compartment and treated the injury. Next he found and worked on a dozen small glass cuts they had both sustained. While he nursed the injuries, they discussed the assault and concluded that their attackers were probably nothing but wild hoodlums in search of random victims.

When they arrived at the Fillmore exit, Paul drove into town and they purchased tape and plastic sheeting from Southfork Hardware. After knocking out the rest of the glass from the two broken windows, they taped the plastic over the space.

Paul checked the car and said grimly, "John isn't going to be happy when he sees these bullet holes."

Steven wasn't worried. "I'm sure he can fix them. He seems to be able to fix anything."

Back on the road, Steven dozed while Paul continued to drive. A half hour later Steven was awakened abruptly by Paul's shouts. "Look at that! Another fire."

Steven looked to the left and saw a city on fire. "What city is that?"

"It's Beaver." Paul said. "Looks like the whole city is burning. Do you want to go over there and find out what is going on?"

"No, we have to find Jennifer as quickly as possible."

"Of course. I'm sorry."

They scrutinized the area for other signs of destruction but saw nothing unusual. After ten minutes, Paul said, "It looks like we'll be dealing with polygamists soon. I know you did a lot of reading about their colonies and beliefs when Selena abandoned you guys, so maybe you can fill me in."

"I'll try. Let's see. There are many different groups and they differ in details, but there are some general ideas which are common to most of them . . . They believe they are following the original command of the Lord to practice polygamy as found in section 132 of the Doctrine and Covenants. They believe that every man and woman must live in polygamy—when called to do so by revelation—to be exalted in the celestial kingdom. Like John said, every faithful patriarch must begin to build his eternal kingdom in this life."

"So they claim to follow Joseph Smith but not Wilford Woodruff. I understand they reject the 1890 Manifesto because they say it wasn't revelation."

"That's right," Steven said. "They say President Woodruff presented it as *advice* only and did not say, 'Thus saith the Lord.' The truth is, they would reject it even if Woodruff did use those words because they believe a later revelation cannot contradict or rescind an earlier one."

"That idea seems ridiculous to me," Paul said. "If the Lord gives a law, why can't he take it away? What do they say about D&C 124:49–52, where the Lord says he will no longer require a commandment at the hands of the saints if they diligently try to obey but are prevented by wicked men?"

"It depends on the group you talk to. They say the saints didn't try hard enough to obey, or the scripture doesn't mean what you said, or they don't accept that part of the Doctrine and Covenants as scripture, or any of several other arguments."

"The saints didn't try hard enough to obey the law of polygamy!" Paul exclaimed. "But they suffered nearly every kind of persecution because of that belief."

"I know," Steven said. "The thing that upsets me most is the hypocrisy of those who condemn the Church for not being faithful to the law of plural marriage, when today they can practice polygamy without any real persecution at all. It's easy to take pride in your righteous obedience when you don't *really* have to suffer for it. Also, while the polygamists claim to place great importance on 'thus saith the Lord,' they have erected an entire doctrinal system from isolated opinions from early church leaders who never claimed they received those ideas directly from God. And that's not all. They take scriptures out of context and misinterpret others in order to fit them into their own doctrinal system."

Paul swerved around a large object in the road. "Whew! That was close . . . It seems to me that from the beginning the Church has pretty much allowed its leaders and members the freedom to express their opinions as long as they don't attack the Church or claim their personal ideas are revelation. I wonder how the polygamists would handle Joseph Smith's statement that a prophet is only a prophet when he's acting as such?"

"I don't know. Why don't we ask them when we get to Arizona?"

Paul laughed. "If they're anything like the apostates I've met, they'll have answers ready to go."

The road seemed endless to Steven in spite of the fact that Paul drove seventy-five miles per hour. Sometimes a lot faster. At first they were worried about being stopped by the highway patrol, but were surprised when they didn't see a single trooper. Steven tried to sleep but found it impossible. All he could do was imagine his precious ten-year-old daughter in the clutches of some old man planning to make her his next wife.

As they drove past Cedar City, Paul broke the silence. "Steve, I really think we should discuss what we're going to do. I figure it would be a big mistake to drive into Colorado City without a plan."

Steven sighed. "All right, what do you suggest?"

"As I see it, our biggest problem is to *find* Jennifer. Once we find her we can grab her and run, even if we have to smash some heads in the process. I'm sure they'd prefer to hide her rather than have a confrontation. It would be easy for them to give us an innocent look and say they don't know what we're talking about."

"Okay, you've convinced me," Steven said. "How do we find her?"

"I've been working on that problem for two hours and I've concluded it's going to be very difficult to do by ourselves. I'm wondering if we should contact the police in Hurricane or Saint George."

"No. The people in Selena's colony are more than willing to defy the police to defend their beliefs. Besides, the police in the cities you mentioned have no jurisdiction in Colorado City. And the police in Colorado City and Hildale are completely controlled by the polygamists. Their last few leaders have either been imprisoned or gone into exile to escape the law. Usually it's because they have abused or sanctioned the abuse of children."

Paul said, "I heard that another so-called prophet took over the Living Church of Jesus Christ of Latter-Day Saints, or LLDS, several years ago, claiming that his predecessor was a false prophet and a sexual predator."

"In any case, we have to rescue Jennifer ourselves."

"Okay, so what are we going to do? Peek into windows at night? Hide ourselves somewhere and watch the streets all day for signs of Selena or Jennifer?"

"Sounds pretty stupid, doesn't it?" Steven wondered if Selena would dare face him or prefer to hide herself away with Jennifer.

"I know. We could always mosey into town sort of nonchalant like, pick some likely people, show them the photos, and ask if they have seen these people."

"Very funny. This is my daughter we're talking about."

"I'm sorry, Steve, but the whole thing seems impossible."

"Difficult but not impossible. I understand that nearly everyone in Colorado City is a polygamist, and if we made inquiries, we might give ourselves away immediately."

"Okay, we'll find someone who isn't a polygamist but who knows all about them."

"That would help, but it would be better if that person—or persons—disliked the polygamists . . . Where can we find such a person? Not in Colorado City I'm sure."

"Now we're getting somewhere," Paul said. "What's the city nearest to Colorado City?"

Steven checked the map. "It looks as though Hurricane is the closest."

"All right, let's stop there and see if we can find the people we need. The trouble is, it'll be dark in about an hour, so we'll have to work on it tomorrow."

After leaving the freeway at the Hurricane exit and driving into the town a short distance away, they stopped at Motel 6 and rented a room.

"This is going to be embarrassing," Paul said, plopping down on one of the beds. "What do we do, walk around town tomorrow and ask perfect strangers if they know anything about the polygamists in Colorado City? They'll probably think we're a couple of weirdos wanting ten wives, and they'll shake their heads in disgust and tell us zip."

"You're right. It's an awkward situation. The trouble is, we don't have time to join this community and win their confidence."

They discussed various possibilities until late in the evening and finally fell into bed exhausted without having decided on a plan of action.

In the morning they went to a nearby restaurant and ordered breakfast. As they were eating, Paul's face suddenly lit up and he grabbed Steven's hand. "I know. Let's hit the local library and go through some old newspapers to see if we can find articles, editorials, or reader's letters on the polygamists."

"All right," Steven said. "I can't think of anything else to do."

After wolfing down the rest of their food, they left the restaurant and located the town library. They asked the librarian for past copies of the local paper, and were directed to six boxes of yellowing newspapers. It took an hour of searching before Steven found a possibility.

"Here's a letter to the editor on polygamy. It was written almost two years ago." Steven began to read the letter. "This guy seems to know what he's talking about. He's complaining about the polygamists who live in the area of Colorado City. He says they claim their church is the only true church of Christ on earth, and they attack the Mormon church in every way possible. According to the writer, they exchange wives at the drop of a hat. Their leader likes to control the men by deciding who can have wives and who can't. It sounds like the group Selena joined." He finished the letter and looked at Paul. "This guy may be our man. He seems opposed to polygamy in general."

"What's his name and what town is he from?"

"Jeffrey Knowles . . . from Hurricane."

"Okay. Let's see if he still lives here." Paul jumped up and went to a phone booth near the library entrance. He checked the directory, wrote something down, and returned to their table. "I think he's still in town." He handed Steven the paper. "I got his address and phone number. Do you want to call him?"

"Yes." Steven went to the phone and dialed the number. After talking a few minutes, he came back to the table. "Let's go. He wants to see us right now."

"What did you tell him, Steve?"

"The truth."

From the directions Knowles had given them, Steven was able to find the address within minutes. As they entered the office building, Steven saw a directory near the entrance. "Here it is. Jeffrey Knowles, Attorney at Law, suite 2B."

"Paul, this guy's a lawyer."

"Uh-oh." Paul murmured.

They entered suite 2B and asked for Mr. Knowles. A pretty secretary ushered them into a nearby office and asked them to sit down and wait. A short time later a tall, balding man in his early fifties came in. He wore thick horn-rimmed glasses.

"Welcome. I'm Jeffrey Knowles. I presume you're the people who called a few minutes ago."

Steven and Paul jumped to their feet. "Yes, I'm Steven Christopher and this is my brother Paul."

He shook their hands. "You said you believe your ex-wife kidnapped your daughter and brought her to a polygamist colony in the area of Colorado City."

"Yes," Steven said. "The truth is, we don't know much about the colony, especially its exact location."

Jeffrey looked at Steven over the top of his glasses and said, "Let me ask you right off, do you have legal custody of your daughter."

"Yes." Steven removed a document from the briefcase he was carrying. He handed it to Knowles. "This is my proof."

Knowles looked it over quickly. "Good. I understand you want me to give you information not legal advice."

"That's right."

"Well, Mr. Christopher, I'm glad you read the letter I wrote to the editor some time ago and came to me. I do know quite a lot about polygamy and the group in question. I wrote the letter hoping they would take me to court, but they didn't. You see, I used to be a polygamist myself until I realized how destructive that lifestyle is. I'd rather not get into the details of my own life but I mention it to show you I have an intimate knowledge of their culture."

"You were a member of the group located at Colorado City?" Paul asked.

"Yes, for about six months . . . Now do you have photos of your ex-wife and your daughter?" Steven removed several photos from his briefcase and handed them to Knowles. After examining them, Jeffrey returned them to Steven. "I've never seen the child before but I know the woman well. She came into the group shortly before I left. She's sealed to the cult's leader, a man named Colton Aldridge. He's their self-proclaimed prophet and has eight wives. A very dangerous man, in my opinion."

"Have you seen Selena recently?" Steven asked.

"Her name was Selena? Not anymore. Now it's Sariah Aldridge . . . and yes, I saw her a week ago. She glared at me and walked in the other direction. I think she has a job in Hurricane."

"Can you tell me anything about Colton Aldridge?" Steven asked.

Knowles rehearsed what he knew of the polygamous prophet and showed Steven several photos of Aldridge from a file of newspaper clippings.

"Do you know where they might have taken my daughter?"

"No, she could be anywhere." He opened a drawer, pulled out a map, and made several circles on it with a yellow felt pen. He consulted the phone directory and wrote some addresses on the back of the map. "I've written Aldridge's address and circled his home on the map and also the address and location of two houses where he used to keep his wives. This map also shows you where the town of Hildale is found. Some of them live in that community."

"Do you have any suggestions as to how we can locate my daughter?"

"It will be very difficult," Knowles said. "But it's logical to assume they expect you to come for her and will hide her."

"Do you think we should get the police in on this?" Paul said.

"If you do that, you'll make a serious mistake. The police in Colorado City are cult members themselves. They would probably arrest you and throw you in jail on trumped-up charges. You might as well walk into one of their meetings with guns and demand they give your daughter up. You'd quickly find yourselves looking down the barrels of ten shotguns. In my opinion, you'll have to do it on the sly or infiltrate them in some way."

"I appreciate that advice," Stephen said. "One more thing. You just suggested that this cult is aggressive and dangerous. Can you explain why you feel that way?"

"Yes, I can," Knowles said. "They latch onto people in the Mormon church who seem to be dissatisfied and they indoctrinate them with lies. In doing so they spread anger and hatred. Also, the leaders promise new people, especially the women, that as cult members they'll receive exaltation in the celestial kingdom. That's how they seduce women into leaving their husbands. The women who are especially vulnerable are those who have unhappy marriages and those who are frustrated with their husbands' lack of spirituality . . . Well, I guess that's just about all the pertinent information I can give you."

Steven shook Knowles's hand. "Thank you. I truly appreciate your advice. I know it will help us get my daughter back."

"Oh. One final thing," Knowles said. "If you go into the country, be very careful. There's a large citizen militia group in the region not far from Colorado City and Hildale. They are dangerous and have been threatening violence against the government. They feel the government, especially Washington, has exceeded the authority granted to them by the Constitution. In fact, the National Guard and the federal government both have several thousand soldiers in that area in case of attack."

"What on earth would the militia attack?" Paul asked.

"Mostly federal facilities in Phoenix and Las Vegas."

"Thanks. We'll be careful," Steven said.

Steven and Paul drove back to their motel to work the problem out. After several hours of considering options, they finally decided to take Knowles's suggestion to infiltrate the new polygamist group.

"Listen," Paul said, "the way I figure it, we're going to need help. Neither you nor I can go to any of their meetings because if Selena is there, she'll recognize us immediately."

"The trouble is, I don't know of anyone else we could get."

"I know of someone."

"Who?"

"Douglas Cartwright." He'd do anything for you."

Steven thought about it for a moment. "Yes, I guess he would."

Paul said, "Okay, we'll try to contact him and ask him to drive down here as fast as possible. Maybe John can get him a good car." He checked his watch. "It's ten o'clock. If he left right away, he could be here by 6:00 p.m. We could fill him in on polygamy tonight and tomorrow he could visit the LLDS compound and ask to become a polygamist."

Steven laughed. "If he did that, they'd run him out of town. Anything we try is going to be risky so we have to make it appear as natural and plausible as possible."

Paul looked surprised. "That's not plausible? All right, Mr. Genius, what do you suggest?"

"He should go in there with two or three women because the polygamists wouldn't resent him if he brought his own females. Actually, if the women are good-looking, it might attract the interest of the leaders."

"And where do we get two good-looking women? Wait. I've got it." Paul said.

"What?"

"It's simple. We ask Mary Fleming and her friend Andrea Warren to come with Douglas."

"Do you think they'd do it?"

"Yes, I do. Mary's got a thing for you, and Andrea follows her everywhere."

"Fine. I'll ask them," Steven said. "I'll do whatever it takes to get Jennifer back. John said the phone service to Grandview might be reinstated soon, so let's try to call his house."

Steven picked up the handset and dialed. When he heard the number ringing, he grinned at Paul. It was Tania who answered and Steven quickly told her what he wanted. She promised that she and John would do their best. After the call, the brothers waited with growing impatience, not daring to leave the room. An hour later the phone rang and Steven heard John's voice. John told him not to worry because Douglas and the two women had been excited to accept and were almost ready to leave for Hurricane. Elizabeth wanted to go also but had to take care of seven children. John said he was letting Douglas use his Ford SUV to make the trip.

Douglas and Andrea were currently unemployed because the companies they had worked for had been destroyed in the flood. As for Mary, since Utah Valley Regional Medical Center had been destroyed in the flood, she had lost her regular job and the Church had hired her to help LDS disaster victims. She had worked so many long hours since the flood that her supervisor agreed to allow her up to two weeks leave of absence, especially when Mary told her why she wanted to go. Steven gave John the address of Motel 6 and the room number and, after relating the story of the attack against him and Paul on the freeway, cautioned him to tell Douglas to be very careful. John reminded Steven, of course, that it was his Mercury that had saved them.

Later Steven and Paul decided to spend several hours doing further research on polygamy in the local library. At five o'clock they bought hamburgers, fries, and drinks at a fast food restaurant and returned to their motel to wait. At seven o'clock they heard a knock at the door and Paul sprang to open it.

"It's you! Thank God." Paul said.

"Sorry it took us so long," Douglas said. "We hit several roadblocks on the highway."

"I appreciate your coming," Steven said.

Mary smiled at Steven. "We're happy to help. We'll do anything we can to help you find Jennifer."

"We understand you want us to pose as people interested in joining an apostate church and entering into polygamy," Andrea Warren said.

"That about sums it up," Steven replied. "It's the only way we could think of to find Jennifer."

"I think it's an excellent plan," Douglas said. "My wife was a bit shaken to think I was going to travel hundreds of miles with two attractive women and pretend I wanted to marry them both in polygamy. What's funny, however, is that it didn't seem to bother me at all."

Everybody laughed, and Andrea pretended she was a starry-eyed convert to polygamy by standing close to Douglas and gazing lovingly into his eyes.

Steven grinned at her antics. "The only thing is, I don't know how long this will take."

Douglas looked at the women and said, "We talked about that on the way down and decided we would stay as long as it took, no matter what."

"I'm grateful to you for that," Steven said. He pointed to some sacks on the kitchen table. "We bought some food in case you're hungry. After you eat I want to tell you what we've learned about the people we believe have Jennifer."

"Yes," Paul said, "and we'll need to brief Doug on polygamy and Mormon beliefs."

"All right, let's get to it," Douglas said.

They spent the entire evening discussing LDS doctrines and practices and the arguments fundamentalists usually give for practicing polygamy. By midnight Steven decided that Douglas understood enough to fool the people they would soon infiltrate.

"Wow! That's a lot of information to absorb in four hours," Douglas said. "I'm not sure I can pull this off."

"Now, now," Andrea said, "don't you worry, Dougie. Like good little polygamist wives we'll serve our patriarch. We'll put you in the middle and whisper clever answers in your ear."

"Hah. I'll be so nervous, I'll probably mess things up."

"You'll do fine," Steven said. "Old Aldridge and his apostles will be staring at Mary and Andrea so hard they'll hardly even notice you."

Paul said, "Who's going to be his first wife and who'll be the one he wants as wife number two?"

Andrea winked at Douglas. "I want to be his first wife."

"Wait," Steven said. "That reminds me of something crucial. We forgot to give you three new names and a history." Steven wanted to kick himself for being so stupid.

They spent another hour creating a background for the amateur impostors and deciding the techniques they might use to discover where Jennifer was. Steven showed them Selena's photo so they could recognize her if they saw her. But ultimately the three infiltrators knew they would have to play it by ear. By one thirty in the morning they were exhausted and decided to go to bed. After accompanying Mary and Andrea to their room several doors away, Douglas returned and climbed into one of the beds.

Steven slept on the floor but remained wide awake most of the night worrying about Jennifer and how successful his friends would be in trying to deceive Colton Aldridge and his followers. For him the most difficult part would be to stay at the motel and allow his friends to do the hard part. He toyed with the possibility of using a disguise and going to the colony with them, but he promptly rejected that idea as foolish and dangerous. No, he would simply have to be patient and put his trust in his friends.

Chapter 9

As they climbed the grade toward Colorado City in John's black SUV, Mary thought about Steven. A week earlier she had realized she loved him, and when he embraced her at Motel 6 she felt an incredible excitement go through her. But she knew his heart was still full of fear and suspicion toward all women because of Selena, and he might not be able to love her—at least not now.

She understood how he felt because she had struggled with the same feelings for over a year after her ex-husband had abandoned her for another woman. Yet when she met Steven, she was impressed by his gentleness and kindness and the way he cared for his children. Eventually she realized he was nothing like her husband, who couldn't tolerate children. She concluded that she was willing to take a chance with this man. When he asked her to help him recover his child, she came without hesitation, not only out of love for Jennifer, but also with the hope of winning Steven's trust.

Before long they reached the city and she began to dread the thought of meeting the polygamous prophet. Steven had described him and his followers to her the night before in some detail and it had frightened her profoundly. Anyone who could be so cruel and so selfish had to be absolutely evil.

As they entered the city, they were surprised at the variety. Some streets were paved while others were dusty dirt roads. There were mansions and trailer parks and everything in between. The trailers and most of the homes had no fences, but many of the bigger ones had fences from ten feet to twelve feet high. The latter looked like enclosed compounds. They noticed many cameras installed just about everywhere: on fences, buildings, telephone poles, and cell phone towers.

They searched for the address awhile and then, suddenly, they found what they were looking for. They parked on the street in front of the house and got out of their vehicle with trepidation. It was a huge, sprawling house surrounded by a brick fence about eleven feet high. As they walked up a long driveway, Mary noticed a blue Porsche and a red Ferrari. They climbed the steps to the porch. Douglas knocked at the door.

Almost immediately the door opened and Mary saw a stocky man of medium height in his mid-fifties. His hair and beard were silvery gray. He smiled and stepped onto the porch. "Good morning," he said in a soft, friendly voice. "May I help you?"

"Hello," Douglas said nervously. "I'm Douglas Hammond. This is my wife Andrea and our friend Mary Jacobsen."

When Aldridge looked Mary directly in the eyes, it sent chills down her spine.

"Are you Colton Aldridge?" Douglas asked.

"Yes, please come in."

They entered the house and Colton motioned to a nearby couch. As she made herself comfortable on the couch, Mary glimpsed several women working in the kitchen. She noticed the room did not look unusual except it had a huge painting of John Taylor on one wall and one of Joseph Smith on another wall. There were several large bookcases stuffed with books, files, and stacks of paper. She was surprised to see an expensive entertainment center and luxurious furniture. This family was obviously extremely wealthy.

"How may I help you?" Colton said.

Mary and Andrea looked at their patriarch, waiting for him to respond. Mary could see that Douglas had forgotten his lines. But then he swallowed hard and said, "We've been anxious to see you for several months. We heard you're the head of the LLDS religion, and that your people follow the original doctrines taught by the Prophet Joseph Smith, namely the doctrine of plural marriage. We also heard that your leaders receive revelations from God and reject the Mormon church because you feel it has strayed from the true path. To make a long story short, we decided to come here to find out for ourselves." Mary was impressed with Douglas's quick recovery.

"What you heard is correct," Colton said. "But let me ask you a few questions, if you don't mind. Where do you come from and who told you about us?" *This is it*, Mary thought.

"We're from Phoenix. We talked to many people about polygamy, and some of them mentioned your church. Also, we recently read some booklets you published."

"So are you LDS?"

"Yes," Andrea said.

"What is it that bothers you about the Mormon church?" Colton said, smiling.

Douglas acted somewhat confused and Mary thought for a moment that he would panic. "Uh, I'm not really sure. I suppose it's the lack of Spirit and the fact that we never see the same kind of miracles which occurred in Joseph Smith's day." Mary relaxed a bit, happy that Douglas had kept his answer vague.

"Mr. Hammond, what is the relationship between the three of you?"

"As I said, Andrea is my wife." He nodded toward Andrea. Then he looked at Mary, who was sitting in an armchair to his right. "And Mary is the person we have chosen to be our second wife."

"I see," Colton said. "So you want to enter into the covenant of celestial marriage. By the way, what you call polygamy, we call the Principle or celestial marriage . . . What brought you to your decision?"

Douglas cleared his throat and seemed more confident now. "The three of us have been very close for many years. We often wished we could be joined together as one family. But our church taught that living in polygamy—I mean celestial marriage—was sinful, and that members who began to practice it would be excommunicated. We prayed often about it. We couldn't understand why the Mormon church would abandon one of its most sacred doctrines just because the government outlawed it and other religions condemned it.

"Several months ago we visited a used bookstore in Phoenix and found six or seven booklets published by your church. We read them avidly and became convinced that the Mormon church had gone astray. We gained a testimony that celestial marriage was a true principle and we wanted to be sealed together by someone having the authority to do so. So we made plans to come here to investigate your church."

"That's good," Colton said, "but why did you come to see me?"

"We feel that it is very possible that you, as the head of the LLDS, are the one who has the power of God to perform the sealing."

Colton stared at Douglas with hawk-like eyes. "The keys of the kingdom of God exist in m—our church and in no other!" Colton glanced at Mary and in a calmer voice said, "But you must realize that the power which can seal is the same power which by revelation must make the final decision as to who is sealed to whom."

What arrogance, Mary thought. All at once she had the unchristian urge to slap him in the face. She steeled herself to avoid showing what she felt.

Colton went on, "Now I would like to introduce you to three of my wives."

"May I ask how many you have?" Douglas said.

"Right now I have eight."

Mary knew that one of them was Selena. The thought made her anxious and curious at the same time, but as the polygamous wives filed in she realized that none of them was Selena. She had stared at Selena's photo for a long time on the trip to Colorado City and had memorized every feature. One of the women was a teenage girl, another was about forty-five, and the oldest was in her mid-fifties. After the introductions, Colton related the story of the three newcomers to his wives and asked them to make the visitors feel welcome. He excused himself, saying he had a meeting with the First Presidency and the Twelve Apostles in the endowment house. Mary studied his face in an effort to determine if he had accepted their story, but his face wore the same enigmatic smile.

Mary prayed that he would not notice their Utah license plate, which they had not thought to replace with an Arizona plate. She tried to make up an excuse for having such a plate.

One of the wives, Martha Aldridge, seemed especially friendly and took charge of them. "I'm Colton's first wife and the matriarch of the family. Would you like to see our church? It's only three blocks away and we can walk there." The three visitors nodded and Mary relaxed a little, feeling that Martha was not nearly as intimidating as her husband.

"I would like to go with you, if you don't mind," the teenager said. Mary estimated that she was fifteen or sixteen.

"You're welcome, Naomi," Martha replied.

"May I ask you a question?" Douglas said to Martha.

"Of course."

"What do you call the other women who are married to your husband?"

"They are my sister wives," Martha said, "and I love every one of them equally. I know Colton feels the same way."

As they walked slowly down the street, Mary saw several men and women and a large number of children in front of their houses. The children and the adults stopped what they were doing and stared at them as they passed. Mary noticed that all the women wore long, high-necked dresses with sleeves down to their wrists, while the men were dressed in ordinary clothes. Some of the men wore beards but others were clean-shaven. Mary looked at every face and every house carefully, trying to spot Selena or Jennifer.

"Why do the women wear that style of dress?" Mary said. "It's so hot today."

"It's to cover their garments," Martha pointed out. "Most people following the Principle wear the original long garments, you know. The garments you're wearing now are a corruption of the true form." Mary didn't understand why her garments were a corruption, but she pretended to accept Martha's assertion without question.

"Are all these people members of your church?" Douglas asked.

"Yes, most of them. There's another fundamentalist community called 'The Work of Jesus Christ.' They live in Centennial Park about three miles south of our communities. They have a membership of about 1500 people. We have a membership of nearly 8,000 people, most of them living here in Colorado City and Hildale. I'm afraid the Centennial Park people don't like us very much."

"Why?" Douglas said.

"For many reasons. They are governed by a priesthood council, while we follow our prophet. They wear modern apparel, while we wear modest, traditional clothing. They reject our practices as being extreme, while we think they are surrendering to the ways of the world."

"I was wondering how so many women can get along living in the same family," Andrea said.

"It's difficult sometimes. It was especially hard when my husband married the first two sisters, but now it's much easier. We share our talents and work together to solve problems. We seldom disagree and we love each other dearly."

"I was wondering, uh, how . . . May I ask you a personal question?" Douglas said.

"You want to know how we handle our sleeping arrangements," Martha said matter-of-factly.

"Uh, yes."

"Every family handles it in the way they prefer. In most families each wife has her own room or sleeping facilities. The men visit them in rotation. In our case three of us live with our husband in the same house while the others live in a separate home a block from here. He also visits each of us in rotation. But for the most part, we don't keep a strict schedule."

At first Mary thought Douglas had made a serious mistake asking such a personal question, but after the woman's explanation, she was relieved and surprised at her openness. They reached the church and went inside. It resembled a large Mormon stake center. The main chapel was large enough for four hundred people. After examining the building for a while, they sat down to talk. Martha pumped them for details of their lives and their beliefs and seemed satisfied with their answers.

"Are you interested in joining our church?" Martha said.

Douglas replied, "Very much. Do you have more of those booklets on your beliefs? I would like to read as many of them as I can."

"Yes, we have them on every subject, and they speak the truth. I can furnish you with as many as you wish. They are only a dollar each."

"We would like to attend your services, if that's okay," Mary said.

"I'll talk to Colton about it, but I'm sure he'll welcome you. I know he is quite impressed with all of you."

"Is Colton the prophet of the church?" Douglas asked.

"Yes, he's a true prophet of God called to bring about the Gathering of Israel, establish Zion, and prepare the world for the Second Coming."

"Where does he want the people to gather?" Andrea asked.

"To this area and certain other sacred locations."

"Wonderful!" Douglas said. "I want to get to know him better, and the rest of you too."

For a moment Mary was worried that Douglas's naive enthusiasm might blow their cover, but Martha and Naomi seemed impressed with his apparent sincerity.

"You will," Martha said smiling. "Come to church this Sunday. Our meeting begins at ten in the morning and ends at noon. I know you'll find great joy when you are in the company of like-minded people."

"I'm sure we will," Douglas said. "I can't wait!"

"It's only four days from now," Martha said. "That will give you time to read some booklets and write down any questions you might have. By the way, where are you staying?"

"That's one of the questions we wanted to ask you," Douglas said. "Is there a hotel or bed and breakfast in town?"

Naomi Aldridge said, "Yes, there's a bed and breakfast six blocks east and four blocks south on the west side of the street. It has a small sign in front of it."

"Is it run by members of your church?" Mary asked.

"Oh no," Martha said. "The owners belong to the liberal sect of fundamentalists."

Naomi said, "And while you're there don't believe what they say about us. We are *not* violent. Just because we have gun permits and store lots of weapons and ammunition, it doesn't mean we want to hurt anyone. We mostly use guns to hunt and defend ourselves."

Mary wasn't sure she bought all that. She decided to flatter them a little. "I think it's terrible that the other polygamists and the media attack you when you show people nothing but love and tell them the truth."

Martha sucked up the sympathy. "Thank you dear. You're very sweet. Unfortunately, I doubt they'll *ever* repent of their sins. But I'm sure the Lord will find a way to cleanse this sacred land of all those who refuse to sanctify themselves. My heart goes out to the unrepentant when I think of what is going to happen to them."

They left the church and walked back to the Aldridge home. Colton had not yet returned. Douglas purchased fifteen booklets and the visitors said good-bye to the three wives. They found the bed and breakfast and rented a room in a building as large as a mansion. The owner looked at them inquisitively.

"One room for the three of you?" she asked smiling.

Douglas's face turned red with embarrassment. "Yes, please."

"You must follow the Principle, unless one of these ladies is your sister."

Seeing Douglas was incapable of answering, Andrea replied, "We're thinking of entering into polygamy."

"Entering into polygamy, huh?" she said. "That probably means you're gonna join the LLDS church."

Mary wondered how she reached that conclusion. "Perhaps. Right now we're just investigating."

"Well, you'd better watch out for that Colton Aldridge. He's as crazy as they come and a lot of other men's wives end up married to him or one of his so-called apostles—sooner or later."

The owner showed them their room. It was old but spotless and had two big beds. After the woman's tirade against Aldridge, Mary decided it might be safe to show her the photos of Jennifer and Selena.

"Have you seen these people?" Mary said.

"What do you wanna know for?" she said.

"Oh, they're old friends of ours, and we heard they moved to this city last year." Mary was shocked at how easily she could lie. "We so much want to see them again after such a long time."

"Nope. Never saw them in my life," the woman said.

Disappointed, Mary put the photos back into her purse. The woman asked how long they were going to stay and requested her money in advance. Douglas gave her what she wanted, and she stuffed the money into her apron and headed for the door.

"May I ask you a question?" Douglas said timidly.

"Suppose so," she said, turning. "What is it?"

"Do you obey the Principle too?"

"Most everyone here does except for a handful of regular Mormons. I've got five sister wives. It's like Relief Society every day. We're all good friends, except for cute little Emily. We clean the house together, manage the kids together, and enjoy recreation together. We all contribute to the family income."

"You earn the living?" Douglas asked. "Does your husband have a job?"

"Heck no! All he ever does is sit around reading scriptures and praying for the millennium. The worthless ole guy never did a day's work in his life. He deserves to be left alone."

"Left alone?" Mary said.

"Yep. You see, he complains all the time that none of us pay him no mind and that he never has anybody to talk to around the house. He says the only way he can talk to an adult is to visit the good ole boys sitting around under the shade trees all day in our little park. I can't figure to this day why I fell for that cuss when he came around to our Tennessee hills doing all that preaching for the Mormons. What's more I can't understand why I was dumb enough to marry him. But that's water under the bridge . . . Look, I gotta go now. The girls are probably sleeping on the job."

Mary figured this woman was so open and frank she would never have lied about not seeing Selena and Jennifer. After they put their things away, the three infiltrators drove all over town as slow as possible trying to spot Jennifer or Selena, but without success. They traveled to Hildale and followed the same procedure. They explored the back country over lonely dirt roads, and when they discovered isolated homes, they stopped and asked the owners for directions. While the occupants were giving Douglas directions, the women scrutinized the living room and the outbuildings from the porch.

While they were still in the countryside and far from town, Mary asked Douglas to stop if he saw an abandoned car. She explained that they needed to find some Arizona plates to replace their Utah plates. Before long they found a junk car still carrying Arizona plates. Douglas stopped and used some of John's tools to change the plates.

At last, they returned to the bed and breakfast before dark, tired and frustrated from the lack of results. They had missed the regular evening meal but the crotchety old owner had saved them some food and brought it to their room. After eating, Mary phoned Steven and reported the successes and failures of the day.

"I appreciate what you guys are doing," Steven said. "You haven't found Jennifer but you're making progress. You met Aldridge and some of his family and apparently won their confidence."

"That's true," Mary said. "And in the next few days we'll try to get into as many LLDS homes as possible. You said infiltrate and that's what we intend to do. On Sunday we'll meet the people in one of their congregations. I hope Jennifer is there, or at least Selena."

"Can Paul and I help in any way?"

Mary thought a moment, then said. "I can't think of any way."

"Couldn't we drive around town and see if we can spot Selena or Jennifer? We could also check the back roads and investigate outlying buildings."

"No. There's surveillance cameras everywhere here. They might have facial recognition capabilities. If so you'd only alert them to your presence and what you're driving."

"Okay. We'll stay put until you tell us to come."

A few minutes later Mary and Steven ended their conversation. "Steven seemed terribly depressed," Mary said to the others. "We simply have to find Jennifer."

"Don't worry. We will," Andrea promised.

In the following days, Martha came every day and led them to some LLDS homes. These people entertained them with suspicion at first but then with increasing confidence. At one of those visits Martha asked them when they thought they might be baptized.

"But we've already been baptized," Mary said. "Do we have to receive baptism again?"

"You were baptized into the Church of the devil like many of us," Martha said. "But now you need to be baptized into the Church of Christ."

"Oh, I see. Yes, that would be marvelous." Douglas and Andrea nodded their heads in agreement.

"So you're definitely ready to make a commitment?"

Andrea answered, "Yes. We've decided to commit ourselves."

"That makes me very happy," Martha said. "You can all be sealed for time and eternity shortly after. Of course, Douglas will first have to be ordained to the priesthood."

Later at the bed and breakfast Douglas asked, "We're not going through with all that are we?"

"Not in a million years!" Mary exclaimed.

"We won't have to," Andrea said. "We'll be out of here by then."

Chapter 10

On Sunday morning they dressed in the best clothes they had and set out for the meeting. As Mary walked into the church she was struck by the noise and enthusiasm. It seemed that half the congregation were children, screaming, climbing onto benches, and running up and down the aisles while their determined mothers tried to quiet them. Martha and several other polygamist wives they had met introduced them to one family after another. The people greeted them with smiles and hugs and told them they were welcome.

At five minutes to ten, Martha escorted the visitors to a row of seats near the center of the room. Mary sat on Martha's right and Douglas and Andrea sat next to Mary. Mary watched as the members hurried to sit together as families. Some of the men were accompanied by only one or two wives but others had three or more. A few men sat alone. The children piled in together as close as possible to their own mothers. Four of Martha's sister wives sat together in the row behind Mary, and the Aldridge children occupied three entire rows. The large room was filled with laughter and happiness and friendship.

As Mary looked at the congregation, she began to understand one of the aspects of this group which made it so appealing to the members: its remarkable community spirit and sense of belonging. She thought about the time years ago when she was sixteen. Her family had been living in West Covina, California and attending church many miles away in an old settled ward in Baldwin Park. One Sunday their stake president announced that a new ward would soon be organized for the people living in West Covina and La Puente. After that, she attended church with her new ward in an old rented building on the side of a hill in Hacienda Heights, California. She remembered how thrilling it was to be part of this new little ward formed from scratch. She knew every person individually and there was an unforgettable spirit of love and community. In that ward she felt she truly *belonged*, more than in any ward since. Now she knew one of the reasons why this fundamentalist church held such an attraction for unhappy Mormons who believed they weren't loved and didn't belong in the wards of the Church.

At ten o'clock the room fell silent as the audience waited for the entrance of the leaders. A few minutes later Colton Aldridge came into the room, followed by his apostles.

"Here they come," one of Colton's wives said in the seat behind. "You can just *feel* the Spirit!"

"Oh yes!" several other wives chimed, tears rolling down their faces.

Mary wondered what spirit they were talking about. The fifteen men filed onto a raised platform at the front of the hall and gravely took their seats, except one man who stood before the congregation.

Martha saw Mary's questioning look. "They are the First Presidency and the Twelve Apostles. My husband is the president of the church."

The man at the podium began, "President Aldridge has directed me to conduct this meeting today. He is presiding. We will begin with the opening prayer, which will be given by Brother Arnold Murray. Then we'll sing from page 256, 'We Thank Thee, O God, for a Prophet.'"

"That's Apostle George Jackson," Martha said to Mary in a low voice.

Arnold Murray came to the stand and gave an extremely long prayer. When he had finished, Martha whispered, "I wish Brother Murray wouldn't give such long prayers."

During the song the audience gazed upon Colton Aldridge with adoration. Mary noticed that his face seemed transfigured by some marvelous, unseen vision. Apostle Jackson returned to the stand, took care of some business, and announced two exciting future events. A murmur of approval went through the congregation. After Jackson noted that the first speaker would be Apostle Hector Paulsen, he outlined the remainder of the program. Mary was surprised there would be no sacrament service.

As soon as Jackson sat down, Hector Paulsen arose and came to the podium. He was 6'7", had a crew cut, and was about thirty-five years old. "First off, I want to thank President Aldridge for the mighty revelation he received. Last Wednesday he revealed to me and the other apostles that the Lord came to him in the middle of the night and told him that I was to take a fourth wife. I've had my eye on this lovely woman for some time now and I've had a powerful attraction to her. I didn't know why at the time, but I felt she belonged in our family. However, I didn't make any proposals because she is the wife of another man. President Aldridge will tell you what the Lord's will is in this matter when he gives his talk.

"Now I'd like to say a word or two about making your calling and election sure. This is a great principle which has been forgotten by the other churches which claim to follow the Prophet Joseph Smith. But Joseph Smith and Brigham Young taught that we must make our calling and election sure in this life or we won't be exalted in the celestial kingdom. And how do we obtain calling and election? By obeying our prophet and leader. And what does he tell us to do? To consecrate our homes and possessions to the church, to enter into celestial marriage, and to live faithful, sinless lives so that we may be sanctified and see the face of Christ. Then Christ will become our second comforter and seal us up unto eternal life. That is getting your calling and election made sure. I want to testify to you in the name of the Savior that every man on this stand is holy and has received his calling and election, and my prayer is that you will follow them into eternal life. Amen."

The audience said amen with enthusiasm and conviction. Paulsen's speech was followed by a tearful testimony from a young woman on the joys of living the Principle.

"What she says about the Principle is true," Martha whispered. "But she has a tendency to gossip about her sister wives and monopolize her husband's time."

Several children gave two-and-a-half-minute talks. During the last of these talks a beautiful young brunette suddenly appeared before Mary with a friendly smile on her face. She pushed past Mary's legs and sat on the other side of Martha. Mary recognized Selena instantly and her throat tightened and her heart beat wildly. She looked around for Jennifer but didn't see her. As the meeting continued, she peeked furtively at Selena several times and felt pangs of both jealousy and fear. But when she caught sight of Colton Aldridge at the podium, she completely forgot Selena.

Colton stared at the audience intently for one minute, saying nothing. Finally, in a low, solemn voice he said, "I will tell you who I am. I am both Joseph Smith and the Holy Ghost, who are one and the same. My name is Baurak Ale. But I am even greater than that. I am the Father of Heavenly Fathers. One of my missions on earth is to be the one mighty and strong who shall set the Church of Christ in order." He held up his scriptures. "These are my words and I know them better than anyone else, for it is I who spoke them. That is why I am able to confound all men, including the leaders of the LDS church . . . Now I give unto you a revelation. Thus saith the Lord . . ." He paused and the congregation held its breath. "It is my will that the woman named Julia Simons, who is now the second wife of one Richard Simons shall be given unto my servant Hector Paulsen as his fourth wife, for I have seen Hector's good works and they are pleasing unto me. Therefore, I commend unto Hector his true celestial wife Julia, and let this be done forthwith. Even so, Amen."

"Lordy! Richard Simons is finally getting what he deserves," Martha whispered.

Mary looked at Douglas and Andrea with her mouth open, unable to comprehend how any man could surrender his wife to another at the supposed revelation of this so-called prophet. Even more astounding to her was the idea that a woman would be willing to leave one man for another without any apparent concern for love. She looked around expecting a rebellion from Richard Simons or the audience, but they continued to gaze at Colton as if they were looking upon the face of God. At that moment she understood that they were hypnotized by the diabolical power of this evil man. What Steven had told her once during one of their discussions was certainly true. The greatest struggle in the last days *was* the battle to win men's minds and souls. The wars of ideology were truly the defining theme of these times, and Colton Aldridge was doing his utmost to win as many people as possible to his side.

But Colton wasn't finished. "The Lord also revealed to me six days ago that Susan, the first wife of James Atkinson, shall become the third wife of Apostle Michael Atwater. Susan is a lovely young woman and I considered taking her as my ninth wife, but Brother Atwater begged me to have her. Therefore, let the marriage take place today. Also, the Lord has shown me there will be further family adjustments in the near future. Now let me review the great principles behind these changes. In the case of Julia Simons the Lord is applying the 'rescue principle,' which means that when any man does not live worthy of the wives he has, the Lord through his prophet has the right to assign her to another, more worthy husband. In other words, the Lord rescues her from an unworthy man."

"That's how we got Naomi," Martha whispered.

"But in the case of Susan Atkinson I am applying the great doctrine of 'prior right.' As you know, this doctrine teaches that in the preexistence the Lord assigned every woman to a man, and she will be his celestial wife forever if they live worthily. However, in mortality women sometimes marry the wrong husbands for various reasons. So it's the prophet's prerogative to reassign that woman by revelation to her true celestial husband. It is this husband who has the prior right."

"That's how we got Rebeccah," Martha confided.

"In this way," Colton continued, "God's purposes are not frustrated. The only thing that can change prior right is when the rightful husband becomes rebellious, and in that case the rescue principle applies. Only the man who holds the keys of the kingdom has the power to direct the use of these two noble marriage principles. The result will be, as always, greater harmony and love in the church and in all the families concerned."

"And believe me, we've got some rebellious men in this church," Martha whispered to Mary. Mary was astounded that Martha, blinded by personal animosity, could forget she was revealing secrets to a new investigator of the LLDS.

Colton continued his speech. "Now the Lord has commanded me to chastise certain members of the church for their disobedience. This is similar to what we do to those who reject our gospel message—we dust off our feet and leave them to the vengeance of the Lord. Now remember, those who will not endure chastening are not worthy of the Lord. Therefore, I publicly chasten Brother Benedict Montgomery for challenging the leaders of the church on how moneys and goods should be consecrated unto the Lord. And in the name of the Messiah, I command him to repent or suffer excommunication. Moreover, to maintain the purity of the church I hereby declare the excommunication of Forest and Blanche Sinclair who refused to allow Blanche to be given to another man chosen by the Lord. They have now returned to the church of Salt Lake City, and like all apostates will receive an inheritance in hell."

After these shocking announcements, Colton's voice softened abruptly and he looked toward Mary. "But all the news today is not unpleasant. We have in our congregation, sitting next to my wife Martha, three young people who desire to commit themselves to joining our holy church and entering into the sacred covenant of plural celestial marriage. Please welcome them with open hearts." The audience turned and looked favorably at the three newcomers.

"Now I would like to make a brief comment on the Lord's command that his true saints follow him and not depend on the arm of flesh. To follow men is to be cursed. We all know that when we were in the Church of the Latter-day Saints, we followed the arm of flesh, not the will of Christ. We know that priesthood leaders made crucial decisions based on their own intelligence or prejudices and not from revelation. In fact, they don't even claim that God guides them to choose people for positions or to solve problems.

"When you were Mormons how many times did you hear the leaders, or the members for that matter, say the Spirit told them to do this or that? How many times did you hear the Mormon prophet say he had received a revelation from God? Never! On the other hand, we say it all the time. Yes, I testify to you as God's true prophet on the earth that the Lord guides us in all things, telling us when to arise, how to fix our food, and what to wear. We live by every word that proceeds from the mouth of God. He tells us how to earn our living, how to guide our families, and what wives to marry. Nearly every day the men on this stand walk and talk with divine beings in celestial realms. No! You do not follow the arm of flesh because you listen to the inspired words of your prophet and his apostles."

Colton continued his speech by railing against the LDS leaders, accusing them of being false prophets. He concluded that they were "damnable hypocrites" and the members were "morons." When he was done condemning the Mormons, he attacked other religious groups: the Christian fundamentalists were full of pride, the old Mormon fundamentalists were completely ignorant, and the New Agers were nothing more than crazies. From the religious groups he turned to the blacks, announcing that he would never baptize or even fellowship blacks because they were under the curse of Cain; their curse would not be lifted until the end of the world.

Next Colton chastened his own people again and described many of them as prideful hypocrites because they thought they knew more than the man who held the keys of the kingdom. He encouraged his members to be more diligent, promising them that if they labored to build the spiritual Zion, the Lord would let them take possession of all the gold he had laid up in store for them. He criticized the men of the LLDS for going out and groveling for a living when they should be spending their time building Zion. He concluded his talk by gravely declaring that he would soon cleanse all their lands of inheritance by sending out a great curse upon the firstborn of the members of the LDS church.

After Colton sat down, the audience sang the closing hymn. As the beautiful music filled the room, Mary could not get Colton's words out of her mind. *He says Mormons obey the arm of flesh by following their leaders*, she thought, *but I've never seen any LDS leader try to control church members through fear and intimidation like he does. All I see is a man full of anger and devoid of any Christ-like love!*

When the prayer was over, the congregation filed out of the building, making a great deal of noise. Like most Mormons or fundamentalists, these people loved to laugh and talk before and after meetings. Outside the building, Martha led Selena toward Mary and her friends.

"Mary," she called. "I want you to meet the missing sister wife. She's been away for a few days. This is Sariah Aldridge. Sariah, this is Douglas Hammond, his wife, Andrea, and their future sister wife, Mary Jacobsen."

"Nice to meet you," Selena said. "I heard what Colton said about you. It will be nice to have some fresh blood around here." The weird image of a female vampire sucking her blood popped into Mary's mind. At the same time Mary wondered why she felt so resentful toward this dark-eyed beauty. Maybe it had something to do with how she was beginning to feel about Steven.

"It's our pleasure," Douglas said. "It's always nice to meet another of Colton's wives." Andrea pinched the back of his arm and he said no more.

After a few more pleasantries, the infiltrators took their leave and hopped into John's black SUV. When Douglas started the motor, Andrea said, "What are you doing?"

"Getting ready to go."

"I know, but why?" she said. "We can't leave now. We have to watch where Selena goes to see if she leads us to Jennifer."

"I knew that," Doug said. "I was just warming up the motor."

Andrea rolled her eyes. "Yeah, right. You were heading back to the inn to chow down and hit the sack." Douglas's mouth fell open in protest.

"Andrea, leave Doug alone," Mary said. "Without him this would be a lost cause."

"Okay, okay," Andrea said. "Look, Selena's walking away with Martha, probably heading for the Aldridge home. They'll see us if we don't follow them on foot."

They got out of the vehicle and strolled along some distance behind Martha, Selena, three other wives, and a pack of children. A short time later they were close to the Aldridge home. They stayed some distance from the house and finally decided they couldn't stand around in the middle of the street all day. Douglas hurried back for the SUV and the women met him at the end of Aldridge's street. After waiting in the car for three hours, they saw Selena leave the house and drive away in the blue Porsche. They followed some distance behind until she turned into a driveway in Hildale. After writing down the address, they watched the house the rest of the day from the confines of the SUV. As soon as it grew dark, Douglas went to the house and spent a half hour trying to peek through the windows for a glimpse of Jennifer. He avoided the surveillance cameras that pointed at the yard and entrances and hid himself as well as possible when the motion-sensing lamps blinked on.

"She's not here," he said when he returned to the SUV. "Or at least I can't see her."

"Could you see into every room?" Andrea asked.

"Pretty much. It's all wide open."

"She's probably not here," Mary said. "I doubt they'd stash her in a closet on the remote chance that Steven might find this house."

After waiting until one in the morning to make sure Selena lived there, they returned to the bed and breakfast and phoned Steven.

"So you found where Selena lives," Steven exclaimed. "That's fantastic."

"Well, I was hoping we could snatch Jennifer away tonight, but we didn't even see her," Mary replied. "I'm so sorry!"

"I know you're doing your best. Please don't get discouraged. Paul and I have decided to come to your bed and breakfast tomorrow at about six in the morning. We all need to talk and make plans."

"Okay, see you then, Steve."

Chapter 11

Steven and Paul reached the bed and breakfast at shortly after six o'clock on Monday and immediately the group began to discuss plans for the day.

"You've been here for nearly a week," Steven said to the three infiltrators. "You know these people. What do you think we should do?"

"I have a suggestion," Douglas said. "You and Paul could stake yourselves out near Selena's house in Hildale. She may leave to visit Jennifer and you could follow her. The main thing is not to allow anyone to recognize you. Meanwhile, Mary, Andrea, and I will try to visit the LLDS members we haven't met yet to see if we can spot Jennifer or at least get clues as to where she might be. These people are so close-knit that I'm sure every family in the colony knows about Jennifer and what happened to her. We've made a list of most of their names and we'll get their addresses from the phone directory. Our excuse will be that we're anxious to see firsthand the joys of living polygamy, or something like that. The trouble is, it may take two or three days to make all the visits."

"That's a good plan, Doug," Steven said.

Andrea looked worried. "The problem is—as I see it—if you sit around all day in John's blue Mercury, the powers that be will get suspicious right quick. Think of all the cameras. Soon you'll be surrounded by big black SUVs with darkened windows. That's their local mafia."

"That's no problem," Mary said. "We'll just let them take our black SUV. It's got tinted windows too. The mafia will just think it's one of their patrols watching out for Selena."

"Good old John," Steven said happily. He noticed that Paul was unusually absorbed. "What's the matter, Paul?"

"I was thinking . . . What if Jennifer isn't here? What if they carted her off to California or some other place?"

"No! She's here," Steven said. "I'm not what you'd call a righteous man, but I've been doing a lot of praying lately and I have the strong impression that Jennifer is here. All we need to do is keep on trying and never give up."

"I believe you," Mary said. "I've had similar feelings. I know we'll find her if we keep trying."

"I wish I had your faith." Paul reached into his knapsack and pulled out two pairs of dark glasses and two baseball caps. "Okay. Let's get to work. I brought our disguises." Everybody laughed.

"Good for you, Paul," Steven said. He put on the hat and glasses. "Tell me the truth. Do you think Selena would recognize me in this getup?"

"Probably not from a distance," Douglas said. The others agreed.

A short time later Steven and Paul drove to the address Douglas gave them and prepared to wait all day if necessary. Back at the bed and breakfast, Douglas, Mary, and Andrea were supposed to wait until nine o'clock and then begin their visits.

One day dragged into another as the visits went on for three days without finding so much as a hint of Jennifer's whereabouts. At 10:00 p.m. on Wednesday the group returned to the bed and breakfast discouraged and frustrated, but determined to continue searching the next day.

Mary said, "All we learned is that Aldridge is getting rich from the tithes of the members and his so-called law of consecration. And we found that some of the members resent it."

Andrea added, "Yeah. And according to one of his apostles, he's purchased property all over town."

"I've got an idea," Paul said. "Let's return the favor."

"Return the favor?" Steven asked.

"Yes, Selena kidnapped Jennifer so we kidnap Selena."

"That's a wonderful idea!" Andrea enthused.

"You don't know Selena," Steven said. "She wouldn't tell us anything no matter what we did. No, it involves violence and might backfire on us."

"That's right," Douglas said. "Her friends would suspect her ex was involved and might take Jennifer farther away. Then they'd come looking for us as the logical culprits."

"What I think we should do," Steven said, "is check every cabin, tent, and house in the surrounding country. Jennifer's got to be around here somewhere."

Andrea agreed. "I don't see what else we can do."

"Okay," Paul said, "we can divide into two teams and inspect the roads and houses in the region north of the towns."

Steven shook his head. "We have two women with us, so I'd prefer we stick together. Remember what Jeffrey Knowles said about the violent paramilitary units in this area. We need to stay together for protection."

On Thursday they left the bed and breakfast at seven in the morning and began exploring the northern roads. By ten o'clock the heat was intense, and on the back roads they choked on the clouds of dust kicked up by the SUV. Finally, they closed the windows and turned on the AC. By two o'clock they had covered the entire region without success. They stopped to rest outside an abandoned cabin they had seen before. Steven walked a few hundred yards away from the others, knelt down, and prayed for help. He repeated his prayer several times and received the same impression each time: keep looking.

As he walked back to the cabin, he caught sight of some military vehicles and uniforms swarming around the cabin. His mind full of panic, he ran forward to help his friends but was quickly surrounded by a dozen men carrying Uzis and high-powered rifles.

"Hold it right there, buddy, or you're a dead man," one of the soldiers warned. He was wearing combat gear and his face was smeared with black paste. "Get your butt over there with the rest of them. Now!"

Steven was dragged to the front of the cabin by two cursing soldiers, where he found his friends sitting on the ground with their hands on their heads. Apparently the soldiers had barely arrived and had not yet questioned their captives. They pushed Steven to the ground next to Mary. Before long, another soldier exited the cabin and walked around in front of them. He had a confident, imperious manner and was obviously the leader of the troop.

"Take those caps off," one of the soldiers said to Paul and Steven. "You ain't showing no respect for the colonel." They quickly removed the baseball caps.

"Who in the hell are you people and what are you doing around here?" the colonel demanded. "Don't you know this sector is going to be a war zone any minute now?"

"We're just American citizens doing some exploring and looking at the sites," Steven said, making his voice sound as innocent as possible.

"Don't you know it's dangerous to be out here?" the colonel growled.

"How could we know?" Douglas said. "We've been sightseeing in the country all day."

"Look, stupid, this conflict has been in the news for weeks. Get your head out of the sand!" After glaring at them for a while, the colonel continued, "Where are you staying?"

"At a bed and breakfast in Colorado City."

"Hah! Wouldn't of done them no good to be in that town," another soldier quipped. "Them stupid Mormons don't pay no attention to the news."

"Yeah," a third soldier said. "They's too darn busy with all them wives."

The soldiers guffawed. Seeing their behavior, Steven realized that this was a citizen militia, not the National Guard or the regular military.

"Shut up or I'll put you men on report," the colonel threatened. He turned again to Steven. "Are you Mormons?"

Steven was about to explain when Douglas Cartwright interjected, "No, sir, we're Methodists."

"Methodists?" the colonel said. "What are good old Methodists doing here in Mormon country? Shoot, Mormons aren't even Christians."

"Shall we tell them the real truth?" Douglas said looking at Steven.

Steven hesitated, wondering what Douglas's real truth was. "Er, yes. I think we can trust them. You tell them."

All at once Douglas's face became deadly serious. "Well, we was staying at a Forest Service campground not far from Snow Canyon over northwest of Saint George when we lost track of my friend's ten-year-old daughter." Douglas put his hand on Steven's shoulder. "This man's little girl. Believe you me, we was frantic. We asked questions all over that camp, and finally some old lady said she saw a woman force a little girl into her car. We asked her to describe the woman. She said she was very pretty, about thirty, with short black hair and an olive complexion. She also said the kidnapper was driving a blue Porsche. We checked the campground registry and got the woman's name and address. Then we tracked her to Colorado City. We've been here for almost two weeks now trying to find her, but them nutty Mormons won't tell us where she is. After searching the town we decided to cover the countryside and here we are."

Steven was surprised at the sudden deterioration in Douglas's English and was impressed with his story, which was calculated to touch the hearts of these rugged good old boys.

"Who are these other people?" the colonel said pointing to Mary, Andrea, and Paul.

"This is my darling wife, Mary," Steven said. "The other lady is my friend's wife, and the boy is my kid brother."

"How do we know they ain't Mormons giving us a line of bull to save their necks?" one of the soldiers asked.

"Good point," the colonel said. "I'm sorry to inform you, but you're looking at a Methodist right now. The real genuine article. I'll ask you a question or two to test you. I *know* no Mormon could answer these questions."

Steven swallowed hard, wondering what the soldiers would do to them if they failed the test. It all depended on Douglas now.

"You know that the Catholics and Mormons believe it takes priests and bishops and all that to do baptisms and sacraments, right?" The prisoners nodded. "Okay, tell me how we Methodists use the priesthood."

Douglas's face lighted up and he answered quickly. "That there's a trick question. Us Methodists don't believe you need any special priesthood to work in the church. We believe the Bible itself is the only authority and everyone can interpret it according to his individual conscience."

The colonel seemed impressed. "Okay, what do we believe about baptism?" He pointed to Steven. "Your turn, pretty boy."

Steven was confused a brief moment but got an idea. "Us Methodists are pretty easy going about baptism. We allow people to sprinkle, pour, or dunk."

"That's right," Douglas said. "And we accept the baptism of other churches; we don't think it's necessary for salvation. We'll even baptize babies if you want. Yeah, like he says, we're kind of nice when it comes to baptism."

"Damn! You're Methodists all right," the colonel said. "We'll get your little girl back if we have to burn every polygamous house in the region. We were sort of debating about whether or not to do that anyhow after we wipe out those government troops."

"Is there anything you can do to help your fellow Methodists *before* things get ugly around here?" Steven asked.

After thinking a moment, the colonel said, "Do you have a picture of the little girl?" Mary handed him the two photos. "Who's the woman?"

"She's the one who kidnapped our child," Mary said without thinking.

"How on earth did you get her picture already?" the soldier said in amazement.

"We stole it from one of the polygamous homes," Douglas said. "We visited a lot of them pretending we wanted to become members of their church. In one home we saw a photo of a black-haired woman standing next to a blue Porsche and we knew it had to be the kidnapper. How many people drive a blue Porsche? She was probably a relative of the family we were visiting. So Mary here secretly grabbed a bigger photo of the same woman and slipped it into her purse."

Steven was astounded at the speed with which Douglas could invent an acceptable lie.

"Good for her!" the colonel said. "We ought to sign her up in our militia. She's a heck of a lot smarter than the dingbats I've got." He stared at the image of Jennifer. "Nope, never seen her." He handed the photos to the militiaman nearest him and shouted, "You men check these pictures and tell me if you've ever seen these people."

Steven watched in desperation as each soldier examined the images and shook his head. Then the last man studied the photos and brought them back to Mary. "No problem," he said.

"What's that, Captain MacGregor?" the colonel said.

"I said no problem. I saw those two walk by one day while we were on patrol. I was sitting there by a trail chowing down—not far from the guys—when those two beauties came prancing along pretty as you please. I checked the woman out and—"

"Captain MacGregor!" the colonel snarled.

"Uh, yes, sir?"

"Where on earth are they?"

"In a cabin several miles into the hills north of here. It's sort of complicated. I'd have to show you."

"Grab that all-terrain over there and lead these people to that cabin. Take Lardner, Carter, and Myerson with you. Use whatever force is necessary to free the child and get back here pronto. We've got a battle to fight."

The four militiamen jumped into the all-terrain and soon skidded to a stop in front of the group. The captain looked at Steven with moist eyes and said, "Good luck getting that little girl, brother. My own little angel was kidnapped three years ago and I haven't seen her since."

Steven and the others climbed into their SUV and followed their guide with Steven driving. Down the dirt road they went, trying to keep up with the speeding military vehicle. They turned and twisted over dozens of bumpy dirt roads for fifteen minutes. Finally, after what seemed forever, the dark green vehicle slid to a stop, almost crashing into a fallen tree. Steven stopped the SUV and climbed out.

"This is as far as we can go in the vehicles," MacGregor said. "Follow me."

"May I ask you a question, Mr. MacGregor," Mary said very timidly.

"You bet, darlin'. Ask away."

"Do you really intend to use any violence necessary as your colonel said?"

MacGregor snorted. "Shoot! That's the colonel for you. Always trying to impress people. We don't attack civilians except to defend ourselves."

"So you weren't planning on burning out the polygamists after all?" Steven asked.

"Heck no. We don't have time for that kind of stuff."

"So there's no battle with the federal troops?" Andrea asked.

"Oh yes, *that's* the truth," MacGregor said.

They began to walk across a wide, flower-swept meadow intersected by several small streams.

"But what can you hope to do against the might of the federal government?" Mary asked.

"Don't you worry none, little darlin'. We've been preparing for this for years. We've got thousands of militiamen in every state and we got equipment and experience and brainpower."

"Brainpower?" Andrea said ironically.

"Yes," MacGregor said with a grin. "It's true that some of our guys are pretty stupid, but we also have a lot of brilliant people. You see, I'm a communications expert. Lardner here is a lawyer. Carter's a diesel mechanic. Myerson is the CEO of a major corporation in California. We've all had military experience. Our colonel was a professional soldier for thirty-five years until he retired four years ago."

They passed through a sparse wood, walked down a long slope, forded a stream at the bottom, and began to climb another hill.

"But why do you want to fight the government?" Mary asked.

"Because the government has destroyed the Constitution of this country and they're trying to control every detail of our lives—just like Big Brother. Soon we'll be nothing but slaves to do the bidding of our masters in Washington. Believe me, we'll die fighting before that happens."

"But why would the government want to do that?" Andrea said.

"It's all part of setting up the New World Order," MacGregor said. "It's the international bankers and intellectual elite who are running this show, and they've made a lot of progress. It's almost too late to do anything about it. Trouble is, they didn't count on us, the American patriots, and today we're going to give them another lesson in what we can do."

Just then Steven saw a cabin in the valley below. He started to run but was stopped by MacGregor.

"Not so fast. If they see us, they'll make a run for it. Let's circle around and hit them from the protection of those trees behind the cabin." MacGregor turned to his soldiers and said, "Remember, men, there's an innocent child in there, so no shooting."

Steven thought they would never get there. He was tempted to rush the cabin in a straight line and smash anyone who tried to stop him from rescuing Jennifer, and it was everything he could do to restrain himself. What if Jennifer and her captors weren't there? What if the kidnappers had seen them and escaped with Jennifer into the hills behind the cabin?

When they finally reached the trees behind the cabin, MacGregor raised his hand to stop them. "You civilians stay here. We'll handle this." He gave the signal and his men rushed forward silently and surrounded the cabin. In seconds MacGregor and Lardner reached the front door of the building with their weapons ready for action. As soon as they were in position, MacGregor kicked the door open and both men charged inside. Steven waited patiently for a while but didn't hear a sound. At last MacGregor walked around the cabin and waved to them. Steven and the others hurried forward and followed the leader into the shelter.

"Dad!" Jennifer screamed, throwing herself into his arms.

"My baby," Steven said with tears welling in his eyes. "Are you okay?"

"Yes, of course."

As he kissed her and hugged her tight, he caught sight of a man and a woman sitting at a table. "Who are those people, Jennifer?"

"They're friends of Selena. They're supposed to watch me until Selena is sure you won't come looking for me. Selena tried to kiss me, but I told her she wasn't my mother anymore and you would find me sooner or later. I said you'd fix her for kidnapping me."

"Did they hurt you?"

"Nope. They were pretty nice. They gave me lots of ice cream and junk food. I think they were trying to make me like it here. Please don't tell Grandma I ate all that stuff."

"Don't worry. I won't tell."

"Okay," MacGregor said. "You folks head back to the vehicles. The men and I have some business to take care of here. Do you know the way?"

"I think so," Steven said. He turned to leave the building.

Mary didn't move. "You're not going to hurt those people are you, Mr. MacGregor?"

MacGregor turned away from the two captives and faced Mary. "Darlin', these people are kidnappers and they deserve punishment, don't they?" He winked at Mary as the couple looked at each other in fear. "As militiamen we don't intend to wait until the government gets around to giving them a trial."

Still uncertain, Mary followed Steven and the others. As they climbed the hill she said to Steven, "They're not going to hurt those people, are they?"

"No, I'm sure they're only planning to scare them a little."

Suddenly there was a deafening noise and Steven and the others whirled to see the cabin engulfed in flames and debris shooting in all directions. Mary and Jennifer screamed and Steven leaped toward them and pushed them face down onto the ground as a shower of dirt and debris fell upon them. When the deluge ceased, Steven looked across the field to his right and saw—a thousand yards away—a line of soldiers heading their way. A spray of bullets pound into the soil all around them.

"Let's get out of here!" he shouted. "They're shooting at us."

"Who are they?" Mary cried as she struggled to her feet.

"I'm not sure. I think it's the regular army." He gathered Jennifer into his arms and raced up the hill. He heard the ping of bullets slamming into rocks and earth near them but he continued to scramble upward desperately, thinking only of reaching the trees as fast as possible. Then they finally entered the safety of the woods at the top of the hill. Steven handed Jennifer to Paul and told him to hurry to the SUV. He turned and saw that the soldiers were moving toward the ruins of the cabin instead of pursuing them. Several were carrying portable grenade launchers. He watched for a minute trying to figure out who they were, but he didn't recognize their ugly light green uniforms. Hearing Paul call his name, he turned again and followed his fleeing friends.

After covering more than a mile over rough terrain as fast as possible, they reached the SUV. Paul jumped behind the wheel and they began the descent to the city below. Jennifer clung to her father. Douglas had been struck in the left leg by a stray bullet and the wound was bleeding badly, so Mary had insisted he sit in the back seat, where she applied a tourniquet and an emergency bandage.

Mary sobbed as she worked on Douglas. "They killed all of them. The polygamists and the militiamen."

"Why did they do it? Who are they?" Andrea shrieked.

"It looked somewhat like the regular army," Steven said. "About thirty of them."

"I'm sure they were government troops," Paul said. "They were after the rebels and the polygamists simply got in the way."

"But they slaughtered all of them without even attempting a capture!" Mary cried. "I can't believe it. The world seems to be going crazy."

"Murdering devils," Douglas said. "It shows what fear and paranoia can do."

"They'd have killed us too if we hadn't left the cabin a few minutes earlier," Andrea said.

They descended the mountain quickly and made a short stop at the bed and breakfast to get the Mercury and their things. After settling with the owner, both vehicles left Colorado City.

Later, as Paul and Steven led the way to Hurricane in the Mercury, Steven fell under the spell of the beauty of the countryside, which was indescribably serene and peaceful. The setting sun lit the clouds on the horizon ahead with crimson and gold. It was as if they had suddenly stepped from a world of violence and brutality to one of exquisite beauty where nothing could possibly go wrong.

The only thing that broke the spell was the occasional appearance of a military vehicle moving in the direction of Colorado City. Steven felt miserable to think that the strange men who had helped them find Jennifer had paid for their kindness with their lives. They reached Hurricane shortly before dark and decided to stay the night at Motel 6 before returning to Provo. While they sat around in the room saying nothing, Mary put a new dressing on Douglas's leg.

Paul broke the silence by saying, "I wonder where Selena was today? Do you know, Jennifer?"

"I think she said she had to go shopping in Saint George." Jennifer still clung to her father's side as if she were afraid he would disappear.

"I'm glad she wasn't in the cabin," Steven said.

Andrea picked up a remote from a night table and clicked on the television. "Let's see if we can find some news on the trouble with the militia," she said.

The images of a man and a woman formed on the screen. Both were wearing a tiny butterfly microphone on their lapels and a canyon scene filled the background. After a moment of silence, the anchorman said, "Please stay tuned to this channel. In a short time we'll go to the white house for a special announcement from the president. While we wait, let me repeat: a few minutes ago we learned that the regular army is engaged as we speak in armed conflict with the so-called American Patriot militia in the wilderness not far from the cities of Hildale and Colorado City. We understand there have been serious casualties on both sides." He paused to listen to something in his earphones and said, "Okay, we are now ready to patch you over to the Oval Office for a special announcement from the president."

Immediately the face of President James Miller appeared on the screen. He was sitting at a huge desk and behind him viewers could see an American flag covering the entire background. "My fellow Americans, several months ago your president learned that a dangerous paramilitary group called the American Patriots was gathering in southern Utah near the communities of Colorado City and Hildale. This group, which possibly numbers several thousand men, claims to be a citizen militia fighting for the freedom of all Americans. They also claim that there are more than three hundred thousand additional militiamen throughout the country who will soon join them in their cause.

"It is because of these dangerous rumors that I have decided to make this short address to you personally. The truth needs to be told . . . From our own sources we have learned there are no more than ten thousand militiamen in the entire country and none of the other groups are showing signs of belligerence except the contingent in southern Utah."

Steven wondered if the president was telling the truth. He had learned long ago that in most matters the government typically told the American public only what it wanted them to believe. He looked around and saw that every person in the room was transfixed by the shocking broadcast.

"Inasmuch as the Utah citizen militia is trained in every kind of warfare, possesses sophisticated weapons and equipment, and has shown evidence of rebellion, I have viewed them as representing a grave danger to the peace and safety of American citizens in northern Arizona and southern Utah. Consequently, three weeks ago I ordered General Adam Ludlow, Chairman of the Joint Chiefs, to send a detachment from the Army Special Forces to northern Arizona on a reconnaissance mission. The reports I received from this elite unit have concerned me gravely. It seems that the intention of these insurgents is to attack and destroy the cities of Hildale and Colorado City, formerly called Short Creek." The president paused to let his startling message sink into the minds of the viewers. "The apparent reason for this violence against American citizens is that the belligerents oppose the religious beliefs of the Mormon fundamentalists who own and inhabit the two towns."

Andrea was livid. "Why can't he get his facts straight? The fundamentalists aren't even Mormons." Everyone shushed her to silence.

"Now it is my duty to report that through the powers granted me by the Constitution of the United States, I have made a strong and rapid response to this threat. Yesterday I ordered the army to deploy five thousand highly trained troops, supported by air and mobile units, and to use whatever force is necessary to protect the citizens of the communities in question. These forces are engaging the belligerents at this very moment.

"But let me make one point perfectly clear. Because of our quick response, the people of Colorado City and Hildale and the surrounding vicinity are in no danger whatsoever. Every effort has been made to secure their safety. Now one last word. I promise you, my fellow citizens, that I will not tolerate any group, no matter how large or small, to take up arms against this country and endanger its citizens. If they do, I will take whatever responsible measures are necessary to bring them to justice. This is my promise to you. It is my hope that together we may continue the work we began three years ago to make this a happier and safer nation. Good evening."

Douglas shook his head. "This is incredible! I didn't know it was that serious. Do you think the militia really wanted to destroy those polygamous towns?"

Andrea shushed Douglas. "Certainly not, Doug. Now please be quiet. We want to hear the rest of the news."

The scene flashed back to the two local newscasters, and the anchorwoman continued the report. "Channel Four has received several accounts indicating that the fighting between the federal troops and the militia is intense and that there are many casualties on both sides. The ability of the insurgents to inflict serious damage to a superior government force has surprised all observers. We have also received another report which claims that the real purpose of the rebels is not to attack U. S. citizens but to engage the regular army in armed conflict. Channel Four will keep you posted as we receive further information on the battle between federal troops and a violent militia body. Now we return to our regular news coverage . . . Texas authorities report that a devastating tornado struck downtown Dallas thirty minutes ago and—"

Andrea turned off the television, and the friends discussed the conflict until midnight. After making temporary beds wherever they could find space, they lay down in their street clothes for some rest. Steven had difficulty sleeping because the night was full of unusual sounds: the rumble of heavy trucks moving through the town, doors slamming, people shouting, cars screeching by at high speed, and the noise of what sounded like firearms. His imagination created all kinds of shocking scenes and he wondered if the pleasant world he had known would ever be the same again.

Chapter 12

Early the next morning Steven drove north on I-15 in John's Mercury. Jennifer was curled up asleep in the back seat and Paul was trying to doze in the front. Behind them Mary, Andrea, and Douglas followed in John's SUV.

Unable to sleep, Paul found a news program on the radio which reported that the struggle between the troops and the militia continued with the death toll mounting. The most shocking news was that dozens of other militia groups had taken to arms and were attacking federal facilities throughout the United States. The paramilitary units claimed that the president had usurped his legal authority by federalizing the National Guard without good reason, by intervening in matters which concerned the states, and by using deadly and overwhelming force to crush a citizen militia in northern Arizona, a militia which was authorized by the Constitution of the United States. A spokesman for the united militias declared that they would gladly fight to the death to protect their freedom and that of all Americans.

The report explained that the uprisings were also taxing state and local authorities because thousands of criminals and other violent people in many regions were using the rebellions as an excuse to perpetrate their own form of violence. These thugs acted individually or in gangs and often took advantage of the chaos created by the recent rash of natural disasters sweeping this nation and other countries as well. They robbed and murdered innocent people, raped women, and pillaged and burned towns. The same kinds of problems were beginning to appear all over Canada, Mexico, South America, and Europe.

Twenty miles south of Cedar City the traffic slowed to a crawl and Steven was unable to proceed at more than fifteen to twenty miles per hour. Through the rearview mirror he constantly checked the position of the SUV, and since it was always following close behind, he began to relax. Then for some time he forgot to check, and when he did look through the mirror, the SUV was gone and in its place was a Jeep with four men in it! Steven felt a panic that was completely unreasonable.

"Steve, what's the matter?" Paul said. "You look like you're having a heart attack."

"Where are they?"

Paul turned to look around. "There they are . . . in the center lane right next to us." He laughed.

Steven felt sheepish. "Why are you laughing? Things are getting dangerous out there and I was worried about them."

"About *them*?" Paul joked.

Steven glanced at his brother without understanding what he was getting at. He was about to ask when he spotted several military vehicles and a contingent of troops on the road ahead. They were stopping every vehicle and, after a short communication, waving them on.

"I wonder what's up," Steven said.

"I don't know. Maybe they're checking for fleeing militiamen."

"Cute, Paul, real cute. Militiamen fleeing frantically up a major freeway at fifteen miles an hour in regular street clothes."

"What's so dumb about that?" Paul said. "It would be a clever disguise."

Steven didn't bother to answer because several soldiers brandishing weapons blocked the road and waved for him to stop.

"Get out of the vehicle . . . very carefully," one of the soldiers ordered through the window.

"Why us?" Paul complained. "They're not making the others get out."

"How do I know?" Steven said as he saw the black SUV roll by out of the corner of his eye. "Maybe we look suspicious." They got out of the car.

One of the soldiers waved a pistol in Steven's face and ordered him to put his hands up and to lie over the hood of the car. Another soldier was giving Paul the same treatment. A third man, after peering through the window at Jennifer, stood back to watch the others. As soon as they had searched the brothers, they ordered them to turn around and answer questions.

"Where are you coming from?" Steven's soldier demanded.

"From Las Vegas. We've been visiting relatives," Steven lied.

"Where are you going?"

"To Provo where we live."

"Do you have any weapons?"

"No."

"Open the trunk."

Steven went to the rear of the Mercury and fumbled through the ten keys on the ring John had given him. He noticed that the soldier was watching him intently and becoming more and more impatient. After trying four keys he finally succeeded in rotating the lock and raising the trunk lid.

"Sorry for the delay," Steven said. "I guess I'm nervous."

The soldier sneered and waved to several underlings standing nearby. "You men, search this car." He approached Steven again, jammed his pistol into his ribs and pushed him toward the car. "Get your registration."

Steven found the registration and handed it to the lieutenant. "Now your driver's license." Steven took out his wallet and handed the soldier his license. After comparing the two documents for a moment, the lieutenant looked at Steven suspiciously. "These names don't match. Why?"

"The car belongs to my brother John. You can see the last names are the same: Christopher. And we both live in the same city."

Six soldiers searched the car thoroughly, even waking Jennifer, who jumped out of the car and ran into Steven's arms. After the search one of the soldiers shook his head at the lieutenant.

"Okay," the leader said. "You can go. Hurry. Move along."

After they had set out again, Paul said, "Good criminy. What was *that* all about?"

"You got me."

The brothers got back into the car with Jennifer between them. The traffic was moving faster now and they hurried to overtake the others. A few miles down the highway they saw the SUV waiting on the side of the road. Steven stopped behind the SUV and walked up to talk to his friends.

Mary rolled down her window. "What happened? Why did they stop you?" He thought she looked especially beautiful as she peered through the window.

"I don't know. Maybe they suspected us of being in the militia."

"We were scared to death," Douglas said. "Mary thought they might shoot you or throw you in jail."

Steven still felt the pain where the soldier had jabbed him in the ribs. "No, they were just rude and overbearing. I suppose they're under a lot of pressure with all the problems with the militia and others. Look, I'm sure you guys are getting as hungry as me. Why don't we stop at Cedar City for something to eat."

At nine thirty they reached Cedar City and stopped at a small restaurant to eat breakfast. Jennifer's eyes grew wide at the stacks of pancakes and the butter and maple syrup.

"I'll have sixteen pancakes buried in butter and syrup," she said.

"Tell you what," Steven said. "Let's start with two pancakes and see how you do."

Jennifer pouted for a while but grinned when the waitress placed a mug of hot chocolate in front of her.

Douglas said, "Did you hear the news reports in the car?"

Steven nodded. "Yes. They said the fighting is bad around Colorado City and that other militias are attacking federal installations in other states. There was one report accusing the president of going beyond his authority."

"I wouldn't put it past him," Douglas said. "It was a shameful day when the people of this country elected James Miller president."

Paul tried to talk while he swallowed a mouthful of pancake and ended up choking. When he had returned to normal, he said, "Whew. Eating too fast. I wanted to say that the courts and the government have been thumbing their nose at the Constitution for over a century now, so what's so surprising about the president exceeding his authority and lying to the American people?"

"He's not the only one who lies," Mary said. "In the last few days I've lied enough for a lifetime. I told the polygamists one lie after another and I was surprised I could do it with a straight face."

Douglas chuckled. "I know. I felt especially guilty when I started to enjoy it."

"And we lied to the militiamen in the wilderness and to the soldiers on the freeway," Paul added.

"I thought we weren't supposed to tell lies," Jennifer said.

"Normally we shouldn't lie," Steven said. "But I'm not sure we owe the truth to criminals and people who wish to harm us. The polygamists were protecting Selena, who was a kidnapper. As for the militiamen, we thought they might hurt us so we were protecting our lives."

Andrea looked at Steven and said, "You're right. I would have told a thousand lies to get Jennifer back from those religious fanatics."

Steven said, "By the way, Doug, how's your leg? In all the excitement I forgot about it."

"I'm fine. The wound bled a lot, but it wasn't serious."

After breakfast they continued their trip, with the two vehicles staying as close together as possible. They saw more fires on this trip than they did heading south twelve days earlier. Many cars blew by them at speeds far exceeding the speed limit and there seemed to be a spirit of recklessness in the air.

Steven gave a sigh of relief when he finally pulled into his driveway on Grandview Hill at two thirty. The SUV pulled in directly behind them. The six weary travelers slowly climbed out of the vehicles with stiff legs and backs.

Within seconds William and Andrew burst from the house and hurled themselves into their father's arms. Next they showcred Jennifer with hugs and kisses. Jennifer fought to get a breath of air but laughed at this unusual display of affection.

Elizabeth followed William and Andrew to the car and wrapped her arms around Douglas. After a few kisses she said slyly, "Are you still my husband?" All five of their children gathered around them, waiting to hug their father.

Douglas joked, "Well, I almost joined that cult with these two women as my second and third wives, but then I got to thinking that you three would probably be fighting over me all the time, so I hesitated. However, when the polygamists told me plural marriage was designed to teach women not to be so jealous and selfish, I almost jumped in. But when—" Elizabeth punched her husband in the stomach before he could finish.

Mary and Andrea decided to stay and visit with Steven and his guests for a while, and everyone laughed and joked as they headed for the house. Without delay Steven phoned as many friends and relatives as possible to tell them the good news and see how they were doing. He was pleased to learn that electricity had been restored to Grandview Hill via a new power station in Orem. By four o'clock the family had gathered at Steven's home and everyone pumped Jennifer and the rescuers with questions for several hours. Steven invited all of them for supper, and while they ate they discussed the civil wars and the anarchy breaking out all over North America, and especially the conflict taking place in northern Arizona between the army and the so-called American Patriots.

It was also during supper that William asked about Selena. "What about Mo—Selena?"

"We don't know," Steven said. "Like we said, she wasn't in the cabin when we found Jennifer."

Mary gave William and Andrew a tender glance. "I talked to her before the cabin disaster."

William looked at the ground and quickly wiped his eyes with his sleeve. "What did she say? How did she look?"

"She looked beautiful," Mary said. "I'm sure she misses all of you. That's why she kidnapped Jennifer."

"Yeah," Paul added. "She probably would have tried to grab you and Andrew too if she had seen the chance."

"I don't think she loves us anymore," Andrew said, his eyes full of sadness.

"Yes, she does," Steven insisted. "She's just been led astray by evil men."

Jennifer looked perplexed. "Do you mean she kidnapped me because she loved me?"

"Yes," Steven said.

Jennifer set her mouth in a straight line. "I guess that means she doesn't know how to love the right way because she took me away from my dad." Steven was touched by his daughter's words and gave her a big hug.

Mary said, "I'll bet she's going crazy right now, wondering what happened to Jennifer. Maybe she thinks Jennifer died in the explosion."

"That's right." Steven said. "That shows you how insensitive I am. I never thought about what Selena might be going through. What do you think I should do?"

Mary thought a moment, then said, "You could call the Aldridge house and tell them what happened. I have their phone number on the LLDS list we made up."

"Yes, of course." Steven took the list from Mary and, going to the phone, dialed the number. Martha Aldridge answered the call. After explaining what happened to Jennifer, he hung up and returned the list to Mary. "I'm glad we did that," Steven said. "All of them, especially Selena, were in the depths of despair, thinking that Jennifer had been killed in the blast. The soldiers wouldn't let them near the cabin ruins and refused to answer their questions."

"It was the kind thing to do," Douglas said.

"Did Martha revile you, Steven?" Mary asked.

"No. She was just grateful to hear that Jennifer was safe."

After dinner everyone went into the living room, and Steven turned on the television to see if he could find reports on the conflict near Colorado City. The face of President James Miller appeared on the screen, holding some papers in his hand.

". . . the belligerents in the area of Colorado City have been dispersed and many of them taken into custody. Some of the rebels have escaped into the Cottonwood Point Wilderness east of the threatened cities, but it is expected that most or all of them will be apprehended shortly. Moreover, it is my duty to announce that there were some casualties on both sides of the conflict, but at this time we have no precise information regarding the number killed or injured . . . Now I must sadly report that several other militant groups are making copycat attacks against federal installations in other regions of the country. But I can assure you that they present no real danger to American citizens. You can trust your president to do everything in his power to apprehend these new belligerents. As you see, I am updating you concerning these events personally instead of communicating them via the usual channels, and that is because I am a hands-on president. My fellow Americans, that is my report and my promise to you tonight. Good evening." After the president's statement, Channel Five brokc for commercials.

"Hands-on president my eye." Robert Christopher said angrily. "He knows he's up for reelection in a few months and he's buying votes."

"That's the first time I've ever seen the president appear on television to report on this kind of event," John said. "You may be right, dad. He's presenting himself as a hero to get votes."

Sarah seldom agreed with her husband, but this time she did. "Robert's right. But why does that sneaky guy always play things down? I've heard there are forty paramilitary groups taking up arms."

"Forty-five groups," John corrected. "And they've got some of the best training and equipment money can buy." John spent the next few minutes reviewing the locations and capabilities of some of the most important paramilitary groups. He stopped when he saw that the Channel Five news had returned.

"Okay, we're back," said the anchorman. "As the president said, the Colorado City War, as people are now calling it, has ended. Channel Five breaking news has learned that there were approximately two hundred militants killed and four hundred wounded. We are having difficulty ascertaining government casualties, but it is estimated that five hundred and twenty troops are dead and almost eight hundred wounded. One soldier of unknown rank admitted to one of our reporters that the rebels outflanked and outguessed an entire company of the regular army. We have asked the army about this, but they have refused comment."

The female anchor continued the newscast. "The president also reported on the uprising of other militant groups in the country. We have received several accounts dealing with this matter, and they all seem to agree that from forty to fifty powerful military groups have begun to engage in guerilla warfare against government installations as we speak. Channel Five will continue to keep the public informed as we learn more about these events. In other news, the Bureau of Consumer Affairs reports that dishonesty and cheating are running rampant in American society today."

Steven turned off the television and said, "Gosh! If things continue this way, the entire nation will soon become one vast battleground."

They spent the rest of the evening discussing national and world events until the gathering broke up at ten. Later, as Steven lay in bed, the image of dark-haired Selena returned to his mind. He felt sorry for her. Poor Selena had forsaken everything worthwhile to follow after a false god. Then to his surprise the image of a blonde beauty popped into his mind—Mary Fleming.

He felt a strange burning in his heart. Quickly, he thrust the image from his mind. In some ways Mary was like Selena—the Selena he had married many years ago. He had also been impressed by Selena's integrity and her loyalty to the Church, and he had never dreamed that one day she would betray their love and the Church. Steven sensed that he loved Mary, but how could he be sure that she wouldn't do the same things as Selena? Why should he take the chance of enduring the agonies of such a hell once again?

Chapter 13

The call came from Josiah Smith, prophet of God and president of the Church. It was read in all LDS wards on Sunday, July 21. Steven was sitting in sacrament meeting with his children when Bishop Justesen read it in the Grandview Second Ward. Steven couldn't believe his ears.

The bishop went to the podium, removed a document from his briefcase, unfolded it, and laid it before him. After putting on his reading glasses, he said, "Last Monday I received a long letter from the president of the Church. It is addressed to all wards and branches throughout the world and is of the utmost importance. I shall read the most important part verbatim."

He picked up the prophet's letter and read, "As the leader of God's Kingdom and Church upon the earth, I have been deeply concerned for the welfare of the saints in the face of the increasing wickedness and violence upon the earth. Knowing that these events are consistent with prophesies regarding the times directly preceding the Second Coming of our Lord and Savior, I recently knelt in prayer to discover the Lord's will concerning his Church. I had no sooner finished my prayer when the voice of the Lord spoke to my heart and mind. He told me that I should instruct the saints everywhere upon the earth to gather to Zion. They are to gather to Zion in two ways. First and most important, the saints must forsake Babylon and renew their commitment to the Lord with full purpose of heart. Second, they must physically gather to the larger and safer stakes of Zion wherever they may be in the world. Included with this letter is a list of locations in the world which the General Authorities consider relatively safe at this time.

"Latter-day Saints living in the United States are instructed to gather to the Rocky Mountains, for that will soon become the only safe region in this country. All saints are to gather as quickly as possible, but they are not to move in haste or without wise preparation. The Church has established a sizable fund to help those who are too poor to bring their families to safe places, and they may obtain such funds easily by simply making their needs known to their local church leaders. We encourage all saints to take with them all their possessions which they can safely transport in order to provide for themselves as much as possible in their new homes. War shall presently be poured out upon all the nations of the earth as never before and if the saints do not act with dispatch, it will soon be too late. The Lord also commands his saints who already live in regions of safety to receive all refugees with open arms and hearts full of love.

"As soon as I had received the Lord's message, I pondered its importance for some time when again I heard the voice of God. In the second communication he told me that some of the nations of the earth had rejected his missionaries and that I should bring them home. Henceforth, he would teach his lessons to those nations with lightning and thunder and great power. In obedience to the Lord's will I have instructed the missionaries serving in fourteen foreign lands to return home immediately or accept assignments in other missions."

After reading the main part of the four-page letter, Bishop Justesen said, "The prophet also explains that he called a solemn assembly two days after hearing the voice of the Lord and during that meeting he presented the new revelations to his counselors and ten members of the Quorum of the Twelve. Those brethren unanimously accepted the revelations as the word of God. Most of them explained that in the preceding weeks they had received the same basic message through the power of the Spirit.

"Now as bishop of this ward, it is my duty to ask every member to search his heart and make up his mind whether or not he or she will obey the will of the Lord. This means we should be willing to welcome and succor those who will soon move into this area. They have already been summoned and the General Authorities are now asking us to get ready to receive them. I know that most of you have made great sacrifices due to the recent flood, but we too have been asked to receive as many saints as we can. We must remember that God will bless us for every sacrifice and will give us the necessary strength if only we will trust in him. I say this in the name of Jesus Christ. Amen."

The bishop sat down and the audience was silent for a short time, but soon the whispering began and filled the room until the bishop had to ask for quiet. Most church members had known this call would come someday, and some had been waiting anxiously for years. It would not be completely accepted by any but the most faithful because it would bring great trials. Steven noticed that some of the ward members seemed thrilled while others appeared to be upset. He glanced at Mary and Andrea sitting together several rows away and wondered what they were thinking.

The meeting proceeded as usual but Steven paid little attention. He vaguely remembered a song, the sacrament, four short talks, and the final prayer. But all he could think about was the vast import of the prophet's call. He was surprised that the bishopric did not spend the entire meeting discussing the great exodus which would soon bring hundreds of thousands of people to the Rocky Mountains.

After the meeting Steven approached the bishop and asked him why they had not spent more time on the letter, but the bishop replied simply that he knew no more than what he had announced from the stand. He added, however, that the letter from the First Presidency promised that the General Authorities would send regular messages to church branches guiding the members as to what they should do. As Steven walked out of the chapel, he waved to his children, who were jumping into John's hotrod to spend the day with their cousins. Steven had guarded his children carefully for the past few weeks and had only agreed to part from them after receiving repeated promises from John and Tania that they would watch them carefully.

"They're not invading my house." Steven looked around and saw that the voice came from Karla Millman, a pretty red-haired woman and wife of the Elder Quorum president, Gregory Millman. He also recognized Michael Stark, Nolan Carson, Lyman and Gertrude Jones, and Quentin and Rose Price. Suspecting that the group was discussing the prophet's call, he decided to join them.

"Gregory talked me into letting two families into our home during the flood and it was the worst experience in my life," Karla continued. "The adults had no education at all and their children. I'll tell you, no one else is moving in with us no matter who says so." Steven knew that Gregory was a man of great integrity and iron will and would have something to say about what went on in his home.

"I agree with you," Nolan Carson said. "My house is so dang small, and I've got diabetes and several other health problems. Besides, my wife divorced me four years ago, and I live alone and wouldn't know how to take care of refugees." Steven remembered that Nolan was the prospective high priest who had been a postal supervisor but who was now living on disability.

"Still, this comes from the prophet of God, and we should be willing to make sacrifices when the Lord requires it of us," Lyman Jones said. Steven was intrigued. Lyman was a sixty-year-old policeman who acted as though he knew everything and gave the impression of being extremely arrogant. Life is full of surprises, Steven thought. You never know who will obey the inspired prophet at all cost until the moment of truth arrives.

Gertrude Jones beamed at her husband. "Oh, I agree with Lyman. We should look upon this with joy because it gives us a chance to show love to our fellow saints. When you think of the blessings the Lord promises us, it's such a little thing to ask." Gertrude was short and chubby and was constantly smiling in spite of the pain of several destroyed disks in her lower back.

Quentin Price smirked. "Yeah, but it doesn't make sense! When Joseph Smith first talked about 'gathering,' it was a physical thing and the early saints were told to go to Missouri. Then the policy changed, and the word gathering meant the honest in heart should gather to the Church and remain in their homelands. Now they're changing it again and the saints must gather physically to major church centers." Quentin was a 39-year-old doctor who always presented the image of piety wherever he went. He was a tall man with coal black hair and, in spite of his sharp features, was strikingly handsome. His petite wife resembled him enough to be his sister.

"The way I look at it," Michael Stark said, "the term gathering always had a spiritual meaning and a literal meaning. In the early Church the physical meaning was stressed because the saints needed to join in large groups for protection. But when the persecution stopped and there was little physical danger, the spiritual gathering was stressed. At that time church leaders also realized it would be impossible to gather millions of people into one region which could not support such a large population. Now the world is becoming very dangerous for the saints, and it's necessary to gather them physically once more for their protection. I believe the leaders are wise men and have made all these decisions through revelation." Steven knew that Michael was the truck driver that John considered to be well informed.

Quentin Price continued his tirade as if Michael hadn't said a word. "The truth is, if the saints in other parts of the country had been faithful and made their stakes strong enough, they wouldn't have to come here and overrun us in times of trouble."

"And that's not the only thing," Rose Price said in a tiny, sweet voice. "We have endured a great disaster here and we're still trying to recover. The prophet's words can't refer to us. I think the bishop is going beyond his authority."

Steven couldn't believe that some of these people were boldly saying such negative things right in front of the church with other ward members walking by.

"What about you, Brother Christopher? What do you think?" Gertrude Jones asked.

Her question surprised Steven. "Uh, I'm ready to help in any way I can. After all, people's lives are at stake."

Quentin glared at him with anger in his eyes. "You don't know what you're saying, Christopher. With all the bank failures and the violence, it's only a matter of time before the stores and markets will start closing. Three major supermarkets in Salt Lake shut their doors in the last two weeks. If this becomes widespread, where do you think we'll get food and supplies? It's going to be hard to survive in Utah even as it is without having millions of people swarming in here begging for help."

"Quentin is right," Rose declared. "The First Security Banks of Utah closed down last month and we lost all our life's savings." Great tears welled from her eyes as she said these words.

"But what about the FDIC?" Lyman Jones asked.

Quentin snorted. "The federal government can't do a lousy thing. There are bank closures all over the country and the feds can't keep up with it. The Bank of America is headed for bankruptcy and they're begging for billions in government bailouts. But they won't get it this time. Too big to fail doesn't cut it anymore."

Steven looked Quentin in the eye with surprising calm. "I'm sorry you lost your money, but I know that hundreds of other people have lost their homes and everything they own. I guess that's the test. We do what the Lord asks no matter what the consequences." At that he turned and headed for his car without looking back. He had difficulty believing his own words. Three months ago he never would have said such a thing.

As Steven reached his car he found the elderly Heber Clark waiting for him. "Hello, Brother Christopher."

"Hi, what's up?" Steven said.

"Oh, I just wondered if Brother Mills and I could come home teaching tonight." Byron Mills was the building contractor who enjoyed being known as an expert scriptorian. Even though Brother Clark was a high priest, Byron, an elder, called on him frequently to go home teaching with him because his regular partner was a truck driver and often out of town.

"No problem."

"Is seven o'clock okay with you?" Clark said.

"That's fine."

"Good." Clark looked at Steven's small red Pontiac. "I see you bought a car. I heard your other car was stolen."

"Yes, by some thugs." Steven was embarrassed. "I know it's not much to look at but it's the best I could afford. I tried to borrow enough to get one of those fancy solar jobs but none of the banks had any money to loan. So I had to borrow nine hundred dollars from my father to get this old Pontiac. Actually, it runs pretty well. Paul and I spent several days working on it."

"I think it's wonderful," Clark said. "It's certainly better than my old buggy. By the way, we missed you in June. I understand you've had some fantastic adventures."

Steven grinned. "Yes, it was quite an experience."

"I'd love to hear all about it tonight," Clark said. "Also, we can talk about President Smith's message to the Church."

"Sounds good. I'm sure every member in the Church will be talking about it."

Steven said good-bye and drove home alone. He saw that the Cartwrights were not there. After fixing himself a sandwich, he sprawled out on the living room couch and spent the afternoon studying the scriptures and worrying about his children. At five o'clock he called John's home to check on them. William came to the phone and begged him to let them sleep over. Steven reluctantly gave his permission after getting John on the line and reminding him over and over that Selena and the polygamists might try again to abduct one or all of the children.

After talking to John, he decided to call Mary and Andrea to invite them to come at seven o'clock to meet with his home teachers, hoping they might be able to help him describe their recent adventure. He sorely missed Paul, who had been staying at their parents' home for several days. Shortly before seven the door opened and Douglas Cartwright walked in, followed by Elizabeth and the kids.

"Oh, you're back," Steven said with relief. "I thought you had abandoned me too."

Douglas looked around and saw that Steven was alone. "No, we were visiting some friends in Orem." Steven noticed that Douglas looked depressed.

"Tell him now, Doug," Elizabeth said.

"Tell me what?"

Douglas hesitated, his eyes cast downward. "Our Orem friends are spending the rest of the summer in California and they've kindly offered us their home while they're gone. So . . . we accepted their offer . . . And by the time they return we should be able to get into our own home in American Fork."

"You're moving out?"

"Yes, tomorrow morning," Douglas replied sadly.

Steven jumped to his feet and, with tears in his eyes, hugged Douglas, Elizabeth, and all their children one by one. "I . . . I'll miss you so much! I think of you as part of my family." Steven was embarrassed because the tears began to flow down his cheeks and he couldn't stop them. Soon the others were bawling too.

"Hey! You won't get rid of us that easily," Douglas said. "We won't be far away and we'll be bugging you from time to time to see if you need us to rescue you again."

"Douglas!" Elizabeth scolded. "Steven's the one who rescued us."

"Yes, of course. I was kidding."

Steven put his hand on Douglas's shoulder. "But it's true that you rescued us too. If it hadn't been for you we may never have recovered Jennifer. I never did thank you enough for all that brilliant acting you did in Arizona. You came up with some on-the-spot answers I would never have dreamed of. Remember our Methodist discussion with the militia leader?"

They both laughed out loud.

Steven checked his watch. "Look, it's almost seven and I'm expecting my home teachers, and also Mary and Andrea. I expect them to discuss a subject which will interest you, so I hope you're not going anywhere tonight."

"Uh-uh," Douglas said, grinning. "We wouldn't miss one of your group discussions for anything."

By seven the home teachers, Heber Clark and Byron Mills, arrived, followed by Mary and Andrea. A short time later Paul arrived unexpectedly with his parents, and Steven introduced them to the home teachers.

"Well, we've got quite a group here," Paul said.

"Yes, the more the merrier," Sarah Christopher said. "But let's get to the thing which is on every Mormon's mind right now—the prophet's call. What are people saying?"

"I understand some church members have come out in open opposition to the prophet," Byron Mills said. "There are rumors that thousands have already asked to have their names removed from church records."

Paul acted disgusted. "But doesn't that always happen when the General Authorities make some major decision? I read that when Spencer W. Kimball announced that all worthy males, regardless of race, could receive the priesthood, many people left the Church."

"That's true," Byron said, "but this time it's much more serious because it has to do with money and personal sacrifice."

"Yes," Heber said, "I heard a radio broadcast from Salt Lake City before we came here which said the station had received unconfirmed reports that there were as many as ten thousand defectors from the Church in the first six hours after the prophet's call was made public. The commentator indicated that hundreds of threats of violence against Mormons had been received in the same period of time. Even the prophet's life has been threatened."

"That's terrible!" Elizabeth exclaimed. "But I don't understand. If your members believe their leader is a prophet of God, why don't they support him?"

"Most of them will when the moment of decision comes," Heber said.

"What reasons do the dissenters have for defying your prophet?" Douglas asked.

Robert said, "I talked to at least a dozen people after the announcement today, and I heard several objections. One brother said that the prophet must not be inspired by God because his revelation is too radical."

"That's incredible," Mary said.

Steven said, "You know, that practice of calling something radical because you prefer not to accept it really bothers me. If that brother would read the scriptures carefully, he'd find that there are many things which are radical in the eyes of the world, but which are nevertheless from God. For example, to the wicked Jews the Lord was an extremist who challenged many of the practices of the Jews and the authority of the rulers. They said he had a devil and spoke blasphemy. In Enoch's day the people called Enoch a wild man. In our dispensation Joseph Smith told the world that none of their churches were accepted by God. What could be more radical than that?"

"As you say, Steven, it all depends on your point of view," Heber replied. "If you're worldly you'll see the words and acts of the prophets as fanatical, but if you're spiritual you'll consider them perfectly natural."

"I agree with that," Andrea remarked. "I believe the dissenters are horrified at the thought that soon there will be floods of people coming here to upset their lives. Many of the refugees will be poor and need a lot of help."

Mary looked troubled. "Personally, I support the prophet's call completely, but I wonder how some of the people can drop everything and find the means to make the trip. They'll have to leave the only homes they've ever known and travel hundreds of miles to places where they'll have no jobs or homes."

"And how will the people who receive them find the resources to bear the burden?" Paul said.

"I suppose it means we'll have to depend upon the power of God," Heber Clark said. "Remember that Nephi said God gives no commandment to man without providing a way for that commandment to be accomplished."

"That's true," Steven noted. "What it all boils down to is whether or not we believe President Smith is a prophet or not."

"And whether or not we have the courage and faith to obey the Lord," Byron added.

"Absolutely," Heber said. "In any event, I think it's too early to know for sure what the members will do and how many will oppose the prophet's call. But we know that someday the Lord is going to build the New Jerusalem at Independence, Missouri. That city will be the capital of a great new nation called Zion, which will eventually spread across the entire American continent. The decent people of the earth will have to flee to that nation for safety."

Byron opened his scriptures. "I think I know which scripture you're referring to, Brother Clark. It's in D&C 45:68." He promptly found the reference and said, "The Lord declares that anyone who lives among the people of the world and who refuses to take up the sword against his neighbor will have to flee to Zion for safety. That has to include a lot of people."

Heber said, "Yes, and if you read verses 66 through 71 carefully, it seems clear that what is meant is a physical gathering. In my opinion, this gathering to the Rocky Mountains—and other safe places—is the first phase of the gathering to Zion, so in a sense this region is Zion too."

Mary's face was full of excitement. "When I was a girl people often talked about the great trip to Missouri to build the New Jerusalem and New Zion, but I seldom hear about it anymore."

Sadness clouded Heber's face. "That's true. I'm afraid the saints have waited so long that many of them don't take the building of the New Jerusalem seriously anymore. It's kind of like the way many saints view the Second Coming. It'll happen someday—they say with a bored yawn—but probably not in their lifetime. In other words, they believe their Master delays his coming."

Steven remembered what John had said in that priesthood meeting back in May. "Doesn't it say in the scriptures that the faithful saints will know the signs of the times and be looking for the coming of the Lord with joy?"

"Yes, that's correct," Heber said. "In Doctrine and Covenants 2:1, the angel Moroni called the Second Coming the great and dreadful day of the Lord because that moment will be great and wonderful for the righteous but dreadful for the wicked."

Andrea asked, "Then shouldn't the saints be excited about this new physical gathering since it's a prelude to the building of Zion and the Second Coming?"

"Yes, they should be excited. In Joseph Smith's day the saints certainly were thrilled about building Zion. It was one of their most cherished goals. In fact, in the Teachings of the Prophet Joseph Smith, Joseph says that the saints should have the building up of Zion as their greatest object. Unfortunately, the Lord postponed it because the early saints weren't righteous enough to do the job."

"Are we any more righteous than they?" Mary said.

"I'm not sure about that," Heber said, "but I do know that in section 105 of the Doctrine and Covenants the Lord promised that Zion would be established or redeemed when his people became a mighty army and sanctified themselves."

"They're certainly a mighty army now," Steven said. "The last I heard, there are over twenty million members. As for the sanctified part, I don't know."

"Often the Lord has to sanctify his people by putting them through terrible trials," Heber said. "That's one of the reasons why the early saints were persecuted so greatly. Now after a long period of peace and acceptance, I'm afraid the Lord is going to test us and chasten us to the utmost because many saints have one foot in Babylon and the other in Zion, and they don't even realize it."

"Trying to serve two masters at the same time," Byron added.

"Exactly." Heber said. "Many will drop away, but those who remain will be worthy to do the great work which lies ahead."

Mary looked at Heber with tears in her eyes. "I hope I'm worthy to stand the test."

After several of those present expressed the same feeling, Heber said, "I don't mean to change the subject, but I'd love to hear about your trip to Colorado City. I understand your daughter was kidnapped and that you recovered her yourself."

"Yes," Steven said, "with the help of my brother here and Doug, Mary, and Andrea."

"How did you do it?" Byron said, intrigued.

Steven related the entire story and the home teachers reacted with amazement and laughter.

When the story was finished, Paul winked at Mary and Andrea and said, "You know, after seeing how happy those polygamists are, I was thinking about asking these two pretty women to join me in polygamy and live in Colorado City. They could support me while I study secret religious documents all day."

Everyone laughed at Paul's suggestion, but Andrea replied, "Fat chance of that, Paul Christopher. I've no intention of robbing the cradle."

"I guess it's okay to make jokes," Mary said, "but I think polygamy is a destructive practice. At least the way it's practiced by Mormon apostates, especially the LLDS. The women do most of the work and are usually little more than slaves. If the men can't get along with one wife, they ignore her and turn to the other wife for companionship and love. From that time on the rejected wife, sometimes the man's first wife, lives a lonely, unhappy life. As a result, the husband never finds it necessary to go through the painful adjustments and sacrifice often required to develop a happy marriage. With the LLDS and other groups, polygamy is truly the doctrine of disposable wives."

"What's the LLDS?" Byron asked.

"It refers to the Living Church of Jesus Christ of Latter-Day Saints," Mary explained.

After the group had discussed the doctrines and practices of the LLDS and other fundamentalist groups for another half hour, Steven went into the kitchen and prepared several root beer floats. All of his guests grinned when he handed them the tumblers, except Sarah, whose eyes shot daggers at her eldest son. She was especially upset because she knew how hard it was for her husband to resist the temptation of junk food.

As they enjoyed the treat, Andrea Warren brought up a new subject. "Did you hear about the Mormon churches that were firebombed?" she asked. "It was on a Channel Two report at six o'clock."

Several shook their heads.

"No, tell us about it," Steven said.

"Well, the report said there have been six LDS churches firebombed in the last few weeks. Two of them took place last Sunday in Idaho while church was in session. Sixteen people were killed and dozens injured. Five of the people killed were children."

"I wonder why we haven't heard about this before?" Byron Mills said.

Andrea shrugged. "I don't know."

"It's probably because a few little firebombs are insignificant in comparison with all the insurrections and anarchy taking place every day all over the country," Paul stated.

"I expect it to become much worse for us when the general public learns of President Smith's call," Heber said.

"I'm sure it will," Robert said. "Do they know who bombed the churches?"

Andrea said, "It seems the authorities suspect it was some Christian organization which accuses Mormons of being in league with Satan because we claim that the destiny of man is to become like God. The news report indicated that some of those people have paid for television time to air documentaries attacking the Church."

"That's unbelievable!" Mary said.

"Speaking of unbelievable," Robert added, "yesterday a customer told me that he had read a news article which reported that some groups accuse the Church in Iowa of polluting the Chariton River so that when it flowed south from Iowa into Missouri, it would poison the crops of farmers in northeastern Missouri. The claim is that Mormons are trying to get revenge for what Missourians did to the saints in Joseph Smith's day."

Byron pulled from his coat a piece of paper. "Yes, I cut this article out of the Tribune. After covering what Robert mentioned, the article goes on to say that the Missouri National Guard attacked the Iowa town of Centerville last Wednesday looking for Mormons. Several people were killed in the confusion, and the guard arrested ten men and hauled them away for trial. But after the Missouri Guard crossed the border on their way home, the Iowa National Guard in superior numbers made a counterattack shortly after dark. A total of fifty guardsmen were killed and the ten prisoners escaped. Now the citizens of both states are enraged and thousands of armed men, mostly civilians, are massing on both sides of the border. Oh, by the way, none of the ten men arrested were Mormons."

Steven saw fear in the eyes of his guests. No doubt they were thinking the same thing he was. Sometimes the flimsiest excuse was sufficient for people to resort to violence. What was to prevent non-Mormons from blaming any problem whatsoever on church members?

Sarah nervously cleared her throat and said, "The violence is not only against Mormons. It seems that people all over the country are finding reasons to attack one another. I've seen television reports saying that many states are now fighting over water rights and the right to use lakes, rivers, and reservoirs. In some situations it involves the right to offshore fisheries. And the arguments are becoming very nasty. The problem seems to be that industrial waste and agricultural runoff have polluted vast reservoirs of groundwater and there is less good water now. The federal government seems incapable of controlling the situation."

"Have they resorted to violence?" Steven asked.

"The reports said there has been a lot of violence. It seems the country is in such chaos that people are using force instead of law to obtain their rights. Sometimes it's the police or the national guards who are fighting, and sometimes it's individual citizens."

"Are any of the states in our part of the country involved in these things?" Heber asked.

Sarah shook her head. "No, it's mostly on the West Coast, the East, and the plains states."

Byron said, "I understand that this region is relatively free from crime and violence in comparison with the rest of the country."

"I suppose we should be grateful we live here," Steven noted.

"Yes, we should be," Heber agreed. He looked at his watch. "It's getting late and we have another family to visit, but thanks for an interesting conversation." As everyone stood, Heber said, "Would it be okay if we had a word of prayer?"

Byron offered the prayer and all the visitors left. Only Paul remained and Steven was grateful to have his company again. They spent half the night talking about what role they would have when the multitudes of homeless saints began to arrive.

Chapter 14

Early in the morning Gerald Galloway drove his favorite grandchildren, Callie and Marcel, to Portsmouth, England where he had found a new position for their father as president of a major investment firm owned by Gerald. He had spent three delightful days with the children and regretted it was over so soon. However, he consoled himself with the fact that now they lived only thirty-five kilometers away and could visit him often. As he returned to his mansion in his Rolls Royce, he wondered if he would arrive in time for the eight o'clock meeting with his associates. This would be the tenth general meeting of the Supreme Council of the Universal Government of the Twelve, or UGOT.

Gerald reached his estate ten minutes early and decided to wait for his people on the front porch of the mansion. The eleven guests arrived within fifteen minutes of one another from all parts of the world, and as they stepped out of their luxury sedans, Gerald greeted each in the same way, first with the words and then the gesture. Two of the guests were women, a beautiful 28-year-old French woman named Lucienne Delisle, and Janet Griffin, the society's associate in Eastern Asia, whom Gerald had always thought of as a man. She was a tall, homely woman in her mid-forties who wore shapeless dark suits and horn-rimmed glasses. Although unattractive, she had a forceful personality, a sharp mind, and was tireless in pursuing UGOT objectives.

When they had all arrived, Gerald ushered them into his study and ordered their favorite drinks from memory. The spacious room was rich in tapestries and French impressionist paintings, and five sumptuous divans made a circle in the center of the room. Gerald sat next to Lucienne and quickly whispered something in her ear, and she smiled her answer. As they sipped their wine, the associates discussed the exceptional weather of Hampshire County and the improvements Gerald had made in his magnificent mansion in the countryside. During these preliminaries, Elenore, Gerald's sedate wife, casually entered the room. Seeing her husband sitting next to the stunning brunette, she approached him from behind and kissed him possessively on the cheek.

"I see you have company, dear," she said. "Am I in the way?"

"Not at all, my dear," Gerald said patiently. "It's nothing but a business meeting. Please don't let us interfere with what you were doing. We'll probably be at this for several days."

Elenore took the hint and left the room. Gerald loved her dearly but kept her completely away from his business dealings. He was amused at her jealousy because they had an understanding. She had known since the beginning of their marriage thirty years ago that he saw other women. At first she had been shocked and hurt, but as time went on she realized she could not change him and had gradually accepted his indiscretions. As long as he kept them discreet.

She and Gerald had raised five children according to the strictest standards, and they had sent them to the best private schools. Gerald had spent a great deal of time with the children as they grew up and gave them everything money could buy. Most of all, he showered Elenore with lavish gifts on regular occasions and provided her with ten thousand dollars in Euros each month as money for her personal needs. They lived in one of the most splendid mansions in southern England. She had concluded that Gerald was, in spite of his amours, an excellent husband. After all, a man has his needs.

"I welcome all of you to my humble abode," Gerald said, smiling. Everyone laughed. "To begin, I want to introduce Ms. Lucienne Delisle. She has been working as an operative in the States for three years and I finally invited her to join our inner circle of associates last month to replace Marlin Parker, who neglected to follow UGOT guidelines once too often." Several heads nodded, for Parker's incompetence was well known. "I appreciate the fact that all of you voted to accept her. She is one of the most qualified people in our society."

Lucienne smiled as she looked around the circle. "I am glad to be here and I hope to get to know each of you intimately," she said with a slight French accent.

"Not too intimately I hope," Gerald quipped. The others laughed knowingly. All of them understood that Gerald and this woman had an intimate relationship. "Even though some of you know Lucienne already, I'll tell you a little about her. As you can hear from her accent, Lucienne is French. She was born in Tours into a traditional Catholic family of seven children. She is trained in medical law and diplomacy and speaks four languages fluently." He looked at Lucienne. "What else can I say?"

"That's enough for now, Mr. Galloway," Lucienne said. "I'll get to know everyone better in the next few days."

"Oh, yes," Gerald said. "One more thing. She's not the kind of person you want to cross." More laughter, but all the associates took Gerald seriously, even when he made jokes. They revered the Chairman because of his brilliance, his genius at planning, and his indomitable will. He seemed almost godlike in his power to control circumstances and dominate everyone he met. However, they also knew he could be utterly ruthless to those who stood in his way.

Gerald introduced the others and told Lucienne something about each of them. Next he gave a short review of the society and its purposes for the benefit of the new associate. "So now there are once again twelve associates," he said with a sigh. "As you know, we are a close-knit family with eternal bonds that go beyond patriotism, religion, money, love, honor, and our personal families. To betray the society or another associate is to invite death from the others. This society was formed twenty years ago, and we are now meeting for the tenth time as the governing body. Of course, we keep in close contact in other ways, usually by secured lines on the phone. The purpose of these general meetings is to report on our activities in person and to plan future strategy. Lucienne has no report at this time, but I wanted her to be here to listen to what the rest of you have to say."

Gerald spent the next two hours receiving preliminary reports from the associates on their progress in their assigned regions. When the reports were completed, he sat back in his seat and looked at the ceiling with an air of satisfaction. "I'm pleased with all of you—except Randolph Benson." He cocked his head to the side and gazed at Benson through narrowed eyes. "Randy, you have the Middle East, the most important area, and you have not finished establishing the proper contacts. Without powerful connections you cannot influence and manipulate the policies and actions of the governments of Iran, the Arab countries, and Israel. I want you to use as much money and leverage as it takes to create an effective network, and I expect you to complete this network within six months and report to me personally."

Benson nodded with an embarrassed look on his face. "I've made a list of the right people, and I'll be contacting them in the next few weeks. As you know, I've only been assigned to the Middle East for six months." Benson was a short, bald man with an enormous paunch. Behind his spectacles his eyes darted back and forth and he constantly dabbed his nose with a handkerchief. Gerald knew that Benson was a gifted planner and would stop at nothing to reach his objectives.

Gerald said, "Yes, that was right after Boyd Murdock, our former associate in the Middle East, died an unfortunate death from food poisoning . . . I regret his death terribly, but I have to admit that he wasn't especially effective in his assignment. Randy, I know you'll accomplish a lot more in a fraction of the time. You haven't had much opportunity, but now I expect you to move swiftly. If we hope to accomplish our goals for the benefit of humanity, we need your operation to do its part."

"It will. Don't worry, it will," Randy said, a slight tremor in his voice.

"Now, tell us about the Arabs."

"They've been building their military power for a decade now, as you know, and soon they'll be ready to attack Israel. Actually, spurring them to act will not be as difficult as I originally thought. They're always looking for the slightest excuse to demonstrate on the streets and to destroy any perceived enemy, especially Israel."

"Yes, yes, I understand," Gerald said. "Most of them are crazy fanatics. There are some moderate Arabs who want peace, but they don't serve our purpose. At any rate, we need to provoke the fanatics as much as possible. Some of them want to attack Israel without making sure the others will back them, and if they do, Israel will achieve another easy victory. Remember what happened in 1967."

Gerald saw the quizzical look on Lucienne's face. "Let me explain this to our new associate. For years we have encouraged the Russians and the Chinese to supply the Arabs with sophisticated weapons and with military training. We know they will never defeat Israel because they are incompetent cowards, but if we can provoke an all-out war, we will exhaust Israel and also kill a lot of Arabs, the second most vile race on earth. In this way our new world army, which will soon be formed from the forces of many nations, will have no trouble crushing the Jews. Incidentally, I expect that the new army will number no more than a ten to twelve million troops."

Lucienne indicated that she understood. "By the way, Randy, how is your work coming with Mahmoud?"

"Great progress! We've used the Egyptian press to help him gain a secure place in the imagination of his fellow countrymen."

Once again Gerald turned to Lucienne. "I don't know how much you know about Mahmoud al-Mamoun, the new president of Egypt. He is a man of great ambition but little intelligence. He is tall and handsome like a Hollywood star. We chose him especially because of his charisma and his stupidity, and we intend to use him as a symbol of the new jihad or holy war against Israel. Already the majority of Arabs in Jordan, Iraq, and Syria see him as a great leader and prophet who will lead them to the complete and eternal destruction of Israel."

Gerald turned back to Benson and said, "Continue your work among the Arabs and the Jews, Randy. As I said before, do whatever it takes: persuasion, bribes, threats, a timely death here and there, and you will soon have the Middle East where we want it."

Randy grinned and his chubby head bobbed up and down. "I suppose I'll have to become more firm with the Egyptian minister of foreign affairs. When I tried to buy his cooperation, he declared he would have nothing to do with foreign conspiracies interfering with Egyptian foreign relations."

"Replace him or assassinate him if necessary." Gerald smirked as he stroked Lucienne's bare arm. "I'm surprised your minister of foreign affairs used the word 'conspiracy.' Our language control unit has spent a great deal of time and money making that word and others like it terms of derision in the popular psyche of the western world." He turned once again to Lucienne. "I started the Language Control Unit, or LCU, myself twenty years ago and in general it has done a marvelous job."

Lucienne lit up one of her favorite cigarettes. "I'd love to hear how you made the idea of conspiracy offensive. Liberals, especially those in the media, seem to use the term 'conspiracy' to pour ridicule upon any person or organization they disagree with. Apparently, their main targets are conservatives."

Julian Kennedy, the associate for South America, said, "Yes, Gerald, why don't you fill us in on that?" Julian was a tall, slender man with black hair slicked back like Rudolph Valentino, the Latin sex symbol of silent films in the 1920s. He was a highly trained physician who had become an expert in biohazards.

"Well, it was easy to do. Just a touch of linguistic mind control. I obtained some of the basic ideas from the Nazis and the Communists, and I made a few improvements of my own. One of the best techniques was to train hundreds of fake right-wing extremists and have them appear on TV talk shows, news programs, college campuses, strikes, civil disturbances, or in any circumstance where they could get widespread media coverage. These plants would act like crackpots and blame just about everything under the sun on some great secret, worldwide conspiracy. As a result no one wanted to be connected with those maniacs." Gerald laughed. "Yes, I admit that I feel an immense pride when I see liberals foam at the mouth when real conservatives declare that some legislation, such as a gun control bill, was passed as a result of a secret coalition of government leaders and the media. The liberal knee-jerk reaction is to discredit the conservatives by calling them 'conspiracy theorists.' "

Marcus Whitman, the society's associate in Western Europe, leaned forward with his hands on his knees. "Yes, I've enjoyed that too. It's as if those liberals have never opened a book on world history and therefore don't realize that conspiracies are a historical fact, not a theory." Several associates murmured their approval.

"That's exactly right," Gerald said. "It never seems to occur to our liberal friends and the brainwashed public that every nation has statutes against the crime of conspiracy. But actually, I feel a certain kinship with some of the genuine conspirators because—like us—they too lust after three superlative things: money, power, and revenge. The truth is, I enjoy the game of turning their energy and assets to our advantage. We now have partial control over terrorist groups like al-Qaeda, the Taliban, Hamas, Hezbollah, and nations that support terror like Iran and Syria. All we need to do is to give them handouts or finance their operations. That gives us dramatic influence over what they do, when they do it, and how they do it. Soon we'll control them completely. We use the biases we created against the so-called conspiracy theorists to disarm one of our most effective enemies—conservative organizations that work for small government and individual freedom and independence."

Gerald's face turned ugly. "Still the greatest threat to our power is the international Jewish confederation. Oh yes, there are a few other powers in the world which could give us trouble, but they don't know we exist, and by the time they find out, it will be too late." Gerald stopped and corrected himself. "No, I should say it's already too late. In a very short time we shall gather our marvelous world army to move against the most despicable and vile race on the planet." He turned again to his associates and smirked. "In the process it will also be a pleasure to feed the Christians to the lions."

Everyone laughed at Gerald's witticism.

"Not all Christians, I hope," said Francis Bonnard, the representative to North Africa.

"Oh no. Only those who are real Christians," Gerald said, "such as evangelicals. You know, the born-again types. Most of the others are Christians in name only."

"Don't forget the Mormons," Lucienne offered. "From what I've seen in the States, most of them take their religion pretty seriously and there are nineteen or twenty million of them if I remember correctly."

"Really? That many?" Gerald said. "From what I've heard about the Mormons, they have a strange religion and used to be persecuted because they practiced polygamy. But it seems they've rejected polygamy since the end of the nineteenth century. In recent decades they've become even more acceptable because they've learned to blend in. Still I didn't realize there were so many of them. Do you really think they're a problem?" Lucienne nodded. "All right, we can always add them—"

"Oh, that reminds me," Lucienne interrupted. "When I was in Utah, I talked to several Mormons and one of them told me something intriguing about conspiracies. I think it might interest this group. Apparently, their scripture book, called the Book of Mormon, talks a great deal about conspiracies, which it calls secret combinations."

Lucienne paused to take a deep breath and to see if the group was paying attention. Seeing their interest, she continued, "It seems that one of the books in those scriptures, supposedly written thousands of years ago, warns that in the last days there will be a great worldwide secret combination which will try to overthrow the freedom of every nation on earth, and that if the Mormons and other good people let it happen, they'll be destroyed by God." She looked sideways at Gerald. "Isn't that fascinating?"

"Yes, it's very interesting! Sounds like that book is referring to our great secret combination. But not to worry. Even if the Mormons believe their book, most of them won't pay any attention to the warning. They'll either ignore it or explain it away. And do you know why?" Gerald hesitated a moment but continued before the others could speak. "Because it's human nature to discredit anything which sounds fantastic and remote, and few of them will want to disturb their lives and take the trouble to investigate it. But I can assure you of one thing: the Mormons will be destroyed someday, or at least enslaved, by those who have god-like power. I'll let you decide who those god-like people are."

As the others stared at Gerald in awe, Lucienne finished her drink calmly and said, "That may be necessary, not only because they're Christians but also because they're sympathetic toward the Jews."

Gerald's face registered surprise and irritation. "The Mormons are sympathetic to the Jews? Unbelievable. Well, if you're right, we'll have to pay more attention to them. Lucienne, I'll let you handle the Mormons for now, and I don't care how you do it. You have at least ten thousand operatives in the States, and I'll give you twice as many if you need them. I suggest you begin by trying to discredit the Mormons. As I said, they have some strange doctrines, and if you portray them as being the enemies of traditional Christianity, you may be able to induce Christian mobs to attack them.

"As you know, it's already getting pretty dicey over there, with all the civil disorder going on. Religious differences have always been the greatest cause of bloodshed, and I think they might work for us in this circumstance. You might also consider the feasibility of provoking the Indians or the government against them. Do whatever you want with the Mormons, if you think they're a problem. But personally, I have difficulty believing they're as much of a problem as you seem to think."

Lucienne replied, "You may be right, Gerald, but I'll still give the Mormon problem some serious thought."

"In the meantime we must present the image of being the best of Christians ourselves," another associate said.

"Oh, aren't we?" Gerald replied, his face showing mock seriousness. After a moment of silence Gerald continued, "Now we need to discuss what we can do to complete the destruction of the American government. It's already teetering on the brink. Huge deficits and debts, corruption in all branches and levels, a burdensome welfare system, a bloated bureaucracy, an incomprehensible and unfair tax system, constant financial crises, a fickle Supreme Court, a defunct Constitution, high jobless rates, and endless government meddling in the lives of everyday people. The government will soon fall from its own weight, or the people will rebel in a nationwide revolution. All we need to do is to push the government over the brink. The US government is still the best support Israel has, and if we don't nullify American power, we'll never be able to destroy the Jewish nation."

The associate from Southeastern Asia, Ernest Hopkins, said, "It appears as though we're receiving help from citizen militias in the United States. But I'm sure Lucienne knows more about this than me."

Lucienne crushed her cigarette in an ashtray. "Yes, I'm familiar with the militia movement and their rebellion against the American government. The ironic thing in this case is that our organization in the States has had very little to do with those uprisings. We've been focusing on other crucial projects and didn't fully realize the potential of the super patriots."

"I've seen several news stories on the militia groups," Gerald said. "How much of a threat are they to the government?"

"Could be a very serious threat. They've inflicted heavy casualties on the state guards, the coast guard, and the regular army. They're masters of guerilla warfare and the government can't seem to handle them. The situation is made worse by the increase in crime and by an unusual number of natural disasters everywhere in the country. I think the so-called silent majority is marching steadily toward anarchy. The situation is similar to what is going on in the European Union and the rest of the world, except that in America it is much worse. Soon there'll be few safe places left in the States."

"Excellent!" Gerald said. "Try to use the militias to our advantage whenever you can, Lucienne. I suggest we bomb some federal facilities and let it leak out that militia units are responsible. Of course, the American government, which largely controls the national media, will try to convince the nation that the attacks are the work of individual radicals. At any rate, do the best you can . . . Now I want to mention something very important. At this point, when the American government is under great pressure, we are preparing to do something definitive to finish it off."

Gerald looked at a huge man with blond hair seated opposite him. "Alexi, in your report earlier on the former Soviet Union, you neglected to talk about your sophisticated propaganda campaign against the Americans in Russia and in the old Soviet republics."

Alexi cleared his throat and said, "For five years we've been working hard to effect a definitive attack on the US. I've placed agents in key places at the highest levels of the Russian government. We've had to bribe many top officials and we've dispatched six or seven who would not cooperate. The tab has come to over five hundred million dollars."

"A small price to pay if we get what we want," Gerald said.

"If you wish, I'll try to convince the Russian government that now is the time for a preemptive nuclear strike against the Americans. I believe there's a good chance for me to succeed because many Russian leaders, some of them former Communist Party officials, despise the Americans and are looking for a way to reestablish their power. They are seeking revenge for America's role in the fall of the great Russian Confederation. But if you prefer, I can encourage the Russians to launch missiles containing lethal biological warheads. They still have a large stockpile of such weapons, and I'm sure you realize that such an assault would be much more devastating than a nuclear attack."

Gerald glanced at Julian Kennedy, the expert in biohazards. "Is that right, Julian?"

"Absolutely. A biological attack is far more disastrous. If you plan it properly, you could kill virtually nearly every American in the country, and there would be little damage to property. The lethal agents are not difficult to obtain and can be delivered to their targets easily and cheaply. On the other hand, such weapons are extremely dangerous, and it requires a great deal of expertise to handle them properly."

Benson's head began to bob again. "As an alternative, we could have one of the Middle East terrorist groups like al-Qaeda make the biological attack. All we have to do is supply them with the means they need. And pay them well, of course. If they infect themselves or incur retaliation, what have we lost?"

"That's an excellent observation, Randy," Gerald said. "We're already financing Asad Fadid, the new dictator of Iraq, and he is developing chemical and biological weapons right under the nose of the UN. Many American politicians are warning the UN of this threat, but after the fiasco with George Bush, they are turning a deaf ear."

"Also, we've given hundreds of millions to Abdul al-Hakim, whose radical sect in Afghanistan—the Muslim Brotherhood—has blown up several US embassies. And in spite of the efforts of Homeland Security, the Muslim Brotherhood has also bombed dozens of US government installations and symbolic sites in the States. We could use that society—or another one—to make the biological attack. If that's the way we decide to go. But it bothers me to think that if we decimate the American population, we will lose trillions of dollars in future manpower."

"That's right." Benson remarked. "It would be nice to have some people left alive over there to serve as our slaves." Everyone in the room burst into laughter.

Gerald grinned at Benson's comment and then said, "As for nuclear weapons, they not only kill people but also damage the infrastructure. If we use them, we'll lose immense sums in property which could be a valuable asset for us in the future. Also, radioactive fallout would render most of the country uninhabitable for months or even years . . . Still, we don't want to rule out a nuclear strike. There's nothing like those lovely mushrooms to intimidate and strike terror into the hearts of difficult people . . . Okay, we don't have to decide this matter today, but soon we must choose a course of action. Let me know if any of you have further suggestions."

The members of the inner circle broke for lunch. An hour later they sat down again and discussed other problems facing them. By eight o'clock they were exhausted and ready for amusement.

"One more thing before we stop for the day," Gerald said. "So far our plans and actions have been done in complete secrecy but, as I told you before, someday soon we'll have to step forward and reveal ourselves to the world. At that time we'll need all the credibility we can get because without it we will never accomplish our goals. We must present ourselves as the only true moral, political, and spiritual leaders of the world and—above all—as the only alternative. To help impress the nations of the earth with my goodness and power, I will need a great man of religion who can convince the world that I alone can give it peace, safety, security, and joy. This should be a man of great spiritual charisma who can perform spectacular miracles or give the appearance of doing so."

"So, when you return to your control centers, I want you to search for such a man. It doesn't matter what he believes or what his status is, but only that he appears to be like Moses or Mohammad or Buddha. Every year I have asked you to search for this man but since none of you have found him, I now give you an ultimatum. Find me a cooperative holy man within six months or there will be grave consequences." At that moment several young men and women appeared at the door to Gerald's study. "Ah! The help has arrived. I invite you to make my home your home. I have many festivities planned for you."

And indeed the party was all they could hope for. They danced and sang, talked and played, ate and drank, until they fell into a stupor. All except Gerald and Lucienne. Knowing what happened at Gerald's business meetings, Elenore had already departed during the day to spend the night with a close friend. At midnight Lucienne took Gerald by the hand and led him to her room.

"Now the real fun begins," Gerald said.

Lucienne smiled. "For a rich industrialist, you're sure a naughty little devil."

Gerald threw her a wicked smile. "But the devil's a god too, isn't he?"

Chapter 15

Three weeks after Bishop Justesen read the prophet's letter to his ward, the president of the United States, James Miller, held an emergency meeting in the Oval Office with the vice president, the director of the NSA, the director of the FBI, the secretary of Homeland Security, the chief of the army, and some of Miller's most trusted aides. As his guests entered the room, he called them by their first names and asked about their families. When all of them had arrived, Miller took his place behind his huge oak desk and surveyed the room. His normally handsome, charismatic face looked weary and troubled.

"Well, people, I'm sure you know why I called you to this meeting," the president said. Several in the group nodded.

Before the president could go on, Simon Nash interjected, "Frankly, I can't figure out when and how it all went wrong." Simon was the vice president.

"It's those damn states," Adam Ludlow said angrily. Adam was chief of the army. "The governors assign the state guards to handle things and what do they do? Sit around and do nothing until it's too late."

"This stuff goes way beyond what the guards are supposed to do," retorted Simon. "Look at how crazy things are. Even some of the local sheriffs are joining the anarchists."

The director of the NSA, Walter Moreau, raised his hand and, without waiting for the president to recognize him, blurted out, "What I can't understand is why the FBI let things get out of hand. It's their job—"

"We investigate crime and enforce laws. We don't do mass revolutions," FBI Director Amos Tucker objected.

"I mean at the start of this mess," Walter said.

"In my opinion the army deserves most of the blame in all this," Nicolas Mason, the secretary of Homeland Security, said boldly. Nicolas knew he had the president's ear more than anyone in the room and that he could say almost anything he desired. "Who else but the army can handle insurgents when they get beyond the control of the guards and the police?"

General Ludlow snapped, "Listen, Mason, if it weren't for the army, you wouldn't even be able to pee in peace right now."

Suddenly, the room was in an angry uproar. The president raised both hands into the air, demanding silence. When the room quieted down, he turned to Margaret Hunt, his press secretary, and said, "Sorry for the language, Margaret."

"No problem, Mr. President, I'm used to it."

"Listen, all of you!" the president said. "Right now I don't care who's at fault. All I want to know is what we can do about it. This country is close to a complete civil breakdown and the welfare of millions of Americans depends on what we decide to do about it today. Our time has run out and I want concrete suggestions, not blaming and bickering."

There was complete silence in the room for almost a minute. Finally, Amos Tucker said, "First of all, we should declare a state of national emergency and martial law. As I see it, we have no other choice."

"I agree," Nicolas Mason said. "Of course, only the president has the authority to declare martial law so it'll have to come directly from this office."

"How do you think the states would see it?" President Miller asked seriously.

"Most of the states will object to losing their power, but after whining a bit they'll be happy to go along," Amos said.

"Except Texas, Oklahoma, and possibly California and Nevada," Robert McNutt added. McNutt was the white house chief of staff.

"That doesn't surprise me," the president noted. "They've always been too independent for their own good."

"After you declare martial law," Amos continued, "we can use the FBI, Homeland Security, the army, and other military forces to watch and control the movement of just about every citizen of the United States. We can confiscate food, guns, ammunition, and anything else we want."

Walter Moreau said, "As I'm sure you all know, by declaring martial law we can suspend habeas corpus and throw anybody we suspect of insurrection into prison. That way, we're bound to catch the insurgents and their leaders."

"That's right," Nicolas Mason said. "Later we can sort out the innocent from the guilty."

The president shook his head. "I don't like the idea of depriving Americans of their constitutional rights, but in times like this we may have no choice."

"It won't be enough," Ludlow stated.

"What?" the president asked.

"It won't be enough. Many of the people causing the trouble, especially members of the citizen militias, are experts at staying under cover. The only way we can ferret them out is to be able to track them wherever they go."

McNutt said, "That's virtually impossible."

Ludlow shook his head. "No, there's a way."

The president looked at Ludlow with surprise. "And what would that be?"

Ludlow hesitated, reluctant to say the words. "We could . . . well, inject every American with a microchip."

There was a stunned silence in the room. The president peered at Adam to see if he was serious, but Ludlow's face remained as inscrutable as ever. Miller noticed that some of his people seemed to approve Adam's suggestion while others were shocked.

"I'm serious," Ludlow added.

Without waiting to be recognized, Amos Tucker said, "I agree with Adam. Declaring martial law is a crucial first step, but it won't give us complete control. But with the microchip we can use remote scanning devices to find any person in the country, as long as that chip is in his body. It's almost impossible for him to escape surveillance. Also, the chip can give us a great deal of personal information, including his occupation, address, income, tax records, and criminal record if he has one. We could pinpoint most of the nation's enemies in less than five or six months."

"I don't see it," the president said. "If we tried that, every loyal American in the country would be against us. I'd never be reelected."

Nicolas Mason shook his head and said, "I'm sorry, Mr. President, but I don't agree with you. All we have to do is tell the people that the purpose of the microchip is to detect and punish rebels and criminals. It's just for their protection and safety. We could also promise certain economic advantages if they accept the chip willingly. For example, they could get food, consumer goods, medical care, police protection, and many other kinds of benefits. But without the chip they can't get those things."

Miller noticed the vice president's agitation. "What do you think, Simon?" The question was surprising since Miller seldom paid any attention to what Simon Nash thought or did.

"It's insane. Implant a biochip in 350 million Americans. There's no way it could be done within the next five years. And what if you get the opposite result from what you expect? What if it incites a general, widespread rebellion?"

Amos Tucker smiled sardonically and said, "I hate to rock your boat, Simon, but we've been inserting biochips into Americans ever since the beginning of the twenty-first century. The program is already in place. I estimate that about fifty million adult Americans have already embraced the chip willingly. And probably seventy million children."

Simon Nash's mouth dropped open. "I didn't realize . . ."

There was general snickering in the historical room. The vice president was notorious for being out of touch with his administration's programs and policies, and with reality in general. He spent most of his time wallowing in one sordid scandal after another. The gamut included sex, drugs, influence peddling, and conflict of interest. He was an embarrassment to the president and was scheduled to be dumped in the next election.

"Yeah, Simon," Nicolas Mason said, "they accept the chip to be safe from crime."

Amos Tucker added, "The government's Find-A-Kid program has convinced millions of parents to permit their children to get the chip in the event they are kidnapped."

"Don't forget the fifteen million convicted felons," Robert McNutt said. "The law requires most of them to be injected."

"Yes, yes, of course," the vice president said. "I'm well aware of all that. It just slipped my mind." More indiscreet snickering.

The president said, "I didn't realize myself that the biochip program was so extensive. It's mostly a product of past administrations. So how many more people would we have to inject?"

Amos Tucker said, "Well, we'd have to implant about 230 million. I know it sounds like a tremendous job but all we have to do is expand the program already in place. Once people realize they can't get pharmaceuticals, food, or consumer goods without the chip, they'll break their necks getting to the nearest implant center."

"I suggest we start with men from the ages of eighteen to about fifty," Nicolas Mason said. "That way we can implant the most probable trouble-makers early in the program."

"That's an excellent suggestion, Nicolas," the president said.

"Is the chip difficult to insert?" Walter Moreau asked.

"Not at all," Amos replied. "It's as easy as going to a doctor's office and getting a shot for the flu. Every chip contains an electronic ID number and a homing device. It can be scanned by a handheld scanner in any store or by a remote device using regular communications satellites. When a person gets a microchip you can locate him instantly anywhere in the world, unless he goes underground."

The president said, "That's remarkable. All right, do all of you think the public will accept martial law and the biochip without too much trouble if we do a good job of explaining to them that it's for their safety and the good of the country?"

"I don't think they have any choice," Moreau said. "What choice do any of us have?"

Everyone in the room agreed that the proposals which had been suggested were the only way to stop the growing anarchy and to save the government and the nation. After each of them had given his opinion, the president concluded, "All right, we'll do it. Martial law and microchip implants. Is there anything else?"

"It's vital we set a time limit for citizens to get the implants," Nicolas Mason said. "Something like three or four months."

"A necessary expedient," the president said. "Does anyone have a problem with four months?" No one objected so the president asked for other suggestions.

"As a part of martial law," Amos said, "I say we include a law requiring the surrender of all firearms and ammunition, and another making it illegal to hoard more than a three days' supply of food."

President Miller agreed. "Definitely. Those two requirements are a must if martial law is to be effective. Is that all?"

"I think those are the main points, at least for now," Amos said.

"I suppose I'll have to address the nation with all this painful stuff," the president said frowning.

Nicolas said, "I don't know who else could do it, Mr. President. I'm sure Margaret can write you an impressive speech which will convince the American people that what you want to do is for their own good."

"When do you intend to give the speech, Mr. President?" Margaret asked.

"Within a week if possible. Is that enough time?"

"Don't worry, Mr. President," Margaret said. "I'll create a special message which combines seriousness of purpose and genuine concern. You'll come across like Abraham Lincoln."

Miller said, "Thank you, Margaret. I know you can do it. In the meantime, Robert, I want you and your staff to start calling on key members of Congress. We'll need their support. As for the rest of you, I expect you to back me in these actions, and never forget that we are forced to take these drastic measures to save this country from complete destruction. Let's pray to God that they work."

At two in the morning Bryan Oliver was still examining the photographs with a magnifying glass. He had studied them again and again. Then for the tenth time he checked the computer readouts. There was no mistake about it. Both of the asteroids were heading on a collision course for the earth at about fifty thousand miles per hour. One of them would impact somewhere in northern Canada and about two hours later the second would smash into the Atlantic Ocean seven hundred miles from the east coast of the United States. Why hadn't they discovered these two rotating mountains before? Were they the same two asteroids astronomers had discovered and then lost in 1932? Both of the nickel-iron asteroids were close to one kilometer in diameter. With such mass they would cause unbelievable damage and there was absolutely nothing anyone could do about it.

Bryan was in the control room of the observatory which housed the 1.8 meter Spacewatch telescope, located on Kitt Peak fifty-six miles southwest of Tucson, Arizona. With all their sophisticated instruments, why hadn't they discovered the two rogue asteroids months or even years ago? Not enough hours spent scanning the skies? Or were the asteroids simply too small to be noticed among the hundreds of thousands of asteroids and comets in orbit around the earth? Yes, they were small as celestial bodies go, but when they hit the earth it would be with the force of hundreds of hydrogen bombs. Various governments, including the American government, had made speculative plans on how to deal with the threat of asteroids, but none had put those plans into operation. Bryan figured there was nothing the authorities could do now but warn the public so evacuations could begin.

Bryan thought about the history of government involvement with asteroid research. At the end of the last century, the U. S. government and the nation's top astronomers and geophysicists had met and discussed the feasibility of deflecting or destroying incoming asteroids, and many experts tried to convince federal officials to fund new technology to accomplish that goal. They presented the idea that sooner or later the earth would be hit by asteroids which could end civilization or even destroy the entire planet. It was a matter of *when* not *if*. As an incentive they promised that the new technology could also be used to mine the vast mineral resources found on hundreds of asteroids. Government officials seemed deeply impressed but because of politics did not produce the funding.

Russ Vincent entered the control room. "Still at it?" Russ combed his unruly red hair with his hand and then gulped a cup of coffee. He had taken a short nap and it would require about ten minutes for the caffeine to begin to chase the cobwebs from his brain.

"Yeah. I've checked the data a hundred times and it looks like we were right the first time."

"Holy cow! What do we do now?"

"We get on the horn right away and call the boss," Bryan said. "And when he gets here we present the facts. Obviously, he'll want to review the data." Bryan and Russ were experienced astronomers with PhDs in physics, but they knew that it was up to their supervisor, Professor Hank Geddes, to verify the facts and the conclusions.

"What do you think he'll do?" Russ said.

"First he'll probably act as though we're bonkers. Next he'll go through the material and probably run his own pet program. After he discovers we're right, he'll get all scared to death and call some of his favorite hotshots in here to go through the data again. When it's all over, he'll get on the phone and call Lowell and Nasa and other associations for confirmation, and then he'll contact the president with the happy news. With the boss's reputation, it probably won't take much to convince the big guy how serious this is."

"Yeah, I can see it now," Russ said. "The first thing the pres will do is ask the chief if he thinks we can stop the asteroids. Of course, when we had time to put watchers in space who could have spotted the danger in time and done something about it, the government had more important things to do. But now that civilization is in danger of extinction, he'll want us to come up with an instant solution."

"Right! And I can imagine how Geddes will answer the president," Bryan said. "I'm terribly sorry, Mr. President, but there *is* no solution. If we had known the asteroids were headed our way a couple of years ago, we could have used nuclear missiles or solar sails or something else to deflect them. But now they're too close. If we hit them with nuclear weapons when they're this close, it would do nothing but shower the entire planet with thousands of radioactive bombs."

Bryan went to the phone and dialed a number. He waited while it rang fifteen times. Finally, he heard the tired voice of Professor Geddes. After explaining the situation carefully, he hung up.

"It'll take him an hour and a half to get here," Bryan said. "You won't believe it, but he doesn't seem particularly upset. In fact, he seems happy that we're the first to make the discovery. Guess what he wants to call the asteroids?"

"What?"

"Geddes-Oliver and Geddes-Vincent."

"Hah! That figures. He wants to put his name first to get the credit for our work."

Bryan poured himself a cup of coffee and began to sip it slowly. "By the way, don't you think you're exaggerating a little when you speak about the extinction of civilization?"

"How do I know?" Russ said. "You're the expert in that area with all your doomsday predictions. I was trying to think like you."

Bryan frowned. "I can give you a plausible scenario. The two asteroids will cause a lot of devastation and change the world's weather patterns. There will be widespread flooding and severe drought in places where they never occurred before. The tsunamis which arise in the Atlantic will flood the entire east coast. And close to the impacts, millions of people will die. The actual number of casualties will depend on whether or not people evacuate the danger zones in time. I estimate the first asteroid will impact us in about 177 hours from now or in slightly more than a week. That's all the time the government has to do whatever it's going to do. In the meantime, what can we do?"

"That's obvious, isn't it?" Russ replied. "We check the data again before Geddes arrives."

Chapter 16

It was Saturday and David Omert sat opposite his friend Chaim Yehoshua in a modern restaurant in West Jerusalem not far from the Knesset Building. They were lucky to find a restaurant open on the Jewish Sabbath. As they ate their kosher dinner, they discussed the many problems which faced the State of Israel. Both of them were members of the Knesset, which is Israel's unicameral legislature and supreme governing body.

David said, "The situation is exactly like it was in 1967! In spite of that, the prime minister is still trying to get the Egyptians to honor the agreement they signed in 1979."

Chaim agreed, "Yeah, and while the Egyptians talk peace, they arm for war. Do you think the Russians are behind it like they were before?"

"There's no doubt in my mind. My uncle has been kind enough to let me examine the secret intelligence reports he has received in the last six months." David's uncle, Menachem Hazony, was the Israeli Minister of Defense.

"You're lucky you have powerful friends, David."

"I do, friends like my uncle and Chaim Yehoshuah."

"Oh yeah, I'm a real heavyweight. If I'm so important, why do my fellow legislators fall asleep when I get up to talk in Knesset sessions? They don't do that to you. When you stand up, they fall off their chairs trying to hear every word you say."

"You're exaggerating," David said. "I know for a fact that many legislators respect you highly. And remember, your constituents gave you a landslide victory in the election."

Chaim stopped frowning and said, "Thanks, for saying that. You're a good friend . . . But tell me about the secret reports you read."

"They prove the Russians have been supplying all the Arabs with MiG fighters and the latest high-tech weapons. And that's not all. They've sent in special teams like they did in 1956 and 1967 to train our enemies."

"That doesn't surprise me at all," Chaim said with anger. "But did you say *all* the Arabs? I thought it was just the Egyptians."

"Not at all. Besides the Egyptians, the reports implicate the Lebanese, the Syrians, the Jordanians, the Iraqis, and the Saudis. All together, the Arabs will have over four and a half million trained soldiers to bring against us, not counting fifty thousand armed Iranians and about twenty thousand Russian advisors."

Chaim was shocked. "Over three million! It seems to me the government should at least share this kind of information with the Knesset. How can we make intelligent decisions without knowledge of the magnitude of the threat? And how many troops do we have?"

"About two hundred and twenty thousand regulars," David said. "We also have the citizen army, which is about one sixth of our population of eight million."

Chaim did some math on a napkin. "Let's see. The total of regular and citizen forces is about one million five hundred and fifty-three thousand." Chaim frowned at the odds. "They'll have us three to one! Does the prime minister know about these intelligence reports?"

"Yes, Hazony told me he pushed them under Eldad's nose himself."

"And what did Eldad do? He begs the Arabs to sit down and talk."

David grabbed his friend's arm in an effort to calm him down. "Take it easy. It's not quite as bad as it seems."

Chaim stared into David's eyes as if he were trying to read his mind. "What do you mean? . . . Wait! You're not saying the Americans—"

"Don't be ridiculous," David said. "The Americans won't help us now any more than they did in 1967."

"At least they kept the Russians off our backs," Chaim said.

"They can't even do that this time. They're having so many troubles in their own country that the American government will be lucky if it doesn't collapse within a year."

"That's incredible," Chaim said. "Maybe we should send an army over to the States to help the American government control their own citizens." The two friends chuckled at the idea of the Israeli military rescuing the mighty American war machine. "Okay," Chaim went on, "tell me why you say our situation isn't as bad as it seems."

"For the simple reason that my uncle the Minister of Defense is a tiger from the school of the great Moshe Dayan." David's eyes filled with pride.

"Remember that Menachem Hazony was the general who stopped the Syrian invasion ten years ago. As the head of defense he has been preparing for an Arab League attack for over five years. He has arranged for the purchase of two hundred of the latest American and French combat planes and state-of-the-art laser technology. He has given the armed forces special training in the lightning strike, which uses every branch of the service in a carefully orchestrated attack. He told me he was confident that when the crisis comes, he can convince the Knesset to approve a preemptive strike against the Arabs before they can begin their invasion, or at least give him complete control of the war effort."

"Fortunately, the Arabs usually give us some warning by their troop movements and by blocking our use of the Suez Canal and the Gulf of Aqaba," Chaim added.

"Yes, the blockade always seems to be their first step."

Chaim's face was animated by enthusiasm, but he hesitated, uncertain. "Do you think the Knesset will back Hazony? He has lots of enemies."

"I hope so. I've been taking a poll and I'm fairly certain Menachem will have the majority behind him. But to make sure, my uncle and I made up a list of legislators who are sitting on the fence, and we plan to do everything we can to convince them to support Hazony."

"Give me the list and I'll try to help," Chaim said.

"That's what I figured." David removed a copy of the list from his satchel and handed it to Chaim. "The names with the checks are the ones you'll contact."

The two friends finished their meal in silence but were reluctant to return to their offices. Chaim gazed across the room and said abstractedly, "It seems to me that the world is going completely crazy."

"What do you mean?"

Chaim looked at him and said, "Oh, I was thinking about the growing anti-Jewish sentiment in the world. Ten years ago it seemed we were finally being accepted as human beings by most people. Except the Arabs, of course. But now the newspapers are full of shocking stories of hatred and violence against Jews everywhere in the world."

David had felt the same apprehension many times in the last few years. "You're right. It's frightening. And it's not only malice against us—it's hatred of the Christians too."

Chaim nodded. "Yeah, now that you mention it, the genuine Christians seem to be the only ones who show us any compassion."

"That's because they're true followers of Jesus Christ, and he never condoned hatred of any kind." David paused and said with conviction, "You know, Chaim, we should be grateful these things are happening because the scriptures teach that the whole world will be at war with Israel at the time when the Holy Messiah comes to save us and establish us as his chosen people forever. It's our eternal destiny."

"Do you really believe there's a Messiah and that he'll save us someday?" Chaim said with doubt in his voice.

"Absolutely. I pray for his return every day, and I believe every faithful Jew should look forward to that day with joy and thanksgiving."

"I wish I had your faith," Chaim said, "but as a people we've longed for the Messiah's return for centuries. And what has been the result? Poverty, hatred, genocide, abject misery, and disappointment."

"But, Chaim! Look at us now. We're a united nation for the first time in almost two millennia. Remember that the gathering of Israel is twofold: physical and spiritual. We've gathered physically and I believe that most of the Jews are secretly, deep in their hearts, preparing spiritually for the coming of the Promised One." David stopped and his face brightened with a sudden idea. "Maybe he'll come during the next war."

"I hope not," Chaim said. "I'm not ready for that. He probably wouldn't be too pleased with the kind of life I lead."

David grinned and slapped his friend on the arm. "Come on. You're a good man. You simply need a little more faith."

"Well, there are so many theories about the Messiah floating around that I don't know what to believe. Some Jews say the term Messiah refers to the Messianic Age of peace and safety which the Jews usher in themselves by their courage and good deeds. Others teach a personal Messiah whose function is to help them gain inner peace. And there's the traditional belief that someday a mighty prophet anointed by God will come to save Israel and bring eternal peace to the earth. It's Elijah who is supposed to prepare the world for his coming."

"I'm familiar with all those beliefs, but I accept the traditional one," David said. "However, I believe the Messiah is more than a great prophet."

"Who is he then?"

David stirred his coffee for a moment without answering. Finally, he said, "I don't know for sure. It's nothing but a personal conviction."

"You're a lot of help," Chaim complained. "By the way, isn't it true that we have to build the third temple before the promised Messiah comes?"

"That's right."

"And we're supposed to build it in the exact same spot where it was anciently?"

"That's my understanding." David knew where Chaim was heading.

Chaim laughed and rolled his eyes. "How on earth are we ever going to accomplish that? You know as well as I do that the grounds where the holy temple used to be are now the third most sacred shrine of the Islamic religion. Moslem pilgrims visit the Dome of the Rock and the Al-Aqsa mosque by the thousands every year. We'd have to destroy those shrines to make way for the new temple, and you know what would happen if we did that."

"Yes. The Arabs would go completely mad and they'd fight us to the death. Any peace we could ever hope for would be gone forever. That's one of the reasons why the official policy of the State of Israel has always been to respect the sacred buildings of other religions."

"That's right," Chaim said. "But do you seriously think the Arabs will ever be thoughtful enough to move the Dome of the Rock a little to one side so we can build our temple right next to it?"

David laughed at Chaim's humor. "Look, I'm not sure how God will accomplish this great miracle, but I have faith that the third temple will be built on the ancient temple grounds and that it will be done in the near future. Somehow!"

"I'll never understand you, my dear friend," Chaim said. "You always believe in the impossible."

"It isn't impossible," David said. "In fact, I have a theory as to how God will bring about the miracle."

"Wow! A theory. Okay, let's have it. I'm all ears."

"In the same way he helped us to enlarge the territory of Israel to its current dimensions."

Before Chaim could respond, David jumped to his feet and headed for the cashier with the tabs in his hand. As Chaim hurried after him, he said anxiously, "What do you mean? That's no answer."

On Saturday, July 27, at1:00 p.m. eastern daylight time, the president of the United States appeared on national television and gravely announced that American astronomers had made a shocking discovery. In about a week, two large asteroids would impact the earth. The government was trying to do everything in its power to deflect or destroy the asteroids but there was no guarantee it would succeed. The president emphasized that since the asteroids were one kilometer in diameter and moving at over fifty thousand miles per hour, it was expected they would cause enormous devastation, but that the damage would occur mostly in the zones of impact.

The first asteroid, named Geddes-Oliver, would probably strike Canada about two hundred and fifty miles northeast of Edmonton in the province of Alberta, close to the city of Fort McMurray. Two hours later the second, called Geddes-Vincent, would plunge into the Atlantic Ocean approximately two hundred miles north of Bermuda and seven hundred miles east of New York City.

The president cautioned viewers not to panic because that would only increase the number of people killed or injured. He advised those living within six hundred miles of Fort McMurray to evacuate the area or to seek underground shelter. As for the ocean impact, the effect on the United States would be catastrophic. Some scientists estimated that the tsunamis might reach a height of three or four hundred feet and computer simulations indicated that the entire east coast of the United States up to the Appalachian Mountains would probably be flooded. Consequently, the president urged all residents living on the eastern seaboard to travel west to locations beyond the Appalachian Mountains. This evacuation should begin immediately but since there was plenty of time, it should be done calmly and in an orderly manner.

The president then gave detailed instructions to authorities and citizens of the east coast concerning how the evacuation might best be accomplished. He concluded his announcement by noting that there was no way scientists could predict the exact spots of impact and both asteroids might strike hundreds of miles from the zones already indicated. The only relative certainty was that the asteroids would strike the earth sometime Friday morning on August 2, unless the US government, with the help of other nations, could stop them.

Shortly after the president ended his frightening broadcast, the prime ministers of Canada and Great Britain appeared on their television networks with similar warnings. The effect of the newscasts was almost immediate. A black fear fell upon the populations of the United States and Canada because many believed their leaders were understating the danger and the end of the world was upon them. Within hours of the warnings millions began making frantic arrangements to evacuate the impact zones. The churches were jammed with people, desperately praying to God that he might spare them. Tens of thousands repented of their sins while thousands of others rejoiced because they hoped the disasters would bring them profit and good fortune.

❧

At County General Hospital near San Diego the hospital staff and the patients gathered in small groups in front of hundreds of television sets Sunday afternoon to watch continuous news reports describing every possible detail of the approaching doom. It was as if the patients' illnesses suddenly became unimportant in comparison with the new danger from the heavens. Only those who were close to death did not know what was going on.

The excitement continued the next day, unabated. However, Doctor Eli Johnson had other things on his mind as he entered room F213. He looked down at his patient in disbelief. The eighteen-year-old boy was dying, and there seemed to be nothing he could do to save him. At eight in the morning, seven hours earlier, Edward Marshall had suddenly been struck by intense flu-like symptoms, including a fever of 104, a severe cough, and headache. Frightened, the boy's mother had brought him to the ER. A doctor on duty had run a test for bacterial pneumonia and had put Edward on IV fluids and oxygen.

Since the test had turned out positive, the intern had put boy on antibiotics. At 9:00 a.m., however, the patient had begun to bleed profusely through the nose, and the frightened intern had asked a nurse to call Dr. Johnson. Within ten minutes Johnson arrived and ordered a complete blood analysis, including a hematocrit test. Fifteen minutes later he received the report which showed that Edward's hematocrit was at 20%, and he ordered an immediate blood transfusion. He suspected that the bacterial pneumonia was only a secondary infection, not the primary cause of the illness. Unfortunately, however, the lab report was inconclusive.

When Edward continued to bleed from his nose and mouth, Dr. Johnson ordered the nurses to start a second unit of blood. All their efforts to stop the bleeding were futile. The boy's fever remained between 103 and 104 degrees and he coughed violently and struggled to get his breath, obviously in extreme pain. A second hematocrit test, taken at 10:30 a.m. showed they were losing ground. Dr. Johnson was at loss as to what to do. He consulted with several of his colleagues and they were as confused as he was.

During the rest of the morning and in the afternoon the patient was given six more units of blood. However, in spite of all the doctors could do, Edward went into a coma at six o'clock and died shortly after. Eli Johnson then had the gruesome job of informing the boy's parents that they had lost their son. After asking question after question that the good doctor was helpless to answer, the grief-stricken parents wept inconsolably as they slowly left the hospital.

Later in his office, Eli stared out his window without looking at anything. He was depressed and angry that he had been incapable of helping his young patient. There was something familiar about Edward's symptoms but he couldn't remember what it was. He went to his magazine rack and searched through the covers. Finally, he saw the photograph of a man lying in bed, covered with blood. He searched for the article and found the title "Zaire Ebola Kills Thousands in Central Africa."

Immediately he grabbed his phone and called several clinics and hospitals in the San Diego area. He was amazed at the results. Ten people had died in the last seven days of an unknown disease and all of them had the same drastic flu-like symptoms. Thirty others had shown the same symptoms but had recovered and been released. He thought, *With a death rate of 25% our disease can't be Ebola. The mortality rate from Ebola is close to 100%. That is, if those forty people were suffering from the same disease as Edward.*

After reviewing every detail of Edward's record, Eli went to the next room and said to his assistant, "June, will you please call the Centers For Disease Control in Atlanta and get my friend, Dr. Judith Jowett, on the phone. It's very important. In the meantime, I'm going to check on several patients, but I want you to page me the minute you make the contact." Eli had just finished with his second patient when he heard his name on the loud speaker.

"Hello, this is Dr. Eli Johnson."

"Hello, Eli, this is Judith. You wanted to talk to me?"

"Yes, thanks for calling me so fast. Sorry to drag you away from what you were doing."

"No problem. We're watching the news reports on the asteroids."

"It's a terrible thing, isn't it?" Eli said.

"It's unbelievable."

Before she could say more, Eli blurted out, "I've got something here that is pretty bad, but I don't know what it is." There was silence on the other end of the line so Eli went on. "Today we had a patient die of a disease which bleeds the patient out similar to the way Ebola does. I checked around this area and found that other people have died recently from a similar disease." Eli gave Judith a complete review of the symptoms and the lab tests.

"One minute, Eli." Eli heard Judith talking to someone but couldn't hear the words. After several minutes she returned to the phone. "Eli, are you still there?"

"Yes."

"Sorry for the delay, but I had to consult with the boss. He wants me to gather a team immediately and head your way. We'll probably arrive early in the morning. As you can imagine, our entire agency here in Atlanta is packing up to escape the tsunami. The government is providing all of us with military aircraft for the evacuation."

"How many people will you bring here?"

"From ten to twelve."

"Okay, I'll make arrangements for you at Holiday Inn, and I'll ask my assistant to call you again with the details as soon as she reserves your rooms."

"That'll be fine," Judith said. She paused and added, "Eli, don't worry. It doesn't sound like Ebola."

"I hope not," Eli said. "See you in the morning. Do you want me to arrange for transportation?"

"No, we'll have our own transportation."

"Okay. As soon as you can, come to my office in the hospital. It's room B30."

"We'll be there as early as we can," Judith said. "Oh, by the way, I suggest you quarantine the body."

"I already took those precautions."

"You're pretty smart for a regular staff physician," Judith quipped.

"Thanks," Johnson said without acknowledging the humor. "Listen, do you want me to warn the other medical centers in this area that you're coming?"

"Only those which have had cases with the symptoms you described. Actually, we only need tissue samples from the people who died. If anyone gives you trouble, remind them we have federal statutes to back us up in cases like this."

"Okay, see you tomorrow, Judith."

Eli felt better as he hung up the phone because he knew he had placed the problem in the hands of one of the world's foremost experts in biohazards. However, he realized the problem might be very serious if the CDC wanted to fly in a special team as soon as possible. That night Eli tossed and turned without sleeping more than an hour or two, his mind full of nightmarish scenes of thousands of human beings bleeding to death on the streets of San Diego.

At 9:10 a.m. on Monday, Judith Jowett and her team stormed through the front entrance of the hospital. One crowd after another turned from the TV reports to stare at the strange group as they hurried through the hospital corridors with yellow bundles in their arms. Before long, they found Eli's office on the second floor. Judith asked her team to wait in the corridor while she and Dr. Johnson made some arrangements. After reviewing the entire situation with Judith, Eli began to call various offices in the hospital to arrange for an autopsy of Edward's body. Judith went into the hall and gave her staff instructions. Two of them slipped into yellow biohazard suits and went to room F213 to get Edward's quarantined body. They took the body to operating room 6.

Special precautions were taken to seal off the operating room so that no one else in the hospital was exposed to the disease. After they had finished this work, Judith's team left to visit every hospital and clinic on Eli's list in order to obtain tissue samples from the recent victims of the fatal flu-like disease. Meanwhile Judith, wearing a protective suit, opened Edward's chest cavity. Shocked at how heavy the lungs were with blood and damaged tissue, she took a sample of the lung tissue and examined it herself in the hospital lab. By 6:00 p.m. on Tuesday she had the results of her lab tests from all eleven tissues samples and she met with Eli in his office.

"It's influenza," she announced.

"Influenza!" Eli stared at her in shock.

"Yes."

"But influenza doesn't kill people," Eli exclaimed. "There are deaths among the very old and young, but not a kid of eighteen."

"You're forgetting the influenza pandemic of 1918 and 1919," Judith said. "It's estimated that it killed somewhere between twenty and forty million people, and the majority of them were between the ages of twenty and forty. It was the worst epidemic in the history of the world, even more widespread and lethal than the Bubonic Plague which killed about twenty million people in the Middle Ages, mostly in Europe."

Eli had read articles on the 1918 influenza pandemic but had attributed its virulence to secondary bacterial infections at a time when antibiotics were unknown. How could influenza be dangerous in the twenty-first century with all the new medicines and procedures?

"So what should I have done?" Eli asked. "I gave the boy Tamiflu." For an important staff physician Eli felt more helpless and incompetent than he ever had in his life.

Judith said kindly, "Tamiflu and Ralenza have proven to have little effect against the most lethal avian flu virus—H5N1—when transmission of the disease takes place between humans. All they do is sometimes reduce the symptoms of regular type A and B flu. But this kid already had the H5N1 virus everywhere in his body when he first came to the hospital. The truth is, there is no known cure for this disease. The government has been stockpiling a vaccine to combat an avian flu pandemic, but there is no definite proof that it will be more effective than Tamiflu.

"Did you say virus H5N1?"

"No, not exactly," Judith said. "It's a version of H5N1. It's H5N1 but with a couple of its genes re-assorted. We examined the workups of the forty-one cases you reported and it seems fairly certain that they all had this new virus. If that's true, the mortality rate would be about twenty-four percent. That would make it much more lethal than the regular H5N1."

"But wasn't H5N1 transferred from animals to people?" Eli asked. "That would make it far more controllable."

"Yes at first, but the virus mutated and was transmitted from person to person. That's why it spread so rapidly. Also, that type of mutated virus is especially dangerous."

Eli felt his stomach knot with panic. "Do you think our new virus moves from person to person?"

"The evidence isn't complete yet, but from the histories we've taken it seems likely that it is airborne and does move from person to person. We'll know for sure when we examine a larger number of cases."

"If it can move from person to person by air and has a mortality rate of twenty-four percent, we may have an epidemic on our hands which will make the 1918 flu look like a picnic," Eli said.

As Judith put her reports into a black leather briefcase, she made a somber prediction. "We estimate—worst-case scenario—that it could circle the globe in a month or so and kill from fifty to a hundred million people if we can't stop it here in San Diego or find an effective vaccine very quickly."

"Do you think it's possible to stop it here?" Eli asked frantically.

"We'll certainly try," Judith replied, trying to maintain her composure.

The horrible thought came to Eli that even now he might be carrying the deadly virus. He forced the thought from his mind and said to Judith, "Where do we start?"

"First we call the CDC and report our findings. I know where the agency is relocating and I have the phone number. I'm sure they'll contact the World Health Organization and other experts in the field of disease control. By tomorrow the city of San Diego will be swarming with yellow biohazard suits."

Eli swallowed hard but he had a question which was nagging him. "What about the boy's autopsy? What did you find?"

"Intense inflammatory edema of the lungs, toxic degeneration of the special cells of all organs and tissues of the body, hemorrhages in the mucus and serous membranes of the respiratory tract and in most other organs. The lungs were the primary organs attacked. In short, the boy bled out." Judith spoke these words calmly and matter-of-factly, but Eli sensed that she too was in pain.

"My heavens. May God have mercy on us!" Eli cried as he turned to look out on the peaceful city of San Diego.

Chapter 17

On Tuesday morning the president of the United States appeared before the nation once again in a special television broadcast. It was clear that he had been under great stress, for his face was drawn and he looked ten years older. He explained to his fellow Americans that the country had reached a state of national emergency which had several causes: natural disasters plaguing the nation in every state, the growing power and defiance of insurgents, rampant crime, anarchy in many cities, and the two asteroids. The government had tried every measure at its disposal to meet the many challenges but without significant results. As a result, it had become the president's sad duty, in order to save the nation, to declare a universal state of martial law, effective immediately. This meant that all local and state authority was suspended and replaced by the power of the federal government.

The president went on to explain that, as a part of martial law, the government would require every American citizen to comply with three important new laws. First, every male between the ages of twenty and fifty must receive a microchip implant within a period of three months, more specifically by the first of November. The biochips could be obtained in a simple and painless procedure at thousands of local medical facilities at government expense. Without them, no male between the ages mentioned would be permitted to work, do business, or make purchases, and would suffer other severe penalties. In the future the implant program would be expanded to include all citizens.

Second, every citizen was required by law to surrender his firearms to government authorities, also within three months. All those who obeyed this law would receive payment for each weapon or amnesty if the firearm was illegal. Third, it was illegal for any person or organization to hoard more than a three-day supply of food and certain other essentials. Those refusing to comply with this law immediately would have their property confiscated and be imprisoned in government internment camps. At that point the president assured the public again that the purpose of these measures was to insure the safety of every citizen in the country against crime, anarchy, and want, and he encouraged all loyal citizens to cooperate with their government for the good of all.

The president declared that he was certain the new order of things would only be temporary and last no longer than one year. He asserted with conviction that he knew most Americans loved their country and hated lawlessness. Consequently, he was confident they would be happy to obey the three new laws during the period of crisis. Finally, with a sincere smile on his face, the president waved good-bye to millions of viewers as he expressed his faith in the greatness of the American people to meet the current crises with courage and fortitude.

The reaction to the president's announcement was immediate. Within hours tens of thousands of Americans rushed to hospitals and clinics all over the country to be the first to receive their implants, while swarms of others invaded local police stations to surrender their guns. However, many citizens openly declared their intention to resist at all cost the government's unconstitutional use of dictatorial force. They used hundreds of local area radio broadcasts, thousands of hastily printed leaflets, and word of mouth to express their views and their emotions. Most of these ideas had a religious fervor to them. The objectors claimed that the microchip was nothing more than the mark of the beast spoken of in the Book of Revelation and encouraged all Americans to save their souls by resisting government tyranny.

Two days after the president's announcement, Texas and five other states declared their independence from the Union and, taking advantage of the weakness and confusion of the federal government, ordered their state guards to seize control of federal facilities. Some federal installations were firebombed by undisciplined bands of state and local police, who had joined forces with violent anarchists. Also, during the first few days following the president's appearance on television, rebels set fire to twenty-seven medical centers and hundreds of smaller clinics in different areas of the country. In the nation as a whole, the president's new policies, instead of promoting peace and order, had the surprising effect of escalating violence and anarchy.

❧

Three days after the president's announcement, Steven climbed out of bed at six in the morning. Everyone knew this was the day when the two asteroids were supposed to hit the earth, and he had invited his family and close friends to watch the news reports with him. Two days earlier he had welcomed into his home a small LDS family from Houston, Texas, which had come to Utah in obedience to the prophet's call, and now he knocked on their bedroom door to awaken them. Ten minutes later José and María Ramírez and their two small children came out of their room and entered the kitchen, where María served her family cold cereal and milk. By eight o'clock the Christophers and the Cartwrights had arrived and made themselves comfortable in the living room. A few minutes later Mary and Andrea appeared at the door. Steven was surprised to see others with them.

Mary explained. "Steve, I hope you don't mind, but I invited the new family that is staying with us."

"No, I don't mind at all," Steven said. "Please come in."

She introduced the husband and wife as Sergei and Margarete Borisovich. They had two children, a nineteen-year-old son named Nicolai, and Anastasia, who was twenty-five. Steven was amazed at the beauty of the young woman. She was tall and slim, with perfect features and silken black hair and captivating eyes. In many ways she reminded him of Selena except that she was younger, taller, and had blue eyes instead of dark brown.

"They are Russian," Mary said, "but they have been living in Paris for the last ten years where Brother Borisovich is director of a museum. They were converted to the Church six years ago." Mary was obviously confused and unnerved by the way Steven stared at Anastasia.

"I *was* the director," Borisovich corrected. "Six months ago I accepted a new position as a librarian at Kansas University in Lawrence, Kansas. But when the prophet made his call, I resigned my position and, after selling as many possessions as we could in such a short time, we came to Utah. We arrived yesterday." He pointed to Mary and Andrea. "These lovely sisters were kind enough to offer us shelter until we can get established."

"I'm certainly glad to meet you," Steven said.

After everyone found a seat, Mary said, "Have the authorities released more information as to where and when the asteroids will strike?"

"No, they don't know any more than they did a week ago," John replied.

"I thought they said they might be able to stop them," Andrea observed.

"Hah. That's no more than government trickery," John said. "The government won't be able to do a thing because it doesn't have the necessary technology. They wouldn't dare try to destroy the asteroids with nuclear warheads because they'd end up shattering them into millions of pieces and creating a nuclear winter."

For a half hour the group talked about the asteroids and how much damage they might do. But soon the conversation turned to the recent government actions to insure order in America.

"What they want to do is unconstitutional," John said angrily. "All this is prophesied in the scriptures. That microchip is no more than the mark of the beast. Anyone who gets it will become a slave to the federal government and sell his soul to the devil."

Sergei looked at John with surprise and said, "Has the Church made any official statements about what we should do? President Miller's announcement was made three days ago and we should have heard from church leaders by now."

"You didn't hear the reports on TV last night at ten o'clock?" Robert Christopher said. Several people in the group shook their heads. "Two of the channels carried an official statement by the Church media rep, Barry Rosenfeld."

"What did he say?" Steven asked.

"First he said that the Church counsels its members to obey the law of the land."

John slammed his fist against the arm of the chair. "But it's unconstitutional to require every citizen to surrender his arms and get that biochip."

Robert ignored his son's anger and continued, "But then Brother Rosenfeld added that even though church members were generally obligated to obey the laws of the land, each member should also read Doctrine and Covenants, section 134 carefully and prayerfully and decide for himself through the Spirit what he will do in this crisis."

"I'm not sure what Brother Rosenfeld is trying to tell us," Steven said. "I understand basically what section 134 says, but the actions we take must depend on the details of the circumstances, and I'm not sure we all have enough knowledge to act wisely in this case."

"I'm warning you now," John said. "Don't get that microchip for any reason. Read Revelation 14:9-11 and you'll know why."

"I don't know what Rosenfeld meant either," Robert said, "but I'm sure the prophet would direct church members to refuse the microchip if the Lord revealed to him it was the mark of the beast. From what I've read in the past, some church leaders feel that a man has accepted the mark of the beast when he knowingly embraces evil and rebellion, so from that point of view, we are not surrendering to evil by getting the bio implant. Yet other church writers say that by forcing every citizen to receive the microchip, the government is taking a step which is clearly unconstitutional, and they leave it up to our individual consciences as to what we should do. Neither the Lord nor the Church will command us in all things."

"So what do *you* think we should do?" Mary asked.

"I believe we should go to the Lord as individuals for guidance as we are supposed to do when we pick a political candidate for office. Then if we decide to refuse the government's injunctions, we should be willing to take the consequences."

"In my opinion, the Church wants us to refuse the microchip and stand up for freedom," Sarah said. "The reason it doesn't say so openly is because the government would crack down on the Church with all the power at its command. It would confiscate church properties, imprison its leaders, blackball its members, and the Church would cease to exist as a viable organization."

"I agree," Paul said. "It's a matter of survival and the Church must stay intact. I believe it's only a matter of time before the government collapses, and when that happens we're going to need spiritual leadership to rebuild society."

"What about the food storage problem?" Steven asked. "At this time the government is saying that if we possess more than a three days' supply, we are hoarding and can be fined or imprisoned."

Robert nodded. "Sarah and I stored enough to last several years, but we used up half of it helping people who had lost everything in the flood. Now, however, I have no intention of volunteering information to the government that we still have storage left. I believe it's impossible for the authorities to check every house in America for extra food."

"No government is taking our storage," Sarah said firmly. "I gathered all that food and herbal medicines for one reason—to help other people!"

Mary said, "At the rate people are blowing up hospitals these days, and raiding pharmacies, we're going to need all the natural remedies we can get. Do you know enough about plants that you could help people find medicinal remedies growing in the wild?"

"Of course," Sarah said. "Robert and I have been studying medicinal plants most of our lives. In fact, all that man wanted to do on our honeymoon was go on herbal walks."

Everyone burst out laughing, and Paul and John couldn't resist teasing their father for another five minutes. Steven was intrigued to see everyone laughing and joking at a time when two asteroids threatened the earth with one of the worst disasters of all time. He had seen this behavior before, when a grieving family laid a loved one to rest, only to enjoy a noisy party afterward. He had not decided whether this incongruity resulted from simple human frailty or from a need to escape unbearable anguish.

After the joking had ended, José Ramírez looked at Sarah and said, "I understand you are a midwife?"

"Yes."

"That is wonderful. When the world collapses in the troubles of the last days," José said, "you will be very valuable to pregnant women because they probably will not be able to find a doctor to help them."

"That's the main reason I got my training."

"I don't mean to change the subject," Douglas said, "but I'd like to ask José and María where they are from."

"We are from Houston, Texas," José explained. "We joined the Church three years ago and when the Lord's prophet told us to come to Zion, we came right away."

"You sure did." Steven said. "The call was made only twelve days ago."

"We believe in being obedient to the Lord's anointed," María said, showing a mouth full of white teeth. "I need to explain that we were wanting to come to Utah ever since we came into the Church and we have been preparing diligently. That's why we speak English pretty well. I think we are one of the first families to come."

"We came immediately also," Sergei Borisovich said. "My colleagues at the library thought I was insane."

"Brother Borisovich," Mary said, "do you think church members in foreign countries will be able to move to large communities of saints in regions where it is safe?"

"Oh yes, most of them will be able to travel to safe places, hopefully in their own countries, without much trouble. Especially since the Church has set up the relocation fund. But some of the saints will find it very difficult to move."

"What do you mean?" Mary asked.

"Well, some of them cannot come because their tyrannical governments will not let them."

"Tyrannical governments?" Paul asked.

Sergei glanced at Paul with great sorrow in his eyes. "Yes, there are many oppressive governments which persecute and murder Christians, and some of the victims are Mormons."

"Which governments?" Steven asked.

"Communist countries and the militant nations of Islam. At the museum in Paris I talked to many travelers, and I have made numerous trips throughout the world myself. What I learned is that there are many of our fellow Christians persecuted and even killed in Russia, China, North Korea, Sudan, Armenia, Turkey, Pakistan, Vietnam, and other countries. The governments of the western nations know this is happening but they do nothing because they want to be good trading partners with those evil nations."

"Is there anything we can do to help those people?" Steven asked.

"For now you can pray for them," Sergei said. "I know that God loves them and will help most of them escape. As for those who do not escape but perish, I believe God will reward them in heaven for their faithfulness."

Steven was deeply impressed with the faith and loyalty of these two immigrant families. He thought that if they were examples of the kind of saints who would soon gather to the Rocky Mountains, the Lord would have no trouble finding good people later to build Zion in Missouri.

Paul decided to tell them something that was bothering him. "I wanted to tell you about a report I heard on the radio this morning. It seems a new type of influenza has appeared in San Diego. They discovered it last Sunday. Apparently it's deadly because it kills twenty-four percent of those infected. At first they believed they'd be able to contain it, but since Sunday they've found over four hundred new cases. That's four hundred cases in five days. According to the report, the disease seems to be moving east from San Diego. The last victim was discovered in Saint George, Utah."

Elizabeth Cartwright looked very worried. "Are we in any danger here?"

"I don't know. It may reach this area, but the government hasn't issued any warnings."

"And I know why," John said with disgust. "The government is afraid that if it warns the people, there'll be widespread panic which would add to the problems it already has."

"You may be right, John," Steven said. "But I didn't know the flu was so deadly. What type of flu is it?"

"It's kind of like the swine flu," Paul said. "They say it originated in some type of animal and for some reason jumped into humans. Now it's being passed from person to person."

"I'm sure we have nothing to worry about," Anastasia Borisovich said. "Even if we get the flu, your mother can heal us with her marvelous herbs."

Steven wasn't so sure. He looked at his watch. Eight thirty. He turned on the television to check for news reports on the asteroids. Immediately, he found an in-depth report on Channel Five. The commentator reported that the top astronomers in the world predicted that the first asteroid would impact Canada around eleven fifteen mountain time and the second would strike the Atlantic Ocean shortly after noon. He said the authorities were encouraged because most of the people living near the impact zones had taken the president seriously and had evacuated in plenty of time. However, on the east coast there were a hundred and eighty deaths attributed to evacuation problems, specifically involving traffic accidents. Also, it was estimated that there were close to one million people who refused to leave the coastal region, either because they didn't believe the flood waters would reach them or because they were taking advantage of the circumstances to loot homes and businesses. The sixty thousand police and national guard who were risking their lives to evacuate people and to maintain order in the region were helpless to control the situation.

Chapter 18

Sal Thomas sat in the swing on his porch and looked off to the northeast. Next to him were several cans of beer, a bowl of popcorn, and a pair of binoculars. From his place on the outskirts of Edmonton he could see the whole thing. No one else was in the neighborhood, for they had all left days ago. But Sal wasn't leaving. He was eighty years old and he'd never seen anything this great in his life. Nope, this was a chance of a lifetime and he wasn't going to miss it. When the local constable had come to his door the day before and ordered him to leave, Sal had taken care of it handily. He had simply reached behind the door and grabbed his 12-gauge shotgun and pointed it at the constable's nose. You never saw a man move so fast as that lawman running to save his hide. It had been years since Sal's wife had died and although he missed her sorely, he enjoyed his freedom and wasn't about to let that whippersnapper of a cop tell him what to do.

Sal peered through the scratched glass of his ancient wristwatch. A bit past eleven. The blooming thing ought to be coming along any minute now if that news guy knows anything, Sal thought. He finished his first beer and grabbed another. Then he scooped up a handful of popcorn and stuffed it into his mouth. Hey! This is like being at the local picture show and seeing the latest disaster movie. They were definitely his favorites—movies full of tornadoes, hurricanes, earthquakes, tidal waves, volcanoes, or some foreign crackpots plotting to blow up the world. This was even better because it was real.

They said the comet—or was it a meteor?—would hit the earth over two hundred and fifty miles away so he figured he was pretty safe. It was just like his wimpy neighbors to turn tail and run at the slightest hint of danger, even if it was four hundred miles away. And so what if this falling mountain did blast him to smithereens? He'd lived almost a century now and every day was getting tougher and tougher. Might as well go out with a bang.

After finishing his second beer, Sal began to feel sleepy, so he let his eyelids droop a little as he hummed a tune and thumped the beat with his right toe. Ten minutes later he jerked awake. Still nothing. He checked his watch and saw it was almost eleven thirty. Stupid reporters. They're as bad as weather men, changing their minds from one moment to the next. Sal leaned back and gazed into the distance with half shut eyes. Then he saw something bright in the sky, slowly rising above the horizon. He sat up and grabbed the binoculars.

"Yep. Thar she blows! A ball of fire getting bigger and brighter and turning down toward the earth."

Then Sal heard the roar as the fireball seemed to bore down on him.

"Woo-hoo! That baby's noisy and coming closer than I thought."

Fascinated, Sal watched the asteroid streak through the sky with a tail of fire streaming hundreds of miles behind it. He could actually feel the immense force of the glowing ball as it grew in size and began to arc downward toward the earth. He followed it—completely transfixed—as it plunged toward the earth, closer and closer. Then suddenly he heard a deafening boom and was hit with a wall of pressure that lifted him into the air and hurled him through the window behind the swing. As he went through the window, the house collapsed around him. He felt an intense heat, but it lasted only an instant because immediately he slipped away into a peaceful, pleasant blackness. As he fell into the abyss, his last thought was that he had finally seen a spectacle worth dying for.

Later the experts gave an official written report on the disaster. The nickel-iron asteroid had smashed into the earth with the force of a thousand hydrogen bombs, and it had pushed billions of tons of dirt and debris thousands of feet into the air. It left a crater twenty kilometers in diameter and two kilometers deep, and the floating debris darkened the sun as it began to spread around the world. The asteroid had smacked down one hundred miles north of Edmonton and had flattened forests and buildings for two hundred miles around. It was predicted that the impact would make the earth's weather colder and affect crop production and the economy of the world's nations for years to come.

Almost an hour later Captain Matthew Korn and Captain Charles Dawson brought their Air Force SR-71 reconnaissance plane slowly down out of the cloud cover twenty thousand feet above the Atlantic Ocean two hundred miles north of Bermuda. All at once the sky was bright and blue around them. They looked off to the east. The last reports said that the second asteroid would impact at about 3:00 p.m. in the Bermuda time zone.

"Don't you think we're getting too close to target zone zero, Captain?" Charles said.

Matthew looked at his copilot and smiled. "You worried?" Charles didn't answer, but was studying the eastern sky. "Take it easy. There's only one chance in a million that the asteroid would hit us."

"But the shock wave and the water it's going to hurl into the sky."

"We'll be up too high," Matthew said. "As soon as we take a gander at what's going on down there, we'll climb to thirty thousand and get above the clouds." Charles didn't look convinced. "Are the cameras turned on?" Matthew asked.

"Yes . . . Captain, I have another question."

"What?"

"Why are we the only ones out here?"

"We're not," Matthew said. "The French and the English have planes in the air east of us."

"I mean, why are we the only ones from our side out here?"

"I suppose they think we can handle it without any trouble."

Charles laughed nervously. "And maybe they don't want to kill more men than they have too."

"Don't be silly, Chuck. This is no big deal. You're nervous because no one's ever taken photographs of an asteroid hit before. The way I see it, we're perfectly safe. The experts have analyzed what we can and cannot do, and I trust their judgment."

After hesitating a moment, Charles said, "I'm not sure they know a lousy thing."

"Hold it. What's that?" Matthew said.

They looked to the east and saw a small fireball rising above the horizon and heading their way.

"The asteroid!" Charles shouted. "Coming right at us. Take the plane up—now!"

Quickly Matthew pulled back on the stick and pushed the throttle forward to increase power. As the airplane began to climb slowly, the asteroid continued to arc toward them. For a moment Matthew was certain they were on a collision course, but soon the asteroid turned downward and to their left. All at once an immense wall of air hit them and they were savagely hurled upward to the right and the plane rotated wildly out of control. When the asteroid had passed, the atmosphere became surprisingly quiet and Matthew was astonished that he had quickly regained complete control of the airplane. All that remained from the violent encounter was a slight vibration as the plane moved upward slowly and steadily.

As Matthew anxiously continued their ascent, he heard a colossal boom behind him. He had the impression that the rear of the aircraft had been blown away by some supersonic missile and he turned to look. When he saw the tail was still there, he realized that the asteroid must have impacted the ocean below. He couldn't see what was happening but he knew that billions of gallons of water must be rising in a ring toward them. All he could do was hold his course and pray. He waited for what seemed forever while the aircraft drew near to the cloud bank above. As he entered the clouds, he felt a powerful wave of air and water hit the airplane and catapult them upward. It was like being overtaken by the wind and rain of a giant hurricane. After a minute of incredible turbulence, the storm at last released the plane—and the resulting calm was shocking.

Matthew flew on through the clouds and soon rose above them to a beautiful sun and a clear sky, and he secretly gave thanks to God that they had been spared. Without waiting he banked the airplane and headed back down through the clouds. He had to see for himself. Within minutes he cleared the clouds again and looked down. A great circle of water, which Matthew guessed was about thirty or forty miles across and contained billions of gallons of water, was falling slowly back into the ocean. The falling water created a series of monstrous waves which billowed up and down. After ten minutes the ocean finally quieted down.

"There's a huge black spot in the middle of the sea," Charles cried.

"That thing must have gone through thousands of feet of water and burned a hole in the bottom of the sea."

"It's unbelievable."

Matthew said, "Look at the rings of water moving outward."

"Tsunamis?"

"Yes, big ones. Right now they're only about ten feet tall but when they hit the coast, they'll be as high as skyscrapers."

"For the first time today, I'm glad to be up here," Charles said.

"Me too, buddy, me too. Now let's head this thing back to base, make our reports, and see what we've got on film."

The two aviators turned west toward the east coast. They were grateful to have escaped with their lives but were deeply troubled too by the realization that they were accompanied below by giant waves which would soon endanger the lives of millions of people.

The asteroids took their toll. Geddes-Oliver filled the atmosphere with dust and the remains of living creatures and dimmed the light of the sun. Geddes-Vincent sent its tsunamis against the east coast, destroyed trillions of dollars in property, and killed more than a million people who had refused to take the waves seriously. Most of the victims had moved away from the seacoast, but not far enough.

Before long, however, the American nation would begin to realize that a more terrible plague was quietly at work. Within weeks the H5N1 flu swept across the country and began its work in Europe and Asia, carried rapidly from nation to nation along the world's airways. At the end of three weeks the death toll reached two million.

In spite of the disasters, the US government moved ahead with its plan to enforce martial law and to insert microchips into American citizens. In August twenty million men willingly received the chip, and eighteen million people happily surrendered their firearms. But the dissenters, though smaller in number, were so aggressive and effective that they became a relentless force in pushing the nation toward anarchy and the complete disruption of society.

Yet in Utah and the surrounding states the situation was relatively stable. Even though the flu was taking thousands of lives, most of the people joined together to face the plague and every other trouble with great courage. In many communities the Mormon church took unofficial control of local government and began to maintain order and direct the distribution of goods and services. Since there were hundreds of packs of murderous brutes who roamed the Mountain West, the Church organized militias of priesthood bearers in every stake. After obtaining weapons and training for thirty hours under good men who had military experience, they were assigned to patrol every community in regular shifts.

The effects were powerful and reassuring. Seeing these results, the federal government made an exception to the rule of citizens possessing firearms, and the official policy soon became that men who were part of the Mormon Guard would be issued special certificates permitting them to possess weapons and carry them while on duty.

Every day hundreds of new saints from other parts of the country moved into the Rocky Mountains and were, in most cases, welcomed with open arms.

Although they brought with them every possession they could, they put a great strain on the economy of the entire region. This crisis inspired tens of thousands of saints to share what they had with those who had nothing. These saints were the ones who had obeyed church leaders and stored both food and supplies.

But those who had ignored the warnings from church leaders ended up groveling for insects, rodents, edible wild plants, or anything they could find to support life. And when they couldn't find enough to eat, they resorted to thievery and violence in order to survive. Eventually thousands of so-called saints apostatized from the Church and viciously attacked church farms, canneries, storehouses, and the homes of individual members. Soon stories began to circulate among the populace concerning people who were murdering their neighbors for a crust of bread.

Chapter 19

During the month of August, Steven spent every morning cleaning up flood debris and searching for dead bodies. Though it had been three months since the dams had broken, the unrest and calamities in the region and the country had delayed the cleanup effort. He was accompanied by Paul, José Ramírez, Douglas Cartwright, and Sergei and Nicolai Borisovich. Several times Anastasia went with them and she always made sure she worked close to Steven, but usually she did more talking than working. Steven couldn't help but feel flattered by her attention. After the dirty labor was done for the morning, Steven spent the rest of the day translating documents for his loyal customers, and in the evening his guests and close friends gathered to comfort one another and to share ideas on the state of the world. Steven refused to admit it to himself but he relished these nightly reunions in his living room because he could enjoy being near Mary Fleming.

After a very pleasant evening near the end of August, Steven reluctantly said good-bye to his guests and friends shortly before ten o'clock, and he and Paul, who was currently staying at Steven's home, grabbed their rifles and hurried out the door. Every evening at ten they joined two other armed brothers, and the four-man team made its rounds in a specific area of the neighborhood. Unfortunately, the local police did not have the manpower to provide significant protection.

Steven knew that at the same time twenty other brethren were also on patrol on Grandview Hill, some of them in cars. There were a total of six shifts and a hundred and forty-four men guarding the community twenty-four hours a day. Steven had heard that throughout the Rocky Mountains the Church had recruited a total of one hundred thousand men for the safety patrol at any hour of the day or six hundred thousand in a twenty-four hour period.

Steven felt a deep sense of peace and comradery as he and his three companions walked along the dark streets of the neighborhood on a summer's night which was unusually cool and dim. He ascribed these conditions to the recent asteroid impact in Canada. He saw the glow of lights behind many closed curtains and felt satisfaction that the people inside were safe. At the same time he knew that José Ramírez was watching over his children, willing to risk his life if necessary to protect them.

Steven shook his head and forced himself to pay attention. He had to study every object around him as the team strolled along because he knew the anarchists had developed an effective attack against the Mormon Guard. In earlier days they had come in large gangs and attacked helpless citizens at any hour of the day. But since the Mormon Guard had been formed, they came as individual snipers and attacked the Guard and others at night. In the preceding week anarchists using that type of guerilla warfare in Utah had shot twenty elders to death while they were on patrol. As a result, Steven was constantly afraid for his life and that of his brethren, especially Paul and John. At two in the morning the next shift of four men replaced Steven and his companions, and the brothers returned home.

"Pretty quiet out there tonight, wasn't it?" Steven said. Paul didn't answer. "Paul, what's going on in that head of yours?"

Paul peered at Steven as if he had just awakened from a dream. "Oh, yeah, pretty night . . . You know, I was thinking. You sure are lucky."

Steven laughed. "Why do you say that?"

"You get all the women."

"What women, you turkey?"

"Mary Fleming, Andrea Warren, and Anastasia Borisovich."

"What? I don't *have* them. They don't belong to me."

"Oh yeah? Every one of them is in love with you."

"For heaven's sake." Steven rolled his eyes.

"Yes, they are. Hey, man, why don't you turn your nose up at one of them so I can have a chance?"

"Okay, which one do you like?"

"Anastasia Borisovich," Paul said. "Mary and Andrea are about thirty but Anastasia's only twenty-five, so she's almost my age. Besides, she's by far the best looking."

"Oh, I don't know about that." Steven grabbed Paul by the shoulders and gazed directly into his eyes. "Listen carefully. I hereby promise to stay away from Anastasia. Does that make you happy?"

"Yes, it does." Paul beamed for a second, but then his face turned into the picture of despair. "What good is that going to do? She's in love with you not me. Every time I cast my adoring eyes upon her, she's too busy staring at you to even notice."

"Tell you what, Paul. The first chance I get, I'll tell her she really needs to pour her affection upon my little brother, a man who truly has the capacity to give her the love she needs."

"Funny, Steve, very, very funny. I'm going to bed. Good night."

"Good night. Please don't tear yourself up over this. I'm sure there are many women out there who'd love to have you as their lover boy."

One day early in September, Anastasia Borisovich came at noon, shortly after Steven had returned from working on the flood damage. She had a basket in her hand, and she looked up at Steven with a glow in her eyes. Steve was shaken by the strange softness and beauty in her innocent face, but fought the sudden feelings of attraction which stirred within him.

"I came to invite you on a picnic," she said.

Steven had just finished a sponge bath and was very hungry. "A picnic? Where?"

"Behind the church two blocks away. There's a nice lawn and a huge maple tree. I have everything we need in this basket. All you have to bring is a blanket."

Steven felt his stomach twist with panic. "I'm really tired. I didn't get to bed until after two this morning and I had to get up at eight to shovel debris."

"Look, Steve, you won't have to do anything but eat good food and lie on your back under the shade. You have to eat anyway."

Steven noticed the determined look in her eye and realized she wasn't about to take no for an answer. "All right, let me tell José and María what's happening."

"Please tell them we're going alone."

Steven returned from the kitchen after talking to his guests and ran into Paul, who stopped him and whispered in his ear that the girl waiting in the living room was the one he wanted and Steven had no right to go off alone with her. Steven scowled at his brother's humor and pushed past him to join Anastasia. He walked with her to the church and spread their blanket in a shady spot. Anastasia unpacked tuna sandwiches, watermelon, and apple pie, and they began to eat immediately. Even though it was still summer, the day was surprisingly cool and the sun struggled to show its dim outline behind the dark haze which filled the sky. Steven knew that the darkness came from the billions of tons of dust kicked into the atmosphere from the asteroid impact thirty-three days earlier.

"I don't know how long we can stay," Steven said. "Sometimes, it rains when you least expect it."

"Oh, I think this weather is strange and wonderful," Anastasia said softly. "It all depends on your attitude. I love it when it rains."

Steven was surprised at her answer. He looked up at the darkened sun and said, "I suppose it does have a sinister charm, especially because it's so different from what we're used to."

"I prefer to believe that the gloominess you speak of is not real, but only an illusion in people's minds. When you think of things that way, you can see everything as beautiful."

Immediately Steven became suspicious. He had heard this type of language before. "If that's the case, doesn't it seem strange to you that so many people have created the same illusion?"

"I see your point, and I know that only a brilliant man like you could make such an interesting observation," Anastasia said sweetly.

Steven saw a trap coming and decided to change the subject. "By the way, I wanted to ask you when you were converted to the Church?"

"My family was converted six years ago in Paris. I was baptized when I was nineteen, but I didn't have as strong a testimony as my parents. It was nice to be a member and I enjoyed doing things with the other young people, but one day I met this remarkable man who taught me a new way to look at life. That was when I was twenty-one. Since that time I have been so happy and at peace with myself. Now I'm full of a great joy that I never experienced before in my life."

"Are you still a member of the Church?" Steven asked.

"In name only. I go to church just to please my parents."

"What gives you all this joy?"

"Oh, I love everybody, and everywhere I look I see nothing but love and beauty. I know that I am one with God and the universe, and that someday I shall reach pure truth and enlightenment."

"This man who taught you, what was he?"

"Do you mean his name?"

"No, *what* was he—his position."

"From your tone I see you already know. He was an enlightened master."

"I see. So you believe in New Age philosophy."

"If that's what you want to call it. But the so-called New Agers don't always believe the same thing. There are many different schools of thought, and all of us believe pretty much what we wish. Originally, I sought enlightenment to benefit from the power it gave me to heal myself and others, but now it gives complete meaning to my life." She looked at Steven sadly. "You don't hate me because I'm not your traditional good Mormon woman, do you?"

"Not at all. I think you have every right to believe as you wish. However, I cannot accept the teachings of the New Age movement."

"Have you studied them with an open mind?" Anastasia said.

"I believe so. Several years ago I purchased some books on New Age philosophy, written by famous believers. One of them was a Hindu guru."

"And you didn't like what you read?"

"Frankly, I thought the books were loaded with falsehoods. All of the authors presented their ideas in extremely esoteric and convoluted language. The claims sounded marvelous and profound, but the arguments supporting the claims were extremely difficult to understand. The biggest problem the writers had was establishing consistent definitions of their fundamental terms. Those basic terms changed meaning constantly, even in the work of the same author, and so they always led nowhere. Once I realized this, I knew their arguments were false and inconsistent."

"Maybe you didn't understand what you were reading or didn't want to understand," Anastasia said.

"Listen, Anastasia, language is my first love and I know when someone is trying to move me emotionally instead of convincing me by reason and solid evidence."

Anastasia gazed into Steven's eyes with a tenderness which made his heart burn and his head spin. "Maybe you should read and listen with your heart and not your head . . . So by using your precious reason, what did you conclude about New Age philosophy?"

Steven looked at her sadly. "I already told you. I believe it's just another false religion."

Anastasia said, "Listen, Steve, I really care for you . . . and I'm willing to listen to your ideas anytime. Maybe we should meet regularly to discuss these things, and if you wish I could play something for you on my violin. I'm an accomplished violinist, you know."

"No, I didn't know that."

"Yes, I am. Also I want to say that I would do almost anything to please you. Anything at all. All you have to do is ask."

Steven didn't know for sure what Anastasia meant and couldn't think of a response. But as he hemmed and hawed, it began to rain. They jumped to their feet, put the leftovers and utensils in the basket, and set out for Steven's house. It was the first time in a long time that Steven had been grateful for bad weather. As they hurried along the downpour ended as fast as it had began, and all that was left was a pleasant drizzle.

Not far from the house they caught sight of two men in police-like uniforms standing guard near the porch. When the men saw them turn into the yard and head for the front door, they ordered them to halt and demanded their names. Steven and Anastasia identified themselves, and while one of the men covered them with his rifle, the other went inside. A minute later the same policeman emerged followed by a man who was obviously their leader. In his hand he carried the two rifles Steven and Paul used during their night patrol.

"Do you have permits for these rifles?" he asked.

"May I ask who you are?" Steven said.

"We are federal deputy marshals." The lead officer flashed his badge in Steven's face. Steven knew that deputy marshals were not local law enforcement officers but were under orders from the United States Marshals Service, whose headquarters were in Virginia. For that reason, he suspected they might not be sympathetic to Mormons. He pulled out his wallet, removed his permit, and handed it to the marshal, who examined it with disgust. "I don't know why we allow you Mormons to carry weapons. You people cause more trouble than you're worth." He returned the document. Steven noticed that the marshal said nothing about Paul's rifle and assumed his brother had already shown his permit.

The chief continued to grumble as he removed a small black device from his belt and passed it across the front of Steven's face and the back of his right hand. "No microchip, huh. When do you intend to get it?"

"Don't we have some time yet?" Steven had decided he would never willingly receive the microchip no matter what they did to him.

"You have until the first of November to get it."

"Certainly, officer, I'll do everything I can to comply by that time. I've been so—"

"I don't want to hear it. Get that chip or face the consequences . . . Now, I want to know if you have a stash of food and supplies."

"We only have enough food for about two days," Steven said. "Didn't you and your men look around?" During the months of June and July Steven and his brothers had dug a small room directly beneath the main basement floor. The room measured eleven square feet and was eight feet deep. After reinforcing and insulating the room, they had installed shelves and filled them with two thirds of Steven's food storage and other supplies, most of which was provided by their mother. The entrance to this room was a small hole three feet square cut into the basement cement. When they were done, they covered the cement floor with a wooden one as if they were building a huge family room, and it was almost impossible to detect that there was a storage room hidden below. As for the other third of Steven's storage, they sealed it in waterproof containers and buried it in a shallow pit in the back yard between the house and the outhouse. These were the items they could reach quickly when they needed them.

"Yes, we checked the house out. Now we'll do your yard."

"Why are you picking on us?" Steven asked.

"We received a report from some of your neighbors that you're hoarding food." The deputy went back into the house and shouted some orders to his men. Immediately four additional officers exited the house. "Check the grounds," the chief shouted.

Steven followed the leader around as he covered every inch of the front yard. He followed him to the back yard and watched while he searched there. It took the officers only a minute to discover the disturbed ground directly over the storage pit. At that moment Steven saw himself behind bars trying to survive on government mush.

The leader pointed to the disturbed soil. "What's this?"

Steven's heart sank but then he had an idea. "Oh, this is the first pit we dug for the outhouse. We used it for a while but had to close it down because it was too close to the house."

"You two men, dig here," the leader ordered. He looked at Steven. "Do you have some shovels we can use?"

"Yes, of course. But I hope your men don't get too much poop on them. It really smells foul." The deputies chosen as diggers screwed up their faces as if they had just swallowed a plate of worms. Anastasia was standing nearby and stifled a laugh. Steven walked to the garage and brought back two shovels.

While the deputies dug, the drizzle became a steady rain and the soil in the pit turned quickly into mud. The diggers, more and more anxious to finish the nasty job, began to throw mud everywhere. They splattered their chief with it several times and he was forced to move back to a safer position. They hit Anastasia with a shovelful and she quickly escaped to the house. After the two marshals had dug for ten minutes, they were slipping and sliding and falling all over each other, completely covered with mire. Their rain gear gave them no protection at all. Steven knew they were only inches away from the top containers of food storage.

"They're almost there," Steven shouted to the head marshal. "In about thirty seconds they'll start slinging poop." Steven's pleasure at seeing the shocked look on the leader's face turned to horror when he glimpsed a white patch on the far side of the hole—the edge of one of the food containers. Fortunately, the frantic diggers had not seen it yet.

"That's deep enough," the head marshal shouted all at once. "Get out of there."

Steven was thankful to see the disgusted diggers scramble out of the hole immediately and begin to scrape chunks of muck from their uniforms. As the deputies prepared to leave, the leader had a few parting words for Steven.

"Watch yourself, buddy. You'll never be smart enough to put one over on us. We're highly trained for this kind of stuff and we'll catch you every time."

With immense relief Steven watched the marshals go, and he expressed thanks to God for blinding their eyes to prevent them from seeing the food container. He went into the house and explained to everyone, including Anastasia and Paul, what had happened. After laughing and rehearsing the details for a while, they discussed what they would do to prepare for the next visit by federal marshals. Steven knew he had told the officer several lies but he didn't feel he owed the truth to officials who were usurping his constitutional rights. Later that night Steven told Paul the story of Anastasia and the picnic.

"I'll never find the girl of my dreams. Good-bye happiness," Paul said after Steven had finished the story.

"What?"

"Good-bye happiness," Paul repeated. "First my brother steals the only girl I ever loved and next I find out she's one of those crazies who float around talking about peace and love and looking for salvation in a flying saucer."

"Funny, Paul. The girl never gave you a second look. When she compared you to me, she had to go for the gold and not the brass. But as for her religious beliefs, I think she'll see the light someday."

"Don't count on it, Stevie boy. I've seen this type before. The more they read New Age stuff and go to encounter groups, the more they become incapable of separating their dream world from reality."

"Maybe you're right, but we still have to try. As for finding the girl of your dreams and getting married, I wouldn't be in too much of a hurry. You may end up disappointed like me. Even if I fell in love with someone, I don't know if I could ever be strong enough to show her the trust that a good marriage requires."

All at once Paul became serious. "You're kidding yourself, Steve. You're a good man, but you don't understand yourself. It tears me up to see you so miserable. I love you but I think you're controlled by fear and selfishness. The truth is you need a wife and your kids need a mother. If I were you, I'd pick

Mary Fleming. She's a wonderful person and she loves you with all her heart. Remember, the scriptures say that it isn't good for a man to be alone."

After his speech Paul added, "Look, I'm tired. I've got to hit the sack. Think about what I said." He dragged himself out of the chair and shuffled off to his bedroom.

He calls me a coward and then gets out of here before I can answer, Steven thought. Yet Paul's words had disturbed him deeply, and he spent the next twenty minutes inventing detailed objections to all of his brother's statements. The thing which troubled him most was Paul's assertion that Mary loved him with all her heart.

Chapter 20

By the beginning of September the influenza virus had swept around the world, and the number of victims increased geometrically every day. It was now clear that the virus was spread by contact with infected blood and mucus, and was also airborne. The US health authorities estimated that within the forty-two days since it first appeared in San Diego, it had infected more than three hundred million of the earth's population. Ninety million of these victims perished of a terrible death within twelve hours of infection. The number of deaths showed that the virus, now called H6N1 by the CDC, was more lethal than first estimated because the mortality rate was almost thirty percent, not twenty-four percent as first anticipated. The ultimate source of the virus was unknown and no one seemed to care. The World Health Organization and the disease-control centers of the world's major nations were too busy trying to find an effective vaccine and had no time to track the virus to its roots.

In every city in the United States, and even in most rural areas, people stayed indoors as much as possible, venturing forth only when it was absolutely necessary. The federal government, as a part of martial law, declared that the people were required to do even essential tasks under a strict time limit. Thus a woman who went to the market was allowed no more than thirty minutes to shop and could do so no more than twice a week. Every person leaving his home had to wear a special mask to lessen the possibility of spreading infection. So great was the fear of the populace that most of the people willingly accepted and complied with these injunctions.

People who were compelled to work together in closed buildings were particularly at risk. As they entered their places of work, they had to change into sterile clothes and be disinfected. They wore special masks and avoided contact with fellow workers as much as possible. In spite of the immense death toll, the average citizen seldom saw a victim who had succumbed to the great plague, unless it was a family member. Whereas in Medieval Europe the victims of the bubonic plague were thrown onto rotting heaps in the streets, the victims of the modern plague died silently behind closed doors, and the infected bodies were carted away quickly and efficiently in sanitary vehicles.

Andrew Christopher, Steven's eight-year-old son, showed definite signs of the plague by Wednesday afternoon in early September. The disease attacked him all of a sudden and grew worse rapidly. Everyone who entered his bedroom wore protective masks. After giving Andrew a priesthood blessing, Steven called Tania, explained the situation, and asked if she and John could take William and Jennifer to their house while he was gone.

Steven had decided to take Andrew to Mountain View Hospital in Payson, and his mother insisted on going with them. When they arrived at the hospital, they saw a scene of inconceivable chaos. The rooms, halls, and reception area were crowded with flu patients, and the hospital staff had been forced to locate recent arrivals outside on the lawns surrounding the building. For a bed they had nothing but one thin blanket. Everyone treating the sick wore the same protective masks.

Steven knelt on the grass and leaned over to kiss his precious son with tears in his eyes. Sarah began at once to give Andrew regular doses of herbs, including goldenseal and olive leaf extract. The nurses who came to check the boy's IV saw Sarah treating the child, but they said nothing because they knew they had no magic remedies to cure this plague. They would have given him morphine for the pain, but as a result of all the sickness and injuries the supply of that painkiller and most others was exhausted at Mountain View. From time to time Andrew looked at his grandmother through bloodshot eyes with the trust of innocence. He coughed almost constantly and fought to get air, while his skin slowly turned blue and a blood-tinged froth oozed from his mouth and nostrils. At first his temperature was 104 and the cold packs provided by the hospital and the kind citizens of Payson could only lower it to 103.

His pulse was unsteady and his tongue thickly coated with mucus. He complained of intense pain everywhere in his body, especially in his head and throat. Sometimes blood would gush from his nostrils or his mouth. Once a harried doctor came and, after seeing Andrew's swollen face and ankles, told his nurse that the patient had nephritis. He admitted to Steven that there was not much he could do, but assured him that all the patients lying on the lawns would be transported to the gym of the local high school before dark, where several nurses would be assigned to care for them. Steven and Sarah spent the next few hours comforting Andrew, making sure he was getting liquids and cleaning up his diarrhea.

At seven o'clock Steven heard Andrew murmur something and leaned close to hear. The boy whispered to his father, "I want to go home."

"He wants to go home," Steven said to his mother. "What do you think?"

"I think we should get out of here," Sarah said. "They're running out of supplies and can't even give him an IV."

"But won't he infect the rest of the family?"

"I doubt it. All of us have been exposed to the virus by this time and bringing him home now won't make any difference. For insurance we'll wear masks."

Steven gathered Andrew in his arms and headed for the car which was a quarter mile away. They reached Steven's home before eight o'clock and put the boy to bed in Steven's bedroom. The same terrible symptoms continued and Steven was afraid to allow Tania to bring William and Jennifer home to see their brother. As for the adult members of the family, they crowded into the bedroom and did everything possible to help Andrew. Sarah made a tea full of healing ingredients, especially vitamin C, and made the patient sip as much of it as he could take.

Around nine o'clock Mary and Andrea arrived. Mary had brought some medicine and equipment with her. "Sorry I didn't come earlier, Steven, but we only received news of Andrew's illness a half hour ago."

"I'm just grateful you came so quickly."

As Mary examined Andrew she asked Sarah what they had done for Andrew up to that point, and was pleased by what she heard. "You've done a lot to help him. However, I can give him some morphine for the pain. Do you agree to that?"

When both Steven and Sarah nodded their assent, Mary set up the IV equipment and inserted a needle in Andrew's arm.

"We've learned that patients who have this disease usually need a fairly large dose of morphine to do any good," Mary said. "It relieves their pain, suppresses bleeding and diarrhea, and helps them relax. But we have to be careful. We don't want to give the patient so much that it depresses his breathing and heart action. It's a matter of balancing the shock the patient might get from the intense pain and the possibility of the depression of breathing from the morphine."

"They didn't have any morphine at Mountain View," Steven said.

"It's understandable," Mary replied. "Most of the hospitals have been hit hard with flu patients. What we have comes from special sources the Church found." A few minutes later Andrew began to relax, his breathing became more regular, and before long he fell asleep. Mary continued to monitor him during this time. Then she took a blood sample and left to have it tested at a nearby hospital lab. When she returned she brought several units of blood to replenish the blood loss suffered by Andrew.

By one in the morning most of the family members had wandered into other parts of the house and found places to sleep. Sarah and Steven remained by Andrew's bed and worked constantly to comfort him and to help him breathe. Mary came in the room from time to time to check him, but there was little else she could do. By one thirty Steven realized that his son was going to die unless a miracle happened. He looked at his mother and saw that she was dozing in a nearby chair. At that moment he made up his mind.

He knelt beside the bed and offered a prayer. "Father in Heaven," Steven said with tears pouring down his cheeks, "please bless my little boy. He has his entire life ahead of him and I know he has a great mission to fulfill. He's always been such a good boy, full of kindness and thoughtfulness toward everyone around him, and he doesn't deserve to die, especially this way."

Another hour passed and Andrew's face and hands began to turn dark purple. A foamy solution of blood and other fluids continued to seep from his nose and mouth and he became deathly quiet except for a continuous rattling sound as he struggled for breath. Steven knew his son was close to falling into a coma from which he would never return. He knelt again in prayer. "What more do I have to do, Father? I'll do anything you ask to help my child." As he continued to pray, he heard a peaceful voice deep in his soul, and in a few words the voice told him what was required. "I understand," Steven said. "Yes, I'm willing to accept his agony and his fear. For him I will give my life willingly and happily." Steven lay down next to Andrew and put everything into God's hands. Feeling a wonderful peace in his heart, he fell into a deep sleep.

Suddenly Steven awoke. He rolled over to check Andrew but the boy was no longer in the bed. He looked at his watch in the dim light of the single lamp near the bed. Five o'clock! He looked for Sarah and saw her still dozing in the chair. He got out of bed quickly, fearing that Andrew had died and someone had taken his lifeless body away. He went into the living room and found family members and friends sleeping in every available space. He searched the house but couldn't find Andrew. At last he checked his translation room in the basement and there he saw Andrew, seated in the big swivel chair and grinning as he turned the pages of his favorite picture book. Steven entered the room softly, but Andrew heard him and looked up.

"You know, Dad, it's sure funny to see these guys running away from Ammon with their arms cut off."

Steven examined Andrew carefully and saw that his color had mostly returned and he seemed to be breathing normally. With thanks in his heart, he took his son in his arms and hugged him tight.

"Take it easy, Dad, you're hurting me. Keep it up and I'll look worse than these guys in the book."

Steven carried Andrew back to bed and held his hand until the child fell asleep. He had an overwhelming urge to kiss his other children but they were staying with John and he would not see them until the next day. He wanted to wake up his family and tell them how much he loved them. Not only because they had stuck by him in the present crisis, but because he knew that soon the Lord would require him to keep his promise. Finally, he decided to let them sleep for now, and he lay down again near Andrew to rest a few more hours.

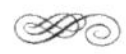

Gerald Galloway, lounging in a luxurious chair in his English mansion, telephoned Alexi Glinka, his associate in Moscow. When he saw his confederate's face, Gerald said, "Is this a secure line, Alexi?"

"Yes, Mr. Galloway, completely secure."

"Good. I understand your son broke his leg. How is that going?" Gerald always made it a point to give the impression he cared about his people.

"The cast bothers him but otherwise he's fine. How is your family?"

"Couldn't be better. Let me get right to the point. Have you been paying attention to events in the United States?"

"Somewhat, yes."

"Then you know the American government is only a step away from complete collapse." He paused to let Alexi answer.

"That's . . . what I understand," Alexi said finally. "The civil unrest, mob violence, anarchy, asteroids, plague. It's only a matter of time."

"Now we need to speed things up."

"Speed things up?"

"Yes. Remember what I said at our meeting here in July. We need to push the Americans over the brink."

"I remember, of course."

"Good. What I want you to do is send the Americans a few friendly gifts with my love."

"Gifts?"

"Nukes."

"So . . . that's what you decided?" Alexi's voice betrayed his nervousness.

"Well, the Americans already have a plague to deal with, and so I thought a little variety might be in order."

"You don't think the plague will be enough to topple the American government?" Alexi said.

"It might, but it's slower and less certain."

"But it's killing millions of people and causing anarchy and disruption. Not only in the States, but in most of the world."

"That's right. And to take advantage of it, I've instructed our friends in the media to broadcast regular documentaries, interviews, and specials designed to produce the impression that the plague was purposely created by the Jews as part of their plan to control the world. The insinuations are subtle but they're so persistent that they are having a positive effect already. Since we started this particular aspect of our campaign, there has been a rash of attacks on Jewish synagogues and communities in many countries and the number is increasing."

"Mr. Galloway, you're a genius."

"I'm much more than that, Alexi, much more. The plague will surely help us in the States, but now I want to have something more shocking, more spectacular, and I believe a few nukes might do the trick. A little pop here and there will have an effect far more devastating than the quiet death. It'll break the will of the Americans and help bring a rapid collapse of their government."

"Whatever you say, Mr. Galloway."

"Thank you, Alexi. It's good of you to be so cooperative," Gerald said ironically. "Now, what I want to know is can you get the Russians to do it? Do you have things under control?"

"My only concern is that dropping no more than a few nuclear bombs is foreign to the Russian ideas on how to wage nuclear war against the United States. They feel nuclear war is total war and they must destroy all US strategic offensive sites to avoid retaliation. Their most likely scenario would be to start by knocking out communications and unprotected electronic equipment with electromagnetic pulses. They'd do that by air bursting some well-placed SLBMs, or submarine-launched ballistic missiles. Then twenty minutes later they'd hit the country with around fifty additional SLBMs and also a large number of ICBMs, or intercontinental ballistic missiles. These would be followed a few hours later by Russian bombers—"

"That's enough. I'm quite familiar with Russian theory on nuclear war. What you must do is convince them that all-out nuclear war with the United States is unnecessary. In the first place, the U. S. government and their military are now in such disarray that it is not likely they'll even be able to detect the incoming missiles, much less where they came from. Ever since the end of the Cold War the Americans, thinking the Russians were no longer a threat, have neglected their missile defense system and radically cut their defense budget. In the second place, the American government is already close to falling and is very vulnerable, and it is doubtful it could retaliate. However, as extra insurance I'm planning a little surprise which will help paralyze the government and make retaliation impossible."

"A surprise?"

"I'll tell you about it in a minute. What I want to know is, can you control the Russians?"

"I'm certain of it," Alexi asserted. "I now have the key Russian leaders in my pocket. It took a great deal of money, but at this moment they belong to us. The amusing thing is some of those leaders were already engaging in secret talks about taking advantage of the current American chaos to finish them off."

"That's good, Alexi, but are you sure you can control things?"

"Yes, I'm sure of it."

"Good, because the attack needs to be at the right time and in the right way."

"Please explain, sir."

"I want you to drop one nuclear warhead on New York, a second on Chicago, and a third on Los Angeles. All three hits should be at about the same time."

"When do you want the bombs dropped?" Alexi asked.

"In fourteen days. Can I count on you, Alexi?"

Although Alexi's face turned pale and his eyes expressed fear and uncertainty, he said rapidly, "I'm certain of it. Months ago I warned the Russians that they might be called upon to strike at any time."

"Wonderful! You've done precisely what I instructed you to do. Now listen and I will tell you my little surprise. I have already given Lucienne Delisle the go-ahead on the termination of sixty-seven key American leaders, including the president and vice president, a number of key political figures, and some top military leaders. She has worked for years to put our operatives into positions where it will be relatively easy for them to do their job. The president and vice president will be killed by a deadly poison delivered by people very close to them. The others will be taken care of by snipers and several other methods.

I have instructed Lucienne to effect the executions on Thursday, September 19 at 2:00 p.m., US eastern daylight time. You'll drop the bombs one hour later, at 3:00 p.m. Even if by some miracle the Americans could track the missiles, there probably won't be any leaders left alive with the authority to order retaliation. I predict that our bombs will cause the US government to disintegrate a few hours or a few days afterwards."

"It's a brilliant plan, Mr. Galloway," Alexi said. "But, are you sure the assassins will be successful in hitting all sixty-seven leaders? There's always—"

"No, of course not. But if they succeed in dispatching the main characters and a good percentage of the others, we'll still get the results we desire. Besides, we've planned for a second wave of assassins to mop up the people who escape the first attack. I assure you that Lucienne is a master at arranging this type of thing."

"Yes, I am quite aware of her reputation."

"She is very good. However, Alexi, there is one thing you must understand. When it concerns the nuclear strikes, there is no room for failure here. If you fail, the consequences for you personally will be extremely grave."

"I realize that, Mr. Galloway. I will not fail . . . May I ask you a question?"

"Of course."

"Do you intend to warn our American operatives as to where we'll drop the bombs?"

"Yes, we may need those people in the future . . . When I told Lucienne to carry out the terminations, I also warned her about the bombs and instructed her to make sure our operatives in the vicinity of the three target cities are in safe areas when the warheads drop. I intend to alert all the members of our inner circle throughout the world regarding our plans because it's vital we work together as a team. Each of them will need to use the media in their regions to make sure the world believes that Russia launched the warheads."

"As for the Chinese, they'll already know that the Russians are the aggressors because of their up-to-date spy network, but I'll work closely with Janet Griffin to convince them that the attack is Russia's first act in a plan to dominate the world. If things go according to plan, the Chinese will attack Russia quickly and appropriately." Gerald stopped and laughed. "You may have to leave Russia in a hurry, Alexi . . . Now I have other work to do. I'll contact you every day between now and September 19 to verify your progress and I expect to hear excellent news."

"You will, Mr. Galloway, you will."

Gerald was amused by the fear in Alexi's voice. "In the meantime you might check the news on Israel from time to time. Soon I'll have another little surprise for you." He hung up without waiting for a reply and walked to where his granddaughter was sitting. He took her hand tenderly and led her to the back terrace. Callie laughed with delight because she always enjoyed strolling through the gardens with her beloved grandfather, and she knew he would give her a special treat when they returned to the manor house.

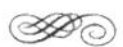

David Omert and Chaim Yehoshua hurried out of David's office in the Knesset Building in Jerusalem and headed for the Plenum Hall on the third floor. Although the parliament did not normally meet on Thursday, the country's leaders had called a special emergency session for ten o'clock in the morning. According to intelligence reports, the Arab states, led by Egypt, would attack Israel with a great united army within a few weeks. Menachem Hazony, the Minister of Defense, was going to ask the Knesset for authority to mobilize the army and activate the reserves. As they approached the Plenum Hall, David noticed that the special security force of the Knesset Building was checking the credentials of every person entering the hall. David knew that only important government leaders and members of the Knesset would be allowed to pass.

The debate lasted five hours. Once again President Eldad and his liberal supporters suggested caution and diplomacy as the best way to diffuse the situation, and they had always won the day in past meetings of the Knesset. But today Menachem Hazony shook the hall with his fiery rhetoric. The Knesset was the ultimate authority in Israel and Hazony fought to obtain its support. He reminded the legislators that historically the Arabs had never listened to reason when they considered themselves united and powerful enough to annihilate Israel. At the end of the session a vote was taken and Hazony, winning by a narrow margin, received the authority to prepare for war. The votes of David and Chaim had helped to give Hazony the victory. David believed that in the weeks to come the fate of Israel would lie in Hazony's hands.

Back in David's office the two friends were anxious to discuss the details of the session they had just witnessed. After shutting the door to his assistants' office, David leaned back in his comfortable chair and said, "That was the most exciting session I've ever witnessed."

"That was something, wasn't it?" Chaim said. "What do you think Hazony will do first?"

"I know he has already prepared the armed forces for this campaign. But I can only guess as to the details. I suppose he'll send orders to all military units in Israel, and they'll mobilize in a matter of hours and wait for the Arabs to do something to justify an Israeli attack. After that he'll hit them with everything we've got. If I understand my uncle, he'll hit Egypt and Mahmoud al-Mamoun first in an effort to completely destroy their air force, and at the same time he'll keep enough forces in the north and the east to hold Jordan and Syria in check in case they attack."

"Just like 1967!" Chaim said. "Don't you think the Arabs will be expecting that?"

"Perhaps, but you know how hard it is for them to learn the lessons of history or to work together in a common cause. Besides, if we give them any serious resistance they'll turn tail and run for cover like they usually do."

"But this time the Iraqis are in it full blast. The US and the UK freed them from Saddam Hussein in 2003, but they're just as much Jew haters as ever."

"I know and that worries me. My uncle told me that Israeli intelligence discovered an Iraqi army of about two hundred thousand men making their way through Jordan with the approval of the Jordanian government."

Chaim got up from his chair and began to pace up and down. "In that case we'll have to deploy a large force around Jerusalem and that means our armies against Egypt will be weaker."

"No, I know for a fact that Hazony will use his elite guard to cover Jerusalem. They are the toughest and the best trained units in the world. One member of the elite guard is worth a hundred Iraqi regulars."

Chaim's face broke into a happy grin. "I know this is stupid, but I can't wait until it starts. By the way, a minute ago you said we'd wait until the Arabs made the first move. Do you think their first move will be to cut off our access to the south like before?"

"Yes, they'll close the Suez Canal and the Gulf of Aqaba at the Straits of Tiran."

"And Israel has warned the Arabs many times in the past that we considered those actions to be acts of war."

"That's right, but they do it anyhow," David said. After a moment of silence, he added, "There's only one thing that really worries me."

"What's that?"

"Well, it's common knowledge that the Iraqis obtained Scud missiles from Russia and used them during the Iraq War. A few years after the Americans pulled out of Iraq in 2011, the Iraqis—when they had breaks in their religious wars—began work on improving the old Scuds. The new missiles have extremely accurate guidance systems and a range of over nine hundred miles. What's to prevent them from blanketing Israel with those missiles?"

"I don't know," Chaim replied. "I've been asking myself the same question in the last few days."

"Look, I'll make an appointment with Hazony and ask him what he's doing about the Iraqi Scuds."

"Do you think he'll tell you?"

"Positively. I'm his favorite nephew and he's convinced I'll be a great leader in Israel someday." David laughed at such a silly idea as he grabbed the phone and tried to get Hazony's office.

Chapter 21

Mary was angry and she let Andrea know it. "That hussy! How dare she sneak out of here and invite my—" She bit her tongue trying to stop that sentence. She had called Steven's house the day before to check on Andrew and was overjoyed to hear that the boy was recovering rapidly. But during the conversation Paul had inadvertently mentioned that Steven and Anastasia had gone on a picnic together several days earlier. Mary had not yet mentioned it to Andrea, but now as they prepared the noon meal at Mary's home, she had to let her friend know how she felt.

"Your what?" Andrea teased. "Your sweetheart? Your lover boy? Hah. You don't have things all *that* wrapped up, young lady. Personally, I think Steven is interested in *me*."

"You?"

"Yes, me. I'm a lot better looking than you and a heck of a lot smarter. And my personality is—"

"Arrogant," Mary mocked. "If you weren't my best friend I'd take you down and sit on you."

"Try it," Andrea threatened. "Hey, sister, all's fair in love and war and, believe me, I'm willing to fight for my man."

Mary looked her in the eye, unsure as to whether she was still joking. "Your man? What makes you think he even likes you?"

"Haven't you noticed the way he hangs around me when we have those meetings at his house? And while we're all sitting around talking, he stares at me from across the room. One thing I'm sure of, when he gazes into my eyes, I don't think he hates women anymore."

Suddenly, Mary felt pangs of jealousy in spite of the fact that she knew Andrea enjoyed teasing her. Especially since she believed it was she that Steven stared at all the time. "Seriously though, Andrea, I'd be happy if he chose you . . . but I don't think Anastasia is good enough for him."

"I agree," Andrea said. "By the way, where is that man stealer now?"

"I don't know for sure. Her parents borrowed my car to go shopping and I thought she went with them."

"I'll bet she's at Steven's," Andrea blurted out.

Mary looked stunned for a moment. Then she growled, "Doesn't she know we're supposed to avoid visiting people unless it's absolutely necessary? Government regulations! Some people have no respect for rules!"

Andrea grabbed their protective masks and flipped one to Mary. "Maybe she thinks visiting Steven is a matter of life and death. Come on. Let's go."

"Now?"

"Yes now. Don't you realize that Steven may be completely alone at this very moment with a woman who's prettier and younger than we are?"

"I'm so glad Andrew is better," Anastasia said as she crossed her long slim legs for the fifth time. "Where is the sweet child now?" Every time she crossed her legs she made it a point to pull her miniskirt down with exaggerated modesty.

"He's sleeping. Yesterday morning he made a miraculous recovery and I found him in my translation room reading a picture book."

"What an angel."

"Yes, of course. Well, anyhow, I took him back to bed right away, and he's only been awake briefly a few times since. I'll be happy to bring William and Jennifer home as soon as I know it's safe."

"Mary told me Andrew was close to death, so it's natural for him to sleep a lot. Is there anything I can do for him or you at this difficult time?"

"No, I think we have everything under control." He looked out the window trying to avoid staring at Anastasia's shapely legs. "I'm surprised you came here with the flu such a danger, especially without your mask."

Anastasia raised her chin bravely. "I'm not afraid. I have the power within myself to heal my body and fill it with life. Besides, I don't like to cover my face with masks." She flipped her black hair back and crossed her legs.

Steven swallowed hard. "Still, it's better not to take chances."

Anastasia put her hand to her mouth to cover a yawn. Then she uncrossed her legs and extended her arms and stretched luxuriously. "Oh, I'm sorry. I didn't get much sleep last night. I was out with Mary until three in the morning visiting neighbors sick with the flu—Mary's a nurse working for the

Church, you know—and the rest of the night I couldn't sleep worrying about you and Andrew."

"You're very kind," Steven said.

Anastasia gazed at Steven sadly and said, "I'm sorry if I upset you the other day during our picnic."

"No, you didn't upset me."

"You were so logical, but I'm not sure you understand the depth of my spiritual beliefs. It's hard for most people to understand someone who is at peace with the universe."

"Yes, it's true that inner peace is hard to achieve," Steven replied offhandedly.

"But in time I'm sure I can make you understand how I feel, if you'll give me the chance." Anastasia paused and crossed her legs again. "However, I know you have a brilliant mind and maybe you'll convince me I'm wrong."

With great relief Steven heard a knock at the door. He went to the door and was surprised to see Mary and Andrea.

"Come in, ladies," Steven said, smiling happily.

Mary and Andrea entered the room and sat together on one of the couches. They seemed almost comical in their masks. Neither of them looked at Anastasia.

Anastasia glanced at them with amusement. "I'm not sure those masks are all that efficient when people are close together for any length of time. Are you sure you need them?"

As they removed their masks, Mary stared at Anastasia's legs, which were almost entirely exposed. Steven expected her to comment on the miniskirt at any second, but she just sat there and stared. Andrea's face betrayed her amusement.

"We came to check on Andrew," Andrea said. "How is he?"

"He's fine. He's in bed now, but I'm sure he'll be tearing around the house in a few days."

"I can tell you, he's a very lucky boy," Andrea said. "The flu has been taking a lot of lives."

Mary tore her eyes away from Anastasia and said, "Yes. As I do my rounds I see hundreds of houses boarded up and I hear cries of despair everywhere. We try to quarantine homes where the flu has struck, but it's very difficult to keep up with the epidemic." Mary picked up her mask. "I'm supposed to wear this mask and take other precautions when I visit the sick, but I'm beginning to feel such efforts are futile. I've been exposed so many times that I'm amazed I haven't come down with the flu."

Steven coughed and his face looked flushed. "I understand it's much worse in other areas of the country."

"There is so much chaos," Mary said. It's hard to know the truth, but there are indications that our survival rate in Utah is higher than in the rest of the country."

"It probably has to do with our lifestyle," Andrea said. "Mormons who obey the word of wisdom put their immune systems under much less stress."

"I think that's true but there is certainly room for improvement," Mary replied.

Steven had trouble following the conversation because he began to experience a terrible pain behind his eyes. He looked from woman to woman but soon their faces began to blur.

"Steven, are you all right?" Mary said anxiously.

"I feel kind of sick all of a sudden."

"Oh, my gosh!" Andrea said. "Maybe he's got the flu! We'd better put him to bed."

Steven had decided that when he became ill, he'd write a quick letter to his family, asking them to take care of his children. Then he'd go off to the mountains east of Provo to die alone. In that way, his children wouldn't see him suffer. But now he couldn't see himself lying on his back somewhere in the wilderness enduring an agonizing death all by himself. He realized also that his family would be frantic wondering where he was and what had happened to him. No, he'd suffer and die, if that was his lot, in his own bed, nursed by his mother and others who loved him.

Mary and Andrea tucked Steven into bed while Anastasia went to the phone to call his family. After giving him as much liquid as he could drink, Mary hurried away to get supplies and equipment. Because of all the attention, Steven felt much better and wondered whether or not he was even sick. But ten minutes later he began to cough and struggle for breath, and pain invaded every part of his body. He knew this virus attacked abruptly and fiercely but he had not really understood how bad it could be.

Knowing his family would arrive soon, he put on a mask. After a few minutes of extreme discomfort, the deadly virus seemed to relent and for thirty minutes he didn't feel too bad. During this time his family began to arrive and soon the bedroom was crowded with people, all of them wearing masks. After embracing his three children, Steven asked John and Tania to take care of them for a few days. He couldn't bear the thought of endangering them or letting them see him die a terrible death.

"Steven, you'll do anything to lazy around," Paul joked.

John eyed Steven with his head cocked to one side. "You're right, Paul, he doesn't look sick to me at all."

"I think he's doing this to get out of late night patrol," Paul added.

As they laughed at their own jokes, Sarah pushed past them, her arms loaded with bottles of liquid and herbs. "Cut it out, you two," she said, frowning. "Can't you see Steven is terribly sick? His face is flushed and his hands and arms are turning blue."

The two tall men jumped to the side to let their mother pass. She was not very big but they had learned years ago not to cross her. "We're trying to cheer him up," Paul objected.

"Listen," Sarah said, "if you want to help, go get the rest of the herbs from the car. After that, you can give your brother a blessing." Sarah put a bottle of foul-smelling liquid to Steven's lips and commanded, "Drink this. It's full of vitamin C and a special herbal combination I prepared yesterday to handle this stupid little virus. Believe me, when this stuff hits those tissues, those bugs won't have a chance." Steven sipped the drink as fast as he could. After he had swallowed most of the concoction, his brothers gave him a priesthood blessing.

A short time later Mary returned with IV equipment, several bottles of IV solution, and other medical supplies. Steven thought his mother might protest, because she usually disliked anything which smelled of traditional medical practice, but he was surprised when Sarah helped Mary set up the equipment. Mary quickly inserted a needle for the IV and then drew blood for blood tests. Each time the needles went in, Steven jerked with pain. He had felt needles before but nothing like that.

"Are you in pain, Steven?" Mary asked.

"Yes."

"Where do you feel it?"

"In my head, chest, throat, and at the ends of my legs and arms."

"Would you like some morphine?"

Steven agreed and Mary took out a syringe and a small bottle from her satchel. "We've had to use a lot of this in the past few weeks." She drew some of the liquid from the bottle, squirted a tiny amount from the tip of the syringe, grabbed a juncture in the IV line, pushed the needle through the rubber center of the branch, and slowly depressed the plunger of the syringe. She looked at Sarah and said, "Have you given him quite a bit of that herbal drink?" Sarah indicated yes. "That's okay but at this point I suggest we wait for a while before giving him more. The morphine often makes the patient sick to his stomach and we don't want him to throw up the drink. Besides, in about three minutes he may become drowsy and want to sleep." After saying this, Mary left to have the blood tested and to obtain as many units of blood as possible. Unfortunately, the supply of whole blood was nearly exhausted throughout the state and the country.

Steven laughed to himself. Fat chance he'd fall asleep with all these people milling around, shouting at the top of their lungs. He'd never been able to sleep on trains or buses or in public places. As he thought about that, he felt the pain mercifully subside and a blissful peace slowly invade his mind and body. And finally, a pleasant blackness.

Steven opened his eyes. Several women were working over him feverishly. He thought they might be Mary, Andrea, and Sarah. He couldn't figure out what they were doing but he perceived several bright lights around the bed which seemed to pierce his eyes and head like the shafts of knives. He thought he saw an IV bag and two or three units of blood suspended above him near the bed. He lifted his right hand to his nose and it came away covered with foamy blood. The pain in every cell of his body was sheer agony. He thought about Andrew and was glad that his child didn't have to suffer this anymore. He was amazed that the boy had endured his own suffering with such patience. Silently, Steven asked God to give him strength to endure the torment and to bring the end as soon as possible.

Steven began to cough and he felt the shock of the coughing in his groin and bowels. All at once, he coughed a quantity of blood from his mouth and it sprayed all over his face and down the front of his shirt. When it was over he felt a little better and he looked around at those trying to help him. He saw that Andrea was not wearing rubber gloves and he said weakly, "Andrea, put your gloves on. That blood is full of the virus."

Mary handed Andrea a pair of rubber gloves and said, "Here, put these on. It's a standard safety procedure."

Sometime later Steven saw a strange face in the room. In spite of his pain, he struggled to see who it was. After gazing at the smiling face for a minute, he recognized the features but he couldn't remember where he had seen the person.

"Steven, Steven," Mary shouted in his ear. "It's Brother Heber Clark. Do you remember? He came to home teach you several times this summer."

"Oh, yes. Brother Clark," Steven mumbled. "I didn't recognize you at first. I guess my brain isn't too clear right now. This flu, you know."

"That's okay," Heber said. "I'm sorry you got it. It seems half the people in our ward have been sick from it." Heber moved from the foot of the bed to Steven's side and took his hand. He watched as Sarah put another glass of liquid to the patient's lips. Steven wondered why the old man didn't show the slightest concern that he might get the deadly virus. After a few minutes, Heber said gently, "How long do you think it'll take you to beat this thing?"

"Beat it? I'm not sure I will."

Heber smiled and said, "You will, my boy. Listen, I don't make promises lightly, but I have it from a pretty good source that you'll defeat this sickness. Would you like a blessing?"

"My brothers already gave me one."

"Maybe they didn't say the right words."

Steven didn't understand what Heber was talking about but he agreed to the second blessing. Paul anointed his head and the old high priest gave the blessing, during which he commanded the disease to depart and he declared that the Lord had a mighty work for Steven to perform. *Clark's a good man,* Steven thought, *but he doesn't know about the promise I made to God.*

Once again blood began to ooze from Steven's mouth, nose, and eyes. He coughed violently until he thought it would tear his lungs apart. He leaned forward and fought to get his breath. The pain was unbearable. Mary grabbed him and forced something into his mouth and down his throat, trying to help him breathe. Steven gagged as his whole body lurched backward convulsively. He was vaguely aware that once again he had sprayed blood in all directions as he quickly slipped away into a blissful unconsciousness. As the darkness covered him he thought numbly, *This is it. Dear God, take care of my children.*

The prophet struggled to get to his feet. His two counselors reached out, took his arms, and gently helped him to a nearby divan. At eighty-five years of age his mind was sharp, but his body was worn out. Josiah Smith had asked his counselors to come with him to the celestial room in the Salt Lake Temple so they might join their voices in prayer to the Almighty. Everywhere he looked he saw misery and death, but also he saw the power of God moving in the Latter-day Saints and in the other noble people of the earth.

"Did you hear it?" Josiah said.

Bennion Hicks, the prophet's first counselor, looked up. "Hear what, President?"

"The voice of the Spirit. It spoke to my heart and mind in a voice as clear as yours."

"I had many ideas rush into my mind, but I didn't hear a voice," Bennion said.

"My experience was the same as Bennion's," Samuel Law, the second counselor, affirmed.

"I heard your voices while I was praying," Josiah said. "The Spirit was talking to me and you were talking too, but your words seemed unrelated to what the Spirit was telling me. However, your presence helped me to hear clearly in a way I don't understand."

"I'm sure you hear the Spirit clearly because you're closer to God than we are," Bennion said.

"Both of you will receive communication from the Lord as I receive it in the days to come because Zion will require it."

"What did the Spirit say?" Samuel asked anxiously.

Josiah smiled at his counselor's impatience. *These youngsters who are only sixty have a lot to learn*, he thought. "The Spirit said that the forces of evil are combining in devilish anger and hatred to bring war in all the nations of the earth. These forces are led by the Antichrist, and the final goal is to destroy freedom and the work of the Lord. Soon the government of the United States will fall and anarchy will reign, and only in the Rocky Mountains will there be found some degree of safety. The time is also very near when the saints must establish New Zion in Jackson County, Missouri, for even now God is clearing that land of its inhabitants. The Spirit gave me the names of seven men who will be called to lead the first groups of saints east to the center place of Zion."

"How will the saints get there, President?" Samuel asked. "It's becoming difficult to travel, even out of one's own town. The highways are being torn up by small armies trying to wage war against the government or by anarchists on a rampage."

"That's right," Bennion said. "Even now travelers cannot obtain gasoline, electric power, or food on some of the highways."

"And it's all happened so fast," Samuel said, sighing. "Four months ago the world had at least some measure of peace and order."

Josiah got up and gazed out of a nearby window. "The saints will go to Jackson County by the same means our forefathers used to come from the east to Utah. It will be part of their testing."

"In the same way as before?" Bennion seemed confused. "Will as many of the saints perish on these trips as they did in the early days?"

"The Spirit did not tell me, but as you know, the trials have already begun.

Large numbers of saints are dying now from the plague and from violence, and many others are suffering terrible persecution."

"But, President, I thought the Lord promised to protect the righteous in these days," Samuel said.

"Not all of the saints are righteous," Josiah said. "There are many wicked saints and we have many traitors. The latter-day prophets have predicted that such would be the case. Even the righteous have no promise that they will fully escape and many of them will perish too. But when the saints die in Christ, their reward will be glorious in the hereafter. You have to understand that all this is part of the chastening. Zion can only be built by a sanctified people, and the Lord often uses persecution, trial, and death to sanctify his people. He did the same thing to the saints in the time of Joseph Smith in an effort to sanctify them at that time."

"It's hard to bear the idea that many of the righteous will perish," Bennion said.

Josiah turned away from the window and said, "The scriptures say they will die, but they will not *taste* death, which means that death will be sweet to them because they die in the Lord." All at once the prophet began to smile. "Besides, speaking from an earthly point of view, death isn't all that difficult."

"What do you mean?" Samuel said.

"I almost died several times. You suffer a few hours or days, and as you approach death you fall into blissful unconsciousness. At that point you don't feel a thing." Josiah grinned at his counselors, who didn't know if he was serious or not. "Furthermore, most people who are going to die within a few weeks don't feel much pain at all because the doctors pump them so full of narcotics that they seem to rather enjoy the experience." Josiah sat down on a bench.

Bennion continued to examine Josiah's face to see if he was joking. He knew by experience that the prophet could lead him on sometimes without ever admitting it. "Still these are difficult times, and I suspect all of us will experience our share of trials and pain."

The grin disappeared from Josiah's face. "Brethren, our job and the job of every Latter-day Saint is to face these times with courage, and above all to look forward to the coming of the Lord with joy and anticipation. If we don't have that joy and anticipation, we're not prepared and we'd better repent. The scriptures speak of the great and dreadful day of the Lord. That means his coming will be a time of joy and triumph for the righteous, but a day of terror for the wicked. This is one of the great messages we must teach our people in the coming years."

"I can see one way that the Lord's coming will be great," Samuel said. "You correct me if I'm wrong, President. The millennium begins directly after the Second Coming, and during the millennium there will be no pain, sickness, or death as we know it. So if a person is still alive at that time and has some terrible disease, he'll be transfigured by the power of the Holy Ghost and will be cured of his disease."

"You may be right, Samuel, but the Lord hasn't given us too many details as to what will actually take place. The only thing I might add to your statement is that the things you describe will happen only to those who are good. That is, to those who are worthy of a celestial or terrestrial glory."

"Yes, of course," Samuel said.

Josiah staggered as he rose to his feet. "We must be off now, brethren. Please remind me to gather the Twelve so they may give their counsel on the revelation we have received. You know how bad my memory can be sometimes." After those words the three elders made their way out of the safety of the temple and reentered the world of men.

Steven opened his eyes slowly and thought he saw an angel leaning over him, her shiny blond hair touching his cheek and framing his head like a golden halo.

"Oh! You're awake," the angel cried with joy. "How do you feel?"

Steven stared at the celestial being for a long time, enjoying the softness of the female face and the fascinating green eyes. Slowly he began to recognize the divine creature—it was Mary.

"I . . . I'm not sure," Steven whispered.

"You've been in a coma for so long. At first I didn't think you'd make it, but when your breathing became regular and your coloring improved, I knew you were getting better."

"I'm not dead and gone to heaven?"

Mary laughed. "I'm afraid not, silly." Her soft cheeks were moist with tears. "You can't get away from me that easily."

Steven was shocked to see her tears. He wanted to express the thing that was in his heart, but he didn't know if she was just showing Christian charity or something more personal. Mary was like that. He felt she usually treated him like everybody else, an object of Christian charity, and for some reason it really irritated him. "Get away from you? I'm not trying . . . Where is my family?"

"Your mother is asleep over there in that chair and the rest of your family is sleeping somewhere in the house. Andrea and Anastasia are here too. Everybody has been so worried about you."

Steven wanted to reach out and touch her face and bring her close, but he resisted the temptation. He was afraid she'd pull away in dismay and he knew he must look disgusting after fighting such a horrible disease. "What day is it?" he asked finally.

"It's Saturday, early in the morning. You've been unconscious all night."

Steven was perplexed. "I don't get it."

"Get what?"

"I'm supposed to be dead and yet I feel much better."

"Why should you be dead?" Mary teased. "You recovered because your body was stronger than the virus. That's normal. And Brother Clark gave you a powerful blessing."

Steven wanted to tell her about his covenant with God but hesitated to trust her. At last he said, "I'd like to tell you a secret, but I don't know if I should."

"You don't know if you can trust me," Mary corrected.

Steven was amazed at her insight and felt embarrassed. "I don't know if I can trust anyone."

"You mean any *woman*."

Steven stared into her eyes, trying to read her mind. After a few moments he gave it up, concluding that no man could figure out a woman. He closed his eyes and started to groan.

"Stop that, Steven. You're not fooling me. I want you to tell me your secret. I promise to keep it between you and me."

"It's rather personal and I don't want people to think I'm pretending to be something I'm not."

After glancing at Sarah to make sure she was still asleep, Mary said, "I know your secret already."

Steven was dismayed. "How could you? I haven't told anyone."

"I know *you*."

Steven figured she had imagined some wild secret and so he smiled indulgently. "What's my secret?" Steven enjoyed looking into her beautiful eyes and watching her soft lips move as she spoke.

"You promised God that you'd willingly surrender your life if he would heal your son from the plague."

Steven was flabbergasted. "How did you know?"

Mary's mouth twisted into a wry smile. "Because I know Andrew's recovery was a miracle. I've seen a hundred people reach his stage in the illness and they all died. So I figured something extra was at work here, and knowing you, there was only one logical conclusion."

"I see you're not only beautiful, but you're also brilliant."

Mary grinned with happiness. "Why thank you, Steven Christopher. That's a sweet thing to say." She leaned over and kissed him on the forehead.

Steven marveled at his nerve. Now it was a matter of life and death for him to change the subject. "Why am I still alive then?"

"You didn't listen, young man. Brother Clark told you the reason."

"Brother Clark? I guess I haven't been too coherent lately. What did he say?"

"He said you weren't going to die because the Lord had a special work for you to do. I guess all this was some kind of test."

Steven thought of the scripture which says the Lord moves in mysterious ways, and he felt a powerful emotion welling in his heart, but he fought to control it. He couldn't let Mary see him act stupid. He wiped the tears from his eyes and said, "When can I get up?"

"Well, I really should take care of you while you stay in bed a few days. After that you can get up on occasion."

"Do you think the disease will come back?" Steven asked.

"Why should it? You've been chosen for some great work . . . What I'd like to know is what that work is."

Chapter 22

All day Saturday Steven enjoyed being pampered by his family, and especially by the three young women, who vied with one another for the opportunity to do things for him. He felt extremely weak and slept most of the day, but when he awoke he was always hungry. Later in the day John brought Steven's three children to see him and he held each of them tenderly and assured them he was all right. Andrew was still pale and weak, and Steven insisted he be put to bed immediately. William asked a dozen questions but soon went downstairs to play video games. Jennifer refused to leave his room and sat on a nearby chair for hours, looking scared.

On Sunday evening Heber Clark and Byron Mills came to check on Steven. Steven's family had gone home, but his three dedicated nurses were still there. When Heber and Byron entered the bedroom and saw Steven sitting up eating soup, they grinned at him.

"It's good to see you feeling better," the old man said. "You were in pretty bad shape Friday night."

"I guess I'm too ornery to die."

"No, it's because the Lord protected you. In fact, his protection is over all the people in the Rocky Mountains. It's true many thousands have come down with this flu—how many, Byron?"

"The last I heard it was about one person in five."

Heber nodded. "That's right, one fifth of our population has come down with the flu, but it seems our mortality rate is only fifteen percent while elsewhere it's about thirty percent."

"I agree with you, Brother Clark," Byron said. "The Lord has a job for the Latter-day Saints, and they can't do it if they all die from the flu."

"And what is that job?" Steven asked.

Heber answered for Byron. "It's to build Zion in preparation for the Second Coming. Actually, there will be two main locations for Zion. The first is right here in the Rocky Mountains and the second will be in the middle of the country, with its capital at Independence, Missouri. Technically, the New Jerusalem at Independence is the center *place* of Zion and all other locations are the stakes of Zion." It was obvious to Steven that these men had been talking about this subject before they arrived at his house.

"When do we return to Jackson County?" Steven asked.

Heber chuckled. "That's the big question. I don't know for sure but my guess is the saints will begin to move to Zion within a few years. If I understand the prophecies, not all them will make the trip to Jackson County, but those who do will be called by revelation. In other words, it will be a special calling like any other in the kingdom of God."

"But the country is too dangerous for traveling now," Anastasia said.

Heber answered, "Yes, but it isn't going to get any safer until the country is organized around Zion. I believe the Lord will protect those who travel east to build the Second Zion and those who come there later."

Byron seemed impatient to say something. Steven had the silly impression that he was like a little boy who desperately had to go to the toilet but couldn't get into the bathroom. "Heber, his appointment."

Heber smiled at his young companion's impatience. "Oh yes, Byron and I have a special message for you."

"A message?"

"Yes. This morning the office of the First Presidency phoned President Howard. The stake president relayed the message to Bishop Justesen, but he can't give it to you personally because he's recovering from the flu. In fact, the whole bishopric has the flu. So the bishop called us as your home teachers and asked us to deliver the message for him. In short, it seems the prophet wants to talk to you."

"Josiah Smith? Talk to me? . . . You must be kidding."

Heber chuckled as if he had inside information. "No, I'm serious. He wants to talk to you personally."

"About what?" Steven wondered what he had done wrong. If the prophet had to handle it himself, it must be bad.

Byron snorted and his eyeballs rotated upward with impatience. "Steve, you know they don't tell us things like that. However, if you want my opinion, they probably want to make you the new apostle. You may not be aware of it yet, but Apostle Donaldson died of the flu a few days ago."

"I'm sorry to hear that because he was such a great man," Steven said. "But the idea of me replacing him is ridiculous. I'm certainly not worthy of that. And from what I've seen, they generally call people already serving among the General Authorities, or people they know personally. No, it's got to be something terrible." Steven was irritated when he saw a pleased look on Mary's face.

All those present had an opinion as to why the prophet wanted to speak to Steven. After debating the subject for fifteen minutes, they finally admitted that none of them had the answer, but they were dying to find out.

"When do I have to meet with the prophet?" Steven grumbled.

"Steven, you sound like you have to go to the dentist," Heber said. "Don't worry. I know it's something wonderful. President Howard talked to the prophet personally and told him you were sick with the flu and might not recover. But the prophet didn't seem worried at all and insisted you'd be fine. He said he prefers you come to his office on Wednesday, September 11th, at ten in the morning. Still if you don't feel up to it, we're supposed to postpone the appointment until you feel better."

Mary took the empty soup bowl from Steven and set it on a nearby table. "That in itself is a miracle," she said. "The only way the prophet could know you'd recover was through inspiration. Personally, Steven, I think it proves he'll tell you something wonderful."

"All right, all right, I'll go, unless the flu hits me again."

Everybody in the room laughed at Steven's excessive fear of the prophet, when most church members were willing to stand in line for hours just to get a glimpse of him. Steven spent the next few days in bed, but insisted on doing some translation work on Tuesday. By Tuesday night he felt much better but was still weak. Every day Sarah made sure he ate good food and ingested a strong dose of the essential vitamins and minerals. To build up the iron in his blood she gave him doses of chlorophyll every four hours.

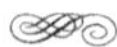

After eating a late dinner on Saturday, Gerald Galloway phoned his associate in China, Janet Griffin. After he had gone through the usual security procedures, he spent a few minutes on pleasantries.

"How is the weather in Hong Kong, Janet?"

"It's normally hot and humid at this time of the year, but since the asteroids hit we have even more rain and we never have a sunny day. It's very depressing."

"I know what you mean. It's the same here in England. The sky is dim and it rains all the time. We seldom go outside anymore . . . And your health?"

"Excellent, and you?"

"Very good, thank you."

"What did you have on your mind, Mr. Galloway?" Obviously, Janet was tired of the small talk.

"How is your operation going in China?"

"We're making good progress in most areas. As I told you at our last UGOT meeting we have managed—in the last two years—to buy the loyalty of most of the key officials in SARFT."

"SARFT?"

Janet answered him with studied patience. "The State Administration of Radio, Film and Television. You know. The government agency that controls the media."

"Yes, of course. Sorry, but I despise all the abbreviations and acronyms which abound these days . . . I understand that agency also controls Internet use in China."

"And doing a good job of it too."

"How many officials have you bought off?"

"Actually, most of them. And we arranged accidents for those who refused us. Gaining control of the media is sometimes a hard task, but here it was fairly easy to do because Chinese society is on the verge of collapse due to inflation and an enormous national debt."

"Well, Janet, I'm happy with your progress. If we control the Chinese media, we will soon have power over their policy. In the larger picture, our control over the global media is just as important as disarming the world's citizens. Continue the good work, but make sure that everything is done in secret. We must remain behind the scenes as much as possible. At least for now."

"Of course, Mr. Galloway."

Gerald smiled. *Janet might be ugly and abrasive, but she never lets silly scruples interfere with the great cause. In fact, she has made great progress in manipulating the Chinese people into hating the very names Jew, American, and Christian. And now that she is gaining control of the Chinese media, her progress will be greatly accelerated. Yes, Janet Griffin is the ideal conspirator and reminds me of myself.*

"Janet, two days ago my confidential secretary called you and told you about the surprise we are preparing for the Americans on September 19. Is that correct?"

"Yes, Mr. Galloway. My colleagues and I have been ecstatic that we are finally taking definite actions against the United States. It's our first truly dramatic maneuver, and it will surely tip the balance of power in our favor."

"Yes, it will. As I indicated before, I want you to make sure the Chinese leaders know about the imminent Russian attack against the United States."

"Naturally. That will not be a problem."

"What do you think the Chinese will do?"

"I'm sure they'll use the Russian attack as an excuse to invade the Russian Federation."

"That's what I expect them to do. But do you think they will use nuclear weapons in their attack?"

"No. I'm sure they won't. They know Russia has the world's largest stockpile of nuclear weapons, and it would therefore be suicide to attack with anything more than conventional weapons."

Gerald believed her and was pleased. He knew that Janet had a profound knowledge of Chinese mentality. He had feared that UGOT might have a gigantic task of cleaning up both Russia and China after it had gained world domination.

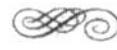

At a quarter to ten on Wednesday morning, Steven and Paul sat in the prophet's outer office. Steven was feeling weak and sick to his stomach. The trip from Provo to Salt Lake City had taken two hours on the bus and had been very difficult. They would have driven there in one of the cars available to them, but it was now nearly impossible to find gasoline. Fortunately, the bus companies still had a limited supply of fuel.

Several times he had wished he would have waited until he was stronger to travel. If it had not been for Paul's support, he would never have made it. At least they had left Provo at seven and were not late. As they sat in the office, Steven hoped that something had come up and the prophet couldn't see him. He noticed the secretary looking at him from time to time with a benevolent smile on her face. He made several conjectures as to what those glances meant and finally concluded she was simply acting the way a prophet's secretary should act.

At ten o'clock she approached and told them the prophet was ready to see them. President Smith met them at the door and instead of shaking their hands, embraced them. Feeling the fragile old body in his arms, Steven was careful to hug him gently.

The prophet immediately knew Steven and addressed him first. "Brother Christopher, it's so good to meet you. How are you feeling after your bout with the flu?"

"A little weak but I'm recovering fast."

"That's wonderful. I knew you would. I certainly appreciate you coming all this way to see me when you don't feel well." The prophet looked at Paul. "And who is this good-looking young man?"

"My brother Paul. Is it okay if he comes in with me?"

"Yes, he is welcome. Two Saint Christophers are better than one, I always say." The prophet chuckled at his little joke. "Please sit down, brethren." The prophet pointed to a couch against one wall of his office. The brothers sat down and Steven surveyed the room. It looked like any other business office except that it had almost no decorations. There was a desk, three chairs, a small couch, and paintings of all the church prophets on the wall opposite the couch. Steven was surprised when the prophet pulled up a chair and sat directly in front of them. "You know, Brother Christopher, I feel I know you already."

"How could you, President? We've never met before."

"The Lord gave me a vision in which he showed me your face."

"My face?" Steven was amazed that the Lord would show the prophet his face. "What was the meaning of the vision?"

"It has to do with the reason I asked you to come to see me. The Lord told me he had chosen certain men for a great work, and he identified the men by showing me their faces and giving their names in a vision. You are one of those men."

"I am? There must be a mistake."

"There is *no* mistake, Brother Christopher."

Steven didn't know what to say and sat there dumbly.

"Don't you want to know what the Lord requires of you?"

"Yes, of course." Steven was thrilled but confused. He suspected that this fragile little man was going to ask him to do something which would change his life forever.

"The Lord has directed me to send many companies of worthy saints to Jackson County, Missouri, one after another. These saints will begin to build New Zion and the holy city. And after they have established the foundations, we will call thousands of others to join them. The men God has chosen will lead those companies to Zion. He has chosen you to head the first company."

"Me? The leader of the first group?" Steven was especially surprised since he couldn't remember having ever been chosen as a leader, except the time he was selected as Elders Quorum president when he was a student at BYU.

"Yes."

"Why me, President? Why not pick someone important in the Church? Someone with experience and wisdom?"

"I'm not sure why God chose you. He didn't tell me. But he always picks people who are strong and have the talents necessary for the work at hand. I believe it's because of your kindness and thoughtfulness and your ability to lead. At any rate, the Lord knows what he is doing."

Steven doubted he had any special qualities that would inspire people to follow him. Yet he dared not question God or the prophet. "When are we supposed to start?" he said without much confidence.

"You will have to wait until next year, sometime near the end of March or in April. That gives you only about six months to prepare. We ask you to choose two assistants and give me their names for approval."

"Is it all right if I pick Paul here and my other brother, John?"

"Yes, that would be more than acceptable to me as long as your stake president, Brother Howard, approves them to go on the trip."

Steven looked at his brother. "What about it, Paul, would you be willing to help lead the first company as one of my assistants?"

Paul's beaming face showed he was delighted. "Absolutely."

Steven smiled at Paul's enthusiasm and said, "What shall we do, President, arrange for caravans of buses or trucks? Wait, I know. Maybe I could set up a system of carpooling. How many people will there be in the first company?"

The prophet looked at him indulgently. "There'll be about a thousand in your company, including men, women, and children."

Steven felt his heart skip a beat. "A thousand! I guess that's the end of the carpooling idea."

Josiah chuckled. "Right. I don't think carpooling would work. Your company will need to take food and supplies for over three months."

"Don't you think it's too dangerous to take women and children on such a trip?"

A sudden twinkle appeared in the prophet's eyes. "You don't think the men could survive without their wives and kids, do you?"

Steven thought a moment and said, "I suppose it might be more difficult. But why couldn't we just take twenty or twenty-five families in the first company? A smaller company would be easier to lead."

"What you don't understand, Steven, is that you will face great perils on your journey, and you will need a large number of armed men to meet those perils. We prefer that your company be composed mostly of families, but we will also call some younger, unmarried people to go too. People like Paul here."

Steven wasn't surprised the prophet knew Paul wasn't married. The Spirit was probably whispering information to him. "When do you intend to send out the later companies?"

"The subsequent companies will be dispatched every three or four months.

It depends on how long it will take us to call them and prepare them. Of course, we won't send out companies during the winter. The prophet paused to let his words sink in. "Your company will be called Pioneer One, the second group Pioneer Two, and so forth."

"I like the name." Steven was glad the prophet didn't want to call the companies by the names of their leaders.

"Now, as to your means of travel, I need to tell you that you won't be able to make the trip in buses, trucks, or cars. Mainly because the fuel supply is seriously depleted. Both gasoline, diesel, and oil are becoming very hard to find, as you probably know already."

"Oh. Uh . . . So we'll travel by train or airplane?"

"No. No trains or airplanes."

"Huh? But how will we get there? Hitchhike?" The second he said it he regretted it. It sounded a bit rude.

Josiah laughed. "No, you won't be able to hitchhike, Steven. You'll have to travel the good old-fashioned way. You'll have to walk."

"Walk? A thousand miles?" Steven wondered if the prophet was putting him on.

"Oh, you can use whatever means you can devise. It may mean you'll have to travel in the same way the early pioneers did when they came west—on foot, horseback, or in covered wagons."

"Why, President? Don't you think that's sort of inefficient?"

"Well maybe but it's the only way you'll be able to get there. It appears you haven't been listening to the news reports lately. Most of the major highways in this country have been blocked, torn up, or blown up by paramilitary groups waging war against the government or by anarchists bent on destroying society. At the same time, insurgents are also destroying the country's major transportation facilities, including airlines, railroads, and bus lines. You're lucky you could get a bus ride to come here.

"And that's not all. Some of the brethren believe that within a few weeks there will be no fuel or electricity available anywhere in the country. Once our primary infrastructure collapses, most Americans will be living in primitive conditions without essential services or medical facilities. It could happen in a very short time."

"I knew these things were happening, but I guess I didn't realize how far it had gone."

The prophet said sadly, "It's already bad and will get much worse. I believe this is happening because of the wickedness of this nation."

For five minutes the prophet reviewed Book of Mormon passages in which the Lord declared that any nation which lived in America must worship the God of this land, Jesus Christ, or they would be led into bondage.

At last he checked his watch and said, "I have another appointment in fifteen minutes so, regretfully, I must hurry. Do you have any final questions?"

"President, I have no experience in preparing people to travel a thousand miles under primitive conditions. How can I gain the information I need to accomplish this task? It seems impossible."

"None of us has that kind of experience, but I know that nothing is impossible if you do your best and depend on God. I think a good place to start is to study the history of the Mormon pioneers and their trek across the plains. Also ask your family and friends for suggestions, and they will lead you to many answers."

"Can I tell them about this call?" Steven asked.

"You haven't accepted the call yet, Brother Christopher. Do you accept it?"

"Yes, of course."

"Good. I'm very pleased. I suggest that at first you inform only your family and close friends. You'll need their advice. But later President Howard will announce your calling in stake priesthood meeting. That's when people will know you have the authority to organize a special company for a very special trip. In addition, I have asked Elder Jason Widtsoe of the Council of the Twelve to give you as much help as he can. He's an expert in Mormon history, especially the Mormon trek across the plains.

"I want you and your assistants to come to his office once every two weeks for instructions, as long as the freeway is still passable. When you come here, the First Presidency will give you further light and knowledge as the Lord gives it to us. We will also instruct you on what you should do once you reach Missouri. Now, do you have any more questions?"

"I can't think of any," Steven said, unsure of himself. "I will probably have questions later."

The prophet went to the door of his office and said, "Veronica, please ask my counselors to come in."

After a short wait, President Bennion Hicks and President Samuel Law came into the room. Steven had no idea why the prophet had sent for them.

"Brother Christopher, please sit in this chair," said the prophet. Steven obeyed and the three men put their hands on his head. The prophet gave him the calling and authority to perform the task of leading the first company of saints to Zion and a blessing which included many details as to how he should accomplish his mission. The blessing lasted five minutes and it gave Steven confidence and a desire to do his best. He no longer felt so unworthy.

Then Josiah said, "We'll also ordain your assistants at a later time."

Later, as the brothers traveled back to Provo, Steven felt weak and faint, but he didn't care. He knew the Lord must be pleased with him or he would not have entrusted him with this sacred calling. The only thing he didn't understand is why the prophet had said, at the end of his blessing, that the Lord had reserved for him an even greater mission than leading the first group of saints to Zion. Without actually saying so, the prophet had implied that this calling was nothing but a test and a preparation for something greater. He was excited that the prophet had accepted his two brothers as his assistants on the journey to Zion, provided that their stake president also gave his approval. Therefore, he asked Paul to find John as soon as they got home so he could talk to him.

An hour after Steven returned, John burst through the front door, his eyes full of questions, and Steven wasted no time in telling him why the prophet had wanted to visit with him.

John embraced him impulsively. "I figured it would be something like that. It's really great news, Steve. One thing I know for sure is that you can handle the job!"

Freeing himself from his brother's bear hug, Steven declared, "Wait, listen to the rest of the news."

"What?"

"The prophet also approved two great assistants to help me lead the saints to Zion."

"Really? Who?"

"You and Paul, if you're willing."

John, who almost always had a lot to say, was momentarily stunned and couldn't utter a word.

"You didn't think you were going to get off the hook so easily, did you? The prophet said he'll be contacting President Howard before you're officially called, but I know there won't be anything to change his mind. There better not be, because I'm going to need you big time. Are you willing to accept the call?"

"Are you kidding?" John said, finally finding his voice. "I've been preparing my whole life for this. We're going to need a lot of supplies—guns, ammunition, food, transportation. It'll take a few weeks to get ready at the very least."

Steven laughed at John's energy and enthusiasm. "I'm glad you can do it so fast. However, I'm sorry to tell you that we won't be able to leave until next April.

John's face fell with his disappointment, but a minute later he recovered and his countenance opened up with excitement and anticipation. "I'd better inform my family and start making preparations. See you later, brother."

Chapter 23

Around eight o'clock in the evening, Alexi Glinka made a desperate call to Gerald Galloway. "Mr. Galloway, our Russian collaborators refuse to go ahead with it."

"Calm down, Alexi." His Russian confederate was calling him from an old-fashioned telephone, and Gerald couldn't see his image, but he heard the anguish in his voice.

"I'm sorry. Forgive me. I'm all right."

"Good. Now what do you mean our collaborators refuse to do it?"

"They refuse to push the buttons. To fire the warheads. The cowards are afraid the Americans will retaliate and destroy Russia. And that's not all. They fear the responses of NATO, the Japanese, the Chinese, and even Afghanistan. One top official complained that Moscow would be the first city annihilated in a nuclear attack against America, because the elaborate missile defense around the city is in a state of ruins."

"Did you try to convince them that the Americans will be incapable of retaliation as I instructed you to do?"

"Yes, my people have taken that message to every friend we have in the Russian government, including their president, but all of them react with terror. They shake their heads vigorously and refuse to discuss the matter further."

"Did you explain to them that attacking America and plundering its resources may be their only chance to save their failing economy?"

"Yes, but it didn't seem to matter."

Gerald was furious at the bungling stupidity of this bragging Russian fool. However, he fought to control his anger. "I thought you told me you had this completely arranged months ago. What about the other members of the former Soviet Union?"

"We went immediately to the Ukrainians, the Belorussians, and the Kazakhs and got exactly the same response. The weaklings all refuse to attack the Americans. We tried everything from calling in their debts to threatening their lives, and still they refused to even consider it."

"And you wait until five days before our planned attack to give me this pleasant news?"

"I'm sorry. We've had so little time and we were not able to talk to the president of Kazakhstan until two hours ago because he has been vacationing somewhere near the Caspian Sea. We put him into the presidency two years ago and I was sure he would do anything we wanted, but when I presented our plan he looked as though I had stabbed him in the heart. Mr. Galloway, is there any way we can set our timetable back?"

"No, it's vital we stay on schedule. The complex and highly coordinated arrangements are already in place. Listen, Alexi, stay where you are. Do nothing until I get back to you. I'll think about this and phone you in an hour or two. Give me your phone number there in Kazakhstan."

Gerald wrote the number down and returned the handset to its receiver. He was angry, but he knew this was the time for cold logic, not emotion, and Gerald prided himself on being a man of reason and science. Passion was the weakness which had destroyed many other great men in history because in a moment of desperation and frustration, they made hasty and unwise decisions which destroyed them and their cause in the end. There was always a way to solve difficult problems. All he had to do was analyze the situation and consider every possible option. After pondering a number of possibilities and rejecting them, he went to his phone and called Lucienne Delisle at her special number in Washington. They had a short intimate exchange, and then Gerald took up the problem of the attack on America. They discussed options for nearly an hour, and when their conversation was over, Gerald knew what he had to do.

With renewed confidence in his genius, he dialed Kazakhstan and his associate answered immediately. "Alexi, we will continue with our plan. We will bomb New York, Chicago, and Los Angeles on Thursday, September 19, at 3:00 p.m., US eastern daylight time."

Alexi was silent for a moment before asking, "How? These people will not cooperate."

"You have loyal infiltrators in sensitive areas in the republics that have nuclear arsenals, don't you?"

"I can assure you we have embedded agents in all those countries."

"Do any of your agents have access to areas where they could create a timely little accident?"

"You mean someone who could aim a couple of missiles and push a few buttons?"

"Yes. Do any of these people have access to the necessary codes."

"Yes. I'm sure of it."

"Alexi, I have always been impressed with your intelligence." Both men laughed and Gerald continued, "Well, can you do it?"

"Hah. That's as easy as pie, as the Americans say. Much easier than getting the Russians or the other leaders to do it themselves. All I need is a little time to make a few arrangements."

"I'm very happy to hear you say that," Gerald said. "Our bombs will have exactly the same delightful effect as if the Russians themselves had pushed the buttons. And just think. We'll be like gods calling fire down from heaven. Now listen, my faithful friend, if you can pull this off, I promise to give you a country or two someday to rule over all by yourself . . . Now, do you think you can give me a progress report on this matter in three days? That means on Tuesday evening, two days before the attack. Remember, I need to coordinate with Lucienne and the others."

"Yes, and this time I'm sure the news will be good," Alexi said. "But, Mr. Galloway, may I pose a few questions?"

"Yes, what are they?"

"What size warheads would you like us to launch and do you wish them to explode in the air or on the surface?"

"Are there any of the old twenty megaton bombs left?"

"Holy moley! Twenty megatons. Most of the Soviet strategic arsenal was converted a long time ago into one megaton warheads, but I think there are twenty or thirty of the big ones left."

Gerald was amused to hear his Russian puppet use an exclamation straight out of a Captain Marvel comic book. He knew that the Russians simply could not get enough of old American pop culture. "Good. I want you to launch three of the big ones if they are available. But five megatons would be sufficient if necessary." Gerald spoke as casually as if he were ordering a steak dinner in a London restaurant. "And I prefer you explode them on the surface. I like the idea of all those millions of tons of pulverized rock being sucked up over a hundred thousand feet into the stratosphere. And the radioactive fallout will be deadly."

"Yes, it certainly will," Alexi said, swallowing hard. "I'm sure those three bombs will kill at least seven to ten million people."

"All I want to know is can you do it?"

"Yes, I have no doubt."

"That's wonderful, my dear friend. Now do you have any further questions?"

"Yes, I would like to know what the allies will do after the bombs fall? You know, the other members of NATO?"

"As I told you before, not a thing. When the chips are down, they'll decide it's not in their own national interest to defend the Americans."

"I hope you're right, Mr. Galloway."

"Don't worry, my friend, I'm always right."

After his conversation with Alexi, Gerald lay on his bed and contemplated the past and the future with great pleasure. Years ago he had beheld a glorious vision late one night—or was it a dream? During that revelation a glorious angel had told him what he must do and how to do it. And at the end of the vision the angel had raised him in great power above all the nations of the earth, and he saw himself enjoying infinite glory and the adulation of multitudes. That same bright being had appeared to him many times since that time to give him further instructions, and because he had followed those directions faithfully, his success had been unfailing. After relishing the memory of those experiences a little longer, Gerald returned to the task at hand.

In five days Lucienne Delisle would give the signal to her operatives to assassinate sixty-seven key figures in the American government at 2:00 p.m. eastern daylight time. An hour later Alexi's warheads would fall from the sky upon three American cities, and the American government should crumble shortly thereafter. The Chinese would blame the Soviets for the attack and give the signal to their colossal army located on their northern border to invade Siberia. Almost certainly, one of their first targets would be the Siberian Railway, which is Moscow's only overland link to the east.

Seeing the superpowers at war, states and ethnic nations all over the world would suddenly feel free to take up arms against their traditional enemies. India against Pakistan. Japan against Russia and China. Somalia against Ethiopia. Turkey fighting Greece. The Irish and the English hating one another again. And maybe, if he was lucky, the Arabs clashing with the Israelis. What a marvelous panorama! Of course, Gerald's thousands of operatives in every region of the world would do their best to provoke these old enemies to anger and war.

In the succeeding months all these nations would exhaust themselves and their resources in the carnage and would seek peace, but find it nowhere. In the meantime, the Americans would wallow in impotent anarchy. At that crucial moment, Gerald Galloway would step forward and, as the richest and most powerful man on earth, seize the leadership of the United Nations and by power and mighty miracles would become the savior of the world.

The idea of miracles gave Gerald sudden pause. *Miracles!* That's it. By producing miracles he could slide into power with much greater ease. While it took the forms of science and technology, supported by well-funded studies, to convince the intellectual elite, it required the mysterious and the miraculous to impress the gullible masses. Maybe he could employ one of those American religious fanatics Lucienne insisted on telling him about as he embraced her passionately that dark night not long ago. Yes, one little guru, prophet, or wizard, carefully instructed and prepared, could go a long way. Then the great prize would be at his complete mercy—the Jews. Hah! He would play with them as a cat does a mouse before he tore them to pieces.

Even now his people were stirring up the Arab nations to attack the Jews. But Gerald knew the result of that type of conflict. Seeing the growing danger, the Jews would probably attack first and have the Arabs on the run within a week or two. But still, such a war could have many pleasant benefits. Not only would it decimate the Arabs, a people whom Gerald hated almost as much as the Jews, but it would also permit him to accuse the Jews of aggression. Then he could gather a mighty army against Israel, motivating them by clever arguments and great promises. The soldiers of his army would be seen as noble heroes because they were punishing the aggressors and saving the world from the worldwide Jewish conspiracy. At the same time, they could feed upon the vast treasures the Jews had stolen from the innocent peoples of the world. Altruism and greed combined. What a useful package.

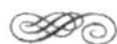

Steven spent the next few days translating a report on the flu pandemic written by experts from the Centers for Disease Control for the French government. The death toll from the virus was so high in France that the French government was anxious to try any feasible remedy as soon as possible. Apparently the CDC scientists, after testing the blood of flu survivors, felt they had developed an effective vaccine against virus H6N1. Dr. Judith Jowett, who had been testing the vaccine, had sought Steven out personally and requested he prepare the translation as soon as possible.

Normally he didn't translate from English to French, but when Judith offered him two thousand dollars in cash from the CDC, he couldn't resist. He awoke early each morning when it was still dark and worked all day on the translation until his mind was numb, anxious to help save as many lives as possible. When he could concentrate no longer, he gathered the children and they took turns reading aloud stories about the Mormon pioneers. He hoped these readings would give him information concerning the trials the pioneers endured in their migrations across the plains and would prepare his children for the hardships they would face in the near future.

On Tuesday night, as he sat alone in his living room, exhausted from a long day of work, Steven thought about what type of vehicles he should use to cross the plains. He figured covered wagons might be best, but he wondered if there was time enough to build them. Besides, he doubted there were many people in the region who had the expertise and equipment necessary to build wagons. He suspected his new pioneers would have to use whatever they had available, especially any vehicle with wheels that could roll across the ground. This meant cars, vans, trucks, trailers of all kinds, and maybe garden carts.

Of course, they would have to remove the heavy parts from the vehicles, including the motors, and they would have to pull the vehicles by any means possible—horses, mules, oxen, or human labor. Steven worried over how they might harness the animals and attach them to the vehicles. No doubt there would be a few fortunate ones who would go in style—people like his brother John, who always seemed prepared for exceptional circumstances. Some modern pioneers would probably plan on bringing their four-wheelers or similar vehicles and enough gasoline to reach the Appalachian Mountains. However, the prophet had told him that people probably wouldn't be able to use motorized vehicles due to the lack of gasoline, so Steven wasn't going to count on it.

On Tuesday, September 17 at 10:00 p.m. Alexi Glinka phoned Gerald Galloway on a secure line.

"What is your report, Alexi?" Gerald said.

"I am happy to tell you that my operatives are in position to fire three missiles at the United States on Thursday at 1:40 p.m., US eastern daylight time. Each missile will be armed with one twenty megaton warhead. The warheads will reach their targets in about twenty minutes and will explode close to the surface for maximum shock and fallout."

"Excellent," Gerald said with pleasure. "Your future is assured, Alexi. Did you have any problems arranging our little nuclear accident?"

"None whatsoever. We have infiltrators in both Russia and Kazakhstan who work in the control bunkers from which the missiles will be launched. They were delighted to have the chance to put the Americans in their place."

"You convinced them that America will not be able to retaliate?"

"Yes, but they didn't seem worried about that. We gave them some fat promises and they jumped at the chance. However, I believe they intend to head for safe places as soon as they push the buttons."

Gerald laughed. "It's amazing what hate and greed can do. The Americans were foolish enough to believe that the Russians and their satellites were no longer a threat after the Cold War ended in 1991, and now the armament of those harmless enemies will soon be the instrument of the downfall of the American government."

"Yes, that shows a curious gullibility."

"I want to know, Alexi, whether or not you have analyzed and rechecked every detail of this operation. Are you sure nothing can go wrong?" Gerald had other ways of verifying the activities of his associates, but he also found it useful to make them commit themselves.

"I'm absolutely positive."

"Good. I'll contact you again after our three presents are delivered. Now I need to break off so I can call Lucienne Delisle in the States to confirm our tactical terminations."

"Yes, yes, I'm happy you remembered that. Good-bye, Mr. Galloway."

Gerald shook his head in disgust as he dialed Lucienne's private number. Why was he surrounded by such idiots? Alexi was a fool to think that he, the master planner, would ever neglect to coordinate with Lucienne on such a vital matter. Was he the only truly intelligent person on the earth? Only the brilliant ones, such as himself and Lucienne Delisle, were worthy of being rulers. The rest were better off as slaves.

Chapter 24

Two days later, at eleven thirty in the morning, Steven was in his study finishing his translation of the CDC medical report for the French government. Indeed, it appeared that the CDC scientists had created a vaccine which showed excellent promise in the fight against virus H6N1. Steven was exhilarated. Not only had he finished the translation within the time limit imposed by Dr. Jowett Jewel, but also he knew the report would offer hope and comfort to the French. The plague had already killed more than one hundred and twenty million people and was characterized in news reports as the worst plague of all time, except perhaps for HIV, which experts believed had infected about three hundred million people worldwide. The difference was that while H6N1 killed twenty-nine percent of its victims within twelve hours, AIDS killed its victims slowly and relentlessly over a period of ten to twelve years.

Steven's thoughts were interrupted by María Ramírez calling him from the top of the basement stairs. "What is it, María?"

"Your brother is here and wants to talk to you."

Steven wondered which brother it was. "María, please tell him to come downstairs to my office. Thanks."

John came plunging down the stairs and hurried into Steven's office. "Hey, Steve. I see the generator is still working like a charm."

"Yes, the new power station in Orem gives us electricity most of the time, but it shuts down several times a week. Fortunately, I have the generator, thanks to you. So what's up?"

"Obviously you haven't heard the news."

"What news?" Steven wondered what he would do without John keeping him up to date on every new development in the world.

"The assassinations," John said matter-of-factly as he tried to read Steven's translation on the flu vaccine.

"Assassinations!"

"Yep. The reports say sixty top U. S. government leaders and military heads were assassinated at about the same time in different areas of the country, many of them in Washington and a few abroad."

Steven was stunned. "Sixty!"

"Yep. Including the president, the vice president, and the speaker of the house. They also got the secretary of state, the joint chiefs of staff, and the head of the NSA. Apparently there were seven other unsuccessful attempts on other officials. Three of them are in hospitals in critical condition."

"But when?" Steven asked.

"Around eleven o'clock mountain time. It looks like someone is trying a *coupe*— . . . How do you say it?"

"*Coup d'état.*"

"That's it. It kind of reminds me of the conspiracy to assassinate John F. Kennedy in 1963. Only this time the conspirators seem to be after the entire government, not simply the presidency."

Steven was numb with shock and he waited for his brother to admit it was all a joke. But John continued to look at him seriously without saying another word.

"Have they found out who was involved?"

"Nope. They say it's too early in the investigation. As usual the feds and the cops are running around like chickens with their heads off and, sooner or later, they'll find some patsies to take the rap. This time, however, they won't get away with denying it was a conspiracy."

"What is President Miller doing about it? Has he appeared on TV?"

"Didn't you hear me? He was one of the first to go. The government is in a state of chaos. Don't you remember how many times I told you that the American government would have to fall as one of the signs of the last days? It was prophesied by Joseph Smith."

Steven struggled to get up from his chair. His terrible illness had left him weak and tired all the time, and he wondered if he'd ever be his old self again. "Let's go upstairs and find some news on TV. This can't be as bad as you're saying."

John took his brother by the arm to help him up the stairs. "I'm not exaggerating. Oh, by the way. I called the family and they'll be here any minute now. I hope that's okay with you."

"Good. Did you invite any of our friends?"

"Don't worry, Steve, your harem will be here too."

"My harem? I thought they were my sister wives." Steven knew it wasn't all three of the women he wanted to see, but only one of them.

"No, Paul and I decided the word harem is more like it."

Jerry Gleason swore as he threw a shovelful of dirt on the family trench shelter. His twin, twelve-year-old Tommy, eyed him from the other side of the mound of dirt. "What's the matter?"

"I'm sick of all this work. Dad gets this idiotic idea to build a bomb shelter and all we do for four days is slave to satisfy him. Mom and Erika don't do a blasted thing to help. Especially Erika. Dad makes her stay home from school to help and all she does is stand around twiddling her thumbs and ordering us around—as if she really knew something. And I've even heard Mom say it's a harebrained idea to build a bomb shelter in a time of peace."

"Yeah, it's not fair." Tommy complained. "Phew! I'm glad we're almost done. The only good thing is we didn't have to go to school this week."

"Oh, yeah, I forgot about that," Jerry said.

The shelter was four and a half feet wide, five feet deep, and twenty-five feet long. Its roof was supported by sixty ten-foot poles. The family had sealed the spaces between the poles with cloth, sticks, leaves, and roofing material. Next they had covered the poles with a sloping mound of earth sixteen inches deep. Over this they had placed a huge sheet of thick plastic. The final step was to cover the plastic with another mound of earth thirty-six inches thick. Elmer Gleason, the boys' father, proudly claimed that his homemade shelter would completely protect ten people from nuclear radiation and blast. The family had also made their own fallout meter and shelter-ventilating pump, and had furnished the shelter with enough food and water and other supplies to last them three weeks.

Elmer came out of his house mopping his face and neck with a towel. Even though the sun was partially covered by dust clouds, the day was very hot and he had taken a short break to make a cold drink. When he reached the shelter he poured some lemonade for the boys and admired his handiwork, pleased that it was almost completed. Fortunately, when the passion to build the shelter had hit him, he was on swing shift at the Longview Fibre Company two miles away, and this allowed him to work on his project from early in the morning until three o'clock when he had to leave for work. He was especially proud of his two sons, who worked on the shelter as hard as their father, even though they moaned and groaned constantly. The two boys always became excited when their father came up with some new and ingenious project.

"Is the roof done?" Elmer asked his sons.

"Yes," Jerry said. "Can we stop now?"

"Not yet. We still have a few details to take care of."

The boys grumbled for a while but finally quieted down. All morning they had discussed the idea of camping out in the new shelter and Tommy had been chosen to make the request. "Hey, Dad," Tommy said, "is it all right if Jerry and me camp out tonight in the shelter?"

"Absolutely." Elmer said. "I think it's a good idea for you boys to get used to being in the shelter for long periods of time. The only thing I ask is that you don't play with the ventilator or the fallout meter. And I want you to leave the blast door open."

The boys promised, and Jerry said, "Okay, Dad. By the way, why in the heck did we build this thing anyways?"

"Yeah, why?" Tommy said. "If the Russians attacked us, wouldn't they blow up Chicago? And that's more than fifteen miles from here. How could the bomb hurt us this far away?"

"Well, it might," Elmer replied. "It depends on the size of the warhead and whether it's exploded at the surface or high in the air." Elmer had been studying the latest government book on nuclear survival and considered himself somewhat of an expert. "At this distance a one-megaton warhead probably wouldn't harm us much, but the blast from a twenty-megaton bomb would destroy most of the houses in this area and kill a lot of people. If the same bomb were exploded at or near the surface we'd get hit with lots of deadly radiation, even though we're upwind of the city. In other words, if the blast didn't get you, the radiation would." Seeing the fear in his sons' eyes, Elmer added quickly, "Unless, of course, you had a bomb shelter like this one. In that case you'd be perfectly safe."

"Hi there, Elmer. Still playing soldier?" It was Luke Small, the next-door neighbor. He had been visiting the Gleasons every day that week to check their progress on the bomb shelter, asking Elmer question after question, always with a sly grin. He especially quizzed him about the ways in which the Russians represented a threat. Elmer answered the questions carefully but always with a red face.

"Funny, Luke," Elmer replied. "You're always full of jokes. The shelter is almost done and when the bombs fall we'll be protected while you'll be burnt toast."

Luke chuckled. "And what do the experts say the chances are of the

Russians or anyone attacking the US with nuclear weapons? The last I heard it was about one chance in a million."

"You have to be pretty dumb to listen to the so-called experts. They're always trying to make profound statements about everything under the sun and more often than not, their predictions turn out to be nothing but the rants of windbags."

After laughing even harder, Luke put on a face of mock seriousness and said, "I know. Your Mormon prophet told you to do it and you're following orders. He's seen the coming destruction in mighty vision and he told the members to prepare for the worst. That's it, isn't it? All the Mormons around here will be saved while us Gentiles will suffer a horrible death from a fire cloud or rot away from radiation poisoning."

Elmer really liked Luke Small. He knew Luke was the kind of man who would do anything to help somebody in need. He was the best possible neighbor, but he still enjoyed teasing Elmer about his religious beliefs. Elmer knew that deep in Luke's heart he respected the Mormons and especially the Gleasons.

"No, you're wrong," Elmer said. "The prophet didn't give us any instructions this time. I felt I needed to do it now. It was a personal thing."

"A personal thing. But I thought the Mormons didn't do anything until their leaders told them to."

"Wrong again, funny boy," Elmer chided. "We believe in following the directions of inspired leaders, but we also believe worthy members—and sometimes even you Gentiles—can receive revelation from the Holy Ghost in special situations."

"Are you saying the Holy Ghost is the one who told you to build a bomb shelter in spite of the fact there's no threat whatsoever?"

Elmer grinned at Luke's trick question. "Yes, I believe he did, and you don't know for sure there is no threat."

"Maybe not, but I do know your Holy Ghost has been very busy lately because there's people all over this neighborhood building bomb shelters, and not all of them are Mormons."

"How do you know that?"

"Hey, I see them every day in my hardware store. Why, we've had so many requests for shovels, plastic sheeting, roofing materials, cement, fuel, and other bomb shelter stuff, that I can't keep up with it. When the rush first began I got suspicious and started asking people questions. The answer was always the same: they're building a bomb shelter just in case. Most of them can't afford professional shelters so they do homebuilt ones."

"When did all this start?"

"About two months ago. And that's not all. We've had a flood of people coming from Chicago and heading west. They bought every bit of camping equipment I had. At least their needs are different from those of the bomb shelter types."

Elmer was amazed. "Have you questioned them too?"

"What do you think? I'm a good businessman and I need to watch the trends." Elmer could tell that Luke was anxious to reveal what he had learned. "Anyhow, I discovered that some of them are Mormons who suddenly got the *urge*, like you did, to go off half-cocked and do something crazy. They *feel*, for reasons known only to the mystic forces, that Chicago is suddenly a dangerous place and they need to head west and not stop until they reach the Rocky Mountains. They tell me they're obeying the words of their prophet to gather to Utah and also the *promptings*—whatever on earth that means—of their Holy Spirit to leave Chicago. By the way, your Holy Spirit isn't a very good planner. On the spur of the moment he tells all these people to drop everything and run and he doesn't even give them time to pack provisions or valuables. Personally, I think if he was going to get involved in all this, he should have started preparing them earlier."

"Come now, Luke, you talk like a pagan but I happen to know you're one of the best Christians there is. The only thing I ask is that you be a little more respectful."

Luke tried to look repentant. "I'm sorry, neighbor. I didn't mean to offend you. But what I'd like to know is why the Holy Spirit bothers to talk to all these Gentiles and tells them to get ready if, as you're always saying, the Mormons are the only ones who have the only true religion."

Elmer mopped the sweat from his face again and then poured Luke a cup of lemonade. "Because they're God's children too and he loves them."

Luke grinned. "Well, I suppose you're right there. So what's the bottom line here, neighbor? Are you going to let us use your shelter too? You know, in the infinitely remote chance that something bad will happen."

"Definitely, if you survive the blast."

Luke's eyes widened all at once. "Survive the blast? How do we do that? How will we know?"

Elmer figured he'd tease Luke a little. "Well, Luke, that's a problem for all of us. Getting to the shelter in time. We might not make it in time ourselves. All I can say is, if you're home and see a sudden blinding light in the east, you'd better come a running. You might just make it in time."

"How much time would we have?"

"It depends on the size of the bomb, the distance the blast travels, and the kind of obstructions it meets. Since we can't be sure of the speed of the shockwaves, we plan to get into our shelter long before the bomb drops."

Luke was puzzled. "But how will you know when to do it?"

"The Holy Spirit will tell us."

"Okay, when that happens, will you let us know?"

Elmer smiled at Luke's change of attitude. "Of course. That's what good neighbors are for."

"Look, Elmer, when will your shelter be done?"

"We just finished it."

Luke sighed with relief. "Good! But I'm still confused about one thing."

"What's that?"

"I noticed you put up a 'house for sale' sign several weeks ago. So why are you building a bomb shelter if you're going to move?"

"Because I got the strong impression the other day that I will need the shelter before the house sells."

"The Holy Ghost again?"

"I believe so."

After mumbling a few words Elmer couldn't hear, Luke said, "Where are you going when you sell your house?"

"To Utah."

"That figures. Look, I've got to go now. See you later." Luke headed for his house, looking back from time to time, as if he were reluctant to take his eyes from the shelter.

Elmer watched him until he disappeared and then turned to his sons. "All right now, let's get Mom and Erika out here to see if they like our masterpiece."

Elmer hurried into the house and called for his daughter and wife. Even though the female members of the family had thought it pretty silly to build a bomb shelter, they had done their share of the work and were anxious to see the finished product. They dropped what they were doing and followed Elmer outside.

"Okay, everybody inside," Elmer shouted as if he were a sergeant directing the movements of his squad. One by one his family walked down the dirt stairway at one end of the trench.

"Mother, will you please light an oil lamp or two?" Elmer asked. "Erika, I assign you to be the first person to pull on the ventilator rope." Erika was an intelligent, athletic girl of seventeen and Elmer knew she would work the KAP ventilator at the other end of the trench for a long time without complaint, while his sons would be whining about being tired in two minutes.

He checked his watch and saw it was almost one o'clock. He still had two hours before he had to leave for work. "Okay, I'm coming down after you." Elmer took one more look around the work site to see if he had missed anything. Satisfied, he started down the stairway when suddenly he saw from the corners of his eyes the entire eastern sky burst into dazzling brightness. Instinctively he covered his eyes and face with his hands and hurled himself forward. As he tumbled to the bottom of the trench, he felt a wave of intense heat scorch the earth around the upper part of the entrance. Although his wife had lit two oil lamps, he could see nothing and he stumbled around trying to get his bearings.

"What was that light?" Tommy demanded.

"Quick! Help me with the door." Elmer screamed, knowing he had less than a minute before the blast wave struck. Elmer had built a massive door five inches thick which fit into a recess in one of the walls of the trench. By rotating the door into place, he would be able to block off the entire end of the trench near the base of the stairway. Elmer's daughter rushed to his side and together they moved the door into place. Elmer still couldn't see, but he knew every inch of the shelter. To secure the door from the inside he inserted several thick blocks of wood into holes dug into the walls of the trench near the door. When the barrier was in place, Elmer sighed with relief, knowing his family would be protected from most of the effects of the blast.

"What's going on, Dad?" Jerry screeched.

"Everyone into your hole," Elmer shouted. Quickly his family found the recesses they had dug for themselves in the walls of the trench. They had discussed this safety measure several times during family home evenings and knew what to do.

"Is this it?" his wife cried.

Because of the horror of it, he had trouble answering. Finally he stammered, "Yes. Nuclear explosion. Over Chicago. A big one. Blast will hit us any second."

All at once the shelter was struck by a tremendous force. It was as if a mighty tornado had fallen from the sky directly onto the homemade structure. The earth shook violently and the wind roared. Elmer feared the shelter would collapse at any moment, and he and his family would be swept away in the holocaust.

But the structure held firm in spite of the savage assault. With great sadness Elmer thought of his neighbors and knew that those who had not prepared wouldn't have a chance. After a few minutes he noticed that things were beginning to quiet down. He felt an immense relief and a deep sense of gratitude toward God for giving him the crazy idea to build the shelter.

"Come on, Dad, it's over," Jerry said. "We can get out now."

"Yeah, Dad, I'm sick of this shelter already," Tommy said.

"Elmer," his wife said. "We've got to help our neighbors."

"I'm sorry—we can't go out. If we do the radiation will kill us." Elmer was relieved that his eyesight was beginning to return.

"There's radiation?" Erika asked. "I thought you said some kinds of nuclear explosions aren't very dangerous in that way, especially at this distance?"

"That's true if the bomb explodes high in the air and downwind, but I'm sure this one was a surface explosion. So the radiation will be deadly. I think we have a few hours before the fallout reaches us but I don't want to take any chances. If we leave the shelter to help others, we may get a fatal dose of radiation. In fact, we'll probably have to stay here for two or three weeks." His family moaned. "Be grateful. At least we're alive and we have plenty of food and water and all the other comforts of home. Don't worry. In a few hours I'll take the meter outside for a radiation check, and I'll do it again tomorrow morning. Maybe we won't have to live here the whole three weeks."

Elmer hunkered down against the cool wall of the trench and grimly imagined the despair and destruction which must have struck his neighborhood. He thought of Luke and his family and said a short prayer in their behalf, but he feared the worst. During the prayer he heard some muffled sounds above him.

"Quick. Somebody help me with this door," Elmer yelled.

Erika hurried to his side and together they removed the blocks of wood and pulled the door open. Elmer heard a voice again and recognized it as that of Luke Small. To make himself heard, Luke had to shout over the screaming of the wind and the sound of distant explosions. "Can we come down?" Luke called.

"Yes!" Elmer hollered back, excited. As Luke and his wife and two children entered the shelter, Elmer was astonished to see they were not injured. "Are you guys okay?" he asked.

"We're fine," Luke said smiling. "How about you?"

"Completely protected." After they had closed off the entrance again, Elmer turned and looked at his guests with amazement in the dim light of the lamps. "What I want to know is how you survived the blast."

Luke looked too embarrassed to answer, so Camille Small answered for her husband. "Well, early this morning Luke put one of his employees in charge of the store and spent the entire morning building a shelter in our basement. A little cubby hole for four made of books, bricks, pillows, sacks of flour, two tables, five chairs, and every piece of junk in the basement. Right before the bomb hit, he made us come down into the basement to admire his work. So when we saw the windows light up all of a sudden, we squeezed inside the shelter and waited it out. Later he had the nerve to force us out of the shelter and rush us over here. Our house was almost completely destroyed and I didn't even have time to look for our photo albums."

Elmer said, "It's a good thing he made you come, or you might receive a fatal dose of radiation." Seeing that Camille had no further interest in complaining, Elmer looked at Luke and laughed. "No chance in the world for a nuclear attack, huh? And while you make fun of my preparations, there you are, building your own homemade shelter."

"Oh, come on," Luke objected. "It only took a few hours this morning. After seeing so many people building shelters, I simply decided to take no chances." Luke sat down on one of the stools Elmer had placed inside the shelter. "By the way, my tiny shelter did a good job of resisting the heat and the blast."

"I'm grateful for that," Elmer said. "Not only because your shelter saved your lives, but also because we may have to remain in this trench for as long as three weeks."

Luke shot Elmer a surprised look. "Why would you be grateful for *that*?"

"Why? Because that should give me plenty of time to convert you to Mormonism and talk you into moving to Utah with us." Everyone laughed at that.

Before long they turned on the battery-powered radio to get news on the nuclear attack. The news was much worse than they had expected. Not only had Chicago been bombed, but also New York and Los Angeles. And shortly before the nuclear attacks, sixty national leaders had been assassinated by terrorists.

Steven's family and friends seemed spellbound as they watched the continuous news stories on television in Steven's living room. The reports on the assassinations went from one city to another, describing the circumstances of the atrocities in detail and returning to the studio regularly to present the opinions of six well-known commentators. Most of them believed the crimes were committed by one or more Middle East terrorist groups—jihadists—trying to destroy the United States, which the terrorists described as the Great Satan. The most likely candidate was al-Qaeda.

One lead newscaster made a short review of terrorist attacks against the

US. He said that militant Islamic groups had been exploding bombs at US embassies and populated sites in the States for many years, and that the US government had been powerless to stop the fanatics in spite of intense military security and continuous retaliatory strikes against terrorist strongholds.

The newscaster went on to say that al-Qaeda terrorists had plunged two passenger airliners into the two skyscrapers of the World Trade Center in New York City on September 11, 2001. Also they had run a third airliner into the Pentagon building a short time later and had unsuccessfully commandeered a fourth airliner. As a result, the US government had declared the War on Terror and had created the Department of Homeland Security. Finally in May 2011, the leader of al-Qaeda, Osama bin Laden, was killed in Pakistan by Joint Special Operations Command forces working with CIA special forces.

The question was now, continued the newscaster, whether or not al-Qaeda was also responsible for the recent assassinations.

At ten minutes after noon, the assassination coverage was interrupted abruptly, and the face of Carlton Morley, an important broadcaster for NBC news, appeared on the screen. "We just received a special news bulletin," he said with studied self-control. "A spokesman for the United States Air Force has reported to this station that three American cities have been attacked with nuclear weapons. Ten minutes ago New York City and Chicago were struck with what the military believes were fifteen- or twenty-megaton nuclear warheads, one in each city. Seven minutes ago Los Angeles was also attacked with a large nuclear warhead. The authorities are unable to determine the origin of these attacks and why they were not immediately detected by NORAD. At first, military experts thought the attacks had come from Russia or one of the former Soviet republics, but all of those nations have vigorously denied any responsibility.

"The government cannot offer any explanation as to why only three of our cities were attacked because any nation making a nuclear attack against this nation would be in immediate danger of annihilation by an American retaliatory response. Therefore, to make a limited attack, as this seems to be, would be an act of suicide. Unfortunately, at this time the authorities do not know for sure who is responsible but are certain that one or more of the nations with nuclear capabilities is responsible.

"Another problem lies in the fact that no one seems to know who has the authority to order retaliatory strikes. As a result, what's left of the government is taking a wait-and-see position. It is the belief of this commentator that the recent assassinations are the cause of the government's confusion and vacillation and that at this time there is, in effect, no government to direct the nation.

Please stay tuned to this channel for further developments." Steven lowered the sound so he could listen to the opinions of those in the room.

"Did you hear the anger in that guy's voice?" John exclaimed.

"I don't blame him," Paul said. "After all the billions of dollars the government has spent on nuclear defense and detection, now it can't even identify who the enemy is."

Steven's father nodded and said, "It's no wonder the government is taking a wait-and-see stance, because the assassinations have left no one with the authority to make decisions."

"All those people killed!" Mary cried.

"And thousands more injured and homeless," Andrea said. "It's too horrible to imagine."

"I think the Russians did it," José suggested.

"Or one of the other communist states," Margarete Borisovich offered.

"I believe it was the Chinese," Sarah said. "It may be their bid for world dominance."

Sergei shook his head. "The trouble with that theory is the Chinese have been on relatively good terms with the United States for two decades now. China wants to continue receiving American goods and technology. Also, Chinese consumer goods have flooded the American market. On the other hand, the former Soviet republics are in a state of economic disaster and this might be their last attempt to remain a world power. Therefore, I agree with José and my wife."

Paul said, "But if any of the old Soviet republics started a nuclear war, they would face retaliation from enemies all along their southern borders. Most of those enemies now have nuclear arsenals."

"I can't explain why," Anastasia said, "but I *feel* that some Islamic terrorist group is responsible."

Steven was not surprised to hear Anastasia analyze the situation by feelings alone. "I could agree with you if it were a biological attack, because even a small group of determined fanatics without vast resources could easily wage germ warfare, but the use of nuclear weapons requires sophisticated technology and extensive means." Anastasia puckered her mouth in protest, but no one paid any attention.

"My hope is that whoever did it will not extend their attack to the rest of our country," Andrea said.

Steven touched the volume control and they continued to listen to the news reports all afternoon, but there was little additional information. At five o'clock Carlton Morley returned to the television screen. "It has been estimated that the nuclear warheads have killed or injured more than eleven million people in the greater metropolitan areas of the three cities. The cities are now on fire and it's expected the death toll will increase . . . At this time, however, there have been no further attacks on American cities.

"In another report we have learned that a large number of people evacuated New York and Chicago in the days preceding the attack and are therefore alive and safe. Some observers believe that at least three hundred thousand individuals escaped destruction in this way." The anchorman paused and listened to a message in his earphones. "All right, I have just received word that we have a special report from Beijing, and we will now join our correspondent Raymond Carter on location."

A young man appeared on the screen, standing in the center of a busy square. "This is Raymond Carter in Beijing, China. Our news team in this city has obtained reports from certain top Chinese authorities that indicate the warheads launched against three American cities originated from Russia and Kazakhstan. Shortly after the launching of the missiles, Chinese officials tried to relay their information to the president of the United States and other American officials but were not able to reach them. Consequently, the Chinese contacted our NBC news team with the information. Chinese authorities have also asked us to report that the People's Republic of China has begun the invasion of Siberia with an army of three million troops to obtain justice for their American allies. It seems the Chinese are not using nuclear weapons at this time but their non-nuclear weapons are highly sophisticated and have great destructive power. The Russian Federation has fifty divisions in southern Siberia and is expected to offer stiff resistance. Now, back to you, Carlton."

"So if we can believe the Chinese government," Carlton said, "the ICBMs were launched from Russia and perhaps Kazakhstan. Our news team in Beijing believes, and this reporter agrees, that the Chinese are using the nuclear attack against the United States as an excuse to invade the former Soviet states with vastly superior forces. It is obvious then that the Chinese have refused to accept the claims of Russia and Kazakhstan that the ICBMs were not launched from their soil. Several of our experts on the old Soviet Union believe that the launchings were acts of sabotage by communist dissidents operating in Russia and its satellites. Let me make an important point, however. These ideas as to who is responsible are nothing but conjecture. The American government is in such a state of disarray that it is unable to issue reliable—"

The picture and sound suddenly disappeared and left a white flickering screen.

"Darn. It's doing that more and more," John complained.

"Is it my television set?" Steven asked.

"No, it's a signal problem from the network," John replied. "The television and radio broadcasting systems are breaking down all over the country. There are only two national TV networks still operating and three radio networks, and even they don't work for more than a few hours at a time."

After dinner the Christophers and their friends continued to listen to news reports on radio and were relieved to hear that there were still no further nuclear attacks on American cities. On the other hand, they were alarmed by continuous descriptions of the tidal wave of violence and anarchy which was rapidly spreading across the country like a deadly plague. Copycat assassins began to execute state and federal officials by the hundreds. Insurgents increased their assaults against federal installations all over the country, and tens of thousands of police and military personnel continued joining the mobs in the looting and destruction.

Indeed, the federal government had collapsed in a day. Even states took up arms against their own citizens and against other states. It seemed the country had gone mad at the spectacle of the collapse of central authority. There was no peace and safety anywhere, except in the Rocky Mountains where millions tried to succor one another, and six hundred thousand armed priesthood holders were on regular patrols.

Chapter 25

The Egyptians made a sudden attack against Israel at 7:00 a.m. on Friday. Five hundred and forty-eight Egyptian MiG fighters assaulted Israeli airbases in an effort to gain air supremacy. Egyptian leaders rejoiced when the reports began to arrive indicating that their pilots had surprised the Israeli Air Force and had destroyed about five hundred F-15 Eagles and F-16 Falcons, and fifty Cobra helicopters on the ground. By 9:00 a.m. most of the Egyptian warplanes had regrouped to provide air support for the Egyptian army rushing through the northern part of the Negev Desert.

Fifteen hundred laser-armed tanks and an army of two hundred thousand troops headed toward Jerusalem and Tel Aviv with the intention of destroying Israel once and for all. Without warning, this army had raced past the UN peace-keeping force of two thousand troops stationed near the Israeli border. Obviously, the Egyptians had not wished to warn the Israelis by asking the UN to remove their forces before the attack. By 10:30 a.m. the Egyptians closed the Suez Canal and an hour later they blockaded the Gulf of Aqaba at the Straits of Tiran. Suddenly, Israel had no southern access through the city of Elat to the Red Sea and the Indian Ocean.

At the same time the other Arab nations, including Jordan, Syria, Lebanon, and Iraq made their assault on all fronts with the mightiest army ever to come against Israel. Syrian and Iraqi MiGs attacked Israeli airfields in the north at the moment the Egyptians began their air attack. The speed and violence of the attacks were far beyond anything attempted before by the Arab Alliance. Iraq controlled Jordan's army and the combined force totaled over three hundred thousand soldiers. Iraq also began to unleash their improved Scud missiles armed with powerful conventional weapons and possessing a range of over nine hundred miles.

The Israeli parliament had almost waited too long. For years a liberal majority had convinced the Knesset and the government to handle the Arabs with caution and diplomacy. But finally, fifteen days earlier, Hazony had convinced the leaders to give him the authority to activate the reserves and to control the armed forces as he saw fit. Hazony, as Minister of Defense, had never trusted the liberals and had been making secret preparations for years.

The Iraqis boasted that the Arab coalition would conquer Israel within four or five days and that their powerful Scuds would terrorize Israel and quickly reduce the beautiful and flourishing state to a heap of rubble. Proud of the amazing accuracy of their new missiles, Iraq began to lob them on western Jerusalem where the Jews had built the prosperous New City. Unfortunately, the Iraqis miscalculated when they launched one volley of Scuds and the missiles fell directly upon the third most holy shrine in the Arab world.

The marvelous Dome of the Rock and its surrounding monastery and temples in the Old City were obliterated in one gigantic fireball. When the news of the disaster became general, all of the combatants in the region, numbed by shock, ceased fighting, trying to comprehend the magnitude of the calamity. During the half hour of calm the Iraqis, unwilling to take responsibility for the monstrous act, released the information that the Israelis had sabotaged the sacred Moslem shrine in their hatred of Islam. Hearing this report, the Arab armies renewed their assault with blind fury.

Friday morning Gerald Galloway arranged a secure conference call with Lucienne Delisle in New York City and Alexi Glinka in Moscow. The worldwide telephone network was becoming increasingly less dependable, and Gerald was concerned that this call and his future communications by telephone or cell phone might soon be compromised. Two weeks earlier he had hired a prominent firm in London to come up with a dependable radio wave system so his business dealings, as he explained it to the company, would not be interrupted.

After giving his secret name Gerald said, "I'm proud of both of you. As you know, yesterday afternoon the American government fell like a hawk pierced with a deadly arrow. And I have you two to thank for it. Lucienne, your assassins terminated sixty essential leaders within ten minutes. Most important, you eliminated the president, the vice president, and the speaker of the House. Only six targets escaped your efforts. As a result, you broke the back of the entire U. S. power structure with one concerted blow and the Americans were helpless. And you, Alexi, you gave them the coup de grâce just at the right moment with three well-placed warheads. Remember when I told you it would be the easiest thing in the world to do, and you doubted me?"

"Yes, Mr. Galloway, you were right as usual," Alexi said.

"Gerald, I never doubted you. Not for a second," Lucienne objected.

"Perhaps . . . but now I have new instructions for both of you. Lucienne, I want you to visit me here in England. I would like you to come on October 17. Organize your flight crew and fly here in your Challenger 604, the jet you retrofitted with machine guns and cannons. The airways are becoming increasingly dangerous, and you may have to defend yourself. Alexi, I want you to follow the plans we developed at the meeting we held here in July. Do your best, according to the plans, to foment war between the Russian Federation and all her enemies. Do you understand?"

"Yes, Mr. Galloway," Alexi replied.

"Good. I have many surprises and rewards for both of you. All you have to do is obey my instructions without question as you have in the past. You should have no problem contacting me and other associates because in a few weeks I plan to supply all our people with our own radio communications system so we do not have to depend upon the regular telephone network. Hurry, Lucienne, I'm waiting for you with open arms. And you, Alexi, I will embrace you also before too many weeks have passed."

"What did you think of the Arab invasion of Israel this morning?" Lucienne said.

"I am very happy that it is going as planned," Gerald replied. "Too bad the pitiful Arabs do not realize that Menachem Hazony has been preparing for an Arab assault for years. And he has done it in defiance of the wishy-washy Israeli parliament. But in spite of his preparations, Israel will have to fight for its life. The Russians have trained the Arabs well and have tried to teach them how to avoid the mistakes of the past. In the end, however, Israel will defeat the Arab invaders. I'm afraid that's inevitable.

"However, the Arabs shall have served our purpose by helping to exhaust Israeli power and Israeli hope of ever finding peace. We'll try hard to use our propaganda machine to turn their victory into a public relations nightmare. Well, that's all I have for now. Good-bye until later, my good friends."

"One more thing, Gerald," Lucienne said. "I believe I've found the prophet you wanted. He's exactly the man we need, and I know you'll be pleased."

"Where did you find him?"

"In Utah. He used to be a Mormon, but now he spends much of his time attacking his former church."

"He sounds promising," Gerald said. "Listen, Lucienne, I trust your judgment. Still we need to continue looking for other holy men to do all the work I have planned for them. Maybe your prophet may eventually turn out to be their leader and their inspiration."

"Yes, I'm sure he will. But when do you want to meet my prophet?"

"Not yet, but soon."

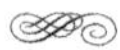

To escape the invading armies, David Omert and Chaim Yehoshua drove westward on the expressway leading away from Jerusalem. As members of the Israeli Knesset, it was important for them to escape from their enemies and join other national leaders in Tel Aviv. If they were captured by the Arabs, they would be executed instantly.

"Why didn't they listen to Hazony earlier?" Chaim said frantically. "Now we haven't got a chance."

"Calm down." David said. "I've talked to Hazony a dozen times in the last few months, and I'm telling you that he was expecting this. He said he was making secret preparations in case the Arabs made a surprise attack. He said he'd have to do it on his own authority in spite of the liberal weaklings in the government."

"Well, he'd better do something fast because in a day or two there won't be any Israel."

David reached out and switched on the radio, hoping to hear the latest news on the war. He dialed until he found a clear station.

". . . three hundred Israeli warplanes are attacking the Egyptian army as we speak. Reports indicate that our F-16s have destroyed one hundred and sixty Egyptian MiG-29s after two hours of fighting, while we have lost only eighteen fighters. At this moment, air and ground battles are taking place north of the city of Beersheba. An unconfirmed bulletin states that the Israeli army has finally stopped the Egyptian advance. Approximately ninety Israeli aircraft are now attacking Syrian and Iraqi units near the Sea of Galilee and west of Jerusalem, and other squadrons of fighters and bombers have penetrated into Iraq and are destroying Iraqi Scud launching sites. In the northwest the Lebanese—" Static sounded in their ears.

Chaim grabbed the dial and tried to find the station again but without success. A moment later he located another clear station.

"The Minister of Defense, Menachem Hazony, told this reporter personally that he had fully anticipated an Egyptian attack at any time. Consequently, he had filled the known airfields with outdated aircraft and hid the most modern fighters in camouflaged airfields built in remote places. The thing that surprises observers most is that Egyptian pilots could not distinguish outdated aircraft from state-of-the-art warplanes. It was Hazony's hidden fleet of fighters which attacked enemy positions fifteen minutes after the Egyptians had completed their massive air offensive.

"The Minister of Defense also told this reporter that he had amassed Israeli tanks and infantry units at strategic locations two weeks before the invasion began. The result is they were ready when the Arabs attacked. After five hours of fighting, Arab armies have been stopped on most fronts and in some locations are in full retreat. So far no Israeli government officials have asked for Hazony to be disciplined for acting without direct authority from the Knesset." After this report the newsman told the story of the destruction of the Dome of the Rock.

David and Chaim cheered wildly. "That uncle of yours is unbelievable. They'll make him a national hero for sure."

"I told you the old boy was a tiger," David said. "He'll do anything to protect Israel, no matter what the cost."

"At least we won't have to destroy the Dome of the Rock. You told me once you had a theory as to how God would help us get rid of the Moslem sanctuary. Was that it? The stupid Iraqis, in their fanatical desire to destroy us, made a mistake and destroyed their own holy shrine with their own missiles?"

"Yes," David said. "I couldn't think of any other way it could be done."

"They'll blame it on us," Chaim said.

"I know, but it should be easy for international investigators to check and find the truth."

"David, nothing those investigators turn up will convince the Arab people that we were not responsible. Their hate completely blinds them."

A month after the American government had fallen, Lucienne Delisle arrived at Gerald Galloway's mansion in the late afternoon. They hugged and kissed each other and then entered his studio. After catching up on what each of them had been doing during the preceding weeks, Lucienne described the new prophet she had found, and they discussed how they could use him to further their cause.

At last Lucienne said, "Gerald, we also need to discuss the Mormons in the United States."

"Weren't they pretty much wiped out during the collapse of the country?"

"Not really. A million of them were killed by natural disasters and mob violence, but there are still about six million left, concentrated largely in the Rocky Mountains. The majority are armed to the teeth. What should I do about them?"

"Most are children, I understand," Gerald said ironically.

Lucienne sneered. "Yes, it's disgusting. Mormons seem to breed like rabbits. All those diapers and mouths to feed. And the screaming! But what should I do about them?"

"We must send an army against them right away. Do the Mormons have any enemies in North America that we could organize to fight against them?"

Lucienne thought a moment, then said, "No I can't think of any enemies with enough power to do the job—wait—the old drug cartels."

"Drug cartels? There can't be enough of them to have much effect on millions of armed Mormons."

"It's not just the cartels. There are also hundreds of bands of anarchists and outlaws roaming the country. There must be at least a million of them in Mexico alone. We could contact the cartels and offer them huge profits to do our work for us. The cartels usually fight with one another, but now they have no drugs or profits to fight over. So we tell them that now they should throw away old enmities and organize to obtain the greater riches which lie in the shattered and weakened lands of the north. And especially in the land of the wealthy Mormons. All they have to do is send out the word and invite the anarchists and outlaws to join their army. We could promise them additional weapons, military vehicles, supplies, gasoline, and the wealth of the north. We could tell them that this is their chance to fulfill their dreams of recovering all the lands they lost from the gringos in the nineteenth century—and much more."

Gerald seemed intrigued. "Yes, of course. I understand that many Mexicans feel that their lands and property in the American southwest were stolen from them by invading Americans."

Lucienne was delighted that her ideas had excited Gerald. "So will you let me go ahead with my plan?"

"Decidedly. It's an excellent idea. The destruction of the Mormons will be a prelude to our prime objective of destroying Israel and the Jews, a goal we're getting closer to every day.

"Okay then. I'll organize a team and travel to Mexico right away. I promise you that by mid-December our Mexican friends will be ready to start recruiting a highly motivated army."

"When do you think our new army might be ready to strike Utah?"

"That's hard to say, but I'd guess we can raise an army and march them into Utah within nine months, probably by July of next year."

Gerald kissed her hand and looked into her eyes. "I'm sure you can do it, but don't you think it's too dangerous to go yourself? Right now Mexico is a wild, savage land. I'm worried I might lose you."

"Don't worry. I'll take a sizeable guard with me. I have to go because I can't trust my subordinates to handle such an important assignment."

Chapter 26

Five months later in mid-March, Steven sat at his desk in his basement study. He had just finished a translation for a Provo firm that was trying to negotiate a business deal with a Japanese computer company located in Lehi. It was the first contract he had received in two weeks and he wondered if he would get paid for it. He had completed fifteen other jobs in the last six months but had only been paid for six of them. As a result, money was very tight and he had to depend heavily on his food storage. The problem was, however, that even if he had earned a lot more money, it was very difficult to find food to purchase. So in order to obtain necessities for his household, and to supplement his storage, Steven, like most Utahns, had to resort to basic survival skills.

In October of the preceding year Steven had borrowed a half dozen books from his brother John on how to survive in the wilderness. He figured this knowledge would help him now and also be essential as he led Pioneer One across the plains to Zion. After pouring over these books, he had agreed to travel with John to the nearby mountains to learn how to survive in difficult circumstances. Several times they had visited the west desert to expand their knowledge of survival in another environment. John had already received a lot of survival training and used his knowledge now to help support his family and to assist his neighbors.

Paul and Robert Christopher, José Ramírez, Sergei and Nicolai Borisovich, Douglas Cartwright, and several neighbors had always accompanied them on these trips. Since bands of savage renegades roamed the wild places in search of prey, it was important to form a sizable group of well-armed men.

On several occasions they had come across the tragic sight of small groups of families murdered and pillaged by outlaws. Those families had sought refuge and safety in wilderness strongholds, but had only succeeded in making themselves more vulnerable to the depredations of monsters.

Steven was especially pleased to have his father go along on these trips because Robert was an expert at finding medicinal herbs, and he taught the men and women how to recognize dozens of useful plants. When the weather had turned cold and snow covered the mountains in December, John focused his attention on teaching the men how to hunt and survive in the winter.

As Steven got up from his desk and sat on a nearby couch, he began to think about the events of the last ten months. In a very short time the world had become an extremely dangerous place, one full of war, natural calamities, disease, hatred, fear, and acts of unspeakable barbarism. Six months ago three hydrogen bombs had wiped out three great American cities and the US government had disintegrated. Other than in the Rocky Mountains, North America became a scene of unending horror, full of mobocracy and bloodshed.

Ghastly plagues covered the land with their clouds of death, and famine was everywhere. In their lust to obtain food and other necessities, formerly decent people betrayed their friends and neighbors and committed murder without hesitation. Even members of the same family frequently fought one another to the death in order to get food. In some regions reports of cannibalism began to surface from time to time.

Outside the United States, it seemed as if the nations and peoples of the earth had gone insane in their desperate attempts to settle scores with old enemies. The only bright image which struck Steven's mind was Israel. The deadly circle of Arab enemies had struck with all their power and yet she had defeated their combined forces in eight short days. And in the process, she had once again enlarged her territory in spite of the squawking of the Arabs, the communists, and the impotent protests of the United Nations. Steven knew that the hand of the Almighty had protected the chosen people in that faraway land.

Then Steven thought about Pioneer One and the trip to Zion. There were still so many problems to solve! He decided to take another look at an especially difficult spot on the road to Missouri and pulled out his detailed maps of the plains states. As he studied the maps with a magnifying glass, he heard María's voice upstairs. "There is a man here to see you, Brother Christopher."

"Ask him to come down into the basement. Thanks, María."

Quentin Price, an elder in the ward and a Provo doctor, came to the door of Steven's office. Steven invited him to come in and take a seat. They spent fifteen minutes chatting about their families and the world situation, and

Steven discovered that since Quentin's private practice had been destroyed by the flood, the state had recruited him to care for victims of the plague and other disasters.

Steven said finally, "What can I do for you, Quentin?"

"I came to ask you questions about Pioneer One. The stake president recently called our family to be part of that expedition and we don't have much time to get ready."

"You're probably among the last called to go to New Zion. President Howard has been hard-pressed trying to do his regular work, handle the problems of these difficult times, and also interview the people recommended by the bishops to join Pioneer One."

"Yes, he's under great stress. After my interview, he directed me to see you if I had detailed questions."

"I'll do my best. What are the questions?"

Quentin took out a piece of paper from his coat pocket, and began to read. "Let's see. I'd like to know when we leave, what kind of vehicle we will travel in, what supplies are necessary, what route we'll take, how long the trip will take, what dangers the caravan will run into, what my role will be on the trip, and what we'll do when we get there."

Steven laughed. "I guess you've asked most of the important questions. May I see your list of questions?" Quentin handed him the page. "Okay, we'll leave in about a month. The prophet has not yet given us the exact date. Most of us will travel in covered wagons. We have good people building them now and we can help you obtain one. Some people are adapting cars and trucks for the trip. We ask that you take enough nutritious food to last your family for at least three months if you can find it. The Church will help us with that. Since it's likely we'll run into polluted lands, we may not be able to obtain nourishment from the lands we cross. We suggest you try to obtain dried meat, fruits, and vegetables, twenty gallons of emergency water, several good water filters, various kinds of grain and beans in cans, flour, salt, sugar, and a selection of seeds for planting in Missouri."

Steven reached into a file and extracted some sheets and gave them to Quentin. "Here is a three-page list of food and other supplies that we ask members of our company to bring with them if they can. If you have trouble finding these items, let me know. The Church has promised to help our people procure whatever is necessary. Now to return to your questions. We expect to take a route that is roughly parallel with I-80 but we may have to alter our course as the circumstances dictate.

"We hope to arrive in about three months if everything goes well. As for dangers, no one can accurately predict what they will be. We request that every family bring at least one weapon and plenty of ammunition for protection. Since you are a doctor, I ask you to act as the official medical officer of Pioneer One. When we arrive in Missouri, we will try to plant late-season crops, build permanent shelters, create a new community, and prepare to build the holy city." Steven paused for a breath. "Well, I guess that's it. Those answers are the best I can give you at this time."

Quentin laughed with pleasure. "That's fine. I'd be happy to be your medical officer. Do you mind me visiting you again if I have additional questions?"

"Not at all. Any time."

After Quentin left, Steven heard María's voice again. "Brother Steven, there's a woman at the door. She wants to talk to you."

"Okay, I'll be right up. Thanks."

Steven climbed the basement stairs and headed for the front door. The door was partly closed so he opened it all the way and saw the back of a woman's head. Suddenly, his heart pounded wildly. There was something familiar about the shape of her head and the color of her hair. The woman turned and he saw Selena.

"Hello, Steve. May I come in?"

Steven was struck by her beauty and the sadness in her eyes. He looked outside fearfully to see if she was alone but saw nothing unusual except an old car parked in front of the house.

"What do you want, Selena? How did you get here?"

"Let me come in and we'll talk."

Steven stepped aside and Selena walked into the room and sat on the couch. Standing in the middle of the room, he gaped at the woman he had loved for twelve years and who had betrayed him. He was so paralyzed that he couldn't even begin to make the recriminations he had rehearsed so many times to himself. "Why are you here?" he said at last.

"I want to see my children, if you will let me. Where are they?"

Steven checked his watch. "My brother John should bring them home anytime now."

Selena trembled. "I'm afraid they hate me for what I did. Do they hate me, Steve?"

"No, they don't hate you. At first they were confused and deeply hurt, but now they're beginning to accept things as they are."

"Maybe they will forgive me eventually. Will you allow me to see them from time to time?"

"Yes, but only in my presence."

"I can understand how you feel. I don't expect you to permit me to take them anywhere, at least not at first. In any case, you don't need to worry. I'm not going to steal them from you."

"Like you did last summer," Steven said with a trace of anger.

"I'm sorry about that. I was so desperate. I knew it would hurt you terribly, but I couldn't think of anything else except to be their mother again. And Colton said they were really our children, his and mine. But now I know we were wrong."

"What was your plan? To take them all?"

Selena continued to gaze at Steven with eyes full of sorrow. "Yes, but we only had time to take Jennifer. You came for the children sooner than we had anticipated." Selena lowered her head and great tears welled in her eyes. "I was wrong in every way. To abandon a wonderful husband and my precious children because of the lies of a monster."

In spite of his anger, Steven began to feel sorry for the pitiful wretch sitting before him. He had always been a sucker for a woman's tears. When he was a child his mother had never found it necessary to discipline him. A little bit of crying and he was immediately repentant and anxious to please.

Selena dried her tears with a handkerchief and said, "I also wanted to tell you how grateful I am for your kindness in letting me know Jennifer wasn't in that cabin when it was destroyed. It saved me so much grief."

"I'm glad for that," Steven said. "So you're not with Colton Aldridge anymore?"

"No, I left the community a month ago, determined to be free of their control and especially to see my children again."

"How on earth did you get here? The highways are almost completely destroyed and the danger—"

"I know. We had to travel on back roads and across open country, and we saw vicious gangs everywhere. We were constantly hiding."

"We?"

"Yes, I escaped from Colorado City with two friends, a man and a woman. The man died from poison water and the woman just disappeared one day."

"What happened?" Steven asked.

"She went down to a river to bathe and never came back. I searched for an hour but couldn't find her. I figured a gang had killed her or took her with them. I walked for six hours to the main highway, where a kind young family had pity on a bedraggled vagabond and drove me to the home of an old friend in Provo. My friend gave me refuge and enough money to buy an old car. It took me several days to get up enough courage to come here."

"Did Colton try to stop you from leaving Colorado City?"

"No, he had already abandoned his wives and the church last September, about a week before the Russians bombed the three cities."

"What?"

"Yes, some French woman came one day and had a long talk with the creep and the next day he was gone. Apparently they flew out of the area together in a private helicopter. One of his apostles told me later that she offered him great wealth and power. I'm not sure what she wanted him to do, but I think it had to do with his ability to perform miracles."

Steven was surprised but then remembered that in the last days false prophets would convert millions of people by performing great miracles. "He actually performed miracles?"

"Oh, yes. He healed the sick and spoke in tongues. He also said he received visitations from divine beings, but I suspect they may have been evil spirits. Or maybe Satan. However, many of his predictions concerning important events did come true. Now I realize he did his miracles through the power of the Devil."

"Well, I hope he's gone forever and we'll never hear of him again," Steven said.

"Colton Aldridge will appear again and I fear the world will suffer because of it," Selena replied with conviction.

Steven wondered why she was so certain, but he wanted to ask her a more important question. "So you're no longer a member of that polygamous church?"

"No, I have completely rejected the LLDS and their lies. All the leaders want to do is attack the Mormon church, steal the homes and property of their members, seduce other men's wives, and control women as if they were inferior creatures. I really don't know why I was so blind. The thing that bothers me the most is they claim to be sanctified and yet they can't even obey the Ten Commandments."

The front door banged open and Steven's children burst into the room.

"Who is that?" Andrew asked, looking at Selena. Steven knew it would take a minute for the nine year old to recognize his mother. It had been almost three years since he had seen her.

"It's your mother," Steven said.

Andrew's eyes bulged as he stared at Selena, but he didn't move or say a word. William glared at Selena and said, "What's *she* doing here?" He stood close to the front room window and refused to look at his mother.

Jennifer's eyes were full of fear. "You're not going to kidnap me again, are you?"

"No, I'm not going to kidnap you," Selena said, almost crying. "I just wanted to see my children."

"We are not *your* children!" William insisted. "We are Dad's children."

"Yes, I know," Selena said. "You belong to your father."

"She *is* our birth mother, William, even though she didn't want us," Jennifer insisted. William turned his scowl on Jennifer. "Actually," Jennifer continued, "you could say we don't have a real mother at this time."

Selena burst out weeping and it took several minutes for her to stop the tears. At that moment Steven was deeply ashamed that he had spent so much time reviling her.

Finally Selena said, "The truth is, I love you and I came to ask for your forgiveness. I know you might not believe me but I have changed and I deeply regret leaving you. If you want me to leave, I'll go, but I'd prefer to visit you and be your mother again."

At those words, Andrew flew into her arms and kissed her on the cheek. "I forgive you and I don't want you to leave again. I want you to stay forever."

Selena could not hold back the tears. Again she wept openly and hugged Andrew tightly, bathing his cheek in her tears. Steven knew she was telling the truth.

"Children, I want you to try to forgive your mother. I believe she is telling the truth and does love you. If you can't do it now, ask your Father in Heaven to help you." Steven was sure Andrew and Jennifer could forgive quickly but it would take some time before William could accept his mother again.

"What about you, Steven?" Selena asked. "Can you forgive me?"

Steven realized he had to give his children a good example and said, "Yes, I forgive you." He felt empty as he said the words, and he saw the doubt in Selena's eyes.

Selena stayed an hour, asking the children questions and looking at them longingly. Andrew sat near her the entire time, but William and Jennifer maintained their distance. At last Selena said she had to leave, but promised to come again soon.

"I need to ask you a final question," Steven said.

"What is it?"

"How could you do it? How could you abandon us?"

Without hesitation Selena said, "It was nothing but spiritual blindness and the insane religious exaltation of the moment. All I can say now is I'm deeply sorry for your pain and the children's pain, and that I deserve the misery and despair I feel." After these words she got up and left in her tiny white car.

"Welcome, Lucienne." Gerald Galloway said as he embraced her in his London town house. As usual Gerald was dressed in a dark business suit, red tie, and black shoes. Lucienne wore an attractive green stretch linen collar dress with a burnished brown leather belt. "It's always a delight to see you. I haven't seen you since the end of last September. That means you've neglected me for almost five and a half months."

"I'm sorry, Gerald, but you didn't ask me to come," Lucienne teased. She motioned to a man standing directly behind her. "I want you to meet Colton Aldridge, from the United States. He is the great prophet I told you about." While Lucienne had told Gerald last September that she had found the holy man he wanted, Gerald had not asked her to bring him to England until now.

"Welcome to London, Mr. Aldridge. I trust you had a nice trip in my private jet."

"Nice? It was the most frightening experience I've ever had. We were nearly blown out of the sky by some warplanes bristling with missiles and cannons. There were two of them. If it hadn't been for our escorts . . ." Colton was upset, but he dared not show his anger. On the flight to England Lucienne had explained to him that he was about to meet the richest and most powerful businessman on earth.

Gerald looked at Lucienne Delisle. "You had trouble?"

"Two fighters about three hundred miles from the English coast. Apparently they came from France. They armed their missiles but didn't fire, no doubt because they spotted our escorts not far behind and knew they were outgunned."

"I'm so sorry, Mr. Aldridge," Gerald said. "But one never knows what will happen in these dangerous times. That's why I sent the Jaguars, the F-20s. At a cost of seventy million each, they are the most lethal warplanes in the world and their pilots have the best training available. It would be rather foolhardy for any enemy to attack them." Gerald pointed to a nearby sofa. "Please sit down, Mr. Aldridge." Colton headed for the couch, but Lucienne remained standing near Gerald.

Colton sat forward on the sofa with his forearms on his knees. "How are we going to get back to the States with enemy planes waiting to shoot us down?"

"You won't return to the United States," Gerald said.

"What?"

"I'm sure that when you hear my offer, you will have no desire to return to such a lawless country."

"Yes, it's lawless in most of the country, but not so much in Utah and the surrounding states," Colton said.

"I heard the streets of Salt Lake City are under the control of roving gangs."

"That's true of Salt Lake City at night. No one dares to venture forth after dark anymore. But in daytime the city is still fairly safe, especially if you have an armed Mormon escort. The same is true for most Utah cities and towns."

"*That* is reassuring," Gerald said sardonically. "It's too bad we'll have to destroy the power of the Mormons."

"Destroy their power? What do you mean? What do you intend to do?"

"Does it worry you? It's my understanding that you are an enemy of Mormonism."

"I certainly am. The Mormon church is an apostate church. It has betrayed the legacy of the Prophet Joseph Smith."

"Yes, I've heard you have good reasons for hating them, and you are right to feel the way you do. But as I see it, the main reason why the Mormons are a problem is because they are out of step with the new order of things. After the present turmoil cleanses the earth, the world will move into a new era of peace and joy. That era will be brought into existence by the effort and will of great men like yourself, and the new order they create will do away with the negative forces of nationalism and sectarianism. It is these divisive elements which have caused all the misery and death which we see throughout the history of the world.

"And the Mormons and the Jews are perfect examples of what is most destructive in those negative forces. It is my hope that you will join me and my organization in our goal to cleanse the earth and usher in our perfect world community. In that great society a glorious new religion will arise, but it will not resemble the old. It will be a religion of joy and freedom and oneness with nature. It will be free from the restraints of useless ritual and sectarian structures. You will become one of the great spiritual leaders of that divine movement."

"What do I have to do to become such a leader?" There was excitement on Colton's face.

"Just what you already do so well. But first you will need to read some materials and attend some training sessions led by special teachers. Most of the time I will guide you myself. Later, because of your talents, we will give you great authority in our movement. Lucienne tells me you have performed some astonishing miracles. Is that right?"

"Yes. I can speak in tongues, heal the sick, and cast out devils."

"Marvelous. Is there anything else?"

"I have the right to receive the mysteries of the kingdom from divine beings."

Gerald was perplexed. "What does that mean?"

"It means that God teaches me hidden doctrines and reveals to me the truths of the universe."

"Incredible. I'm sure those things will be vital to our society. So you can perform spectacular, visible miracles? You can predict earthquakes and other natural events?"

"I have done so often in the past. All I need to do is go to God in prayer and he gives me the power and knowledge I need."

"I can see you are exactly the kind of leader we need. I admit to you that sometimes God tells me things also. Oh, nothing compared to you, but little things. And I can tell you now that God has revealed to me that you will astound the world with your miracles and they will be an everlasting source of good. You will obtain great riches and all the desires of your heart." Gerald paused. "Don't be surprised if I speak of riches. Isn't it the Bible which says that the laborer is worthy of his hire?"

"Indeed."

"You will receive wealth and power and kingdoms beyond your wildest dreams. All you have to do is help me usher in the new era."

"Your proposal is certainly intriguing, but I need time to consider it."

"Take all the time you need." Gerald picked up some books and pamphlets from a table and handed them to Colton. "You can start by reading these materials. I had them prepared especially for the people of our organization. They detail our history and our goals. Read these things and embrace them with all your heart. My only caution is that you must never lose them or give them to another. Do you understand?"

"Completely."

Gerald was sure that Aldridge would accept his offer in time. He nodded to a beautiful girl who had appeared in the doorway. "This young lady will show you to your room. She will be your private consort and will supply you with anything you need. I hope you will accept my hospitality for many weeks to come. Now I need to speak to Lucienne in private, so please excuse us."

"Of course." Colton turned and followed the girl out of the room.

When Colton had disappeared, Lucienne said, "What do you think?"

"He certainly looks the part with that beard and long gray hair. My question is, will he do what we tell him to?"

"I'm sure of it. He's the kind of man who would sell his soul to the devil for profit and fame. Throw in a few women like your pretty little consort and he'll be our slave for sure."

"Good. And that miracle stuff, does he really do miracles?"

"Absolutely," Lucienne said. "As I told you before, I've seen it with my own eyes. While he was visiting me in Salt Lake City he healed a child's withered hand and restored a blind man's sight. I don't know whether he gets his power from God or the devil, but it sure works."

"Does it really matter as long as it works for us?"

Chapter 27

During the first week in April, Steven's parents paid him a special visit.

"Steven, I don't understand why Sarah and I can't go with you, just because we're a tad older," Robert said with moist eyes.

"Dad, this comes from the First Presidency, not from me. The Brethren know that this expedition to Missouri will be fraught with hardship and danger and that it will be terribly difficult even for young people. I know it's no consolation, but Utah and the Rocky Mountains are also a land of inheritance for the saints. In fact, the Prophet Joseph Smith said all of America is Zion, and I know it will be so in reality someday. Because of that, the Lord will need faithful people here to build a safe place for the saints and the other good people of the world." Steven knew his parents were disappointed but, in the final analysis, they would not question the wisdom of church leaders in the matter.

It was one week before the scheduled departure of Pioneer One to Missouri. The Christopher family had gathered once again at Steven's home to discuss their final plans. They had also invited Mary, Andrea, the Cartwrights, and the Borisovich and Ramírez families, all of whom had been chosen to go to Missouri.

"They won't let us go either, Dad," said Julie Godet, Steven's thirty-four-year-old sister, who lived with her husband Mike in Mt. Pleasant. Present also at the gathering was Steven's other sister Christine Renwick, who was twenty-nine. Christine and her husband Chad and their three children had moved from California to Lehi five months before. California was a scene of continuous bloodshed, especially in the large cities, and the Renwicks had barely escaped with their lives. They too were disappointed that they had not been called to join Pioneer One.

"I'm pleased you all want to go with us." Steven said. "Your faith is certainly greater than that of many people in Provo who were called but declined. Don't worry. I'm sure you'll be called someday. It was the prophet's decision to pick people from this section of Provo to make up the first company, and I'm sure he has his reasons. Maybe the brethren will choose people from Mt. Pleasant or Lehi to go in one of the later companies. There will be many companies leaving this year and next. I understand the Church will eventually call hundreds of thousands of people to travel to New Zion."

"Yes, but it would be more exciting to be a part of Pioneer One, as you call it," Christine said, her lips drawn in a pout.

Paul said, "That's true but the first group will face greater dangers and hardships. One day you'll be able to travel to New Zion as easily as when we used to travel by car from Provo to Los Angeles. There will be lots of motels, restaurants, and exciting tourist sites along the way. You'll be as safe as in your bed at home."

Chad Renwick laughed. "Paul's exaggerating but he does make a good point. After what we went through coming here, I'm not sure I'd relish walking or driving a covered wagon to Missouri. A large convoy of us made the trip from California in cars when the freeway was mostly still intact, and our lives were in constant danger. It'll probably be much more treacherous to trudge across a thousand miles of bleak and polluted prairies full of savages and gangs of thugs."

Steven said, "It certainly will be perilous, but we've tried to prepare for every contingency."

"You sure have changed, Steven," Julie said. "You've become a lot more spiritual and self-confident in the last year."

Steven felt embarrassed. Yes, for the first time in his life he was close to God and respected himself. He looked at Mary and saw a subtle smile cross her face. That made him even more flustered. He was relieved when Chad changed the subject.

"So the First Presidency and the stake president decide who goes. But who makes the other decisions?"

"The First Presidency makes all the other basic decisions," Steven said. "Two weeks ago the prophet told me that Pioneer One was to leave on Friday morning, April 14."

"Are you going to follow the old Mormon Trail?" Julie Godet asked.

"Not really," Steven said. "The brethren believe our path will be easier if we try to stay on or close to the interstate highways. First we'll go north on I-15 and then head east through Parley's Canyon until we reach I-80. We'll follow

I-80 to Lincoln, Nebraska and then travel southeast to I-29. We'll follow I-29 south to Kansas City. From there it's only a short distance eastward to Independence, Missouri. We expect to travel about eleven hundred miles."

"That route isn't as romantic as the old Mormon Trail, but I'm sure it's much more *practical*," Mary said with irony.

Steven smiled. "Well, I don't want to disappoint you completely, Mary. We'll parallel the Mormon Trail closely for about two hundred miles while we're in Nebraska." He was delighted that Mary and Andrea had been called to go with Pioneer One.

"Oh, no," Mary said, laughing. "I was thinking that we'd miss out on the historical pioneer sites and we'd have it so easy we wouldn't be able to understand what the pioneers went through."

Paul fired back, "Are you kidding? We'll have it much rougher than the early pioneers. They didn't have thousands of cutthroats waiting to murder them and steal their provisions at every turn of the road. And they didn't have to deal with polluted rivers and grasslands. Yes, they ran into disease, especially scurvy and malaria, but they didn't have to worry about the terrible plagues we have today. And that's not all—"

"Didn't the Mormon pioneers have to deal with dangerous Indians?" Douglas asked.

Paul shook his head. "Not really. They had to feed a lot of Indians and some of the tribes stole their cattle, but they weren't attacked by the Indians as they journeyed west. In fact, the Indians kind of liked the Mormon pioneers."

Steven said, "I don't know if we'll meet hardships as great as the pioneers did. But I do know we'll need God's help to survive the trip. I don't want to frighten you, but the trail from Utah to Missouri holds many kinds of unpredictable dangers for us. One of our most difficult problems will be to feed ourselves. The pioneers had the buffalo and edible wild plants and they were able to obtain food by trading with the Indians and other groups traveling on the same trails. We probably won't have any of those advantages. We'll have to carry as much food with us as possible because it's not likely we'll get much help from the land."

"Didn't the pioneers have all kinds of animals with them?" Chad asked.

"Yes, they took horses, mules, oxen, sheep, cows, and poultry. So they had a walking supply of milk and meat. We're not even sure our animals will have safe grass on the plains."

Sarah's face became more and more pale as her sons described the dangers of the trip. Finally, she said, "Steven, you'll be going through some big cities on this trip. I'm sure there'll be good people in those places who can help you."

"It's possible. We'll travel close to Laramie, Cheyenne, Lincoln, and dozens of smaller cities. I understand those cities have been devastated. But I'm sure there'll be good people still alive in some places who can help us—and whom we can help."

"They'll probably be in hiding, and you may find it difficult to find them," Robert said.

"True, but the prophet told me I should seek them out, and they'll help us reach Zion."

Sarah relaxed visibly when she heard her son say that the prophet had declared they would reach Zion safely.

John said, "I heard a report on the shortwave radio that a bunch of renegades attacked the city of Rawlins in Wyoming and slaughtered most of the inhabitants."

Steven saw the pallor return to his mother's face and felt irritation toward John.

John went on. "I also wanted to say something about the food problem. Through my connections I have tapped into a supply of army rations. I should be able to obtain several thousand units by the time we head out. They aren't great eating, but since food is so scarce, they'll help us survive."

Steven had tasted army rations before and wasn't excited at the prospect. Still he had to admit that the rations would be better than nothing.

"I don't know what I'd do without John," Steven said.

Mike Godet grinned. "I understand you're converting modern vehicles for the trip."

They all burst out laughing. Steven chuckled and said to his brother-in-law, "Every family called to go has the basic responsibility of providing its own vehicle. But the amazing thing—in my opinion—is all the other people who suddenly offered their help when they heard we had to travel across the plains using whatever conveyances we could find or make. Ranchers, farmers, sheep herders, experts on pioneer culture, and others. They even contributed horses, mules, and oxen to pull the vehicles. Some of them donated sheep and milk cows. Others helped many of our travelers build excellent wagons, showed them how to care for the draft animals, how to hitch them to wagons, and how to drive them. It has been exciting to see all those good people step forward to help us when we needed them."

"Yeah," Paul said, "I don't know if all of you know it, but last October we got an invitation from a Mormon rancher in the Price area to spend a week at his ranch. Now this is the kind of guy who has always taken his cattle to market the old way instead of using cattle trucks. Four hundred miles of driving those critters on horseback. Of course, it's the only way you can get them to market nowadays. So listen to this. He invites Steve, John, and me to come to his ranch to learn the ropes. Everything you can imagine: herding, roping, driving, branding, and crossing streams. He even gave us lessons on how to survive in a hostile environment. When the week was over we all had such a love of the wide open spaces that we were considering becoming ranchers and cowboys ourselves."

Everyone laughed at Paul's story and the way he told it.

"But I heard that some of your pioneers are not going to use wagons or hand carts," Mike said, returning to his earlier question. "I understand they're converting their cars and trucks into pioneer vehicles by stripping them of unnecessary weight."

"I'm afraid a few people insist on doing that," Steven said. "I've tried to convince them that wagons would be lighter and more durable, but they disagree with me. Even many of those building covered wagons plan on using modern axles, wheels, and rubber tires. I only hope they don't have trouble on the trail."

"I'm not so sure they're wrong," John said. "It's possible the converted vehicles and the wagons with up-to-date wheels and axles may be better. With rubber tires they may cover the damaged highways easier."

Steven replied, "Maybe so. I guess time will tell." He looked at Tania and saw tears in her eyes. "What's the matter, Tania?"

"Oh. I was just thinking about all the horrible things that are happening in the world."

"Tania's right," Robert said. "Terrible things are happening. There are wars everywhere on the earth. Yesterday I made a count and found that forty-seven nations are currently at war."

"It sure didn't take long for China to overwhelm the Soviet Union," Paul said. "China's army of fifteen million swept over Russia and the other communist republics in less than five months. And now we have Ho Lung as the mighty new dictator of Russia and the East."

"He may not be the worst tyrant we have," Robert said. "In my opinion, Asad Fadid, the butcher of Iraq, is the most dangerous man on the planet. Already he has conquered Kuwait, Saudi Arabia, the United Arab Emirates, and Iran. Now he is threatening Pakistan and India. Like Adolf Hitler he stops at no lie or atrocious act, including the use of chemical weapons. There are rumors that he is in league with al-Qaeda."

"Yes, so far he's the only leader who has used atomic weapons," Chad said. "If he hadn't dropped two hydrogen bombs on Iran, he would never have had the strength to defeat the Iranians."

"What about the bombs dropped on New York, Chicago, and Los Angeles?" John said.

"Well, I think it's fairly well known by this time that those missiles were launched by mistake," Chad said.

John replied, "I don't believe it. I think they were launched by saboteurs. It was a conspiracy conceived by some immensely powerful organization. Possibly to initiate the worldwide chaos we see today."

Steven noticed the sudden silence of his family. They were used to hearing John say outlandish things, but none of them would openly disagree with him. Though Tania usually went along with her husband, even she seemed embarrassed. After seeing all the terrible things happening in the world, Steven was beginning to see that John was usually right.

Robert quickly changed the subject. "In any event, the turmoil has brought a lot of new leaders into prominence. Many people believe there's an obvious move from democratic governments to dictatorships. I understand Argentina has a new dictator who is preparing to invade Uruguay and Chile, and even Canada and Mexico are now controlled by tyrants."

John said, "I've heard radio reports saying that herds of rogue Mexicans have attacked cities in California. It seems they want to get their share of the booty. In my opinion, they would have conquered the entire western half of the country if they hadn't lost most of their military capability in their own civil wars. As it is, they don't seem as well equipped as the Mormon Guard."

"That's unbelievable," Robert said. "Also, there's that guy in the United Nations. What's his name?"

"You mean Gerald O. Galloway," Steven said.

Mary asked, "What's the 'O' stand for?"

Steven didn't know, but John said, "I think it stands for Osborn."

Robert continued. "I don't know how he did it, but in a very short time after the fall of Russia and the United States, he formed a coalition which gained complete control over the UN. Right now he's the virtual dictator of the UN and the European Union."

"I have a theory as to how he did it," John said. "When the superpowers started fighting last September, many nations took advantage of the chaos to attack their traditional enemies, and ethnic nations rebelled against the states which controlled them. Because of this, there was a widespread collapse of economies and governments, and the UN was powerless to help. Then at the darkest hour, Galloway steps forward and declares that if he's given control of the UN he can save it from dissolution and lead all nations back to peace and prosperity. He promises to use hundreds of billions of dollars of his personal fortune to help stabilize the economies of the warring nations and to reestablish order. To control those who oppose his grab for power, he uses blackmail and assassination."

Steven saw a certain logic in John's scenario. Before the Collapse, he had seen Galloway in many news stories and had been impressed with the power and charisma of the wealthy industrialist. Every time the Englishman had appeared in a panel debating some important issue, Steven had been fascinated by his incredible brilliance and self-assurance. His strange eyes had made a shiver of fear go up Steven's spine. Steven had concluded that here was a man who would stop at nothing to get what he wanted.

Mike asked, "How do you know all this, John?"

"It's been in the news. All you have to do is follow it closely. Also, I've read dozens of essays by political analysts."

"The most surprising thing is that Galloway achieved his amazing feat in less than six months," Robert said.

Since there was a break in the discussion, Sarah said, "I think it's time we stop talking about all the terrible things going on in the world. I want to talk about something pleasant. Something that concerns our family."

"What's that, dear?" Robert asked.

"Selena." There was an abrupt silence and some of those present glanced at Steven but said nothing. "She came to see me last week," Sarah continued. "She told me she was living with a family somewhere in Lindon and had broken all ties with the apostate polygamous group she was involved with. She went to her bishop and asked to be reinstated into the Church and the bishop gave her a plan and a schedule to follow. She said she wanted most of all to be forgiven by her children and by all those she had hurt, especially the Christopher family." Steven began to feel very uncomfortable.

"Do you believe she's sincere?" Julie asked.

"Yes, I do. I think we should all try to forgive and forget. Most of all, I think it's important for Steven's children to spend time with their mother. It might ease some of the pain and anger they have endured since she left."

"I'm willing to give her a chance," John said.

The rest of the family also seemed willing to forgive. Steven said nothing.

"How do you feel about it, Steve?" Robert asked.

He was a little annoyed at being put on the spot. "If she has really repented, I will forgive her. I already told her that."

Mary's face took on a worried look.

Elizabeth Cartwright said, "You saw her, Steven?"

"Yes, she came to see the children about three weeks ago." Steven told them how his children had responded to their mother. Then, feeling increasingly uncomfortable talking about such a painful subject, he suggested they have refreshments and enjoy themselves by playing board games.

Chapter 28

At one o'clock, six days before Pioneer One was scheduled to leave for Missouri, Selena came to take her children on an outing. Steven called the children in from the backyard, and Andrew rushed into his mother's arms. She had brought a picnic lunch, and they headed for a shady little park not far away. In the last few weeks the sky had become clearer and the sun more bright, and swarms of people, after being under the gloom of half-light for more than eight months, rushed outdoors to enjoy every bit of sunlight, as if it might soon disappear forever. Selena and the children returned shortly after three, and Steven noticed that both William and Jennifer had warmed considerably toward their mother. Instead of leaving, Selena sat nervously on the couch listening to Jennifer relate every detail of their picnic.

When Jennifer paused briefly in her endless rehearsal, Selena looked up at Steven and said, "I wanted to tell you I have to go out of town for a few days. I'm leaving today and I might not see you again before you and the children leave on your trip to Missouri."

"Leave town? Isn't that dangerous?" Steven said.

"I hope not. I'm only going to Salt Lake City. I need to consult frequently with a lawyer I've hired and so I'll stay at the Holiday Inn for about a week."

Steven panicked, wondering if Selena was trying some legal maneuver to gain custody of the children. "A lawyer. Why do you need a lawyer?"

"When I joined the LLDS in Colorado City, I turned over some valuable personal property to Colton Aldridge and I want to get it back. I talked to my lawyer several times on the phone and he thinks we may be able to get Colton for fraud. Colton seems to have disappeared, but if we can get him into court, I hope to get a judgment against him."

Steven was relieved. "I hope you can, Selena. I understand a lot of polygamous leaders steal their members' property under the guise of religion. The new members are asked to consecrate all their property to the church, not knowing the leader *is* the church."

"Yes, they do. At any rate I wanted to see the children before I left and to talk to you—mostly about the children."

The front door opened abruptly and Mary Fleming stuck her head inside. "May I come in?"

"Please do," Steven said. For some reason he couldn't understand, his face became crimson as Mary took a chair on the opposite side of the room from Selena. Steven noticed that Selena looked upset, and the children were gazing at the adults as if they were seeing some strange new spectacle. Steven couldn't decide which woman was the most beautiful.

Mary looked straight at Selena and said to Steven. "So this is Selena, the children's mother and your *ex*-wife . . ." She emphasized the word "ex." "It's nice to meet you again."

"Meet me again?" Selena stared at Mary blankly for a moment, but soon her eyes showed her recognition. "Why, you're the woman who came to Colorado City to join our polygamous church."

"Yes, but my name is Mary Fleming not Mary Jacobsen. I helped Steven infiltrate your cult to recover the child you kidnapped."

Steven swallowed hard. He had never seen Mary so aggressive before.

Selena's eyes widened as if she were going to burst into anger, but then she paused and smiled. "You were all very clever and your scheme was a great success. So you're Steven's girlfriend?"

Mary's composure suddenly broke down. "No, Steve and I . . . and I are just good friends," she stammered.

"But you're such a pretty thing. What's the matter with you, Steve?"

Steven shrugged and said nothing. He was disappointed that Mary had spoken of him as being no more than a "good friend." He had not specifically planned it, but when he saw Mary and Selena in the same room, he had hoped that Mary might become jealous and unintentionally admit what Steven knew in his heart—that she loved him. For the next thirty minutes they talked about one insignificant thing after another. Toward the end of this time, Selena began to drum her fingers impatiently on the arm of the couch and stare at Mary with narrowed eyes. Steven figured she was impatient for Mary to leave, but Mary seemed to be perfectly happy to stay right where she was until Selena left, even if it took all day. Tired of hearing the boring talk, the three children wandered away to engage in more interesting activities.

After another twenty minutes, during which Steven described in detail how to hitch a team of horses and drive them properly, Selena turned toward him and, completely ignoring Mary, said abruptly, "Steven, I've been giving things a lot of thought lately, and I've made some decisions. Your mother told me how much you and the children suffered because of me. I don't blame you for hating me all those years because what I did was terribly wrong, but now I have repented and I'm determined to rebuild my life. I'm grateful that my children and your family seem willing to forgive me. Most of all, I'm grateful for what you said the first time I came here."

Steven was confused. He had said many things to Selena and wasn't sure what she was referring to. "What did I say?"

"You said you forgave me."

"Uh, yes, that's right."

"That means a great deal to me, Steve." As she searched for the right words she stared at the floor in front of her. Finally she said, "Many years ago President Spencer W. Kimball said that an essential part of forgiveness is to forget."

"That's right. It's in his *Miracle of Forgiveness.* To forgive is to forget."

After glancing at Mary nervously, Selena returned her eyes to the floor. "Can you *forget* what I did, Steven?"

The question stunned him. After thinking about it for a while, he said, "Well, I think forgetting is not something you can do by simply deciding to do it. The offense must not be repeated. A new relationship must be made. All that takes time. Sometimes years. All you can do is say you'll *try* to forget, and you have to avoid dwelling on the misdeed." Steven had no idea what Selena's point was, but if it helped her rejoin the Church and straighten out her life, he was willing to help.

Selena smiled wryly. "I see your point. You always were good at analyzing things from one end to the other. But let me ask you a simple question. If you forgive me and are willing to try to forget, do you think you could someday let me back into your life?"

Steven's throat and chest tightened. He was startled that Selena could be so bold, especially in front of Mary. If she had come a year ago and had made the same offer, he might have flown into her arms joyfully. But now he simply didn't care anymore. He glanced at Mary and saw her staring at him, waiting for his decision.

Trying to think of a kind answer, Steven coughed a few times and waited for the tightness to disappear. When he did speak, he was amazed at his own words. "I'm sorry, Selena, but there's another woman in my life." He looked at Mary and then at Selena. Mary's face was transfigured by shock and Selena's by despair. Seeing they were waiting for him to explain, he said, "She's one of my best friends and my children love her dearly."

"That's very nice but you haven't told us her name," Selena said, her voice low and sad.

At that moment Steven realized that he really did love the woman who was one of his best friends. Now he was ready to tell her so. "Mary knows who she is," Steven said, thinking that would make things perfectly clear.

"You're in love with Andrea Warren!" Mary cried, her face crumpling.

"Well, I—"

"I'm . . . so happy," Mary said with tears in her eyes. "She's my best friend. But why don't you *tell* Andrea? She really cares for you."

"But I don't—"

"Oh, I see. You're too bashful. Do you want me to tell her?" Mary said, wiping her eyes with her hand.

Selena rolled her eyes and tapped her fingers impatiently against the arm of her chair. "Why don't you just be quiet and let him explain?"

"No I—" Steven began.

"I'll do it if you say so," Mary said. "Andrea will be so surprised—and delighted. And I am too. To think that you're in love with my best friend."

Steven got up and went to her side. Leaning over, he put his hands on her shoulders. "Mary, I don't want . . . I can't . . . I was talking about *you*."

"I knew you liked each other, but I never realized—" Mary broke off, her eyes suddenly wide with shock.

"I knew it all the time," Selena said in a low voice as if she were talking to herself.

Mary caught her breath and looked into Steven's eyes. "What did you say?"

"I said I was talking about you—Mary Fleming." Steven felt good to finally have it out, to have admitted to himself and Mary how he felt. But now he released her shoulders and stood there in front of her, unsure what would happen next.

"Me? You're in love with me?" She bounced to her feet.

She was so beautiful staring up at him that Steven could barely talk. "That's what I said."

Again Mary wiped the tears from her eyes, this time tears of joy. "Oh, Steven! I love you too."

Selena smiled, despite her reddening eyes. "Well, you've given me your answer and now I'm leaving. I'll try to return to see the kids before you leave, but if I can't make it, I'll see you again when you return from Missouri or when I go there. Can I go outside to say good-bye to them now?"

"I think that's a good idea," Steven said sincerely. Noticing that she held a handkerchief to her eyes as she left the room, he wondered whether she was crying because he had rejected her proposal or because the children would soon be out of her life again. He took Mary's hand and pulled her down to the couch. "I hope I wasn't cruel. I didn't mean—"

"You weren't cruel. Don't worry about it. She tried to bait you with that forgive and forget stuff and you didn't fall for it. For that I'm grateful. In my opinion, she had a lot of nerve expecting you to take her back."

"Well, I can forgive a woman for cheating on me and abandoning our family, and maybe I'll forget those offenses someday, but that doesn't mean I have to remarry her. Today is another day and there are new people in my life."

Her hands tightened on his. "Do you mean me?"

"Yes, I mean you. You're right. Selena has no right to expect me to take her back. If your friend raped your child, you might forgive him one day, if he repents, but you don't have to let him take your daughter off alone to the ice cream store."

She laughed. "I get the point, Steve. You don't have to analyze it to death."

"Oh, I'm sorry." After sitting there for a moment, feeling like a fool, he said, "Mary, there's something I need to tell you."

She moved closer to him. "Yes, what is it?"

He paused, unable to say the words. But then he remembered Paul's words, describing him as being controlled by fear and selfishness, and he knew he had to do it. He looked down into her upturned face and, seeing her eyes full of love, his heart melted. "I . . . I think I was taken by you from the first moment I saw you standing in the church foyer next to Sister Goodrich, but I didn't want to admit it to myself."

"Taken by me? That's a quaint expression. Are you trying to say you love me?"

"Yes."

"So what do you intend to do about it?"

Man! This woman can be pushy when she wants to be, Steven thought. "I want you to be my wife, if you'll say yes."

Mary didn't hesitate. "My answer is yes. I accept your proposal. I first knew you were the man I wanted when we went to Arizona to get Jennifer, and I was fairly certain you cared for me too. The only thing I couldn't figure out is how to make you realize it and tell me. I guess it took your ex-wife to do the job."

Steven took her into his arms and kissed her respectfully at first, and then with increasing passion. He delighted in how soft and warm she felt in his embrace, especially when she met his passion with equal eagerness. But he released her quickly when he heard a loud bang. It was the children charging through the back door. As they hurried in and plopped on the first seats they could find, Steven's face turned red, and he remembered what it was like to try to show affection to a woman when children were around.

Steven and Mary were married in the Salt Lake Temple, two days before Pioneer One was scheduled to depart. They decided to take their vows as soon as possible because they knew the times were dangerous and they might not have many hours together. They agreed to consider their trip to Independence, Missouri as their honeymoon. Steven explained to his children how he felt about Mary, and they seemed to take it very well because they too had come to love her in the past year. Steven didn't know how, but they already understood that he could never love Selena in the same way as he did before. Jennifer alone showed some signs of jealousy toward Mary, but Steven hoped that problem would resolve itself in time.

The Christophers, especially Sarah, were pleased and relieved that Steven had at last found a good wife. Andrea also admitted she was delighted because Steven had chosen her best friend. But she couldn't resist teasing them, claiming that they only succeeded in getting together because she had withstood Steven's advances and convinced him to take Mary instead. Anastasia was disappointed that Steven had been foolish enough to choose another woman, but she seemed to get over it almost immediately and turned her attention to Paul. After all, he was only two or three years younger than she. Since she and her family had been called to go to Missouri, Steven suspected that she hoped to have plenty of time to cultivate a relationship with his brother, or perhaps one of the other bachelors in the company.

During the week before the departure of Pioneer One the excitement was unbelievable. The neighbors chosen to make the trip were packing their wagons or other conveyances with the greatest care. They were soon joined by friends and relatives who made valuable contributions to their supplies. The air was full of congratulations, suggestions, warnings, weeping, and laughter. Every person knew that the modern-day pioneers were making history and their mission would be the vital prelude to the coming of the Messiah.

Steven decided that his wagon should lead the caravan. It was a covered wagon of good size and made of the lightest and strongest materials available. It was more than large enough for his family and their supplies. A master craftsman in American Fork had helped him construct it. It would be pulled by four powerful mules, noted for their endurance. Douglas and Elizabeth Cartwright would drive the second wagon.

Although they were not yet LDS, the Cartwrights had become sincere investigators, and Steven had obtained special permission from President Howard to permit them to join Pioneer One. The third wagon would be occupied by Paul Christopher and two other young bachelors. Steven wanted Paul close to keep his eye on him and because he was his second assistant. Since Steven believed John was one of the most trustworthy and resourceful men in the wagon train, he had assigned him to bring up the rear of the caravan.

At last the great day came—Friday, April 14—the day of departure! The noise and the enthusiasm were intoxicating as hundreds of people watched the new pioneers set out on the dangerous but glorious voyage to faraway Missouri, to establish New Zion. Bennion Hicks, first counselor to the prophet, offered a prayer, pleading with the Father to bless the travelers in their dangerous endeavor. Next an apostle reviewed the prophecies concerning the building of the New Jerusalem.

When the apostle referred to a prophecy that spoke of the Second Moses, who would lead the saints to Zion in power, the Prophet Josiah Smith, seated next to Steven, whispered to him that the Lord had told him that he, Josiah Smith, was that Second Moses, and since Steven was his special agent, he too was the Second Moses. Soon the prophet himself stood and promised the brave people of Pioneer One that even though they would encounter terrible hardship, if they trusted in the Lord, the Holy Spirit would go with them as their guide and protector. He especially encouraged them to follow the counsel of their leader, Steven Christopher, or they would fail in this enterprise.

After the brief ceremonies, Pioneer One left Provo at eight in the morning, heading north on Interstate 15. It took them two days to reach Salt Lake City. Saturday morning they arose at six o'clock and started off by eight, and in the evening they stopped on the freeway at seven o'clock. After preparing the evening meal and socializing a while, they retired around eight. On the third day they turned into Parley's Canyon and began the long climb upward. That night they camped for the first time in the wilderness.

On the fourth day Steven and Mary sat together on the driver's seat of the covered wagon. They were on I-80 in Parley's Canyon about three miles from Parley's Summit, and the scenery was spectacular. But Steven was more interested in the scenery sitting beside him. He felt a strong need to kiss her regularly when he saw the children were not paying attention. And Mary didn't help matters any. Each time he turned to kiss her, she grinned and moved her lips toward his and surrendered to his tenderness. When he wasn't engaged in his favorite activity, Steven flipped the reins lightly against the rumps of his four mules to encourage them to maintain their pace. A quarter of a mile in front five riders roamed, investigating the terrain ahead and watching for marauders.

As the wagon train rounded a curve in the freeway, Steven looked back and saw a fascinating sight: a moving stream of handcarts, wagons, cars, vans, trucks, a bus, men on horseback, and animals and people trudging steadily along. In all, 398 men, 267 women, 359 children, 250 wagons, 48 handcarts, 75 stripped motor vehicles, 620 horses, 98 mules, 40 teams of oxen, 38 cows, and an undetermined number of sheep, chickens, and dogs. Steven had instructed his people to keep their vehicles close together for the sake of safety, and they were doing a good job of it. Several times he had given the reins to Mary and jumped on his horse, which was tied to their wagon, and had headed back down the canyon to check on the progress of the wagon train.

When Steven turned once again to the road ahead he felt an incredible exhilaration and a confidence he had never experienced before. He knew that the people of Pioneer One were risking their lives to bring about the redemption of Zion, and that the Lord had changed his heart and blessed him by allowing him to play an important part in that great undertaking. He believed he was equal to the task, as the prophet had promised, and he would do everything to fulfill the Lord's purposes. Most of all, he gave thanks to God that he would be facing the trials of the future with his family nearby and a beautiful new companion.

"Dad," Andrew asked, pushing his face between Steven and Mary, "are we there yet?"

Steven laughed. Some things never changed. "No, Andrew, we're not there yet. But do you want to take a turn at driving the mules?"

"Yeah!" His eyes shining, Andrew squeezed in between them. Steven met Mary's eyes and grinned.

THE END

We hope you enjoyed *Gathering Storm.* The first chapter of *Pioneer One,* the next novel *The Last Days* series begins on the next page. Or you can read more about the author and his books after the sample chapter.

THE LAST DAYS
VOLUME 2

Pioneer One

Kenneth R. Tarr

Chapter 1

When Pioneer One left Provo at eight in the morning on Friday, April 14, heading for the Promised Land, the modern pioneers were full of energy and enthusiasm. As they hurried along Interstate 15 toward Salt Lake City, they chattered, laughed, danced, and sang, enjoying themselves to the utmost. After all, they faced, as they saw it, an unbelievably exciting and fulfilling journey ahead of them, traveling in the name of God. But to many of the thousands who watched them embark on that dangerous trek, it was a shocking sight to see the strange assortment of vehicles the travelers had chosen and the unusual clothes they wore.

The spectators stared in amazement at the bizarre mixture of old-fashioned wagons and handcarts, modern cars, vans, pickups, trailers, and a swarm of two- and three-wheeled bicycles. Those who rode bicycles pulled children or provisions in bike trailers. One brother had even converted a small bus for the occasion. The onlookers might have thought they were seeing the strangest Fourth of July parade ever.

Since there was no oil or fuel to be found anywhere, the pilgrims couldn't simply *drive* to Missouri. But when some travelers saw how difficult it would be to build new "authentic" covered wagons, they decided to use the "modern" vehicles rusting away in their driveways or in wrecking yards, or they accepted more functional ones from friends. They stripped the metal carriages of every unnecessary part, such as the engine, and then packed the empty spaces with food, bedding, and other necessities. Their greatest challenge was to figure out how to attach tongues and hitches from the frames of the vehicles to the poor animals destined to pull the weird contraptions.

As for those who had built—or had someone else build—covered wagons, or "prairie schooners," they gazed at those transformed modern vehicles with amusement or disdain, depending on the bent of their minds. These wagoners were extremely proud of their wooden works of art, which they had furnished with every kind of modern convenience. There were spring seats—some with shades—fancy braking systems, exterior tool boxes, double board boxes, full suspension springs, and even steel covered wheels with spokes. At least half the wagon crowd tried hard to hide the fact that their supposedly "authentic" covered wagons had axles, wheels, and steel-belted radial tires pirated from modern vehicles.

Some of the builders and the converters made bets as to which type of vehicle would best survive the arduous journey. But, of course, there was no money involved in those bets. As time passed, the two groups adopted names to describe themselves and their rivals. The wagon builders used the terms "Creators" vs "Converters," while those who drove gutted vehicles preferred "Ancients" vs "Moderns." It was never hard to figure out what they referred to, if you knew who was doing the talking, and you had any sensitivity at all to vocal tone.

All those conveyances, except the bicycles, were pulled by mules, work horses, or oxen. And in order to spare the draft animals, which had to pull wagons heavy with supplies, most of the travelers walked or tried to walk—at least at first. But reasonably good drivers were always needed for any type of vehicle that was drawn by mules or horses. As for conveyances pulled by oxen, someone had to walk beside the leading team and control the animals with whip or goad.

Steven Christopher, the leader of Pioneer One, rode up and down the caravan on his sturdy mustang to check the progress of the company, amazed at the surprisingly brisk pace of the people. He decided to let them go, figuring there was no way to hold them back. After all, they were the courageous ones who would make history by being the first to reach Missouri and by building New Zion. And yet he felt a certain trepidation, seeing all that exuberance and overwhelming self-confidence. He noticed many were not wearing proper clothing, in spite of the guidelines he and his assistants had given them. Most had bare heads and arms, and wore shoes that would be more appropriate at a dance than on an 1,100-mile trek under the most trying circumstances.

Steven was especially surprised to see many teenagers—and adults too!—wearing T-shirts and shorts. Some of the beautiful daughters of Zion pranced along merrily, although awkwardly, on platform shoes. It was as if they were going to a party or some exciting outing at a nearby shaded campground. Steven wondered if they had remembered to bring their homemade sunblock and mosquito repellent.

"They don't look too prepared, do they?" Steven's brother, John, called as he rode up on his rugged horse. "You know, the way some are dressed."

"I'm afraid not. I guess a lot of them didn't take our guidelines seriously."

"Well, it won't be long before reality hits them," John declared with a grin. "They'll get more blisters and sunburns and whatnot than they ever dreamed possible . . . But there are other things that worry me more than clothes."

"Like what?"

John struggled to control his frisky horse. "Some of these people don't look too fit. We warned them to take long hikes and trim up as much as possible, but it doesn't seem as though they paid much attention."

"Don't worry. The trail and the sparse diet will shape them up in no time." Steven felt guilty as he touched his own belly. He certainly wasn't as trim as he could be.

"I guess you're right. I only hope they don't suffer too much before that happens. And I suppose it's only a matter of a few miles before they get the idea to maintain a slow, steady pace."

"Yes, I know what you mean. Some of them act as if they're frantically trying to get to a special sale before everybody else does." Steven gazed at one chubby guy chugging along as fast as his stubby legs would permit.

"Okay then, I'd better get back to my post at the rear." John turned his horse and trotted down the caravan.

A mile farther along the freeway, Steven noticed many of the pilgrims eyeing their wagons with longing. Soon, along the entire length of the caravan, they began to hop onto wagons, desperately seeking rest. A rest which would last a long, long time. The draft animals slowed their pace with the extra weight. A mile later, nearly every pioneer was hitching a ride, and the wagons slowed even more. At first Steven was irritated to see such laziness, but then a pang of guilt hit him. He had to admit that he was no paragon of physical fitness, and he started to worry about whether or not he'd make it through the day without embarrassment. After all, he was supposed to be a good example. Thank heavens he had to ride around on his horse for a while—to check on the welfare of his people, of course. He wondered how long he'd get away with *that* excuse.

On that first day of the journey, Steven asked himself if he'd already made a mistake. He had planned to increase travel time by one hour a day every two weeks: first ten hours, then eleven, and finally twelve. In that way, he had hoped to break the pioneers in gradually, to make the transition from unfitness to fitness less painful. But from the looks of the saints, maybe he should have asked them to walk no more than three or four hours a day at the beginning, and increase the time gradually. He might have to make a quick change of plans.

Four days later, as Pioneer One struggled up the six-percent grade on I-80, three miles from Parley's Summit, Steven knew for sure he had made a mistake in expecting the pioneers to maintain such a grueling early schedule. He was grateful that he and the other leaders had decided to call a halt for a day and a half after they reached the summit, and then proceed at an easier pace. But they still had to traverse the next three horrible miles. He continued on slowly, walking beside his wagon, his legs and feet hurting terribly. Mary, Steven's bride of six days, drove their wagon and glanced at him often with sympathy. He couldn't imagine a worse way to spend a honeymoon. It was only 11:30 a.m., and already the temperature was ninety degrees. And since there was no breeze and the skies were cloudless, the heat was sizzling on the hot freeway surface. John had informed him that the temperatures of the last few days were twelve degrees higher than normal for this time of year. Steven wasn't surprised, because the weather had been erratic and extreme around the world for a long time. The peaks to the south were covered with snow, but that seemed to have no effect in moderating the temperature.

"Do you want to take the reins for a while, sweetheart?" Mary said, looking down at him. "You need rest."

"No, I'm okay. Maybe later." Steven agonized over what the other pioneers must be going through. At least he was wearing sneakers which gave his feet good support. They were two sizes too large so he could fill the bottom with foam pads to absorb as much shock as possible. He had wrapped his lower legs with Ace bandages just tight enough to give his muscles a measure of support. He wore a long-sleeved shirt and a wide-brimmed hat. Yet, in spite of this preparation, he had shin splints, aching muscles, blisters, dry skin, red eyes, and chapped lips.

He knew others must be suffering even more than he, because some were older and less fit. Many had not made careful preparations nor worn the right clothes. Already most of the company was smitten by sunburn, blisters, pulled muscles, fatigue, dry skin, and a multitude of other ailments. Steven and his brothers had instructed the pioneers from the beginning to take regular doses of water, but many had not done so and were ill with heat exhaustion and dehydration.

Steven knew that even the early Mormon pioneers, who were used to hard labor and physical exertion, had endured great physical exhaustion and pain as they made the journey to Utah. But most of the new pioneers had led lives of ease and inactivity. After only four days, several families had already given up and returned to the city, protesting that nothing was worth the agony they were going through. A few had no choice: they had developed such severe symptoms that the caravan doctor, Quentin Price, had warned they might die if they didn't return to civilization.

Steven was proud of those who persisted despite great distress. He felt especially sorry for the ones who were overweight. Their initial brisk pace had soon turned into painful trudging. Their torment was so great that they moaned from pain during the day and also at night instead of getting the sleep they needed so badly. Many saints still found it necessary to hop into wagons or mount horses to continue the journey. This added to the burden of the animals that had to pull overloaded wagons. Steven wondered how many more saints would have to go back to Salt Lake City, and how many draft animals would perish from exhaustion.

He was surprised to see that the people driving converted vehicles did not seem to have more difficulties than those using wagons. But the bicyclers had given up trying to climb the steep road, and had fastened the bikes to hooks on their wagons. Since the people hauling handcarts experienced the hardest going, every family member had to pull to keep the carts moving. Steven knew their struggle would ease as the highway leveled out.

The Prophet Josiah Smith had warned Steven that not all the pioneers would have the strength of character to endure the trials the Lord would send them on the road to Missouri. Some would abandon the wagon train, and others would become traitors before the trip was over. One of the purposes of the difficult journey was to prepare a sanctified people worthy of establishing New Zion and the holy city. He told Steven that he must use his own judgment in solving problems, after seeking the counsel of his assistants and the wisdom of the Lord, but he advised him to maintain reasonable company rules and to travel as fast as the saints could bear.

The previous evening, on Monday, Steven had called a meeting with the caravan leaders, including his brothers—John and Paul—the four colonels, and a number of captains. They had decided to allow the company to proceed somewhat slower for a while and have a rest day after they reached Parley's Summit, which would occur around noon on Tuesday. So on Tuesday morning, before the pioneers had hit the trail, Steven announced that after reaching the summit, which was only a few hours away, the entire company would stop shortly thereafter to rest for the remainder of the day and the next day too.

When they began the journey again on Thursday, they would travel no more than five hours a day for about a week. At that welcome announcement the entire company cheered and rejoiced.

"Steven, please take these reins," Mary called down. "You've been walking almost three hours now. I can see your legs are hurting you."

"Don't worry. I'll be fine. It isn't far to the resting place." Steven saw a sign on the right indicating that Parley's Summit was only a mile ahead. He knew they could rest shortly after reaching that point. Then the road would descend and the going would be much easier. He looked at his three children walking on the highway and felt a wave of pride as he saw them maintaining the pace without complaint. Only Andrew, who was nine, found it necessary to jump into the wagon at times. Jennifer, his eleven-year-old daughter, doggedly kept up with William, who at thirteen, was proud of being a teenager.

He looked back and saw his non-Mormon friend, Douglas Cartwright, plodding wearily beside his wagon, his eyes staring at the road in front of him. Apparently this march was taking its toll, even on a man as strong as Douglas. Steven gritted his teeth and steeled his mind to the idea that he was going to set a good example for his children and the others in the company, no matter what the cost. His legs had always been one of his weak spots, his Achilles tendon. In past years they had prevented him, during workouts, from running too fast or jogging more than three or four miles.

He looked at Mary again and called out, "We can stop in about two hours. Within three miles we come to a wide valley, where there will be plenty of room to place the wagons into circles. It's near Jeremy Ranch." Mary nodded and threw him a kiss.

The next few miles seemed endless, but finally the road began to level out and turn downward. Steven felt a huge relief. He looked to the right and saw a community of cabins and other buildings on the side of the mountain, not far from the freeway. He was astonished to see that all of them were demolished, and there was no sign of life. It reminded him of the housing developments he had seen on the bench east of I-215 on the third day of their journey just before the wagon train turned northeast into the canyon. They too had been flattened by some gigantic force. At the time Steven had wondered if the devastation had been caused by the great earthquake that had struck the Cottonwood Fault nearly a year ago in May. Or was it the result of the massive mud slides which had occurred this year after three weeks of ceaseless rain? Perhaps both disasters had taken their toll.

In the case of this mountain community, marauders may have been involved also because many of the cabins looked as if they had been burned out.

A sudden chill went up his spine. He remembered the words of the prophet, who had warned him several weeks ago that Pioneer One would face dangers from wicked men that would be almost insurmountable.

After the wagon train had traveled another mile, Steven's thoughts were abruptly interrupted.

"We can camp over there," a voice said. It was Paul, who appeared beside him on his horse as if from nowhere. Steven looked in the direction indicated by his brother and saw a wide-open space on the left, large enough for hundreds of wagons. It was about a mile south of Jeremy Ranch. Inasmuch as the ditch on the side of the freeway was shallow, Steven knew they would have no trouble crossing it to reach the site.

"Looks good, Paul," Steven said, climbing into his wagon.

Paul waved and rode away. As Mary slid to the right on the seat to make room for her husband, she handed him the reins. He drove the mules toward the field and turned his wagon into a wide circle. If the other drivers followed him, as they knew they should, they could form a ring of about a hundred wagons. As soon as he finished the first circle, he jumped from the wagon and, with the help of Paul and Douglas, guided the second line of wagons into another circle.

They repeated the procedure until the final section of wagons formed the last circle. The result was three complete rings, one inside the other, of about a hundred wagons each, with openings at opposite sides. Seeing this company all together in one spot for the first time, Steven was amazed at how huge it really was. The prophet had told Steven that the brethren realized that such a large body of travelers would be extremely difficult to oversee and to lead. But they had purposely planned it to be large to provide the pioneers with a vital measure of safety on such a dangerous journey.

The handcart pioneers parked their carts in the center of the circles. Most of the livestock was herded to forage on the north side of the camp, where Paul posted several bachelors as guards. John put sentries around the entire encampment.

It was the first time Steven had tried to form the wagons into such large circles. When they had stopped for the night on the first few days, they simply had stopped where they were on the freeway because there wasn't enough room to form protective circles. But today the pioneers spent a half hour to complete the three circles. This time-consuming task was frustrating to the leaders, but they knew the circles would provide them with greater protection.

It was 2:30 p.m. when the saints finished the work of organizing the encampment. Most of the travelers found a shady spot and fell asleep immediately. But many found it necessary to nurse their aching bodies before they were comfortable enough to rest. Only a few showed any interest in visiting neighbors, telling stories, or playing games, as they had that first night on Interstate 15.

Paul, John, and Douglas gathered at Steven's wagon as soon as their chores were completed. They hugged Mary and Steven's children. A few minutes later, Jarrad Babcock and Leonard Reece, Paul's traveling companions, turned up. Like Paul, they were not married.

"I suggest we mount up and check the region east of here," John said. "There are several communities farther along the freeway. Or at least there used to be."

"I agree. We need to check it out," Paul said.

Steven saw anxiety in the eyes of the other five men. He guessed that they too had seen the destruction at the entrance to the valley. "All right. Let's go." He turned to Mary and said, "We won't be long."

"Please be careful," she said.

"We will." He gave her a kiss.

Mary said no more but Steven saw the worried look on her face. He knew she feared for their safety but realized, at the same time, that it was something they had to do.

"Can I go, Dad?" William said.

"Not this time, son, I'm depending on you to stay here to help protect the camp." Steven was afraid for the boy's life if they ran into trouble. William frowned, but didn't protest. Steven knew his son was secretly pleased that he had expressed confidence in him.

The six men mounted their horses and trotted east on the freeway. Each carried a rifle. With great caution they spent two hours exploring the area several miles from the encampment. Desolation was everywhere, evidence that some great natural disaster had struck the region. Nearly every building was smashed and covered with a thick layer of hardened mud. Yet the searchers found something even more sinister.

Some of the buildings had been consumed by fire, and there were dead bodies everywhere, including women and children. It was clear they had been shot or stabbed to death. Whoever had committed these atrocities had also poured out their rage upon pets and farm animals. The situation became even more frightening when they realized that the tragedy had taken place only a few days earlier. Finding no life and sickened by what he saw, Steven called off the search, and the men headed back to camp.

Before they reached their destination, they agreed to report the destruction in general terms, but to avoid revealing the violence committed against human beings. Steven did not want to provoke terror in the hearts of the pioneers. As they reached the outskirts of the camp, they were met by two colonels and seven captains. The colonels were in charge of fifty families, and the captains oversaw ten families. Steven told them what they had found and asked them to be cautious as to what they told the families in their charge. He also asked John to make sure he doubled the guard. The leaders left immediately to do what he requested.

After saying goodbye to Douglas and the others, Steven joined his little family, who had gathered around a campfire not far from their wagon. It was nearly 6:00 p.m., and Mary was preparing supper. Steven sat on a log beside his wife and kissed her gently on the neck. The children snickered at his display of affection. As he sat there looking into the fire, the feeling suddenly came to him that he wouldn't want to live another minute if his wife and children ever suffered the kind of violence he had just witnessed not far away.

Even though Mary was his second wife and not the mother of his children, Steven knew that she already loved them almost as much as he did. She had no children of her own because her first husband hated children and eventually abandoned her for another woman.

Mary stopped her work and insisted that Steven take off his shoes and roll up the legs of his pants. The children giggled at his white legs, but Steven didn't care, because Mary knelt in front of him and began to rub his legs with pain-relieving ointment.

"Why don't we invite the Cartwrights and the bachelors for supper?" Mary asked as she worked on him, her facing glowing like that of a typical newlywed.

"Good idea," Steven replied. The Cartwrights and the three young men sometimes ate meals with them, and Steven was especially anxious to have their company tonight.

"I'll go get them," Andrew yelled enthusiastically, not waiting for his father's approval.

Andrew had become the unofficial family courier, and Steven didn't mind as long as the boy didn't stray too far. He watched as his son ran the fifty feet to where Douglas was doing some chore. Hearing Andrew's message, Douglas smiled and waved his acceptance to Steven. The boy ran to another wagon and spoke to Paul. Paul said something to Andrew and the child quickly sped away toward the center of the camp. Steven figured he was hurrying to find Leonard and Jarrad. No doubt the two bachelors were hanging around the best-looking young ladies of the camp, hoping to score points. Steven was sure that Anastasia Borisovich would be one of them.

Mary had just finished working on his legs, when Paul and the Cartwrights arrived and sat around the fire. Elizabeth Cartwright, Doug's wife, had brought a huge bowl of potato salad. She and Doug had five lively children. Like her husband, Elizabeth was not a member of the Church.

Steven was growing concerned that Andrew had not yet returned, and he was relieved when he finally saw the boy hurrying toward them, pulling on Leonard and Jarrad's arms. "What took you so long, Andrew?" Steven asked.

"Well, Dad, to make a long story short," he said with disgust, "I couldn't get these two lover boys away from the chicks."

"Hey, what's the problem, Andy boy?" Jarrad said with a twinkle in his eye. "We were merely having a profound religious conversation with two serious young women."

"Yeah, right," Andrew said, smirking. "You looked pretty googly-eyed to me."

Everyone laughed at Andrew's choice of words. Steven was astonished to hear his son use terms like "lover boys," "chicks," and "googly-eyed."

By that time Mary had finished preparing fried chicken with pork and beans. Doug offered a prayer. Steven looked at all the food and wondered how long they'd be able to enjoy such feasts. He felt guilty that he hadn't done a good job of encouraging *everyone*, even his own wife, to ration food. Obviously, other people were ignoring the guidelines also. Maybe he'd have to do what John said—put the food in special wagons and give every person a specific allotment every day. Another thing to bring up in the leadership council.

As they ate, the friends discussed the difficult trip up the mountain, the ailments of the pioneers, and especially the terrible destruction around them. At 10:00 p.m. Mary asked the children to go to bed, but William begged to stay up until midnight. He said he had the right, as a teenager, to stay up later and listen to the adults talk. Steven agreed in spite of the frown he saw on Mary's face. At that moment John and Tania Christopher joined the group and were greeted warmly by everyone.

When everyone had settled down again, Paul said in a mysterious voice, "I wanted to tell you all that I think something very strange is going on."

Steven looked at him in surprise. "Like what?"

Paul gazed around the campfire as if to make sure he could speak freely in this group. Seeing William, he declared, "William, what I'm about to say is a secret. It's important that you don't repeat it to anyone, no matter what."

Normally, Steven would have considered Paul's attitude to be no more than one of his usual jokes. But after the terrible things they had seen that day, he sensed that Paul was serious. He noticed that no one in the group was smiling.

"Don't worry, Uncle Paul," William said, "I'm an expert at keeping secrets."

"I'm sure you are . . . Okay, as everyone here knows, Leonard and Jarrad have spent a lot of time in the last few days visiting the available females in the caravan."

"Hey, we were only doing a little quality home teaching," Jarrad protested.

Paul smiled. "That's understood. Anyhow, Jarrad and Leonard tell me that some of these young ladies couldn't resist pouring out their tender hearts to them. To make a long story short, these young ladies inadvertently revealed that they've heard a lot of murmuring."

"Murmuring?" Douglas asked. "What kind of murmuring?"

Paul leaned forward and placed another branch on the fire. "Well, it seems someone is spreading rumors about us, the leaders of Pioneer One. According to the gossip, we are dangerously incompetent. The brunt of the attack seems to fall on Steven."

"You're joking!" Douglas said angrily.

"No, I'm serious."

Steven felt the heat of shame flow from his neck to his face. The idea of incompetence was particularly embarrassing, since he had always believed that someone else, almost anyone else, would be better qualified than he to lead Pioneer One. "Incompetent in what way?" he asked nervously.

Jarrad answered for Paul. "In lots of ways. Not establishing rules that are strict enough. Neglecting to enforce the rules we have. Supporting the weaker saints, who are slowing us down. Refusing to make the people ration their food more carefully. Not posting enough guards at night. Choosing a poor route . . . And believe me, that's only the beginning. Those sisters just couldn't stop talking."

"The attitude seems to be," Leonard added, "that you—all of you—are endangering the lives of everyone in the company by not doing your jobs properly."

"But it was the prophet who chose this route for us, not Steven," Elizabeth objected.

In spite of his humiliation, Steven was pleased to hear Elizabeth, who was not a member of the Church, refer to Josiah Smith as "the prophet."

Mary was visibly upset. "Paul, do you think these criticisms represent a general opinion, or just gossip spread by a few individuals?"

Before Paul could respond, John said, "It's obviously a conspiracy. I've talked to a lot of the pioneers. Most of them like Steven and have complimented us on the way we're handling the trip. I believe someone is purposely trying to corrupt the others and undermine our authority by circulating lies."

"But why?" Douglas said. "What do they hope to gain?"

"That's what we need to find out," Paul said. "Also, we may have another problem. Several people have told me that someone is stealing supplies."

"I've heard the same thing," John observed.

Steven was stunned. "Stealing? Are you sure?"

"Yes," Paul replied. "Two wagoners told me this morning that someone stole tools and ammunition from their wagons. They've no idea when it happened, but both are fit to be tied."

"And what did you hear, John?"

"What I heard came from Byron Mills."

"Oh, yes. I remember him," Steven said. Byron had been an elder in the Grandview Second ward. He was thirty-eight years old and considered himself a scriptorian.

"Well, Byron said he had a sack of wheat and a rifle stolen. He doesn't know when it happened either."

"Do you think these people simply made a mistake? Maybe they forgot to bring the items they believe were stolen."

Both Paul and John shook their heads. The group discussed the matter another half hour without coming to any firm conclusions.

Finally, Steven said, "Listen, everyone, we're not going to find the truth without more information. I want you to keep your eyes and ears open. I suggest you enlist the aid of as many people as possible, if you know you can trust them. I especially want Paul, Leonard, and Jarrad to use their special talents and connections to uncover some solid evidence. We need to resolve these problems quickly."

After the guests left, Steven and Paul walked around the camps to check the guards, who reported that they hadn't seen or heard anything unusual.

"You sure are lucky," Paul said as they trudged back to their wagons.

"Lucky. What do you mean?"

"You get to go home to a beautiful, tender wife, while I have to put up with two dirty bachelors who burp constantly and think it's funny to let smells."

"You poor boy. Look, I happen to know that your companions are pretty high up on the cleanliness chain, so don't give me a line of bull."

When they reached the wagons, Paul let out a profound sigh. "What a life without a wife," he moaned. "How can I bear it?"

Steven laughed. "Good night, Paul."

"Good night, you lucky devil."

Later, as he snuggled close to Mary, Steven couldn't sleep. He struggled to think of something pleasant but failed. He was tormented by the problems of the wagon train and the murdered people he had seen in the nearby communities.

"Can't you sleep, sweetheart?" Mary whispered. "You're tossing and turning constantly."

"Sorry to keep you awake."

"Listen. There's no problem we can't solve with the Lord's help. Maybe we should ask him."

"Yes, of course." Steven was grateful for the suggestion because he had forgotten to have prayer that evening except over the supper. Another thing to feel guilty about. They kneeled, and Steven asked God for protection and help in solving the troubles of Pioneer One.

After putting more balm on his legs, Mary said, "Now, roll onto your stomach, so I can rub your back."

The gentle touch of his wife and the warm ointment made him feel better immediately. He remembered how Selena, his ex-wife, had rubbed his back sometimes when they were first married. Strange how it was that you never seemed to forget completely a woman you once loved. And yet, because of Mary, he could think of Selena now without the terrible pain he had felt before. What would his life be like today if Selena had not abandoned him and the children three years ago to join a polygamous cult? Would it be *her* rubbing the pain out of his legs instead of Mary?

At last the great fatigue of the day gradually overtook him and he began to relax and feel sleepy. He hoped that he and the other company leaders would be equal to the task of solving their current problems and perhaps even greater ones as they continued their trek eastward.

Kenneth R. Tarr taught French language and literature at Brigham Young University for fourteen years, and French and Spanish for three years at Snow College. He received a master's degree in French and Spanish at Brigham Young in 1965, and a doctorate in French at Kansas University in 1973, with a minor in Medieval history.

Kenneth was born and raised in southern California and has been a member of the LDS church all his life, serving in many capacities. He and his wife, Kathy, have been married fifty-five years and have eight children and thirty-two grandchildren. Currently they live in Utah where they operate an herb store. Kenneth enjoys writing, reading, exercising, doing repairs, and listening to good music.

Gathering Storm is Kenneth's first published novel and the first in his *The Last Days* series. He has also written three sequels, *Pioneer One*, *Promised Land,* and *End of the World.* The author welcomes questions and comments. You can contact him at krtarr015@gmail.com.

Made in the USA
Middletown, DE
18 December 2022

19255690R00176